Bread and Wine

Ignazio Silone

BREAD
AND WINE

Translated from the Italian by
GWENDA DAVID *and* ERIC MOSBACHER

HARPER & BROTHERS PUBLISHERS

New York and London

1937

Bread and Wine

Chapter I

OLD Don Benedetto was sitting on the low wall of his little
garden, in the shade of a cypress tree. His black priest's
habit seemed to absorb and prolong the shadow of the tree.
Behind him his sister was sitting at her loom. She had placed it
between a box hedge and a rosemary bed. The shuttle bobbed
backwards and forwards through the warp of red and black wool,
from left to right and from right to left, to the accompaniment
of the rhythm of the treadle that lifted the warp cords and of
the lamb that lifted the warp. It was a warm afternoon towards
the end of April, and one's thoughts followed the movement
of the shuttle, from left to right and from right to left. The right
led towards the town; the left led straight into the mountains.

On the right was the railway, and the national road that followed the course of the ancient Valerian Way, between fields of
hay and wheat and potatoes and beets and beans and maize,
leading to Avezzano and Tivoli, and eventually to Rome. On
the left, between vineyards, and fields of peas and onion beds,
ran the provincial road, clambering up into the mountains,
straight into the heart of the Abruzzi, the region of beech trees,
the haunt of the last wild bears, leading towards Pescasseroli,
Opi, and Alfedana.

The priest's sister threw the shuttle with the red bobbin in
and out of the warp.

A young peasant woman, riding a donkey and carrying a baby
in her arms, came down the local road, which was stony and
winding, like the bed of a dried-up mountain stream. The road
was white, and beside it a peasant was tracing brown lines with
a small wooden plow drawn by two donkeys.

Along the national road down on the right a lorry, full of soldiers, clattered by in a cloud of dust. Life, contemplated from the priest's garden, seemed an ancient children's pantomime.

Today was Don Benedetto's seventy-fifth birthday, and he sat contemplating the valley from his garden wall, awaiting the arrival of his guests; for some former pupils of his had promised to visit him in honor of the occasion. They would arrive separately, from the right and from the left, from the city and from the mountains, from wherever life had scattered them since the end of their school days.

The few poor cottages of the village of Rocca huddled beneath Don Benedetto's garden. In their midst was the narrow village square, with grass growing between the stones, and at the other end of it the low porch of the church, and over the porch an ancient stucco filigree rose. The houses, the streets, the small village square might have been uninhabited. A beggar passed by in rags and went on without stopping. A tiny girl appeared at a cottage doorway and peeped about her. Then she slipped behind a hedge and went on peeping from there.

"Perhaps I should have bought some tamarind," the priest's sister said. "And you might have shaved, since it's your birthday party today."

"My birthday party? A fine time for parties, to be sure. Strawberry juice will do for the young men," Don Benedetto replied. Tamarind came from the city, in bottles. Matalena Ricotta, with her strawberries, her mushrooms, and her eggs, came from the mountains.

Shoe polish and cuff-links and Pantanella macaroni, flavored with saffron, and Donna Evangelina's Oriental Nights hair dye, and celluloid collars, and the preparation Marco Tuglio Zabaglione used for starching his unruly mustaches came, of course, from the city. But Bonifazio Patacca, with his sheep's-milk cheese and pressed curds and his *mozzarelle* cheeses, and Sciancalla with his wood and charcoal, came from the mountains. Such was the vivid pantomime in which Don Benedetto lived.

"Sciancalla has reverted to trade by barter," Don Benedetto's sister announced. "All he'll take for his charcoal nowadays is beans and onions."

"I've been suffering from heartburn after every meal for some time past," the old priest replied, "and bicarbonate of soda is three times what it was. Don't you think those young men are late?"

Bicarbonate of soda came from the city, like insecticide and safety-razor blades.

"Safety? Rubbish!" observed Marta. "When you shave with them you slash yourself worse than with an old-fashioned cut-throat."

"Safety, Marta, is always relative. I suppose it wouldn't be a bad thing if the Department of Public Safety were called the Department of Public Danger. And besides," Don Benedetto added, "when you talk at the top of your voice don't forget that the razor blades you are talking about are Italian national blades, and therefore the wounds you receive with them are, in a sense, patriotic wounds. Perhaps, on reflection, my old pupils would prefer wine, after all. They aren't boys any longer."

The former pupils whom Don Benedetto was expecting had finished their schooling soon after the end of the Great War, and so now they were thirty years old or more.

Marta went into the kitchen to fetch the refreshments. She carried them carefully to the granite table in the middle of the garden, between the tomatoes and the sage. Her action was partly a propitiatory one, to cause the young men to hurry.

Then she went back to her loom, and threw the shuttle full of wool between the threads of the warp.

"Do you know that there's a new sub-prefect?" she said after settling down to her work again. "Another stranger, of course. And there seem to be a lot of other changes in view, because of this new African war."

"War time is career time," said Don Benedetto.

Transfers and changes always came from the city. Sub-prefects, inspectors, controllers, bishops, prison governors, speakers on behalf of the corporations, Jesuit preachers for the spiritual exercises, always came from the city, just like newspapers and songs of the type of "Tripoli, Lovely Land of Love," and "Valencia," and "Giovinezza," and gramophones and the wireless and novels and picture-postcards. From the mountain there came Brother Antifona, the Capuchin friar, with his wallet for alms; and Cassarola, the wise-woman, with her herbs and badger's hair and snake-skins against the evil eye; and the philosopher of Pescasseroli, Benedetto Croce, with his four different kinds of awareness; and every year the bagpipers for the novenas before Advent, and every Thursday Sciatàp for the market, and every Saturday Magascià for salt and tobacco.

"Have you heard that Clarice is engaged to a mechanic at the sugar factory?" said Marta. "To marry in war time is to sow among thorns."

There was a knot in the warp-cords of the loom, and Marta had to get up to free them.

Don Benedetto reflected for a few moments. Then he said:

"You know, some women are born to be war widows. . . . Poets are made, but war widows, like bishops, are born. Mind, I don't say that with reference to Clarice, who seems to me to be rather on the stupid side."

"Clarice owns some good land. Hemp land," Marta remarked.

"Does the mechanic want to leave the factory and grow hemp?" Don Benedetto asked.

"On the contrary," said Marta. "Clarice wants to sell her land. Hemp isn't any good any more."

Formerly hemp had gone down to the city, but now it did so no longer, for it was held to be expensive, primitive, and crude.

"Truth used, more or less, to go down, too," mused Don Benedetto. "It was more or less tolerated. But now it is tolerated no longer. Monsignore finds it expensive, primitive, and crude; while hypocrisy is smooth, always up-to-date, and not only cheap but profitable."

Marta had to get up to turn the warp beam under the loom. There was a web of sad memories under her heart. Those had been the exact words that Monsignore had used. "Your brother, dear madam," he had said, "is so crude and primitive that we cannot possibly tolerate him as a master in a college to which the richest, that is to say the best families, send their sons." There was no doubt that Monsignore was neither primitive nor crude, and therefore, knowing that Don Benedetto was timid and resigned so far as his career was concerned, he had dismissed him on the grounds of ill health.

Since then Don Benedetto had lived in seclusion in the house above Rocca dei Marsi, with his sister, devoting himself to his beloved classics and poetry and plants, to everything that beautifies the world and does not change with changing fashions. He took no interest in politics, and perhaps the classics did not help him very much to understand the events of the day, but they certainly helped him to abominate the most recent forms taken by the collective life about him. Don Benedetto was a quiet and good and humble man, slightly captious, and averse to vain excitement, and all he let strangers see of his inner life was an ingenuous love for a few Latin and Greek authors and a slightly provincial attachment to his own countryside and to the cafoni, the poor peasants who lived in it and made it fruitful. But his country shyness concealed a liberty of spirit that was rash for his station; this liberty of spirit went hand in hand with a great humanity. But the warmth of Don Benedetto's heart was not sufficient to earn him the forgiveness of the few priests of neighboring parishes with whom he still sometimes dared to talk openly. Thus he was reduced to living between his garden and his library, abandoned even by his relatives, members of an old-fashioned landowning family who had known better times but had been ravaged and ruined by the earthquake and the Great War. His family resented the fact that he did not possess the influence with the authorities which they expected of him, which he would have possessed had he not been primitive and crude, and which he might have used to their advantage in an age in which honest work was useless without influence and wire-pulling. Lacking all other close ties apart from his aged sister, Don Benedetto's affections were centered upon a few young men who had been his pupils, and he followed their changes of fortune in the complicated and paradoxical circumstances of their careers with paternal care.

Marta had warmly invited a few of them to come to Rocca
to visit their old schoolmaster in his retreat in honor of his
seventy-fifth birthday. She had asked them to bring others, whose
addresses she did not know, and she was worried. Had she prepared sufficient refreshments, and would the dozen glasses of
different shapes and sizes that were ranged upon the granite table
be enough? Marta went on with her weaving, and between one
shuttle and the next kept looking down the valley at the roads
and the footpaths along which the guests would come.

On the right were the railway and the national road that led
from the city, on the left the provincial road descending from
the mountains, and in front the vast chessboard of the Fucino,
furrowed by long lines of poplars and canals. Right and left,
city and mountain, engineer and peasant, met in the Fucino.

"If the boys are late it's because the trains and the post-buses
don't run on time," said Don Benedetto. "Since foreign tourists
don't come to our part of the world, there's no such thing as a
time-table. After all, for us mere Italians such a thing would be
too much to expect!"

From Rocca dei Marsi the land slopes gently down towards the
immense hollow of the former lake of Fucino, now reclaimed and
the property of a so-called Prince Torlonia.

All round this huge hollow, which is green with wheat and
beets, there rises a great circle of gently sloping hills, with tiny
villages cradled on them all, with here and there the clustering
towers of old, smoke-black towns, some girded by high walls,
some with houses carved out of the slope, like caverns; places
with ancient names and venerable histories, but largely destroyed
and badly reconstructed since the last earthquake. Behind the
circle of hills the mountains rose steeply, cut by floods and tor-
rents. Towards the railway the mountains were as bare and
desolate as burned bones; towards Pescasseroli they were green
and wooded.

The confused noises that floated up to Rocca from the Fucino
towards sunset only increased the sense of distance and solitude
in the little village. A few women, clothed in black, squalid and
unkempt and aged before their time, appeared in the dark

doorways. Other women returned slowly from the fountain, bearing copper vessels on their heads, with handkerchiefs knotted under their chins. A peasant woman, dressed in black, crossed the tiny village square, pulling, almost dragging, behind her a little girl dressed in yellow, and disappeared into the church. An old peasant passed by on a donkey, urging it forward with his heels. Then the little street emptied again and Rocca resumed the appearance of a village of the dead.

Meanwhile traffic had multiplied along the national road. Army lorries were passing in a continual stream.

"I don't understand why the Holy Father doesn't denounce this new war they are preparing in Africa," said Marta. "Concetta, the baker's wife, stopped me after Mass this morning and said her son had been called up, and she wanted to know what the Pope says about the war."

"The Holy Father knows, my dear, that it's unhealthy to talk with a bit in one's mouth," answered Don Benedetto.

He suddenly rose to his feet, attracted by loud cries and shouts from the provincial road. It was not easy to see what was causing all the hullabaloo. A long cloud of dust was overflowing from the narrow highway on to the neighboring vineyards and gardens. In the midst of it a flock of sheep was slowly advancing, like a small river of little yellow waves. Next there came into sight a donkey loaded with its usual equipment, its straw canopy, its saucepan bag, its milkpails and cheese-molds. Behind the donkey came a shepherd, with his sheep-dogs, and behind him a small open motor-car, the occupants of which were shouting to the shepherd, urging him to make way and let them pass. But their cries were vain. The only effect they had on the man was to make him gesticulate eloquently, indicating that he could not hear a word they were saying, that he was not only deaf but dumb, and that all he wanted was to be left in peace. But since even a deaf-mute ought to be able to understand that a motor-car cannot dally forever behind a flock of sheep, the young men went on shouting furiously at him. They would probably have abandoned words for deeds had the shepherd not been escorted by three silent, ferocious-looking dogs, with docked ears and bloodshot eyes, wearing metal, nail-studded collars as a defense against wolves. One of the young men in the motor-car was in the uniform of an officer of militia. He kept on standing up at the driving-wheel, shouting imprecations and gesticulating at the deaf-mute, begging, beseeching, and commanding him to make his flock move over to one side of the road to allow room for the motor-car to pass. But the shepherd plodded on, using equally expressive gestures to show that he hadn't the slightest idea what all the fuss was about, that it was no affair of his, that he couldn't imagine what on earth the two young men wanted, and that they should leave him alone. This had been going on for some time. Don Benedetto walked towards the center of the disturbance with a cordial greeting for the shepherd and for his two old pupils in the motor-car.

"Welcome, welcome," the old priest called out, and, turning politely to the shepherd, he introduced them to him.

"They are friends of mine who have come to visit me," he said.

The shepherd abruptly regained the power of speech.

"Why didn't you tell me you were going to see Don Benedetto?" he calmly said to the occupants of the motor-car. Then he gave an order to the dogs, and in a trice the flock had elongated and moved over to the right side of the road, leaving plenty of room for the car to pass.

By this time Don Benedetto's sister had approached.

"This gentleman in uniform," said Don Benedetto, introducing him, "is not the charcoal man, but only my dear friend and former pupil, Concettino Ragù. And this gentleman, who looks like an unfrocked monk, is nothing of the sort, but a real doctor, Doctor Nunzio Sacca. Both are excellent young men at heart."

The two excellent young men, however, had not yet swallowed their amazement at the deaf-mute's sudden recovery of speech.

"What's the rascal's name?" Concettino asked.

"I have reached the age of seventy-five, and I have never yet acted as an informer," the priest answered, laughing, "and it's too late to start now."

He took his two old pupils by the arm and led them towards his garden.

Meanwhile the shepherd, evidently believing himself to be entirely in the right in this affair, went on shouting from the middle of the road:

"Why didn't you tell me you were going to Don Benedetto?"

"Sit down and rest," Marta said to the two young men, to distract their attention from the shepherd. Then she quietly and patiently resumed her work at the loom and added:

"The others won't be long now."

But Concettino Ragù had not yet recovered from his astonishment at the false deaf-mute. He was so amazed that he was not even angry. Don Benedetto saw this, and gave an explanation of the incident that perhaps he would have preferred to avoid.

"My dear Ragù," he said, "there's no need for you to be surprised. There's no need for me, who take no interest in politics, to explain to you what your uniform represents to the poor people, the cafoni, the shepherds. That they pretend to be deaf-mutes when they meet an officer of the militia on a lonely road is the least thing you ought to complain about. The day when the ears of those who sham deafness are opened and the tongues of those who sham dumbness are loosened will be a terrible one, and I should like to see you spared it."

At these words Concettino looked at the doctor. Wasn't this just the kind of thing Don Benedetto might be expected to say? His glance reproached the doctor for having persuaded him to come. Dr. Sacca, however, tried to save the situation.

"We came to visit you here in your retreat," he said to the priest, "to show you that you are not alone and are not abandoned, and that all those whom you taught . . ."

"*Deus mihi haec otia fecit*," answered Don Benedetto, and there was tenderness in his voice. "Your presence here gives me much pleasure and makes me forget all bitterness. And now sit down and rest. Not there on the ground. That is not grass, but thyme. This is basil, *ocimum suave*. That yonder is parsley, *apium petroselinum*, as you know. This at the side is mint. Good, ancient, and honest things."

The three men sat down on a granite seat, at the foot of a graceful and delicate olive tree. The old man sat between the two younger ones. For a while there was silence in the peaceful garden, save for the alternating rhythm of Marta's loom, the sounds of the treadle and the shuttle.

"What has become of Luigi Candeloro? I have had no news of him for a long time," the old man said.

"He died of typhoid fever two years ago, in Libya," Nunzio Sacca answered. "For me it was like the loss of a brother. After qualifying as an engineer, he worked for a short time on his own account, and then for three years he was unemployed. Finally he took a job as a civil engineer in Libya. He would have gone anywhere, to hell itself, for the sake of earning a living. He died two weeks before sailing for home to marry a cousin of mine. His family, who had bled themselves to the bone to help him finish his studies, were left without any support."

The old man said nothing. Then he spoke again:

"What is Battista Lo Patto doing?"

"He plays Scopone—a card game, you know," Concettino answered. "At scientific Scopone he is absolutely unbeatable."

"But what does he do in the daytime?"

"He sleeps all the morning. He gets up when his mother has lunch ready. Then he goes out and plays Scopone. He comes back when his mother has dinner ready. Then he goes out and plays Scopone again."

"Doesn't he ever vary his program?"

"On Sundays."

"Does he work on Sundays?"

"On Sundays he plays billiards."

The old man shook his head. Then he asked:

"And Antonio Speranza?"

"As perhaps you know, he didn't go on with his studies after he left school," Sacca replied. "For a while he earned a meager living from the little provision shop his father left him. He spent ten years struggling to meet his accounts and pay his fines for bad sardines, rancid oil, moldy flour, and inaccurate scales. In the end he lost patience and tried to get rich quickly; he contracted substantial debts and went straight into bankruptcy. So now he can't go out at night, because some of his creditors are after him and want to skin him alive. But he's even more afraid of the carabinieri."

"And Carlo Caione?"

"He died of consumption and left his wife with two children."

"Has his wife anything to live on?"

"No, but she's pretty."

The old man was silent. Marta's loom had stopped now. The first shadows of evening were gathering in the Fucino. Don Benedetto spoke again.

"Tell me what Verdone is doing. It's a long time since I heard anything of him."

"He's a clerk in the tax office at Colle, the village he was born in," Concettino said. "He wanted a political career, so as soon as he left school he got in with the Socialists, and in 1924 he was, of course, a member of the Aventine and belonged to a lodge. In the end he tried worming his way in among us, and in 1927 he succeeded, but it hasn't helped him very much. He intrigues, he petitions, he writes letters to the authorities denouncing everybody who has been more fortunate than himself, but he still remains at the counter of the tax office. Rage has made him as green as his name implies."

"But his father is well off. Can't he help him?"

"His father is dead and his property had to be divided up among nine children, six girls and three boys," Concettino answered. "Each of the six girls is uglier than the others, so they are known as the six monkeys."

"Is Pietro Spinacci still mayor?" Sacca asked Concettino.

"How's that!" asked Don Benedetto. "Isn't he a lawyer any longer?"

"He took his lawyer's diploma," Concettino answered, "but he had very little work, so he managed to get appointed mayor of Ortona dei Marsi, a poor town, where the pickings are very small. And now he's a mayor, he's not allowed to practice his profession and drum up clients. So the first administrative mischance that deprives him of his job will leave him in the gutter."

"Tell me what Di Pretoro is doing now," said Don Benedetto.

"All I know is that he spent two terms at the university and then got a job on the railway. I think he must still be employed at Rome Station," said Sacca.

"He was dismissed from the railway some years ago," Concettino said. "Di Pretoro was the best of us at Latin, I don't deny, but in my opinion he was always a muddle-head and half a Socialist. Anyway, he had an affair in his village with a poor little dressmaker who owned nothing in the world but her sewing-machine. She knew the kind of man he was, so she promptly presented him with a son. He married her. She has regularly presented him with a son every year since. They have been married for four years now, and they have five sons, including the one born in advance. And in the meantime he has been dismissed from the railway because of his vague anti-national ideas. No one dismissed from the railway can get a job in any other public service, and private employers have to engage their staff from the employment exchanges, who are obliged by law to reject anyone who is politically suspect. He is too proud to do any kind of manual work. You don't study for ten years to become a carpenter. And besides, his wife, the little dressmaker, is always pregnant or suckling her last-born. So obviously there is often nothing to eat in the house. Then Di Pretoro goes to the tavern and drinks, and when he's drunk he comes home and beats his wife and children until the neighbors intervene and reëstablish peace. And people say that's what comes of sending boys to the priests' college."

Don Benedetto rose to his feet, with an effort. There was a look of affliction on his thin, pale face, with its light, blue veins. He walked a few paces up and down the garden, and, without saying a word, went into the house. Marta had finished her weaving. Her warp-beam was empty. But she remained in her place, bent over her loom, as if her back were aching. Then she passed her hand over the work she had done, which was still around the cloth-beam, and said gently to the two young men, who remained silently sitting beneath the olive tree:

"This rug is my birthday present for Don Benedetto."

She said "Don Benedetto" simply, with distance and respect.

"My dear lady, you make your brother a greater present every day," said Nunzio Sacca. "You have made him the gift of every single day of your life."

Marta blushed to the temples and shook her head. She walked slowly over towards the two young men and sat down between them, beneath the graceful olive tree. Then, in a gentle voice and with many pauses, she said:

"Every one of us is given the gift of life, and what a strange gift it is. If it is preserved jealously and selfishly it impoverishes and saddens, but if it is spent for others it enriches and beautifies. But I do not say that for myself. He who has the good fortune to live at Don Benedetto's side receives a thousand times more than he gives."

"Can't it happen that if one gives everything to others one may remain poor and empty and never enjoy the gifts that life has offered?" Concettino said.

"The gifts that life has given us are truly precious," Marta said. "They are strange and precious. He who wants to enjoy them, and strives to enjoy them, and frets from morning to night to enjoy them, does not enjoy them at all, but burns them up and consumes them rapidly. But he who forgets them, and forgets himself, and gives himself entirely and devotedly to somebody or something, receives a thousand times more than he gives, and at the end of his life the gifts nature has bestowed upon him are still flourishing in him, like May roses."

"That's how Don Benedetto used to talk to us in school," said Nunzio Sacca. "But what good did his teaching do? How did it help Battista Lo Patto and Luigi Candeloro and Antonio Speranza and Di Pretoro and Carlo Caione and the rest?"

Don Benedetto reappeared at the threshold of his house, with a bundle of yellow, faded papers in his hands.

"To what shall I liken you?" he said to his two former pupils sitting on either side of Marta. "To what shall I compare your unhappy generation? You are like children sitting in the market place, calling one to another and saying: 'We have played the flute, and ye have not danced; we have mourned to you and ye have not wept!' Everything has turned out in a manner contrary to what was promised you."

His shining eyes, illuminated by the rays of the setting sun, gave a noble and serene appearance to the old priest's face. His voice was grave, slow, and sad, as of one who has long and vainly been seeking an explanation, and has begun at last to doubt whether any explanation exists.

"I have here an old photograph we had taken fifteen years ago, just before we parted," he said. "I also have here the last Italian essays I made you write for me. The subject I set you was: 'Say sincerely what you would like to be in life, and what purpose you would like to have in life.' I have just re-read the essays written by you two, and by Caione and Di Pretoro and Candeloro and Speranza and Lo Patto and the others of whom you told me. I confess to you, in all confusion and humility, that I am ceasing to understand, and am even beginning to doubt whether it is worth while seeking an explanation. A Frenchman of the last century, who, like you, was educated by priests, said that perhaps the truth is sad. My friends, perhaps the explanation is sad."

Don Benedetto's voice was lower now, and he spoke with a certain hesitation, as though he were thinking out loud, as though there were an internal censor checking his words, or as though he were a short-sighted man moving among unfamiliar objects and fearful of hurting not himself but them. Don Benedetto spread a few of the yellowed papers on the table and said:

"In judging compositions of this kind all sorts of allowances have, of course, to be made. They are full of literary frills in the manner of Pascoli, d'Annunzio, Sem Benelli, and they also contain naïvetés peculiar to a school conducted by priests; then, too, they reflect the illusions of the time at which they were written, and overtones of the recently concluded armistice. But beneath all that, beneath all the frills and furbelows and falsities and impressions of the moment, there was, and you can still hear the echo of it, something essential and characteristic of you, something that fitted in closely with the observations I had made of you, individually and collectively, during the long years of upper and lower school. Later, when you left school and entered the world, that something was not developed and was not satisfied, but was side-tracked, suppressed, thwarted, corrupted, poisoned, subjugated. Now you are between thirty-two and thirty-four years old, and already you look like aged cynics. I speak, of course, of the best of you, of those who are sufficiently intelligent to realize your own failure."

"School isn't life, my dear Don Benedetto," Concettino interrupted. "At school you dream, in life you have to make adjustments. You come up against a reality older than yourself, to which you have to adapt yourself. You don't become what you would like to become."

"And if the adaptation is carried out with new ceremonies and new uniforms," interposed Nunzio Sacca, "you try to convince yourselves and the masses that there has been a revolution."

"You're a great friend of mine, but a miserable cynic," exclaimed Concettino. He rose to his feet and started pacing up and down the garden to divert the conversation from this awkward topic.

Don Benedetto was leaning against the cypress tree and said nothing.

Nunzio Sacca, who had remained seated by Marta's side, attempted to lead the conversation to safer ground.

"The last lesson you gave us," he said to Don Benedetto, "was on Greek tragedy. Your comments were unforgettable."

"Nevertheless, the study of Greek tragedy and my comments did not help you, could not help you, to face and understand the obscure tragedy that was about to overwhelm you," Don Benedetto said. "The idea that man, in our modern age, can play his rôle only in dramas, and never in tragedies, is a piece of stupidity that we may leave to the newspaper critics. When Concettino confessed that you don't become what you would like to become he expressed crudely, without realizing it, the essence of the modern tragedy. Certainly we are no longer victims of the ancient Fate of the Greeks, *Anangke,* Nemesis, but what is this new Fate that prevented you from being what you wanted to be? What is this obscure and pitiless destiny that has played havoc with your generation in the last fifteen years, from the occupation of Fiume to the occupation of the factories, from the smashing of the Socialist Leagues to the liquidation of the Fascists of 1919—this destiny that caused many of you, who were Catholics, to become, first, Nationalists, then Socialists, then Fascists, then advocates of the corporate state, and now, if many signs and tokens do not deceive me, Socialists again? What is this new and inexorable demon, this new and ferocious destiny, that has taken the place of the Fate of the ancients and plays with your lives like a drunkard playing with dice?"

Marta rose briskly to her feet and went towards the table where the dozen glasses were standing, and the bottles containing the refreshments.

"Do you still think the others will come?" she said.

"They certainly intended to come, but they may have missed the train or the post-bus," Concettino said.

Marta made as if to carry the superfluous glasses into the kitchen.

"Leave one of them," said Don Benedetto. "For Don Piccirilli."

"But we didn't invite him," his sister protested. "We left him out on purpose."

"For that very reason he will not fail to appear," Don Benedetto replied. Then he turned to the two young men and went on:

"Of course you remember Piccirilli, the only member of your class who chose to enter the Church. His people were small landowners who lacked the means to enable him to continue his studies; so he went to the Salesians, studied theology, and took orders. As soon as he was ordained he abandoned the Salesians and returned to his diocese. That was not a very proper way to behave towards the Salesians. Now he is a priest in a little parish near here, but he is discontented, because he would like to be a master at the seminary and a canon. In order to ingratiate himself with the bishop he acts as his secret informer. He never fails to put in an appearance on occasions when he believes something may be said that he can denounce to the bishop. As you imagine, therefore, he pays me the honor of frequent visits."

Meanwhile evening had fallen, and Marta had difficulty in filling the glasses in the semi-darkness.

"Sit down and drink," she said.

"My sister would have liked to offer you tamarind, but she remembered too late," Don Benedetto remarked.

"What a charmingly maternal idea!" said Concettino. "Do you believe, dear lady, that we need a purge?"

A cool breeze had begun to blow from the mountains, and Don Benedetto coughed.

"We had better go indoors," said Marta, and the two young men helped her carry the bottles and glasses inside the house. On the ground floor there was one big room, which served as kitchen, as workroom on wet days, and as the room in which guests were received, just as with the peasants. A yarn-windle was hanging on a nail over the door. A distaff was leaning against the doorpost. On the shelves of the bookcase was some coarse crockery ornamented with flowers. On either side were cooking pots and pans and copper kettles. Over the big fireplace were red rows of peppers, brown rows of rowan berries, bunches of garlic, and strings of onions; on the mantelpiece there were a lot of dusty old books; in one corner, no doubt Marta's, was a small recess decorated with lace paper, with a little plaster Madonna, surrounded by paper lilies. The room smelled vaguely of stale biscuits and of fruit preserved in vinegar.

"Sit down and drink," said Marta.

Some one knocked at the door, and Don Piccirilli came in. Don Benedetto received him leaning against the fireplace. Don Piccirilli went up to him, embraced him, cordially offered him his congratulations. Don Benedetto returned his embrace and invited him to join the others.

"Sit down and drink," he said. "There is a glass for you."

Don Piccirilli was rather fat and looked well fed; he had an expansive and jovial air. He said he was late because he had had to finish an article for the diocesan journal.

"The article is entitled 'The Scourge of Our Time,'" said Don Piccirilli.

"Was it about the war and unemployment?" asked Don Benedetto.

This remark annoyed Don Piccirilli.

"Those are political questions," he answered. "Only spiritual questions are dealt with in the diocesan journal. From the purely spiritual point of view, the scourge of our time, in my opinion, is immodesty in dress. Don't you think so?"

"The scourge of our time," calmly replied Don Benedetto, emphasizing each word and looking Don Piccirilli straight in the eye, "is insincerity between man and man, lack of faith between man and man, the pestilential Judas Iscariot spirit that poisons public and private life."

Don Piccirilli changed the subject.

"There has been enormous spiritual progress in my parish in the last few years, thanks be to God," he said. "The number of confessions has increased by forty per cent, and the number of communions by thirty per cent."

"Poor Piccirilli," said Don Benedetto. "You talk of pure spirit and of spiritual progress, and you express yourself in calculations and percentages, just like a baker."

Dr. Sacca was seized with a violent fit of coughing. Marta took from her brother's hands the old photograph dating from 1920, in which he was surrounded by his pupils. She held it well in the light in the recess of the fireplace. Dr. Sacca, Concettino, and Don Piccirilli gathered round and looked at it. Each looked first for himself, then for friends not seen or heard of for many years. Each spoke of past memories, contrasted them with present-day hard facts. In the photograph Concettino Ragù was in the front row, sitting on the ground with his legs crossed. His head was shaven, and there was a catlike expression on his small, dark, gray face. His eyes had remained the same, but fifteen years before nobody could have foreseen that he would ever look like a provincial drill-sergeant, which was what his goatee beard and the way he brushed his hair made him look like now. Nunzio Sacca was one of those who had changed least. But his forehead seemed broader, because he had lost hair over his temples. In the photograph he was sitting behind Don Benedetto, on a step, and you could see his thin neck, his rather narrow shoulders, the deep-set eyes, and the timid and slightly absent-minded air that he still retained.

"Who were your favorite pupils?" Concettino suddenly asked Don Benedetto.

"My favorite pupils?" the old man replied. "Those who were not satisfied with what they found in the textbooks, the insatiable ones."

"Who were they?" his three old pupils exclaimed, their curiosity thoroughly aroused. "Who were they?"

Don Benedetto smiled, then answered:

"Where is Pietro Spina now? What has happened to him?"

In the photograph Pietro Spina was seated on Don Benedetto's right, and Don Benedetto had one hand on his shoulder. Spina had untidy hair, a wild and sullen expression, and his tie was all askew.

When nobody answered, Don Benedetto asked again:

"Where is Pietro Spina? What is he doing? Where does he live?"

The three young men looked at each other in embarrassment. Marta's nerves had been on edge all the afternoon, she had been on the alert the whole time to avoid disagreeable subjects of conversation, but now she looked like one who is tired and resigned and believes that nothing can be done. Don Benedetto turned to Concettino.

"Pietro Spina was your best friend," he said. "You admired him so much, you might almost have been in love with him. Where is he? What news is there of him? What is he doing?" he asked, with eagerness and affection in his voice.

"How should I know? Am I my brother's keeper?" the young officer asked, avoiding Don Benedetto's glance.

The old man was standing near the fireplace, and the reply made him go pale. He almost staggered. He walked slowly over towards Concettino, took his head between his trembling hands, looked him in the eyes, and said, quietly, almost with tears:

"My poor boy, is this the pass to which you have come? You don't know how terrible are the words you have just spoken, the most terrible words in Genesis, and Genesis is a terrible book."

Concettino looked at him, startled, without understanding. Don Benedetto went on, still more quietly, almost whispering into his ear:

"And it came to pass, when they were in the field, that Cain rose up against Abel his brother, and slew him. And the Lord said unto Cain, Where is Abel, thy brother? And he said, I know not. Am I my brother's keeper?"

Don Benedetto walked slowly away from the young officer and sat down in the extreme corner of the room, on a stool beneath the recess in which the little plaster Madonna stood among her colored paper flowers.

"Pietro Spina," said Don Benedetto, "was my favorite pupil. He never knew it, but he was. He was not satisfied with what was in the textbooks, he was insatiable, restless, and often undisciplined. But the most severe punishments he received during all his years at school were invariably provoked by his protests at what he believed to be undeserved punishments inflicted upon others. When he believed himself to be in the right no consideration of expediency could make him hold his peace."

Don Benedetto searched among the yellow papers for the last school essay written by Pietro Spina.

"Listen, this is Spina," he said. " 'If the prospect of being displayed on altars after one's death, and being prayed to and worshiped by a lot of unknown people, mostly ugly old ladies, were not very unpleasant, I should like to be a saint. I should not like to live according to circumstances, environment, and material expediency, but I should like, ignoring the consequences, in every hour of my life to live and struggle for that which seems to me to be right and good.' Fifteen years ago, when I read that confession," Don Benedetto went on, "though I did not doubt Pietro Spina's sincerity, I did not know to what extent he might have been carried away by his own rhetoric. At that time he was devouring the lives of the saints. He had lost his parents some years before, and family misfortunes had reinforced his tendency to meditation."

Don Piccirilli had been waiting for the old man to pause, and now he interrupted.

"In 1920 Spina wanted to become a saint, but in 1921 he joined the Young Socialists—who were atheists and materialists," he said.

"I am not interested in politics," Don Benedetto answered, dryly.

"You are not interested in atheism and the struggle against God?" the young priest asked, curiously.

"He who does not live according to expediency or environment or convenience or for material things," the old man answered, calmly, "he who lives for justice and truth, without caring for the consequences, is not an atheist, but he is in the Lord and the Lord is in him. My dear Piccirilli, you can teach me many things, for example the art of making a career, but I was your master in philology, your master in the science of words, and I am not afraid of them. Nunzio Sacca, tell me what you know of Pietro Spina. Where is he and what is he doing?"

This time Dr. Sacca replied.

"In 1927 he was arrested and deported to one of the islands," he said. "A year later he escaped and fled to Tunis, and then to France. He was expelled from France and went to Switzerland. He was expelled from Switzerland and went to Luxemburg. He was expelled from Luxemburg and went to Belgium. If he hasn't been expelled from Belgium he must be there still. How he manages to live I do not know, but he is bound to be hungry. I have also heard from a relative of his that he is suffering from lung trouble."

Don Benedetto remained silent. Then he turned to Marta and said:

"Foxes have holes, and birds of the air have nests; but the son of man hath not where to lay his head. He goes on living according to the pure dreams of his adolescence, and the Christian countries hunt him like a wild beast."

Marta looked at her brother, frightened.

The three young men rose and took their leave.

"It's late," they said. "We must go."

Don Benedetto accompanied them to the crossroad. Don Piccirilli took the path to the left, towards the mountain. Concettino and Nunzio went to the right, in the direction of the railway.

The old man watched them as they drove away.

After they had gone some distance Concettino murmured to the doctor, without looking at him:

"Spina is in Italy. He returned from Belgium surreptitiously. The police are already on his track. He may have been arrested already. But what can I do if he is mad?"

On the horizon, over the ravine of Forca Caruso, there had appeared a small white cloud. A big and threatening cloud followed close behind it. There was a clap of thunder, a light wind arose, a shudder went over the fields, and it started to rain.

Chapter II

O NE morning Dr. Nunzio Sacca was called to the bedside of a sick man. A young man from Acquafredda came and fetched him in a carriage. The doctor looked at him and said:

"We know each other."

"I am Mulazzo Cardile, of the Cardile family of Acquafredda," the young man said. "Yes, we know each other. My grandfather used to rent Monsignore's mill and lands. It was good land, dear land. For three years my father rented a vineyard belonging to your family, doctor. Then came misfortunes, quarrels, and illnesses. Two of my brothers are in Brazil and do not write."

"We know each other," Dr. Sacca said. "Who is the patient?" The carriage was going against the wind. There was rain in the wind.

"Rain at the end of April is good," said Cardile. "I remember hearing you make a speech in the public square at Acquafredda when I was a boy, Doctor. The speech you made was for the Church and the People. The word 'Liberty' was written on the banner. Our family were on the same side. It was immediately after the war, and liberty was allowed. Then the Church was not for the government, but for the people. We were on the same side. After that the wind changed."

The carriage was now driving into the rain. The rain was coming from the pass where the Campi Palentini broaden out into the Fucino basin. It stretched like a gray veil over the villages of Magliano and Scurcola.

"Now the women and the old folk are for the Church, and we look after our own affairs," Cardile went on. "My father is sixty years old and is still a prior of the Confraternity of the

Holy Sacrament. On Sunday mornings he sings at mass, on Good Friday and Corpus Christi Day he walks in the procession in a red cassock and makes the responses to the *Oremus*. Every year we give two casks of wine to the parish of Acquafredda for masses. All our dead are buried in the Chapel of the Holy Sacrament in Acquafredda cemetery, on the right-hand side as you go in. All these things do not mean that we are any better than the rest, but I have a reason for recalling them. The reason I recall them is that I want to show you we are on the same side."

"We know each other," said the doctor. "We know each other. Who is the patient? Some one in your family?"

The carriage left the national road that led to Acquafredda and entered a side road, full of puddles, running between fields of beans and peas.

"Nevertheless, people have many ways of knowing one another," said Cardile. "We peasants know the better kind of people through the land they own, and from recommendations. But is that a way of knowing people? You work, you buy, you sell, you rent, and you need papers and recommendations. You go abroad to work, and see lots of officials and meet a lot of people. But is that a way of knowing them? Once, when I was working at Estaque, near Marseilles, where a big tunnel was being built, some one said to me: 'There's a countryman of yours here, an educated man.' It'll be some one wanting to get something out of me, I said to myself. My papers and certificates were all in order, I had paid all my dues, and what could he want? Anyway, the man came to me and said he had not been to the Marsica for several years, and he started asking me about Acquafredda and the Campi Palentini, about the people here and about their lives, and he spoke of his own village and of the Fucino. We went on seeing each other in the evenings after that. We used to go and sit on the quay at Estaque, and we would talk till late at night. After a few evenings, when we had told each other everything and knew each other well, we started talking about things that neither he nor I had ever thought about before, simple things, and we started thinking about them together. Sometimes I said the better things, and sometimes he did. It would be impossible to repeat them aloud here now, because you would laugh at me, Doctor. Anyway, during the daytime I worked in the tunnel. It was an eight-hour day, but everybody worked two or three hours extra, to earn more. But after eight hours I used to stop because I knew that that man, whom I enjoyed talking to, was waiting for me. We talked about man, about the earth, and about life. And then I thought to myself, here is a person from whom I get nothing whatever in a practical way, either for work or for my testimonials, or for any of the other papers. Nor does he come to me as a priest or as a schoolmaster or as a propagandist. He is not one of those people who know everything and are paid to convince others. Here is somebody who comes to me like a man. One day he went away and I heard no more of him."

"I can imagine who it was," the doctor interrupted.

"Now I must tell you that two years ago, on my way back with the handcart from the Feast of San Bartolomeo, I found a dog that had been run over by a motor-car on the Magliano road. Its leg was broken and it was howling pitifully. I put it in my cart, tied its foot with a handkerchief, and took it home. Two months later a carter came from Scurcola and took it back. Last summer I found a lame sheep on the road, and I took it home and put it in the shed, between the cow and the donkey. Later its owner came and took it back. That is the custom. And now, last night, the man whom I met at Estaque came and knocked at my door. I didn't recognize him at first."

"Is Pietro Spina here? Are you taking me to him by any chance?" Nunzio Sacca asked, scared out of his life.

Cardile drew the carriage to the side of the road and stopped. The two men jumped down. Cardile tied the horse to an elm tree and covered it with a red rug. The doctor looked all around him anxiously. It was not raining so hard now, and the clouds were drawing away towards Tagliacozzo, but fresh clouds were advancing from the direction of Avezzano. The countryside was deserted. The two men went on talking beside the carriage.

"Well, that man knocked at my door," Mulazzo Cardile went on, "and he wouldn't come in, although he was feverish. So we went for a short walk along a country lane and talked a little about Estaque. And then he started telling me that he had returned secretly to Italy, and that it was only with the greatest of difficulty that he had succeeded in escaping from the police. He said he had lost touch with his party friends, and that for a time he would not be able to get in touch with them again, for fear of being arrested. He told me he had been wandering about the countryside in the rain for some days, but now he couldn't go on, because he had a high fever. He said that after much hesitation he had come to me to ask me to hide him until he got better. He said to me: 'You are a worker, and it is for the party of the workers that I have returned to Italy. Do not betray me.' Last night I hid him in a shed, and now I am wondering what we can do for him. Can we let him die like this?"

"He only had to stay where he was, abroad," the doctor said, in a dry voice.

"But now he is here. I found him on the doorstep, as you might find a dog or a sheep, a dying animal. Can we let him die like this?"

"He has nothing to lose. He is alone. I have a family. Our political ideas are not the same," the doctor said.

"This is not a matter of political ideas," Cardile said. "He is a dying man. They made me learn the catechism by heart when I was a boy. The catechism says: The works of mercy are these: to give drink to the thirsty, to clothe the naked, to give shelter to pilgrims, and to succor the sick. The catechism does not say: to succor the sick who are of the same way of thinking as you. All the catechism says is to succor the sick. But in those days the Church was for the people and not for the government. But perhaps they have changed the catechism now, too."

"Did he send you to me? Did he tell you he knew me?" the doctor asked.

"He said he was at school with you, Doctor, but he told me not to fetch you under any circumstances," Cardile answered.

The two men went on talking in the roadway beside the carriage. Then they stopped. A peasant passed with a donkey laden with wood. A little later an old woman went by with a goat. Cardile did not know whether to speak the whole truth. Then he made up his mind.

"The truth is this," he said. "He did not want me to fetch you. Last night he said to me: 'I returned to my country for the party of the workers, and I asked you to help me because you are an honest worker. But Dr. Sacca is an intellectual, with a career to make. Moreover,' he added, 'he is an intellectual who frequents the episcopate, and for the sake of ingratiating himself with the authorities he might be capable of handing me over to the militia.' But I refused to believe that. He also said that there was only one man who would not be afraid to help him, a priest who had been his master at school, but he said the priest was too old now, and he did not want to involve him in any risk. That was how we parted last night. This morning, when I saw him in daylight, he looked much worse. So I came to you, Doctor, without asking his opinion any further. It would be our duty to help him if he were only a sheep."

Nunzio Sacca was leaning against one of the shafts. He looked anxiously all round him. He seemed very scared. Then he plucked up courage and said:

"He must leave at once. I shall try to persuade him to leave at once. If he needs medicine I shall write out a prescription in the name of some member of your family. May the Lord direct us out of this."

"He is down there," Cardile answered, "in the shed behind the nut tree. You can go down there alone, Doctor. I'll stay here and keep guard."

Dr. Sacca entered the shed behind the nut tree and found a neatly dressed and unassuming little old man sitting on the floor. This annoyed him, for Cardile had not warned him that anybody else would be there.

"Where is the patient?" he asked.

"Who sent for you?" the old man answered.

"Mulazzo Cardile told me there was some one here who was ill," the doctor said.

"I told him to do nothing of the sort," the old man answered, rising to his feet and looking Nunzio Sacca in the eyes.

To his amazement Dr. Sacca recognized his former school-fellow, Pietro Spina.

His big, deep-set, flashing eyes, his thin lips, his thin, bloodless, transparent pink ears, his thick, untidy hair were all that were left of his former features. The skin of his face was like lined parchment.

"You're the same age as I, thirty-three, and you look like sixty," the doctor barely dared to murmur. "How did you manage to reduce yourself to this state?"

Spina laughed loudly and happily, like a child who has played a successful practical joke. He then explained that before returning to Italy he had treated his face with a special iodine mixture, in order to give himself the lines, wrinkles, and complexion of premature old age, and thus make himself unrecognizable to the police.

"It's my own invention," Spina said, "and it is capable of the most widespread application. When the average young Italian stops wanting to become the lover of every American or Swiss tourist and starts applying himself to more serious aims, perhaps it will be necessary to open an artificial disfigurement institute for the handsomest and daintiest dandies, to take the place of the present beauty parlors."

Dr. Sacca looked in astonishment at the disfigured and aged face of his contemporary. Pietro Spina had never been considered good-looking, but his impetuous nature and his sincerity had always made him attractive to women. He had never been an idle petticoat chaser, but he had the reputation of having a passionate temperament and of being a violent and tenacious lover. Dr. Sacca found it hard to understand how political sectarianism could have driven him to disfigure himself, so that he looked like an old man while still in the prime of life.

"The police succeeded in recognizing you in spite of your precautions," he remarked.

"Not at all," Spina replied. "I was denounced to the Rome police, obviously by some spy, almost before I had time to get in touch with the organization. The only reason I escaped was that the Rome police distributed a copy of an old photograph of me. In any case I had no intention whatever of staying in Rome. I returned to Italy to work among the peasants."

This stratagem of Spina's, so like a device out of a novel of the romantic 1848 period, recalled Dr. Sacca to a sense of the childish and dangerous situation into which he had allowed himself to be drawn. The noise of a lorry passing on the national road made him start.

"Don't be frightened," Spina said, with a smile. "Sit down." The noise of the lorry faded away.

"I have no need to sit down," said the doctor, "because I have no intention of remaining. I came only to advise you to leave here and go abroad again as quickly as you can, in our interests and your own."

"Thank you for your advice, but I am not going abroad again."

"Why did you come back to Italy? If you love liberty, why didn't you stay in one of the countries where there is liberty?"

"I came back here to be able to breathe," said Spina.

Sacca tried to find language that Spina would understand.

"The greatest revolutionaries," he said, "your masters, who worked for their ideals for decades and destroyed tyrants, spent their whole lives in exile. Why can't you?"

Spina was familiar with this objection.

"You are perfectly right," he said. "I do not know how to spare myself in the expectation of playing a great political rôle. I am a very bad revolutionary. But I shall not go back into exile."

"And if they catch you?"

"There's certainly a danger of prison, but that's not enough to keep me away from my country. I'm an internationalist, but out of my country I feel like a fish out of water. I have had enough of exile. I don't know how to wait."

"Then it is an affair that does not concern me, and I wash my hands of it," said Nunzio Sacca, going through the motions of washing his hands as he spoke.

"I'm glad to hear you express yourself in such biblical fashion," said Spina. "It's obvious that your religious education wasn't wasted."

Then he went on:

"I spent the other night in a cave on Monte della Croce. I was hungry, thirsty, feverish, and drenched to the skin. In the distance I could see the school where we spent eight years together. The flower-beds we looked after together must still be in the garden. Do you remember my geraniums? The big dormitory, where we slept with our beds so close together that we could talk nearly all night without the prefect noticing it, must still be on the second floor. Do you remember the fantastic plans we used to make? Don Benedetto expounded the symbolism of ancient poets, Don Sillogismo expounded the laws of logic, and Don Zaccheo held forth on the texts of the Holy Fathers and the deeds and sayings of heroes and kings. During meals in the big refectory each of us in turn used to have to read aloud the life of a martyr or a saint. When we emerged from that fantastic world we found a society, a Church, a state that were very different from the world we had grown up in, and each one of us had to make his choice. Either we had to submit to it or be crushed by it, either serve it or rebel against it. Once upon a time there were middle ways. But after the war, for our generation, those ways were shut. How many years have passed since then? Fifteen. Nobody, seeing us here now, would imagine that up to the age of twenty our lives ran parallel and that we dreamed the same dreams for the future."

Nunzio Sacca was embarrassed.

"It is true," he said, "that we belong to different parties now."

"Different humanities," Spina corrected him. "Between free men and slaves, in the long run, there is more than a difference of party, there is a difference of humanity. I would say a difference of race, had that word not been compromised by the Germans. I talk like this because there are no other terms for what I have to say. In a situation in which I am completely in your hands, to pretend esteem towards you and those who have conducted themselves like you would cost me an effort of which I am not capable. Besides, the day of reckoning is not yet. You may go."

Pietro Spina walked back into the empty shed and sat down

on a donkey's saddle. The doctor hesitated, then went towards him and said:

"At least let me examine you. I can get you some medicine through Cardile."

Spina reluctantly bared his chest. The lined and faded parchment of his aged-looking head and face contrasted strangely with his body, which was clean, white, and graceful, like an adolescent's. The doctor bent over his sick friend and started tapping each rib of his narrow, hollow chest, to which he repeatedly applied his ear, observing the desperate hammering of his heart, trying to fathom from every side the anxious panting of his lungs. The examination exhausted Spina's strength and he slowly slid from the saddle and lay full-length on the straw-covered floor, with half-shut eyes. Nunzio Sacca was filled with a sense of warmth and good-fellowship.

"Listen, Pietro, my friend," he said. "Don't let us quarrel. You must not die."

Sacca held one of his hands and talked of the illusions, the disappointments, the wretchedness, the lies, the intrigues, the nausea of his daily life.

"All our life is lived provisionally," he said. "We think that for the time being things are bad, that for the time being we must adapt ourselves, even humiliate ourselves, but that it is all just temporary, and that one day life, real life, will begin. We get ready to die, still complaining that we have never really lived. Sometimes I am obsessed with the idea that we have only one life, and spend the whole of it living provisionally, waiting for real life to begin. And thus the time passes. Nobody lives in the present. Nobody has any profit from his daily life. Nobody can say: On that day, on that occasion, my life began. Even those who enjoy all the advantages of belonging to the government party have to live by intrigue, and are thoroughly nauseated by the dominant stupidity. They too live provisionally, and spend their lives waiting."

"One must not wait," said Spina. "In exile one spends one's life waiting too. One must act. One must say: Enough! from this very day."

"But if there is no liberty?" said Nunzio Sacca.

"Liberty isn't a thing you are given as a present," said Spina. "You can be a free man under a dictatorship. It is sufficient if you struggle against it. He who thinks with his own head is a free man. He who struggles for what he believes to be right is a free man. Even if you live in the freest country in the world and are lazy, callous, apathetic, irresolute, you are not free but a slave, though there be no coercion and no oppression. Liberty is something you have to take for yourself. It's no use begging it from others."

Nunzio Sacca was thoughtful and troubled.

"You are our revenge," he said. "You are the better part of us. Try to be strong. Try to live. Take real care of your health."

"Nunzio," said Pietro, speaking with difficulty, "if my return to Italy achieves nothing but to have revived that voice of yours and to have regained a lost friend, it will have been worth the cost. That was how you used to speak during those nights at school, when the rest of the dormitory was asleep."

Cardile appeared in the doorway, dripping from the rain.

"It's still raining, and there's not a soul to be seen," he said.

The doctor and Cardile went to one side and discussed the immediate measures to be taken on Spina's behalf. Cardile took the sick man in his arms and carried him up a ladder to the hayloft overhead.

"For the time being you'll stay hidden here," the doctor said to Spina. "You must lie down all day long. Cardile will bring you what is necessary. Meanwhile we'll try to find you a more comfortable hiding-place."

"I shall not go back to exile," said Spina.

"You wouldn't be able to even if you wanted to, I'm afraid," said the doctor. "You're not in a state to make a long journey, or to cross the Alps surreptitiously. We shall have to find you a hiding-place for a few months, somewhere safe and quiet and not far away. After that you can do what you like."

Pietro Spina was left alone, buried in the straw. After the last few days of flight and danger, he could now rest, comforted by the warmth of his fever. These were his first moments of peace since returning to his country, his first moments of nervous relaxation. That Cardile had given him shelter, as he had expected he would, gave him great pleasure. You had to trust people. That Nunzio Sacca had helped him, contrary to his expectations, gave him still greater pleasure. You had to have faith in friendship.

The thought of these things made him feel like jumping with joy on the straw, particularly as there was nobody there to see. Then he remembered that he must stay quiet, because he was engaged in a difficult struggle with death. So he sank back into the straw, like the Child in the Manger. For the analogy with the Child in the Manger to be complete, he should really have a cow and an ass on either side of him. Indeed a cow and an ass did share his roof, but they were down below in the shed, and only at night-time because during the day they had to be out working for their straw. By the time the animals came back at night the outlaw upstairs was fast asleep. The soft straw made him go to sleep and dream of expanses of summer fields rich with fruitful crops, and poppies, and the noise of crickets. Disgust and exasperation at the police for having wormed their way into his organization, thus forcing him to break off his connection with the comrades to whom he had presented himself on returning from abroad, yielded now to a sense of fellowship and unity with the people of his own countryside, and this feeling was reinforced by the behavior of Cardile and Nunzio Sacca. The new mood gave him strength as he lay there on the straw; it was like a resumption of physical contact with his own earth, like returning to the breast of mother nature. He was burning with fever, yet felt well. After the uncomfortable years of exile he felt he was starting to breathe again.

Behind the hayloft there was a crystal-clear, chattering brook, winding its way between clean, polished stones and tufts of water plants. The chatter of the brook was the most important sound that came to his ears as he lay in the straw. It was his lullaby during the long nights, with its old song that yet was always new. Thus were myths and fables born. Trout, whisper a pretty tale to this man of your own countryside, this man whom the townsmen are hunting!

Spina slept a great deal. He only woke up when he knew Cardile was coming with food and medicine. He ate, took his medicine, then sank back into the straw and went to sleep again.

Cardile came three times a day. He came on his donkey, dismounted, unloaded it, tied it by the halter to a ring fixed in the wall, entered the shed, and climbed to Spina's hayloft. Spina recognized every one of his movements. Cardile never remained a moment longer than necessary. They would exchange a few words and Cardile would go away at once.

"Have you any news from Dr. Sacca?" Spina would ask every time.

"No," Cardile would answer.

Spina waited. He was not in a hurry. The loft had a big window, through which the hay was brought after the threshing. Through it Spina, remaining in the shadow, could see a wide expanse of fields; wheat-fields of tender green, fields of beans with black eyelets showing among the silver leaves, and low vines. In the distance he could also see a stretch of the national road. One night a line of carts passed, a long procession with little twinkling lights dangling between the wheels, going to some fair. Spina dropped off to sleep and went to the fair too.

Between one sleep and the next Spina was an interested observer of the life about him. The feelings he experienced were curious and difficult to describe. What struck him most was the astonishing naturalness of everything his eyes beheld. Everything was in its place; not in the fictitious world of his diseased exile's imagination, with its unreal countryside and its unreal peasants, but in its place. Spina thought of the articles and pamphlets he had written in exile. In every one of them he had striven after realism to the uttermost; they all seemed to him now to have been woven out of moonshine. He was overwhelmed and astonished at the naturalness of what he saw. The fields, the peasants, the donkeys, were real and natural. There they were before his eyes, in three dimensions, outside him, independent of him, no longer merely the products of his heated imagination. He looked at his own sick body as a natural object among other natural objects; as a thing among other things; no longer the central, fundamental object in relation to all the rest, but a natural object among other natural objects; a concrete, limited thing; a product of the earth. On one side of Spina's body, stretched on the straw, was a row of rolls, on the other a bottle of red wine. That was what Cardile had brought him for a meal. The straw was yellow, the bread was brown, the wine was red.

Spina had with him some crumpled notebooks he had filled with jottings on the agrarian question. These might have been dangerous to him in the event of a chance examination by the police, but he had been unwilling to part with them. He had believed his notes might be useful as the basis for a larger work, especially if he should have to remain for some weeks apart from the active struggle and the work of the organization. Now he glanced casually through them, read a few sentences here and there, but could not go on. They might have been written in Chinese. At heart, theory had always bored him. He had come to Italy not to think, but to act.

One day Dr. Sacca read Cardile a long lecture about vitamins, the point of which was that Spina needed a more substantial diet. From that day on Cardile brought Spina a double row of rolls and a double quantity of wine. Spina had never been a drinker, but to cleanse his palate of all memory of the *moules* and the *choux braisés* of Charleroi and Seraing he now drank gladly. Every now and then Cardile managed to steal some cheese or salami without his mother noticing it, and those occasions were real feasts for Spina.

The wine kept Spina in a state of perpetual exhilaration. One day, when he was feeling particularly happy, Cardile arrived with a letter from Dr. Sacca mysteriously and guardedly describing a plan which would enable him to spend two or three months in safety in a village in the mountains. Two or three months would give him time enough to recover. Spina did not immediately grasp all the details of the scheme by which these months of safety were to be assured, but he understood enough to realize that the idea behind it was fantastic. It appealed to his sense of humor. He therefore agreed to it. Dr. Sacca arrived next evening, after he had gone to sleep. Spina descended the ladder and lit the oil-lamp. He found that his friend had brought a big bundle of priestly robes and other ecclesiastical objects. At this sight Spina was unable to conceal a certain feeling of embarrassment.

"I have been outside the Church for many years," he said. "But I must confess I don't like the idea of disguising myself as a priest. I'm afraid such an act of irreverence is inconsistent with my character."

Dr. Nunzio Sacca seemed actually pleased at these scruples.

"If I didn't know you, and if I believed you capable of putting these garments to irreverent use, I should not have suggested them," he said.

The investiture took place in the shed, to the feeble light of the oil-lamp, with the cow and the donkey as spectators. The cow apparently did not understand, for it lay down, shut its eyes, and went to sleep, or at any rate pretended to. But the donkey remained standing and staring. Its gaze seemed to worry the doctor. He took the beast and turned it round the other way. It allowed itself to be treated in this fashion, but promptly turned its head and stubbornly went on gazing at the man who had descended from the loft and was now putting on a long black soutane with a row of little buttons in front.

"The lamb hides beneath a wolf-skin in order not to be torn to pieces," Nunzio remarked.

The eyes in Spina's burnt face assumed a childlike gravity.

Dr. Nunzio Sacca improvised a speech, in a semi-serious voice.

"These vestments," he said, "are descended from the primitive mystery religions, from the priests of Isis and Serapis, as, of course, you know. They were inherited by the first monastic communities in the Catholic Church, who tried to preserve the Christian mysteries from worldly contamination and to assure the essential charismatic virtues to a minority living apart from the world and opposed to the world. Thus do usages outlive the age in which they were born, and pass from one religion to another. And now, here are you, a man dedicated to the new revo-

lutionary mysteries, to the mysteries of revolutionary materialism, donning the dark vestments that have been the symbols of
sacrifice and supernatural inspiration for thousands of years."

A smile came into Spina's eyes.

"I do not understand," Nunzio went on in the same tone,
"why Karl Marx did not introduce a similar costume, or at least
the tonsure, for members of the Workers' International, to distinguish the functionary, depositary, and interpreter of the
sacred texts, from the ordinary mortal. . . ."

Time was pressing.

"What will you call yourself?"

Spina considered for a moment and then said:

"Spada."

"All right," said Nunzio. "Don Paolo Spada."

"Why Don Paolo?"

"Pietro Spada would be too much like Pietro Spina. Well,
reverend Don Paolo, let us go. Have you forgotten anything?
Have you got everything in your bag? Your calotte, your breviary, your rosary, your scapular?"

"Let us go," answered Don Paolo Spada. *"Procedamus in
pace."*

Chapter III

D
ON PAOLO SPADA, curled up in Annibale Soffritto's small open cab, which was drawn by a bay horse, left the broad corridor of the Campi Palentini behind him and entered the hollow of the Fucino. It was the hour when the Constellation of the Serpent rises with its forked tongue from behind Mount Parasano. The clip-clop of the horse's hooves woke the dogs in every barn the cab passed and made them howl. Curious faces appeared at windows in which there was still a light.

Thus did Don Paolo Spada return, after ten years, to the region in which he was born and grew to manhood. The great pyramid of Monte Velino, its two summits still white with snow, rose on his left in a livid light. The hills and alluvial deposits at the foot of the mountains dwindled and faded away into the darkness of the plain. The cab passed through Avezzano, with its mansions and villas next to agglomerations of squalid hovels. Twenty years after the earthquake of 1915 many of the houses were still broken skeletons, and often grass was to be seen growing among the ruins.

Don Paolo was curled up in the shaky cab, and he was filled with astonishment at being able to return to his native region without anyone taking notice of him, at being able to enter and leave a place without anyone giving the alarm.

Annibale was sitting on the box, smoking in silence. All he had to do to keep the animal at a trot was to shake the reins every now and then. Now, however, he turned to Don Paolo and said:

"The Acquafredda blacksmith, master Letterio, used to shoe a horse for one lira. So I used to pay him one lira. Then he said he would rather have two eggs. Eggs are women's business with

38

us; however, my wife agreed, and every time he shod my horse
I gave him two eggs. Yesterday I went to him with my horse
and two eggs, as usual. Master Letterio said he wanted three
eggs, because iron had gone up on account of the new war. He
shod my horse and I went back to my wife and said I owed one
egg, and so on and so forth, because of the war. My wife started
scolding and grumbling and wouldn't hear of it. Since then I've
passed the blacksmith's twice, and each time he's called out:
'Well, isn't that egg laid yet?' 'Wait till tomorrow,' I told him.
Tomorrow the weather will change. Do you see that cloud over
Pescina, sir?"

Annibale turned to see what the priest had to say about it,
but found he had gone to sleep. The cab had reached a crossroad. To get to Fossa dei Marsi, where Don Paolo was going to
spend the night, by the route arranged, Annibale should have
gone straight on and taken the empty roads of the Fucino. This
was not the usual way, but Don Paolo had agreed to pay extra
for the sake of avoiding the road running round the edge of
the Fucino. The latter was shorter, but it went through a number of villages.

"I have heard a great deal about the plain of the Fucino and
the modern manner in which it is cultivated, and about its
canals, so I prefer to take the longer route," he had said to Annibale.

But now he was asleep, and if he wished to see canals he
would have to dream about them, because Annibale took the
shorter way. The road continued with short ascents and descents.
During one of the ascents Don Paolo awoke. High over the
Fucino the Constellation of the Serpent had been joined by that
of Serpentarius. Don Paolo saw he was on the wrong road.

"Is this the road we agreed on?"

"The weather will change tomorrow," said Annibale.

"Is this one of the roads of the Fucino?"

"If you are cold, you only have to say so, sir."

"Can any canals be seen from here?" Don Paolo persisted.

"There's one," said Annibale, calmly pointing to a stream

that came tumbling down the hillside and passed under a bridge beneath the road. Then he went on:

"Well, the Acquafredda blacksmith now wants three eggs to shoe a horse, because iron has gone up on account of the new war. . . ."

Don Paolo did not fall asleep again, but neither did he listen to what Annibale said. His mind withdrew into a sudden and profound silence, from which memories of his childhood and adolescence emerged one by one. The road had been freshly graveled. The carriage plunged on in space and time. Don Paolo began to recognize every bridge, every vineyard, every stream, every tree, everything in that landscape that was old, and also that little which was new. At the Orta crossroad he recognized Acquasanta's tavern in the darkness. The landlady was taking in the chairs, and a girl was helping her. Could Acquasanta's daughter be as big as that? Acquasanta must be getting on herself. In another ten years the girl will be the land-lady, and she'll have a daughter of her own to help her take the chairs in. Thus the wheel turns. The wheels of the cab sank in the gravel of the roadway and turned only with difficulty. Suddenly, at a bend in the road, there appeared the first houses of Orta, only a few steps away, and there was the electric light outside the wheelwright's dark shop at the entrance to the vil-lage.

Don Paolo closed his eyes. He did not want to see. Nero, the wheelwright's mastiff, was the first to notice the cab's approach. Nero barked two or three times, as usual. Then he started listen-ing behind the shop door. He growled a few times, in an uncer-tain and interrogative manner. The cab passed so close that it almost grazed the shop door. Nero let forth a long and piercing howl. Favetta, the bitch on guard in the garden behind the church, answered in alarm. She wanted to know what was the matter. "What is it? What is it?" she barked. Nero answered, indignantly: "What do you mean, what is it? Can't you hear it?" Favetta, behind the church, could not tell what it was, so she barked again. "What is it? What is it?" This made Nero angry, "Can't you hear it?" he howled, three, four, five times. The carriage passed over the cobblestones of the little village square. Thereupon Favetta started barking like a maniac. She awoke her puppies, who were asleep in their kennel. She started jumping against the garden gate, together with her brood, and barked and barked and barked. "What is it? What is it? What is it?" the sleepy puppies yapped and whined at their mother. This made her angry. "What do you mean, what is it? Can't you hear it?" she barked back. Other dogs added their voices to the chorus one by one. Leo, a sheep-dog, woke all the dogs in the neighborhood of the mill, the brickyard, and the stables. Calvino, a wolf-dog, roused all those at the little villas up on the hill, the sporting dogs and the ladies' pets.

Don Paolo still had his eyes shut. Thirty or forty dogs were snarling, growling, barking, and howling in all parts of the village. They were still barking when the cab left the last houses of Orta behind, and then, one by one, they stopped. Calvino was the most persistent. When at last he stopped, too, Don Paolo opened his eyes. The cab came to a fountain with a big drinking-trough for cattle returning from the fields. On the fountain was a bronze plaque with the words: "Built by the Spina family."

"I'm thirsty," Don Paolo said to the driver. "Stop!"

He got out of the cab, and drank from the hollow of his hands. He passed his wet hands across his burning brow. There was no more gravel on the road now, and the horse could trot again. Don Paolo sat with his back to the horse, and looked at the last lights in the windows of his native village. There were still lights in about a dozen scattered windows, and they started going out one after the other at irregular intervals. One went out on the hill, then one in the valley, then one by the river, then one by the cemetery, then one on the hill, then one by the cemetery, then one by the river, and then another by the cemetery. In the end only three lights were left, and, since the hour was late, these were doubtless in sick-room windows. Then the night breeze shifted and the trees rustled towards the east. The moon rose. Don Paolo's head drooped and he went to sleep again.

Annibale woke him up at Fossa dei Marsi, outside the Girasole Hotel.

Before taking his leave, Annibale asked the priest a favor.

"Couldn't you write me a recommendation, sir?"

"To whom and for what?"

Annibale thought a moment and said:

"I can't say just at the moment, but there are plenty of occasions when it will come in handy. You could write me a general recommendation, sir."

"But I don't know you," said the priest.

"Good-bye!" said Annibale, and set off back to Acquafredda.

Don Paolo climbed wearily up to his bedroom and went to sleep. Next morning he awoke early, but felt so tired that he stayed in bed. Dr. Sacca had given him some typewritten instructions entitled, "How a Priest Should Conduct Himself Outside His Diocese." Don Paolo Spada belonged to the diocese of Frascati, and had come to the dei Marsi diocese to recuperate in the mountain village of Pietrasecca. The typed instructions covered ways of dealing with difficult situations that might arise. Don Paolo read and re-read them. The carter who was going to take him to Pietrasecca was not coming to fetch him till the afternoon, so Don Paolo spent the whole morning in his bedroom. He noted with satisfaction that the bedroom contained a washstand with running water. After living in a hayloft it is pleasant to have a washstand at one's disposal. Besides, the washstand indicated that progress was taking place in his country. Over the washstand there was a notice in beautiful handwriting.

"Gentlemen are requested not to urinate in the wash basin because of the smell," it stated.

Nevertheless, the washstand stank.

Don Paolo observed himself in the mirror. Before leaving Acquafredda he had had his hair cut short. He looked very funny with his black cassock and his shorn head, and he almost started weeping. The cassock had twenty-eight buttons in front. The idea of having to fasten or undo twenty-eight buttons every time he put it on or took it off plunged him in despair. Then he discovered that if he unbuttoned it only from the head to the waist he could either pull it over his head or let it fall and step out of it. The idea of these feminine expedients made him laugh. Then he was plunged in despair once more at the thought of having to lift his skirts whenever he wanted something from his trousers pockets. How absurd to lift one's skirt in public! However, he eventually discovered a slit near the pockets. This discovery filled him with joy. He ended by deciding that it wasn't so very difficult to pretend to be a priest, after all. At lunch he made the acquaintance of Berenice Girasole, the widowed proprietress of the hotel.

The dining-room walls were entirely papered with colored illustrations from a well-known illustrated weekly. Among other exciting incidents a signalman's daughter was to be seen in the act of saving a train from certain disaster, an airplane was being assaulted by an eagle, and terrified pedestrians were being chased by wild beasts that had escaped from a menagerie in the middle of a town. Signora Berenice sat down at the priest's table to recount her personal misfortunes. She wore no corsets and was perspiring freely, and her vast breasts were drooping, like poor things that had grown tired of standing up. When Berenice started talking of the Church Don Paolo interrupted.

"I am sorry," he said, "but I do not belong to this diocese. I come from Frascati, and am here for a rest."

Berenice stopped, offended.

The sun was shining, and Don Paolo went and sat on a seat outside the hotel. Five or six flashy young men were sitting around a small table, dozing, with extinguished cigarette stumps in their mouths, with their trousers half unbuttoned, looking as if they were dead. Other idle youths were sitting at another table farther away, playing cards and spitting in every direction. Nearly all of them had government party emblems in their buttonholes. Among the card-players was an older man who looked like a retired actor, with mustaches sticking up and a little pointed beard sticking down, playing cards and noisily drinking his coffee. At the sight of the strange priest he gave the sign against the evil eye.

"Iron! Iron!" he called out.

The sleepers awakened, and everyone hastened to find some iron object to touch. Those who were last put their hands into their left trousers pockets. Don Paolo was well acquainted with this rite. He nearly responded with an outburst of profanity, but restrained himself and held his peace. After all, the behavior of these idle people confirmed his status as a priest.

The hotel overlooked a small cobbled square; at the other end of it were the beflagged government party offices and the town-hall, which was adorned with a medallion of King Humbert with his big mustaches. On one side was a small draper's shop, displaying materials and handkerchiefs printed in vivid colors. The draper, who had immense handlebar mustaches, was sitting outside his shop. He was surrounded by flies, and from time to time he cleared his throat and spat, in a wide arc that sometimes reached the very middle of the little square. Posters in honor of a noted cycling champion were suspended from the telegraph wires. The presence of the strange priest attracted a swarm of fly-infested beggars. A cripple advanced on crutches and begged for alms in the name of them all. Don Paolo retired into the hotel. Berenice approached him, plucked up courage and started again:

"You look so kind, and there's a dying girl. . . ."

"I am sorry," said Don Paolo, "but I do not belong to this diocese."

Berenice could restrain herself no longer and burst into tears.

"Let me at least speak," she said. "The girl won't have the priest from here, because he's a relative. So I told her there was a strange priest here and she agreed."

"I am sorry," said Don Paolo, "but I do not belong to this diocese."

Berenice wept and wailed and rocked from side to side.

"How can a girl be left to die like this, without a priest and without a doctor? If a horse is ill, the vet comes and the neighbors are there to help."

"Why without a doctor?" said Don Paolo, his curiosity aroused.

Berenice feared she had said too much. She looked about her in alarm.

"Can I speak under the seal of silence?" she said.

Don Paolo indicated that she could.

Berenice started whispering, between her sobs:

"The girl isn't married and was going to have a baby, so she tried to get rid of it, so as not to be dishonored and shame her family. The law does not allow it, and if a doctor or a midwife or anybody else helps her, it means prison. Many cases like that have ended up in prison. You only need read the papers. There are some who end up still worse. The daughter of the Fossa notary drank nitric acid when she was four months gone. A girl who was maid to the mayor went to Tivoli and threw herself over the waterfall. But this poor girl tried to get rid of it herself. She had to choose between death and dishonor. She risked her life, and she's dying. It's impossible to send for the doctor, because he would report it and the whole thing would be known. She won't let me send for the priest, because he's a relation. She has sinned, certainly, but there is pardon for us all. Christ died on the Cross for us all."

It was impossible for Don Paolo to refuse. Berenice beckoned him to follow her, as though there were something else she wanted to tell him. In alarm he followed her to the first floor. Berenice went into a small room, with Don Paolo behind her. The room was in semi-darkness and smelled of disinfectant. In a corner was a small iron bedstead, under a big crucifix.

"Bianchina," Berenice whispered.

Something moved on the bed. A small, white, sharp-featured, childish face, disfigured by pain, appeared among the thick, black tresses strewn over the pillow. Don Paolo became aware that Berenice had gone. He remained standing by the door. A moment passed. He thought of slipping away on tiptoe, but he was held by the dying girl's large, staring eyes. Suppose he went away and she started screaming? How could he make the dying girl understand that he was not a priest like the others? The idea of lending himself to an imposture was repugnant to him. Don Paolo did not move and did not know what to do.

This was an eventuality not provided for in Dr. Sacca's instructions. The dying girl went on looking at him with her great big eyes. Then Don Paolo said:

"Good morning!"

He walked slowly, on tiptoe, towards the girl, bent over her, and kissed her hand. Her eyes filled with tears. The light blanket that covered her revealed the outline of her graceful, wasted form, the shape of her breasts, like two lemons, and her thin legs, all skin and bone.

"My dear girl," the priest said. "My dear girl, I know everything. I beg you to tell me nothing. I beg you not to humiliate yourself and not to renew your sufferings. You have no need to confess. You are confessed already."

"Will you give me absolution?" the girl asked.

"You are forgiven," said the priest. "My dear girl, how could I not forgive you? You have already done penance, and it has been too hard."

Don Paolo held the girl's hands in his own. His hands were burning.

"You have fever, too. Are you ill?" the girl asked.

Don Paolo nodded.

"I am doing penance, too," he said.

The voice of Magascià, the carter, was heard from the street.

"Where's the priest who's going to Pietrasecca?" he said.

"And now I must go," the priest said to the dying girl. "Have no fear; you are forgiven. What will not be forgiven is this evil society that forced you to choose between death and dishonor."

Old Magascià, the carter, was sitting at the threshold of the hotel. He had finished his soup, and now he was dipping his bread in his wine. He was a big, bearded man, broad-chested and massively built. The left sleeve of his coat hung empty from his shoulder. He made the priest take his place beside him, and the two-wheeled cart went off slowly, drawn by a she-ass.

"How long ago did you lose your arm?" the priest asked.

"Two years last Candlemas," said Magascià. "But it's no use complaining. God sends flies to plague old asses."

Magascià tied the reins to the brake and lit his pipe.

"There's no need for me even to hold the reins," he said. "The she-ass has taken this road every week for the last ten years, and never makes a mistake. She knows where she can stop to drink and where she can stop to relieve nature, and she knows how long it takes up every hill and down every slope."

Magascià had bought a new hat at Fossa and was wearing it on top of his old one. First he put his two hats on the back of his head, then on one side, like a policeman, and then on the other side, but could not get comfortable and kept on fidgeting.

"Her name is Bersagliera," he said, indicating the poor, scraggy beast that was pulling the cart. "Bersagliera means that she ought to go quickly, but she's old now and goes at a walking pace."

"We all grow old," said the priest.

"A donkey's a lucky beast, all the same," said Magascià. "A donkey works till it's twenty-four, a mule till it's twenty-two, and a horse till it's fifteen. But a man works till he's seventy or more. God took pity on animals, but not on man. But He's got the right to do what He likes."

The cart passed a shed. Bersagliera started braying at the top of her voice, and slowed down till she almost came to a standstill. More braying answered her from inside the shed.

"That's an old sweetheart of hers," Magascià explained. "She had some adventures with him when she was young. They greet each other every time they pass. Of course they are both old now, but the heart doesn't grow old."

Outside the town the road started ascending. Mountains, valleys, hills, fields, and roads once more came into sight. Every moment the priest had a more commanding view of the green bowl of the Fucino, which, from above, looked like a great volcanic crater. The villages that dotted the crater's rim still bore signs of the earthquake. They looked like a lot of wretched beehives that had been shivered and smashed and only partially repaired. The earth still smelled of fire and water.

Magascià's cart proceeded at a walking-pace. A cart with a load of grass and a man lying asleep on top of it, caught up with it and passed it. Later it was overtaken by a cart drawn by an ox and a cow. The ox was licking the cow's ear as it went along. Magascià's cart was next overtaken by a family of poor peasants, father, mother, and child, all on the same donkey. The mother was suckling her child.

"How are the crops?" Magascià asked the man on the donkey.

"Bad, very bad," was the answer.

"That means he'll have a good harvest," Magascià whispered in the priest's ear.

"Then why did he say the opposite?"

"To save himself from the evil eye, of course," said Magascià.

"And how are *your* crops?"

"Terrible, absolutely terrible!" said Magascià, making the sign of the Cross.

"But so far the weather has been very favorable," the priest observed.

"It's all the fault of these motor-cars," said Magascià. "The smell they make destroys the crops."

Every now and then they came upon heaps of stones at the side of the road. Behind them stonebreakers were sitting on the ground, sheltered by screens of fagots, hammering away at the biggest stones. Magascià's cart passed through the village of Lama dei Marsi. Ox-horns were fixed on the outsides of the houses and cottages as a protection against the evil eye. The usual women with their jugs and pails were gathered round the fountain; the usual youths with their bicycles were hanging about the café; the usual old men were smoking at the thresholds of their houses; and the usual policeman was walking up and down the single village street in a resplendent uniform worthy of a Mexican general.

Just beyond the village there was a chapel to the Blessed Virgin. Magascià made the sign of the Cross.

"That is a chapel of Our Lady of the Roses, and it commemorates an ancient miracle," he said. "One year roses bloomed and cherries ripened and sheep lambed in January. Instead of rejoicing the people were terrified. Did not all those blessings portend some great disaster? Sure enough, that summer the cholera came."

"Why was the chapel built?" the priest asked.

"To keep Our Lady quiet," Magascià replied. "And this year's a good year, too," he went on. "Not for me, of course. I mean for others, for most people. Who knows what misfortunes are in store?"

Beyond the chapel the road wound between two hills, crossed a bridge, and entered the valley of Pietrasecca.

A group of women were pulling a thin little old cow, which had stopped dead just at the bridge and refused to budge.

"You've crossed it dozens of times! Why won't you now? What's the matter with you?" one of the women was saying.

The cow refused to budge or to discuss the matter.

"Aren't you ashamed of yourself?" the woman went on. "Really, you ought to be ashamed of yourself. Is this a way to behave without any reason at all?"

Magascià's cart advanced slowly into the valley of Pietrasecca. The valley at first was wide, then narrowed, and the road wound its way between steep stopes of gray, sun-baked rock. Between the rocks, in the hollows filled with alluvial deposits, were tiny fields cultivated with maize and potatoes, farms measured not in acres, but in ells and feet. Similar tiny fields were visible on the mountainside; they looked as if they were stuck on like plasters. Wherever there was a clod of cultivable earth there were traces of man's handiwork. Carts had worn deep ruts, like railway lines, along the little mountain road, which now skirted the rocky bed of a stream. As the cart went slowly on, the rocky slopes on either side seemed ever more rent and riven by storms and torrid heat, and ever poorer in vegetation. A herd of goats, nibbling at a few blades of new grass, turned their diabolical bearded faces towards the strange priest riding in the cart.

The slope became steeper, and Magascià got down to lighten the load.

At a turning they came upon a villa in the Renaissance style built on the bare rock. The doors and windows seemed to have been hermetically sealed.

"That's Don Simone Scaraffa's villa," said Magascià. "He lived in Brazil for thirty years, making his fortune out of coffee growing, and came home to enjoy his wealth in peace. So he built that villa. But he went raving mad the first week he lived in it, and had to be taken to the lunatic asylum at Aquila, the one called Santa Maria di Collemaggio, and he's there still. He really might have saved himself the trouble of making his fortune."

Clouds were advancing from the top of the valley, moving from the mountain to the plain, from the country to the city.

A wooden cross had been erected on a cairn of stones. A date, August 22, 1909, was inscribed on it.

"That's where Don Giulio, the Lama notary, was murdered and robbed," said Magascià. "At the post-mortem they found he had been stabbed to the heart seven times, but they never discovered who did him that evil service. Don Giulio lent money at thirty-per-cent interest, but after his death usury disappeared."

The first houses of Pietrasecca came into view.

"It's a village of adversity," said Magascià. "It has been destroyed once by earthquake and twice by floods."

"How many people still live there?" the priest asked.

"About forty households. Those who could, went down to the plain," said Magascià.

Another cairn of stones with a wooden cross appeared at the side of the road, this time with the date, May 15, 1923.

"That is where Vincenzino Sapone was killed," said Magascià. "It was because of jealousy. Vincenzino was carrying on with the wife of an American. When the American came home he cut his wife's throat in bed with a razor. Then he came and hid behind that rock, waited for Vincenzino to pass on his way to work, went for him with a reaping-hook, and cut his head off. He fled to the mountains, but a few months later he was caught and sentenced to thirty years' imprisonment. He had a daughter, and she's grown up now and, speaking with respect, she finished up in a brothel in Rome, near the soldiers' barracks. She wasn't a bad girl."

They came to another cross.

"There . . ." Magascià started saying.

"Another tragedy happened," the priest interrupted.

"How did you know, sir?"

"You don't tell me anything but tragedies. Are you trying to frighten me, by any chance? Are there nothing but tragedies in this part of the world?"

"The good things are forgotten," Magascià replied, "but the misfortunes are remembered and handed down from father to son. If a good man dies, he goes to Paradise. If a sinner dies a violent death, he stays here, in the valley. That's why he goes on being talked about. The spirit of a murdered man has no peace. During the first few years after his death passers-by throw a stone on the site of the crime, so that his spirit may have rest. You priests say it isn't so, but it is, all the same."

The road skirted a precipice overhanging the stream.

"That is where my brother went over, with his cart," said Magascià. "He was coming back from Fossa with salt and tobacco, at night. The Evil One suddenly appeared before him at this spot. He had no time even to make the sign of the Cross. The mule reared and plunged to the left to avoid the Evil One, and fell over the precipice."

A small house now came into sight, built on a level patch of ground beside the stream.

"That is the house of the damned," said Magascià.

"Did the damned actually build themselves a house?" said the priest. "Then they can't be so badly off!"

Magascià was in no mood for a joke.

"The house was built by the Colamartini family of Pietrasecca," he said. "But as soon as it was finished the souls of the damned took possession of it and no one has ever been able to live in it. Everyone in the valley calls it the *refugium peccatorum.*"

At last the cart arrived at Pietrasecca. It was a collection of about sixty cracked and grimy cottages, some of them with closed doors and windows, having evidently been abandoned by their occupants. The village was built in a kind of cavity hollowed out of the mountainside. Some of the cottages were of the shock-proof type which had been made compulsory after the last earthquake. They were surrounded by hovels built of mud and stones, with roofs of lead or slate. Only two decent houses were to be seen, one of them immediately above the little bridge. This last was Matalena Ricotta's inn, where the priest was going to stay. The other, which was at the end of the village, was bigger and older, and was surrounded by a large garden with a stone wall. This was the patrician house of the Colamartini family, and was the only one in Pietrasecca which had survived the floods and the earthquake.

Near the Colamartini house was the cemetery, next to a little church with a porch facing the valley.

"Are services held there?" Don Paolo asked.

"Pietrasecca has had no priest for the last thirty years," Magascià replied.

All round the village and the cemetery the earth was divided up into many small plots. The plots were so small and the walls that divided them so high and so numerous that from the distance they looked like the foundations of a destroyed and abandoned city. A few hundred yards beyond Pietrasecca the valley came to an end. The road went no farther. Two rivulets united above Pietrasecca and formed a stream that divided the village in two. These halves were joined by a wooden bridge. In front of the inn stood a fountain. A child with a bleeding nose was bending over it, washing himself, and the water was already quite red.

Women and girls were kneeling at the edge of the stream below the bridge, tirelessly washing clothes on rubbing-boards.

Magascià stopped outside the inn, where Matalena was waiting for him. An old gentleman, wearing a long, black, woolen cloak also appeared. His hair and beard were completely white. He was carrying an iron fork on his shoulder, but this instrument of labor served in no way to diminish the nobility that emanated from his person. Everything about him was ancient, even the courteous words with which he welcomed the priest to his poor village. The wool of his cloak still smelled of sheep. Magascià introduced him.

"This is Don Pasquale Colamartini," he said.

Don Paolo Spada excused himself. He was not feeling well and he was dead tired. Matalena took him straight to his room. Sleep! Sleep!

In the darkness Don Paolo heard the voice of a woman calling. It was the voice of a mother calling her child who had stayed out late, playing with older children. "Wait a minute, mother, I'm coming, I'm just coming!"

Chapter IV

ONE Sunday morning a donkey just bought at market was christened outside Matalena Ricotta's inn. A young man held it by the halter while an old man beat it with a wooden cudgel. After each blow the two shouted, "Garibaldi!" into the beast's ear at the top of their lungs.

Garibaldi was to be the donkey's name. In the minds of the peasants it stood for strength and courage. As the two men wanted to be absolutely sure the donkey knew it, the christening naturally lasted a long time. The old man beat the animal on the crupper, without anger, without impatience, without resentment, but with emphasis, as though he were beating a mattress, and shouted "Garibaldi!" after every blow.

The donkey looked at the two men, and each time the stick descended it shook its head. The old man aimed each blow at a different rib, and when he had been all round he started again. The heroic name of Garibaldi resounded dozens and dozens of times across the little square of Pietrasecca, alternating with the thudding of the stick against the poor donkey's ribs. This went on until the old man grew tired.

"That'll do," he said. "He knows it now."

To make sure, the young man tried an experiment. He took a handful of hay, walked over to the wooden bridge, held up the hay, and called out:

"Garibaldi!"

The donkey trotted towards him.

"Yes, he knows it," the young man said.

Don Paolo was lying in bed, with a high temperature. He was puzzled and alarmed by this persistent invocation of the name

54

of Garibaldi, the sound of which reached him through the open window. Could the Republican Party be as strong as all that at Pietrasecca?

"What is happening?" the priest asked Matalena Ricotta.

"Nothing unusual," she said. "Old Sciatàp has been christening his new donkey."

Old Sciatàp was known by that name throughout the Pietrasecca valley. In fact his christening had resembled that of his own donkey. He had worked in America in his youth, as porter and general handy man to a fellow-countryman of his, one Carlo Campanella, who sold coal in winter and ice in summer on Mulberry Street, New York. But in New York Carlo Campanella, who came from Sciatàp's own village, had become Mr. Charles Little-Bell, Ice and Coal, and he treated his servant like a beast of burden. Whenever the poor brute complained, Mr. Little-Bell would lose his temper and shout, "Shut up!" When the ill-used fellow returned to Pietrasecca after several years in America, "Shut up" was the only English phrase he knew, and he used it on every possible occasion, right or wrong. If his wife so much as dared open her mouth he would immediately shout "Sha-tap!" put his forefinger to his mouth, and kick her.

Thus the phrase, rendered in Italian as "Sciatàp," passed into local idiom. It was all the English that was known at Pietrasecca, the solitary example of a modern, foreign culture grafted on the ancient culture of the peasants.

Don Paolo's curiosity was roused. He got out of bed and went to the window to look at the man. Sciatàp and his new donkey were going down towards the wooden bridge by a path beside the stream. A notice posted on an old board just where the path began read "Rubbish May Not Be Dumped Here." But there was a great heap of litter at that very spot—kitchen refuse, old boots, and garbage of every kind. This did not indicate any great respect for hygiene on the part of the inhabitants of Pietrasecca, but at least it proved that they could read.

Don Paolo could not only read but write, and write in a cultivated fashion, but all his attainments did not help him to solve a pressing problem of personal hygiene which confronted him now. This would certainly not be the place to speak of it had it not been symbolical of conditions of life in the villages of southern Italy, and had it not, alone of the physical hardships to which Don Paolo found no difficulty in adapting himself, proved intolerable to him. At Pietrasecca, as in most of the neighboring villages, there were no such things as private lavatories. But custom had created three public lavatories, in the shape of three clumps of bushes, situated some way along the stream. In spring the bushes were covered with leaves and flowers, which provided excellent cover for those who resorted to them. In autumn and winter, however, the situation was considerably more delicate. By immemorial custom, each class of the community frequented a different clump. The peasants frequented the first clump, the small landowners frequented the second, and the women the third. Children usually went behind the church. This tradition had always been observed, and was only violated in the immediate post-war period, at the time of the so-called Red Peril. During the Red Peril poor peasants would ostentatiously go to the second clump instead of the first. In the beginning this caused amazement and incredulity, which quickly yielded to indignation on the part of the small landowners, who uttered dire threats and asked what the world would come to if things were allowed to go on like this. "Really, there's no religion left," was Matalena Ricotta's comment at the time.

Fortunately for religion, however, the spiritual ferment caused by the war subsided. The Red Peril passed, and the old order was reëstablished. The ancient hierarchy reigned once more among the bushes.

Don Paolo, as a priest and an invalid, for reasons of decency and for reasons of health, could not possibly use any of the three clumps of bushes or go behind the church. He felt humiliated and annoyed at having returned to Italy in the revolutionary cause, with his head full of scientific facts and plans for dealing with the agrarian problem, only to find himself confronted daily with the most primitive problem of all.

Matalena had given Don Paolo her own first-floor room. It

contained an immense widow's bed, which occupied nearly three-quarters of the floor, and barely left room for a tiny table, a chair, and an iron washstand. Over the bed there was a crucifix; the limbs were livid, flabby, and twisted, and the face was that of a poor, famished peasant. A niche in the wall facing the bed contained a blue-and-white statuette of the Blessed Virgin in the act of trampling on the Evil One's head. It was now the end of May, which is the month of the Serpent and of the Blessed Virgin, and Matalena lit an olive-oil lamp every evening to invoke aid in the struggle against the Enemy.

Meanwhile Don Paolo's health was no better. The mountain climate had brought him no perceptible relief. All day long he was alone, and he turned and tossed in the vast widow's bed but found no rest. The days and nights seemed interminable.

To complete his priestly equipment Dr. Sacca had given him some devotional books: the breviary, the *Eternal Maxims of San Alfonso Maria dei Liguori*; the *Introduction to the Devout Life of St. François de Sales*; a *Life of San Camillo de Lellis*, a seventeenth-century Abruzzi saint; a *Life of San Giovanni Bosco*, a Piedmontese saint of the end of last century, and a ritual book. Don Paolo started idly turning the pages, as he would have turned the pages of a detective novel or a chemical prospectus or anything else in print, for the sake of momentarily escaping the oppressive monotony of his surroundings. Some of these books had passed through his hands before, in his years of adolescence, and many of the pages and illustrations on which his eye rested stirred forgotten memories within him. Memories of childish fantasies and infantile terrors started gradually emerging from oblivion. Don Paolo found himself constantly more attracted by his collection of devotional books, and he ended by reading them every evening until his eyes ached. Imperceptibly the adolescent who had gone to catechism every evening to prepare for his first communion was resurrected; the schoolboy who had devoured the lives of the saints and argued with Don Benedetto about ways of living without compromise. Imperceptibly a colloquy started between the revolutionary who had been superimposed upon his adolescent self and the adolescent in him who was not yet dead. The extreme weakness to which his illness had reduced him unconsciously led him back to the years of his youth, when he had often been ill, and had always been pampered and looked after by his mother, grandmother, aunts, and the family servant because of his delicate constitution and because he was an only son. In those years he had been constantly enveloped in the warmth of feminine tenderness and affection.

Although the environment into which chance had cast him now was, from the social point of view, several grades inferior to that in which he had grown up, the only living souls he talked to were women, and the only signs of life that reached him all day long, when the men were at work, came from women and children, who spoke the same dialect as he and his mother.

Matalena considered the presence of a priest as a blessing to her house, and consequently was always finding some excuse or other to come and talk to him. Misfortune, fear of which kept Matalena in a perpetual state of anxiety, ought to shun a house that sheltered a priest. A cow's skull, with two big curved horns, was planted at the top of the inn, where the two rain-pipes met. Don Paolo asked what it was for.

"It's a protection against the evil eye," said Matalena, "but it's no good as a protection against anything else. The only thing it protects you against is the evil eye."

Sure enough, in spite of the horns, Matalena's house, like many others, had collapsed in the 1915 earthquake.

"The old house was bigger than this one," she said. "My husband, God rest his soul, toiled for seven years in the Argentine in order to be able to build it. Three months after it was finished the earthquake came and it was completely destroyed. I was buried alive in the cellar for a whole week, and I had no idea there had been an earthquake at all. I thought it was the evil eye, and I didn't know that other people's houses had collapsed too. After a week, when they had cleared away the débris and made a hole big enough for me to crawl through, I refused to come out. I didn't have the courage. 'Let me die here,' I told them. 'I don't want to go on living.' But they cheered me up.

'Practically the whole village has been destroyed,' they shouted down the hole to me. 'Nearly the whole of the Marsica has been destroyed, thirty towns and villages have been razed to the ground, and fifty thousand dead have been counted already.' So it hadn't been the evil eye, but a visitation of God. As the proverb says, everybody's misfortune is no misfortune. My husband, God rest his soul, came back to Italy to serve in the war, and when it was over he went back to the Argentine, and toiled for another five years to scrape enough money together to have the house rebuilt. When it was finished and he was just coming back, he suddenly stopped writing. Six months later I was sent for by the commune, and I thought it must be for a new tax. So I went, and a clerk said: 'Your husband is dead. It was an accident that might have happened to anybody. He was run over by a motor-car.' I started weeping and wailing and crying that it was the evil eye that had got him because he had just been coming home to live in the new house. But the clerk insisted that it wasn't the evil eye, but an accident that might have happened to anybody. But it must really have been the evil eye. Of course priests say they don't believe in the evil eye, but if they really didn't believe in it they wouldn't wear black!"

Apart from all this Matalena used to observe Wednesdays and Fridays, and she dedicated the month of March to St. Joseph, the month of May to the Blessed Virgin, the month of June to the Sacred Heart, and the month of November to the dead. She had long since given up all thought of marrying again and would go about the house unkempt, untidy, and with her corsets undone. She took great pains preparing the priest's meals, and after each one she waited for compliments that never came. Don Paolo had never been a gourmet, and in any case Pietrasecca did not offer a great variety of dishes. But every morning Matalena would go up to the priest's room to ask him what he would like that day. To Don Paolo these interviews were a daily torment. One day he lost patience, and to put an end to it he told Matalena that in future she must give him what all the other inhabitants of Pietrasecca ate every day. Matalena was hurt, but she complied. For breakfast she gave him corn bread and an onion, for lunch corn bread and raw peppers seasoned with oil and salt, and in the evening bean soup. This diet lasted only two days. Apart from the soup in the evening Don Paolo could not stand it any longer. Matalena had won, and exploited her victory. The regular morning torment was resumed. Matalena had inflexible ideas concerning the treatment and cure of lung trouble.

"The best thing for lung trouble is raw eggs," she would say.

Matalena kept a dozen hens in the garden behind the inn. No sooner was an egg laid than she brought it to the invalid. If a hen was late in laying, Matalena would look for it, find it, seize it, and feel it with her little finger to find out whether an egg was there. After concluding the examination she would call up to the priest:

"She's going to lay in half an hour!"

Half an hour later the egg would be laid. Among the hens was a black one, named Pitella, who was the most punctual of them all. Pitella liked roving about the house, and sometimes she actually entered the sick-room. Sometimes she managed to hide under the big bed, and then all Matalena's threats and the ferocious wielding of her slipper completely failed to make her emerge, and Matalena would be forced to call the cock. Pitella would hear the cock coming upstairs and jump out of the window to escape him.

Matalena had a boy, named Americo, who looked like a toothless little old man. He howled in a loud and nerve-wracking manner at every trifle. Americo could not exactly be described as a young eagle.

"Go to Magascià and fetch a kilo of salt," his mother would tell him.

The boy would get up, walk ten paces, stop to pick up something, then come back, and sit down outside the front door.

"What did I tell you?" his mother would yell at him.

Americo would look at her in stupefaction.

"Go to Magascià and fetch a kilo of salt!"

Americo would get up, walk ten paces, stop, start picking one nostril, then the other, and suddenly burst into tears. His crying sounded as though it would never stop.

All the women would come out of their houses to see what was the matter, and all the children would gather round, too, and Americo's lamentations would grow more and more acute. Then Matalena would intervene and beat him with some kitchen utensil until he had no breath left to cry with.

In the morning Chiarina Patacca would come to the inn with a nanny-goat. Matalena would take a basin and milk it to the last drop. By this time the men had gone to work and the women all stood by the windows or came out of doors, to draw the insects out of the house.

At midday Filomena Sapone would come to the inn, with her baby in her arms and a lettuce for Don Paolo. After handing the lettuce to Matalena, Filomena would sit down outside the inn, unbutton her blouse, and publicly suckle her baby. She asked the priest to confess her, but he said he could not, as he belonged to another diocese.

In the space between the inn and the wooden bridge the bigger boys would imitate the drill of the Balilla. A quarrel broke out among them concerning the identity of the enemy. They all complained that the enemy was changed too often. A delegation was formed and three boys approached Don Paolo.

"Who is the enemy now?" they asked him.

"What enemy?" the priest asked, in surprise.

"The hereditary enemy," one of the boys answered, with assurance. The priest did not understand, or pretended he did not.

"In our drill there are two sides," one of the boys explained. "The Italians are on one side and the hereditary enemy is on the other. For a long time our teacher said our hereditary enemy was France and Yugoslavia. Then she said it was Germany. Then she said it was Japan. But this morning she said: 'Children, the new hereditary enemy is England.' But there's a chapter in our schoolbook with the heading: 'The Age-Long Friendship between England and Italy.' So now we're completely puzzled. Who's wrong, our teacher or the book?"

"The book," said Don Paolo. "It was printed last year, so it's out-of-date."

"All right," said the boys. "Let us destroy the English hereditary enemy."

"The English don't fight on land, but on water," the priest pointed out.

So the boys decided to have their battle in the stream. Don Paolo observed the struggle from his window. The new hereditary enemy was rapidly defeated, but both sides emerged from the fray drenched to the skin.

The boys of the village constituted a kind of community apart, with its own laws, its own rites, and its own dialect. It had its own champions at stone-throwing, jumping over the stream, lizard-hunting, and pissing against the wind.

The favorite game of the smallest boys was "campana." They would draw a long campanile on the ground with a piece of charcoal, divide it into sections, and jump from one to the other, kicking a stone before them and taking care that it did not land on any of the lines. If it did they had to start all over again. Don Paolo had excelled at this game when he was a boy.

From morning till night mothers could be heard calling their children, and often the village would resound with the most terrible curses. But they were so frequent that nobody took any notice.

"May you be martyred like San Bartolomeo!" Filomena Sapone would shout at her eldest son.

"May they tear your eyes out and make you hold them in your hands, like Santa Lucia!" Chiarina Patacca would yell at her daughter.

Curses alternated with lullabies and expressions of endearment.

"Sleep, my dear son," Annunziata would murmur, rocking her new-born baby to sleep. "My mother's pride, my riches of riches, my morning star!"

"Sleep, my angel of paradise," Antonia, the dressmaker, would whisper, bending over her daughter, "my royal bride, my fairy pearl."

In the afternoon all the women would do their housework in

the street. Some would hang out the washing, others would
clean potatoes, others would darn, another would de-louse and
scratch her child. Those who had nothing to do would sit down
on the wall outside the inn; barefooted women, clothed in rags,
with oily, greasy hair, looking as stupid as milked nanny-goats.
One of them was an old woman named Gesira, who was worn
out with hunger and child-bearing, and always complained of
the same pains. Child-bearing was the women's chief topic of
conversation. Annunziata was expecting her fourteenth child.
Lidovina had had eighteen. The first was always the hardest,
they said. The others found the way by themselves. One of the
women, Annina Stradone, who was pregnant, touched her belly
and said:

"Here's the head, here's one foot, and here's the other. It
must be a boy, because sometimes it kicks."

"That is in the hands of God," said Gesira. "God acts according to our sins. Every pain is a punishment."

A crowd of half-naked young children, completely covered
with mud, played round a dirty pool formed by the sinking of
the stream. They fled only at the appearance of the school-
teacher, Signorina Patrignani.

When the weather was fine most of the women would cook
the soup for the evening meal in the street, waiting for the return of the men. They cooked the soup in copper pots—some
of them actually used old petrol-cans instead—on tripods over
fires encircled with stones. As soon as it was dark Signorina
Cristina would come to the inn with oil for the lamp of the
Immaculate Virgin. Don Paolo soon learned to recognize the
girl's voice. She would come in, ask solicitously after the invalid's health, give Matalena any amount of advice about what
to do for him, and then hurry away. Don Paolo had not yet
seen Cristina. Matalena had told him that she belonged to the
only well-to-do family in Pietrasecca, had studied for many years
in a convent college, and was about to leave to take the veil.
Dr. Sacca had spoken of her as an extremely intelligent and
cultivated human being. At home Cristina was kept extremely
busy, as she did all the housework herself, and had to look after

her grandmother, who was nearly a hundred years old, besides her parents and an aunt, who were also old, to say nothing of a brother who was a wastrel and a good-for-nothing. But her convent education caused her to be held in great respect by all the villagers, and she often had to go to their houses to help and advise the poor people about most insignificant affairs.

Cassarola, the wise-woman, came to see the priest, and offered him magic herbs for his cough. He refused them. She was a revolting hag with a snub-nose and negroid blubber-lips. To show the priest how religious she was, she started mumbling prayers, exorcisms, and responses in Latin. She unbuttoned her blouse to show him the medallions, scapularies, crosses, and rosary that she wore round her neck.

"God rules over good but not over evil," she said. "Otherwise would He not cure His priests when they are attacked by illness? Why do you not pray to God and rise cured from your bed?"

Don Paolo gave the old witch a piece of good advice.

"Go to the devil," he said.

Antonia's baby girl was ill. Cassarola prescribed a glass of wine for her every morning.

"But she's only three," the dressmaker protested.

"Is she as old as that?" said Cassarola. "Then you must give her another glass in the evening as well."

One Tuesday Lidovina's baby died, and of her eighteen children only two were left. One Saturday Chiarina Patacca's little daughter died, and that left her with three children out of nine. Both had died of coughs. The two mothers filled the village with their lamentations. One Tuesday morning Annunziata's child was born; one Thursday Annina Stradone's. Such were the village happenings. Each one of them was described in the most minute detail. Mastrangelo fetched old Don Cipriano, the village priest of Lama, in time to bless the body of Lidovina's child, but when Sciatàp went to fetch him to do the same for Chiarina Patacca's he made an excuse and refused to come.

"When babies die they go to Limbo," he said, "and so nothing can be done about it. It's not really a priest's business at all."

A baby's funeral is a very simple thing, even with a priest. The tiny corpse is taken to the cemetery by a woman, nearly always a relation. She walks all by herself, without any escort, carrying the tiny coffin on her head, and goes quickly, with the natural and easy gait of one who is carrying a basket of fruit. Lidovina's baby was taken to the cemetery by her sister, Marietta. Since the priest was present, Lidovina insisted on having music. So Marietta walked in front, with the coffin on her head, with Don Cipriano following in his surplice and stole. Three musicians brought up the rear, with trumpet, clarionet, and trombone. All five walked in step with a dance tune, an old pre-war ditty, which began with the words: "When the cherries are ripe, I'll tell you, darling." After the ceremony at the graveside Marietta invited the four men home and offered them wine.

Don Cipriano, the parish priest of Lama, was responsible for the religious observances of the people of Pietrasecca, their christenings, weddings, and funerals, but as he grew older his visits gradually grew rarer and rarer.

Fortunately for him, religious ceremonies in mountain villages tend to be concentrated in certain periods of the year. Marriages take place in October or November and children are expected between May and July. It was a kind of universal levy from which very few escaped. Innumerable babies died in the first few months. It was a kind of massacre of the innocents.

Teresa Scaraffa was expecting a child, and one night she dreamed that it was going to be born blind. The poor woman came to Don Paolo, and went down on her knees at the foot of his bed.

"I dreamed last night that my child was going to be born blind, and only you can save it, sir," she said.

"I am very sorry, my poor woman, but I do not belong to this diocese," the priest said.

The woman started weeping and imploring him.

"I don't want my child to be born blind," she said. "Why should the others have eyes and not he?"

Don Paolo tried to persuade her that this would not be so, but with no success.

"I dreamed it," she said. "I saw it with my own eyes. If you don't help me, my son will be blind!"

The woman would not go away. Don Paolo knew perfectly well that if he consented to say prayers and recite exorcisms for Teresa, the house would immediately be filled with people who wanted to be helped in the same way, and it would be impossible for him to refuse. They would all say he had helped Teresa Scaraffa, and why shouldn't he help them, too? Apart from the imposture, it might end by his attracting the attention of the authorities and being found out. So he called Matalena.

"I want you to remove this woman from my room, by kindness if possible, or if necessary by force," he said. "I am not interested in her dreams."

But Teresa rose like a fury.

"Why should my child be born blind?" she shrieked. "Can anyone tell me the reason for such an affliction? Why should other children be able to see and not my child?"

Teresa stopped and waited for a reply, but Don Paolo had no desire to be involved in an argument.

Once more Teresa went down on her knees. She started weeping, beating her head on the floor, tearing at her hair, pulling out handfuls of it, and shrieking the most irrational things.

"Why should he be blind?" she cried. "Tell me why? All the others will be able to see, and not he. All the others will be able to go to school, and not he. The others will all steal from him, and he won't know it. The others will laugh at him, and he won't be able to see them, and when he's big, no woman will have anything to do with him!"

Then she rose to her feet. She suddenly looked quite calm.

"Now I know," she said. "I shall throw myself out of the window. He shall die with me."

She walked towards the window. In the state of exaltation she was in there was no doubt that she really would throw herself out of the window. A cry from the priest stopped her when she had reached the window sill.

"I shall do what you want," he said. "What do you want me to do?"

The keys of the church were kept at the house of the Colamartinis. Matalena ran and fetched them. She also brought a glass of holy water from the church. Teresa held out her swollen belly to the priest.

"The head must be here," she said. "This is where the eyes must be."

The priest twice made the sign of the cross at the place Teresa pointed to, one cross for each eye, and he moved his lips, as though he were muttering prayers.

"Now he's all right," the woman said with satisfaction. "The calamity has been averted."

She went away. A little while later she came back with a dead hen.

"It's to show my gratitude," she said, laying it on the priest's table.

"I cannot accept it," Don Paolo answered. "Priests are not allowed to accept presents in my diocese."

"Then the whole thing's no use!" the woman protested. "Unless you take the hen the grace won't work and the baby will be born blind."

"Grace is free," said Don Paolo.

"There's no such thing as free grace," said the woman.

She left the propitiatory sacrifice on the table and went away.

On Sunday mornings a number of women would go all the way to Lama to Mass. They wore black shawls over their shoulders, and black handkerchiefs over their heads, because it would be immodest to show their hair, and black shoes and stockings. Don Paolo watched them from his window. The oldest women walked with their rosaries in their hands, letting the beads run slowly between their thumb and first finger.

One Saturday night a girl from Fossa dei Marsi arrived at Pietrasecca in Magascià's salt-and-tobacco cart.

"There is the inn, on the right before the bridge," Magascià said to her. The girl had a bundle under her arm. She came in.

"Does Don Paolo Spada live here?" she asked Matalena.

Matalena was jealous of her priest.

"Why?" she asked, before answering the strange girl's question.

"He saved me when I was on the point of death, and I want to thank him."

"The Don Paolo who lives here is not a doctor, but a priest," Matalena replied.

"Perhaps he is neither priest nor doctor but a saint," the girl said. "I was on the point of death. He came, he looked at me, he touched my hand, and I was saved."

Matalena was proud of having a priest from another diocese in her house, but the idea that her visitor might be a real saint who performed miracles worried and distressed her.

"Yes, he is a real saint," she replied, not wishing to appear unable to recognize a saint on her own account. "He is living here doing penance, like a true saint, a true man of God."

"Perhaps he is even more than a true saint," the girl from Fossa said. "I fear he may be Jesus Himself."

This was too much for Matalena. She sat down on a stool.

"Are you mad?" she murmured. "How could he be Jesus Himself? Why should Jesus come to my inn, of all places? Is He not in Heaven, sitting on His Father's right hand?"

Matalena spoke almost in a whisper, lest the man on the first floor, if he were really He, should hear her doubting words.

"It would not be the first time Jesus disguised Himself and came down to earth to see how the poor people live," the girl from Fossa replied. Then, in a tiny little trickle of a voice, she added: "Have you noticed whether his hands and feet are pierced? That would be the most certain sign. He could not hide the stigmata left by the nails when He was crucified, however much He tried to disguise Himself."

The two women remained silent. The priest's evening meal was lying ready on the table. It consisted of two eggs and a lettuce. Matalena blushed at such a miserable repast. It was shameful to offer two eggs and a salad to the Only Begotten Son. One ought at least to have killed a chicken. But supposing it wasn't He?

"What makes you think it is He? What gave you the idea? Tell me the truth! Aren't you mad?" said Matalena, in a torment of doubt.

"I recognized Him by His voice," the girl replied. "When He appeared before me, He took me by the hand and said: 'Courage, I know everything.' Then I felt that it was no human voice. The men I know do not talk like that. I have an uncle who is a priest. He is the parish priest of Fossa. He does not talk like that."

"Tell me," said Matalena. "Supposing it really is Jesus, what ought we to do? Tell the police?"

The regulations for hotel-keepers were displayed behind the front door, but no provision had been made for the possible arrival of Jesus.

The two women went up to the first floor on tiptoe and with bated breath. They knocked at the door, and there was no reply. They opened the door and the room was empty. Matalena felt she was going to faint.

"He's vanished!" she murmured. "He's vanished!"

No ordinary mortal who went to an inn could have vanished into thin air like this, even if he didn't want to pay the bill. The two women looked at each other in awe. Then they heard a cough in the garden. The two women dashed downstairs. Don Paolo was sitting under a fig tree. He was motionless, and as pale as a corpse. The tree was dead. It had been condemned to be cut down and thrown on the fire.

"Who wants me?" he asked.

The two women approached him timidly.

"It is I, Bianchina," the girl said. "Bianchina Girasole from Fossa dei Marsi, Berenice's niece. I was dying and abandoned by everyone, and then some one I had never seen came and touched my hand and saved me."

Don Paolo coughed again. The sun had set. The long shadows were emerging from the bottom of the valley. Don Paolo rose to his feet, and the two women helped him back to his room.

"You may go," the priest said to Matalena.

Don Paolo was tired and lay down on his bed. Bianchina sat down near the door. Then she plucked up courage.

"Show me your hands," she said.

"Do you want to read the future?" Don Paolo said, with a smile.

Bianchina looked closely at his hands. There was no trace of stigmata. There was no trace of crucifixion. He was not Jesus. He was a saint, but not Jesus. Bianchina was disappointed, and remained silent. After an interval she said:

"My aunt Berenice has turned me out. She wouldn't have anything more to do with me."

"Why?" the priest asked.

"Because I am for liberty. My aunt is against liberty. You, as a saint, are against liberty, of course."

Don Paolo interrupted.

"I am not a saint and I am for liberty," he said.

Bianchina seemed not to believe her ears.

"If you, a priest, are for liberty, why does the Church threaten us with hell?" she asked. "Why is love-making forbidden?"

The priest made no reply, but Bianchina persevered with her questioning.

"If I make love, is it really true that Jesus is angry?" she said. "Why should He be angry? Who tells Him to be angry?"

"Let us change the subject," the priest suggested.

"All right," said Bianchina, laughing. "But love-making is so nice that I don't understand how anybody can do anything else. Don't you agree with me?"

"Listen, Bianchina," answered the priest. "I am sorry, I am really very, very sorry, but I do not belong to this diocese."

Bianchina started laughing. Her pretty face looked even prettier against the dark rectangle of the door. Perhaps her neck was a little too thin, and her mouth was large and red; when she laughed it was really too large; although she certainly knew this, she laughed all the same. She had tiny ears. She picked up two pairs of cherries from the table and hung them over her ears, like a child. Then she started laughing again. Then she grew serious.

"You mustn't think ill of me," she said.

Round her neck, under her chemise, she wore the scapular of the Madonna del Carmine. She unbuttoned her blouse, opened her chemise and showed it. The scapular was green and her breasts were milky white.

Don Paolo felt his heart beating faster at the sight, after long abstinence, of this tender and fresh fruit of his own country. It was a pity, it really was a pity, that he had to be prudent.

"Don't believe I'm lying to you," the girl went on. "I'm for liberty, but I'm for religion, too. God gave us all that we have. God created humanity, half men and half women. Just imagine what it would be like if God had absent-mindedly made men or women only. Speaking with respect, it would have been really hateful!"

Bianchina made the sign of the Cross.

She had brought a small bundle with her.

"What have you got there?" the priest asked.

"All my worldly goods," the girl replied.

She took the bundle on her knees, unwrapped it, and displayed the contents, which consisted of a porcelain coffee-service and a pile of embroidered handkerchiefs.

"That's not very much," the priest remarked. "It's not enough to live an independent life on."

Bianchina was offended.

"But I'm still young!" she answered. "And besides, a saint shouldn't be so materialistic."

"What do you propose to do, now that your aunt has turned you out?" the priest asked.

"That's what I came to ask you," Bianchina replied. "What can I do? I can't do anything. If I knit I muddle the stitches. If I sew I prick my fingers. If I garden I bang my foot with the hoe. The nuns taught me to make sweets, and to embroider, and to sing the Gregorian Chant. Can I go and sing the *Magnificat* and *Salve Regina* in the music-halls?"

Bianchina burst out crying.

"For the moment let us forget the more distant future," said Don Paolo. "Seeing that you cannot stay in my room, where do you intend to find a roof over your head for tonight, tomorrow, the day after tomorrow?"

Bianchina's sobs redoubled.

"A fine thing to save a person on the point of death, and then show her the door," she said. "Why didn't you let me die? You ought to have let me die! What a shameful way for a saint to behave!"

"If you go on crying like that your nose will get as red as a tomato," said Don Paolo.

Bianchina stopped crying.

"Anyway, there's an old school friend of mine here at Pietra-secca, Cristina Colamartini," she suddenly said. "She's a kind of saint, too, but perhaps she'll help me."

It had grown late and Cristina came to the inn, bringing Matalena the oil for the lamp of the Immaculate Virgin. Matalena told her of Bianchina Girasole's arrival, and Cristina appeared at the sick-room door, which had been left open. Bianchina promptly fell on her neck, embracing and kissing her and accompanying her caresses with a murmur of inarticulate sounds.

Matalena brought another chair, and eventually Cristina was able to sit down and tidy her disarranged hair. So far Don Paolo had only heard Cristina's voice, but he had already made up his mind that her appearance would be as attractive as her voice. He thought he detected a strange resemblance between her and a girl cousin with whom he had played as a boy. Cristina's face was thin and emaciated, as though she were being consumed by an inner fire. It was a face of ancient race, imbued with subtle despair, conscious of the futility of vulgar things. She wore a black apron, closed at the neck and wrists, like a schoolgirl, and her black hair was parted in the middle, slightly waved at the temples, and gathered at the nape of the neck in a large knot of tiny little curls.

Cristina bade the priest good-evening.

"We have just finished telling our beads at home, and we added a prayer for your health, as we do every evening," she said.

"For my health?" said Don Paolo.

"My father came home one night and said a strange priest had come to Pietrasecca to recover his health, and we pray that the air of our village may do him good," said Cristina.

"What, haven't you met before?" Bianchina said. "Cristina was my first love," she went on. "We were at the same convent school for three years. She was at the top of the class and I was at the bottom, of course, and that made us like each other all the better."

Then she added:

"There's always a time in life when you go back to your first love. Do you know what the Mother Superior's nickname for Cristina was? She called her Miss Music. She was so fond of music that it made me quite jealous."

Don Paolo studied Cristina carefully. Her face and her hands had the pallor of old white roses.

"Magascià told me you were still at Pietrasecca," Bianchina went on. "To be perfectly frank, for one reason I was very pleased to hear it, because it meant you might be able to help me. But apart from that, surely it's a disgrace for a girl like you to stay in a den of wolves like this? Miss Music ought to be the head of a conservatory or the abbess of a rich convent."

Don Paolo excused himself and started reading his breviary, in order to leave the two girls in peace.

Cristina waited for Bianchina to pause, and then asked:

"What has happened to the others? What has happened to Incoronata?"

"Incoronata took her teacher's diploma, but she hasn't got a job yet," Bianchina said. "There were one hundred and eighty candidates for twelve vacancies at the last provincial competition. Incoronata did her best, she even slept with the prefect's chauffeur, but she didn't get a job. She was going to marry the communal secretary of Fossa, but the day before the wedding she discovered he was carrying on with her sister, so nothing came of it. That secretary is a swine, anyway, he tried to seduce me, too."

Bianchina's stay at the Girasole Hotel had evidently made her very free in her speech. Her way of talking, particularly in the presence of a priest, made it hard for Cristina to conceal a certain feeling of discomfort. But Don Paolo looked as though he were really reading the breviary and not listening to the girls' conversation.

"What has happened to Anita Pietrangeli?" Cristina asked.

"Anita Pietrangeli of Acquafredda? She had the misfortune to lose her father. They must be very hard up, but her mother won't let her look for a job, because office work would be inconsistent with the family dignity. The family dignity of the Pietrangeli means that the girls have to stay at home and rot, waiting for some rich landowner to come and marry them."

"How do you manage to know all these things about other people's private lives?" Cristina asked.

"Down in the plain you know everything," said Bianchina. "And, besides, if you live in the Girasole Hotel you end by knowing the truth about everything, and very often more than the truth."

"What is dear Colomba doing now?"

"She married a station master, a widower with three children, and she has practically become the family servant," said Bianchina. "The station master doesn't want any more children, and his means of preventing them offend poor Colomba's religious susceptibilities, and she complains about it to everybody. In the end the parish priest had to intervene; consequently there is great tension at present between the station and the parish church."

Cristina listened to Bianchina's stories of her former schoolfellows with ill-concealed distress. A slight flush appeared on her cheeks and temples and encircled the graceful curve of her hair. Don Paolo was still reading his breviary.

"I've heard Adalgisa is married, too," Cristina said.

"For some time Adalgisa Colantuoni and I were engaged to the same man, one of the heads of the government party in the Fucino region," Bianchina said. "He's a complete bounder. I don't say so because he preferred Adalgisa. As a matter of fact, I am forced to confess that he went on staying at the Girasole Hotel every Tuesday night for a whole year after he got married, and I had to put up with him in order not to create political difficulties for my aunt. Everybody knows he married Adalgisa for her father's money. Her father, you know, was a director of the Banca Agricola Mandamentale, and when it went smash Adalgisa had to sacrifice all the money her mother had left her to save him from going to prison, and she hasn't seen her husband since. Now they are legally separated because of incompatibility of temperament."

"But how does she manage to live? What does she do if her father has no money left?" Cristina asked.

"She has just been appointed to superintend the distribution of government soup for the unemployed," said Bianchina. "She distributes the bread and soup with the dignity of a fairy godmother. What is left she takes home to feed the poor old broken banker."

Cristina listened to this news with eyes nearly popping out of her head. Her thin nostrils were trembling like butterflies' wings.

"What has happened to Evangelina?" she asked.

"Donna Evangelina now directs the local Piccole Italiane.[1] Consequently she thinks the country's destiny is in her hands. She behaves as if she knows everything, but cannot speak. Secrets of state, you know. When anybody asks her whether there will be war or not, her only answer is a superior smile. She went to Rome for the government party anniversary celebrations, and the head of the government, you know whom I mean, seems to have looked at her. He was two hundred yards away! Ever since Donna Evangelina has done nothing but talk of the devastating glance that penetrated her from two hundred yards' distance. It made the poor girl pregnant. Her father started a frantic search for some one to act the part of St. Joseph for her future child. In times of unemployment philanthropists can always be found, so Donna Evangelina found her St. Joseph. To make the analogy complete, the man is an unemployed carpenter."

Don Paolo had finished reading his breviary. He saw that Cristina was profoundly disturbed. She almost had tears in her eyes.

Cristina had known Bianchina when she was much younger.

[1] Little Italians. A Fascist organization for girls.

She remembered that Bianchina had always liked to shock her friends. That did not justify one in thinking evil of her. One must never think evil of anyone. Appearance was always worse than reality.

"Giuseppina Sraffa has been the luckiest," Bianchina went on. "She lives in a magnificent flat in Rome. She helps a brother in his studies, and every month she sends her mother, who has stayed in her village, enough to live on."

Cristina was glad to hear that at least one of her friends had had good fortune, but she was unable to conceal her surprise.

"Giuseppina was always a good-hearted girl," she said, "but she didn't give one the impression of being very active."

"She hasn't got a very tiring occupation," Bianchina said. "She's kept by a rich, married manufacturer. Since this has been known in her village, her mother, to save her reputation, would like to refuse the monthly money-order her daughter sends her, but that would leave the old woman with nothing to live on, so she goes on drawing it. All her relations refuse to have anything to do with her, and when she goes to church the congregation leaves an empty space all around her."

"We are tiring Don Paolo with our idle chatter," Cristina remarked, rising to go. Bianchina followed her example, so as not to let her escape, and, with her, her only hope of shelter for the night.

"I shall come back tomorrow morning," Bianchina said to the priest. "There are many things I want to discuss with you."

Next morning, however, she did not come.

Two days later there was great excitement at Pietrasecca. Sciatàp, coming home with Garibaldi, discovered that smoke was issuing from the chimney of the *refugium peccatorum*, the abandoned house of the Colamartini down in the valley. The house couldn't be on fire. The smoke was issuing from the chimney in a long, slow, regular line. But who on earth could be cooking in an uninhabited house? Could the souls of the damned be making soup?

Sciatàp's story left the people of Pietrasecca frankly incredulous. Filomena Sapone, old Gesira, Lidovina, and some boys hurried down the valley to see for themselves. They had no need to go far, because at the second turning they could see a trail of white smoke issuing from the chimney of the *refugium peccatorum*. The windows and doors seemed to be closed, as usual. The house was uninhabited. What on earth could be causing the smoke? Could the souls of the damned really have been given permission to cook soup? The women and boys hurried back to Pietrasecca. Other people gathered. The strangest theories were evolved. Eventually it was decided that the Colamartini family, the owners of the house, must be informed at once. They went and knocked at the door, but nobody answered.

"Donna Cristina! Don Pasquale! Donna Adele! Donna Cecilia!" the women called out from the street. They went on knocking at the door. They could hear voices, and people moving about inside the house, but nobody answered the door. What on earth could be happening? Why didn't some one come to the door? The women and boys outside went on knocking and shouting:

"Don Pasquale! Donna Cristina! Donna Adele! Donna Cecilia!"

Eventually old Don Pasquale appeared on the balcony. He was pale and distressed.

"Let everybody mind his own business," he said.

"There's smoke coming from the chimney of the house of the damned!" the people shouted.

Don Pasquale knew it.

"Let everybody mind his own business!" he repeated.

It was useless to persevere. The crowd was forced to disperse and continue with its conjectures at home.

That evening Cristina came to Matalena's inn, in her usual hurry, bringing the oil for the lamp of the Immaculate Virgin.

"Don Paolo told me to ask you how the girl from Fossa dei Marsi is. She hasn't been here since," said Matalena.

"She has gone to our house in the valley, with my brother Alberto," Cristina answered, simply.

"Are they in the *refugium peccatorum* together?" said Matalena, making the sign of the Cross. "But the souls of the damned will eat them!"

Cristina gave Matalena the oil, asked how the priest was, and went away without saying another word. Matalena waited just long enough for her to disappear before she started running from door to door.

"Do you know who are in the *refugium peccatorum?* What? You don't know? Haven't you any idea?"

She told them all about it and hurried on to the next house.

The day on which Cristina was to leave for her novitiate was approaching, and her father said to her:

"I had a son and I have lost him. Now you are going, too, and your father will be left with your grandmother, your mother, and your aunt—three old women, incapable of any kind of work. And so we shall have to intrust the end of our lives to some servant who will rob us of what little there is left to us."

"You know I will do nothing against your wishes, father," Cristina answered.

Her father was very fond of her and dared not oppose her vocation, and thus he let the days pass without making up his mind. The people of Pietrasecca said a girl belonged first to her home and then to the Church.

Her father said:

"I had a son and I have lost him. I have a daughter left. But supposing that, because of us and our selfishness, her life is wrecked, too?"

He could not make up his mind. Besides, the decision was not his alone. Above him there was his mother.

Cristina went on uncomplainingly doing the housework. She looked after the chickens, made the beds, swept the rooms and the staircase, did the washing, and attended to the bees in the garden.

One morning Don Paolo was sitting beneath the fig tree in Matalena's garden when Cristina arrived with a bunch of onions to transplant. The morning light wrapped the girl as in a mantle. Some bees were buzzing about her head, as about a flower rich

with pollen, but to the priest the flower looked a little wilted.
He plucked up courage and asked:

"Forgive me if I am indiscreet, but are you perhaps suffering because you have not yet left for the convent? Are there perhaps difficulties which you cannot disentangle?"

Cristina smiled and answered:

"Don't think me discourteous if I answer with three great words, which were taught me as a child and I have never forgotten. *Jesus autem tacebat.* Those words impressed me more, perhaps, than any others in the Bible. Jesus taught us to be silent when our individual destiny is at stake."

"All the same," the priest replied, "it cannot be indifferent to you whether you live in a convent or in your own home, whether you are shut up all day long or free to go about as you will."

"It is not eating or drinking or dressing or going for walks that can make one happy," Cristina said.

"Oh!" said the priest. "So you aspire to happiness? Do you really believe that it is possible to be happy?"

Cristina looked at Don Paolo in slight perplexity. It was impossible for a priest to be making these objections seriously. Or probably he was playing the part of devil's advocate, desiring to test her religious maturity. Cristina did not want to gainsay a poor sick priest, living in solitude in such backward surroundings.

"Don't you think that silence itself is an anticipation of happiness?" she replied. "Internal silence means that everything is in its place, that everything is listening. Silence varies in intensity, and complete silence does not last long, because that would be death. It lasts only for a little, but what joy there is in those moments when everything is listening."

Don Paolo felt he was listening to a little girl reciting a pretty poem.

"Is it not possible to have inner silence even in the uproar of a great city?" he said. "Can one not be alone even in a crowd? Must one be mistrustful of oneself to the extent of shutting oneself up in a convent?"

"We are not called upon to be bold, but to be docile and to let ourselves be helped," said Cristina. "I read in a book written by a French nun: 'Does a new-born child raise itself to take its mother's breast? Or does the mother take her little one and bend gently over it to nourish it and calm its wailing?' All of us on this earth are newborn children. Everything about us is older than we. But the Evil One is older than it all."

Cristina's freshness and simplicity lent a peculiar fascination to her words, a fascination that Don Paolo had to make an effort to resist.

"I do not wish to embark on a theological discussion with you," he said. "But we are in a country which is still primitive in many ways, a country in which there is great economic distress and still greater spiritual distress. If a peasant ever succeeds in overcoming his animal instincts, he becomes a Franciscan friar; if a girl ever succeeds in freeing herself from bondage to her own body, she becomes a nun. Do you not think that that is the source of many evils? Do you not think that this divorce between a spirituality which retires into contemplation and a mass of people dominated by animal instincts is the source of all our ills? Do you not think that every living creature ought to live and struggle among his fellow-creatures rather than shut himself up in an ivory tower?"

"He who has faith is never alone," Cristina replied. "But the atheist is always alone, even if from morning to night he lives in crowded streets. The soul that does not know God is a leaf detached from the tree, a single, solitary leaf, that falls to the ground, dries up, and rots. But the soul that is given to God is like a leaf attached to the tree. By means of the vital sap that nourishes it, it communicates with the branches, the trunk, the roots, and the whole earth."

Cristina's voice recalled Don Paolo's own internal dialogue between the adolescent and the revolutionary in him. Thus he had himself been greedy for the absolute and in love with righteousness when he had cut himself off from the Church and gone over to Socialism. But much time had passed since then. What had remained in him of that generous impulse towards the masses of the people? He had broken with a decadent Church, rejected opportunism, and declined to compromise with society. But had he not succumbed to another kind of opportunism, the opportunism dictated by the interests of a political party? He had broken with the old world and all its comforts, cut himself off from his family, abandoned his favorite studies, set himself to live for justice and truth alone, and entered a party in which he was told that justice and truth were petty-bourgeois prejudices. Did he not feel himself betrayed? Had he, perhaps, taken the wrong road?

Thus, while Cristina spoke, did Don Paolo oscillate between one pole and the other. The dialogue between the adolescent and the revolutionary became an altercation. The revolutionary won.

"I do not want to engage you in a political discussion," he said. "Nevertheless, permit me to ask you this. Can morality be purely contemplative? Are not morality and contemplation contradictions in terms? Is not practical every-day life the very basis and foundation of morality, that is to say, the virtuous life? Has morality any valid field of action but that?"

"You cannot serve two masters," Cristina answered. "Between spirit and matter there is an irreconcilable conflict. To search for a compromise means to sacrifice spirit to matter, to betray spirit in the interests of matter."

Don Paolo had tried to express himself in language compatible with his ecclesiastical habit. In any case it was the only language accessible to Cristina.

"Is the examination over?" Cristina asked, with a laugh.

"It was not an examination," Don Paolo replied. "You have suggested to me the subject for a meditation which I shall continue by myself. In my first days at Pietrasecca I found the enforced solitude very trying, but now I am beginning to like it. In my diocese life is very busy, and this silence does me good. I now have leisure to think of many things of which it is not easy to think in the tumult of active life."

"One must let oneself be carried along by the silence," said Cristina, with a smile, "like an unconscious man carried by a deep current of water. Only then does God talk to us. The word of God in the silence is more piercing than a double-edged sword, and reaches down even to the division of the soul from the spirit, down to the joints and the marrow."

Cristina shook the priest's hand and went.

Don Paolo was left alone beneath his tree, and let himself be carried along by a stream of memories, like an unconscious man being carried along by a deep current of water.

Before going back to bed he sat down at his table, took a notebook, and wrote "Dialogues with Cristina" on the cover. At the top of the first page he wrote: "Comments on the First Dialogue." After much thought he wrote as follows:

"At a moment in my life when I feel more alone and abandoned than ever before, my stay in this village, my contact with these primitive people, my meeting with this girl, force me to think of myself as I was fifteen years ago. In Cristina I see many features of my own adolescence, I might almost say I see a portrait of myself, an embellished, a feminine portrait. At least it is a spiritual image of what I felt and thought myself. If I compare myself with that image now, I feel gravely troubled and seized with doubt. Perhaps I too have been a traitor to myself."

He stopped writing and thought of the naïve illusions with which he had entered his first Socialist group. His real reason for leaving the Church while still so young had been not because he had grown out of it spiritually or criticized it intellectually, but because of the profound disgust with which he reacted to the abyss which he perceived between its practical actions and the words it preached. That disgust had provided his sole impulse for joining the Socialists. He had not been a Marxist then, having only become one after joining the Socialist fold. But now he had been a Marxist for fifteen years, and it had become his profession. Alas for all professions that have for their ultimate aim the salvation of the world! For the sake of saving others, you ended by losing yourself. . . . Don Paolo saw clearly now that his return to Italy had been at heart an attempt to escape from that profession, to get away from the Marxist bureaucracy, to return to the rank-and-file and recapture in action

the enthusiasm that had originally led him into the movement.
This discovery left him perplexed. What had those fifteen years
devoted to the political struggle been worth? He went to bed,
but the question would not let him sleep. He got up again, sat
down at the table, reopened his notebook, and wrote:

"Is it possible to take part in political life, to devote oneself to the service of a party, and remain sincere?

"Has not truth, for me, become party truth? Has not justice,
for me, become party justice?

"Have not party interests ended by deadening all my dis-
crimination between moral values? Do I, too, not despise them
as petty-bourgeois prejudices?

"Have I escaped from the opportunism of a decadent Church
only to fall into bondage to the opportunism of a party?

"What has become of my enthusiasm of that time? By putting
politics before anything else, before all other spiritual needs,
have I not impoverished, sterilized my life? Has it not meant
that I have neglected deeper interests?

"There are remarkable potentialities in man. Think, for instance, of Cristina. These potentialities are now exploited by all
the reactionary institutions. If, as in my case, they are directed
towards the proletariat, what becomes of them in professional
politics? Is it right that they should be stifled? Is it right that
they should be combated? Is a true and lasting revolution possible without them?"

When he came to the end of the page Don Paolo read through
what he had written. He noticed that all he had done was to
draw up a list of questions to which his divided mind could give
no certain answer. He went on sitting for a long time with suspended pen, but he was not able to write anything else.

Chapter V

CRISTINA had the gift of creating beauty out of nothing. It was remarkable to see how bright and cheerful Don Paolo's room became under her care. As his encounters with her became more frequent, so did they become more open and sincere. At first Don Paolo felt himself rather hampered by the strain of having to avoid saying anything that might rouse the slightest suspicion concerning his identity, but in face of Cristina's ingenuousness this preoccupation eventually disappeared and he started talking to her without restraint, telling her of his youth, his native village, his first religious experiences, and his first steps in adult life, taking care only to place his reminiscences in the diocese of Frascati and not in that of dei Marsi. Gradually and imperceptibly he became more and more completely absorbed by his fictitious rôle, which he nurtured with the still living dreams of his youth. He became a prisoner of his own fantasy. He spoke with so much spontaneity, sincerity, and warmth that Cristina was completely captivated.

"If I wrote down what you said and somebody read it who had no idea who you were, I wager he would say you were eighteen years old," Cristina said once.

Mutual liking made them more conciliatory in the arguments that often broke out between them. What Don Paolo could not say to her aloud, he wrote down in his diary. Thus he had secret conversations with her. He confided to his diary all the things with which his heart inspired him, and he used the tender expressions of a lover. He often sat up writing till late at night. His "Dialogues with Cristina" developed into a kind of examination of conscience, a kind of audit of his past life. He de-

84

scribed in full the spiritual crisis that had made him a Socialist
in 1921, and recalled the efforts made by his relatives and friends
to dissuade him from such madness. Uncles, aunts, and older
cousins of both sexes, all respectable, conventional, church-going
people, had admonished him, sermonized, implored, and threatened. When the sentimental arguments had been exhausted, and
the disgrace his behavior was about to bring upon the whole
Spina family had been described in full, each one of them got
down to bedrock. They all asked the same question: "What
object have you in declaring yourself a Socialist? What will
you gain by it?" "No material advantage whatever," he had
answered, "but . . ." "Then you're mad!" those excellent and
honest people had replied. His internal conflict was rekindled
and became almost unbearably acute, under the influence of his
reliving and rethinking of the past, his imaginative reconstruction of the crisis that had sundered him from his friends, his
relatives, and his religion.

There was a kind of cleavage in him, dividing his being into
two. As long as he had been active the two parts had coalesced
and dovetailed, giving an impression of solid strength. But no
sooner was he immobilized than the two parts fell asunder.
Here he was, with inactivity thrust upon him, and the wood-
worm of his brain took advantage of it to gnaw obstinately at
the weak cartilages that still linked the adolescent to the revolutionary.

Cristina gave Don Paolo a book on Catholic colonial missions.
It contained many stories of the lives of missionaries, many
tales of suffering and difficulties borne with biblical fortitude.
The fate of these men seemed in many ways similar to his own.
They had resolutely turned their backs on ordinary family life
in order to live without compromise. They also had wished not
to serve two masters. But in reality they had served two masters,
the Bible on the one hand and the interests of colonial capitalism
on the other. Life had betrayed them. Their intentions had been
betrayed. They believed themselves to be servants of the spirit,
but in reality they were docile middlemen between the Church

and the imperialist powers, many of them without realizing it. Was it perhaps impossible to avoid serving two masters?

Don Paolo ended by convincing himself that that was the drama of every sincere revolutionary. He had once asked many militant members of his party what had led them to Marxism, and nearly all of them had confessed that their original impulse, as in his case, had been moral condemnation of existing society. He had read the biographies of many revolutionaries, and he had never yet discovered anyone who had become a revolutionary out of scientific conviction or economic calculation. But in actual political life these idealist impulses were submitted to a severe test. Don Paolo thought of the moral degradation that professional political life imposed even on the best characters. He was now completely convinced that his real reason for having decided to abandon his life of exile and cast himself into illegal work had been an instinctive need to escape from this examination of conscience and avoid having to admit his capitulation, his betrayal, and live at such a pitch of intensity that he would not even have time to think of such things. Unforeseen circumstances had brought his plan to nothing. He was cut off from action and had been immobilized. He had been brought back to the land in which he had grown up and put face to face with himself. His internal mechanism had broken down. The two parts of which it consisted no longer coalesced. He knew it was impossible even to think of ridding himself of one for the benefit of the other. Both of them were he. He knew that it was impossible to revert to his adolescence and the mythological tenets of religion, and hand his problems over to a transcendent God. He could not, even if he wanted to, retire into private life, shut his mind to the inhuman fate of the poor, and accept the dictatorship. And it seemed impossible now to go on with his party life, accept its rules and customs, intrigue, lie, consider the interests of the party as the supreme good, and judge moral values as petty-bourgeois prejudices. What was he to do?

Well, he said to himself at one point, if I go on like this I shall go mad.

He became obsessed with the fear of going mad. He had to

repeat his real name to himself, his real, true name; he hid all
his priestly garments, and put them out of sight; he touched his
knees, his shoulders, his face, he bit his hand to find a last refuge
against his moral perplexity in the fact of his physical existence.
One day, in order to escape from his spiritual torment, he dressed,
left his room, went down into the garden, spread a blanket on
the earth, and lay down on it. The warm earth, which had only
recently thawed, sank beneath his weight, like a woman's breast
swollen with milk. He rejoiced in its warmth, and tried to wrig-
gle closer to it with movements of his legs and shoulders. A procession of ants was descending from the fig tree and making its
way along the ground quite near him. Every insect was carrying
something. If only I could go to sleep and wake up tomorrow
morning at dawn, put a stick to my donkey, and go to the vineyard, Don Paolo said to himself. If I could go to sleep and wake
up, not only with healthy lungs, but with a normal brain, free
of all intellectual abstractions. If only I could go back to real,
ordinary life. If only I could dig, plow, sow, reap, earn my living,
talk to other men on Sundays, read and study; fulfill the law
that says, "In the sweat of thy face shalt thou earn thy bread."
On further reflection Don Paolo decided that the root of his
trouble lay in his infraction of that law—in the irregular life he
had been living, in cafés, libraries, and hotels, in having rudely
broken the chain that for centuries had bound his forefathers
to the soil. He was an outlaw, not because he had contravened the
arbitrary laws of the party in power, but because of his infringe-
ment of that more ancient law that said, "In the sweat of thy
face shalt thou earn thy bread." He had ceased to be a peasant,
and he had not become a townsman. It would never be possible
for him to return to the soil. Still less would it be possible for
him ever to forget it.

An unexpected diversion from his torment was provided by a
fearful storm that descended on Pietrasecca one night. The
weather had been oppressively hot and sultry, and the sun had
been blinding, glaring, and relentless. Pietrasecca was like a fur-
nace. The earth burned, as if veined by subterranean fires. "Lord,
send us a little water," the peasants prayed, and the Lord granted

their prayer, but in over-abundant measure. Clouds came swelling up from the plain of the Fucino and massed themselves above the valley. A sulphurous light made the inhabitants shudder. The village was seized with panic. People gathered from everywhere. Mothers called their children and their hens at the tops of their voices. It seemed an attack of collective madness.

"Not a drop of rain has fallen yet. Why is everybody so terrified?" said Don Paolo.

Before a quarter of an hour had passed the cataracts of heaven had opened. The sky burst over Pietrasecca. The storm laid siege to the valley and advanced relentlessly to the assault of the mountain at the head of it. Continuous lightning flashes rent the clouds, while a thunderous barrage, with cascades of water, crashed down on the mountain and on Pietrasecca. For three days and nights the deafening bombardment continued. The mountain was successively attacked from all sectors, but it did not yield. Miraculously it remained intact. Pietrasecca, nestling to its side, tried to hold out, too. Don Paolo helped Matalena and Americo to barricade the doors and windows, but water came in everywhere. The night was full of noises and cries for help, but no one dared move out-of-doors for fear of being overwhelmed by the storm. Not till morning came did they learn that the wooden bridge had been swept away and a dozen houses flooded. Matalena was nearly beside herself.

"If the house collapses again, who will rebuild it now that my husband is dead?" the poor woman wailed, in despair.

A few peasants succeeded in reaching the tower and ringing the alarm on the church bells. Kettles were put outside the houses upside down, and mothers exposed their babies in swaddling-clothes at the windows. These rites were designed to beseech pity of the supernatural powers. But they had no pity. The violence of the storm did not abate. There was no intermission in the onslaught on Pietrasecca and the mountain. Reinforcements kept on advancing from the valley and being hurled against the mountain. The mountain held out. But would it be able to hold out much longer? Bulls, wolves, and snakes seemed to be dancing an infernal jig round Matalena's inn. Water came pouring in

everywhere, and the wind howled and whistled. Every now and
then there were cries and calls for help, but they remained un-
answered. Matalena dashed hither and thither, like a slovenly,
unkempt fury, trying to stop the water that ran in through
every crack. Not till morning came was it known that Gerametta's
stable had been completely carried away by the storm. Of the
donkey and the goat there was no trace. Nicola Ciccavo's house
had collapsed, and he and Marietta, his wife, had managed to
find refuge in a neighbor's house. The roof of Gervasio Amatore's
house had caved in. Gervasio and his daughters had been in bed,
and one of the girls had been seriously injured.

On the third day the rain continued and the thunder went on
growling and roaring along the valley, but the violence of the
storm had passed. The valley was like a sodden gourd. The village
was full of water. Every alley was a rivulet. The cellars and
ground floors of every house were flooded and littered with sand
and stones brought in by the water. Road-menders came from
Lama to repair the road from the valley, parts of which had
been made impassable by landslides, and they threw up a temporary structure to replace the wooden bridge. Everyone started
grubbing among the débris for household property that had been
carried away by the water. Mud had penetrated everywhere. The
men crawling about in it looked like monstrous reptiles, croco-
diles, or great turtles. Mastrangelo's cart had ended up in the
stream. Father and son spent hours trying to drag it out.

"Heave!" the old man cried.

"Stop!"

"Heave!"

"Stop!"

They heaved and stopped and heaved and stopped, but the
cart refused to budge. The wheels just slid in the mud. Young
Mastrangelo started whistling, and lit a cigarette.

"Don't smoke! Pull!" the old man shouted. But the young man
went on smoking.

"Stop! Didn't I tell you not to smoke?"

The father made for the young man as if to strike him.

"Curse you and the mother that bore you! I told you not to whistle and not to smoke!" he shouted.

Don Paolo attempted to intervene on the young man's behalf. "Whistling isn't a sin," he said.

"When you work you don't whistle, or smoke, either," the old man answered. "Work isn't a form of entertainment."

"Supposing he wants to whistle?"

"He must wait till work is over. Work isn't a form of entertainment. Do you know the story of Giant Orlando, sir? He walked a mile at every step. One day he thought he would till the soil, just for fun. He plowed without ever getting tired, and when evening came he loosened the oxen from the plow, put them in one trousers pocket and the plow in the other, and went to sleep. Time passed, but nothing grew from Giant Orlando's fields. Nothing might have been sown in them at all. Why? Because they hadn't cost him any effort. To get any return from work, you have to suffer and sweat blood."

Father and son resumed their efforts to recover their cart. Meanwhile some one noticed a trout in the swollen waters of the stream. The whole village dashed to the stream, armed with baskets, reaping-hooks, sticks, and hoes, and started hunting for the trout, with savage cries and mutual incitements to the slaughter, but the trout had disappeared, and perhaps it wasn't a trout at all.

Meanwhile the peasants who had gone to see what damage the storm had done to their fields were returning.

Pasquale Gerametta approached the priest, took off his hat, made the sign of the Cross, and said, with tears in his voice:

"Please explain to me what God is doing!"

Don Paolo was at a loss for an answer.

"If your crop has been ruined, it is the fault of the storm," he said.

Gerametta shook his head. He apologized, and said he had no intention of taking the name of the Lord in vain. He was not angry, but he wanted to discuss the matter.

"If rain is not God's business, what is His business? If He has power over the rain and allows a storm to ruin poor people, what sort of God is He? Is there no justice He has to be afraid of?"

Poor Gerametta had lost his stable, his donkey, his goat, and the entire crop of two fields at a single blow. He considered himself ruined for the rest of his life. He wanted to know who was accountable. If it was not God, who was it?

"If God allows poor families to be ruined, is it possible that He's not accountable to anybody?" he asked.

Pasquandrea came up and said:

"A man goes and works at the Fucino for fourteen hours a day, good weather and bad, for four lire a day. He lives on bread and onions. He lives like an animal, all for the sake of buying a piece of land. After sweating blood for ten years, he manages to buy a piece of land. A storm comes and destroys the crop. He loses the land. There's no money to live on, to pay the taxes, to buy seed, so he has to sell it. He sells it and starts all over again. He works like a beast of burden for another ten years to be able to buy it back."

Mastrangelo interrupted and said:

"A poor man spends his whole life struggling for a little security, but he is never secure. He builds a house, and there's an earthquake or a flood and he's left without a roof over his head. Fine security! He imperils his immortal soul for the sake of getting a piece of land and a little security for his family. A storm comes and ruins the crop. He is never secure, but always lives in fear."

Giacinto Campobasso's crop had been ruined, too. He sought help of his brother-in-law, who had saved a little money. He brought him to the priest and said:

"My crop has been destroyed. The storm has uprooted everything. My land looks like a quarry. This was to have been the first harvest since I bought it. That piece of land has been the ruin of me. I gave up smoking, I gave up drinking, I went barefooted in summer, I wore nothing but rags. I let my sixteen-year-old daughter die without calling the doctor, without buying medicine, without sending for the priest. I lived on nothing but bread, and sweated blood, all for the sake of that piece of land.

You are my brother-in-law and know these things, but I remind you of them now in the presence of a priest. After buying that piece of land, I had no money left. I had to borrow to buy seed, two tubs, and a donkey. How can I repay now that the crop is destroyed? How can I buy seeds for the next sowing?"

Scaramelli shrugged his shoulders.

"Really, that is your affair," he said.

Campobasso wanted to put the matter beyond all possible doubt. He went on:

"I shan't sell the land, that's certain. If anyone has his eye on it and wants to take it, I shall shoot him. That land is a piece of my flesh. Rather than sell it, I'll sell myself and my wife. But if I don't pay the debt, the land will be seized. You are my brother-in-law and have some money, and you can help me."

"Really, on my word of honor, we all have our own troubles to think about," Scaramelli said and went away.

The priest and Campobasso stayed talking a little while longer. The priest forgot he was a priest and opened his heart to Campobasso.

"There is a great country," he said, "where for the first time in the history of man the peasants are trying to find security by other means than private property."

The priest and Campobasso were still together when Scaramelli came back on his donkey. He crossed the bridge and took the road down the valley.

Campobasso went livid with rage.

"He's going to the money-lender who lent me the money," he said. "He's after my land!"

Don Paolo tried to calm him.

"Perhaps you are mistaken," he said. "How do you know his intentions?"

"He has wanted that land for a long time," Campobasso said. "He hated me for being able to buy it before he could. Now he's got a good opportunity of getting it. The swine!"

"Wouldn't you do the same?" Don Paolo asked.

"The swine!" Campobasso repeated.

He ran home.

"Light the lamp before the Madonna at once!" he ordered his wife. "Go down on your knees and pray that disaster may overtake anyone who wants my land, whoever it may be!"

"Who wants to take our land?" his wife asked.

"Pray!" her husband ordered.

She lit the lamp, and under her husband's eye started praying to the Blessed Virgin to bring misfortune upon anyone who dared think of taking her husband's land.

Don Paolo went back to his room, tired. On the table he found the notebook containing his "Dialogues with Cristina." He opened it, re-read a few lines, and was seized with great disgust for himself. Under what he had written he wrote "meanderings of an idle mind." He went back to bed, but could not sleep. It must have been late when he heard excited voices outside the inn. Matalena came up and told him the news.

"Scaramelli has been brought back on a stretcher," she said. "He fell into the stream with his donkey, at a place where there had been a landslide and the road hadn't yet been repaired. The donkey's dead, and he's got a broken leg."

Next day Teresa Scaraffa's child was born. It was not blind. It was christened Paolo, out of gratitude to the priest who had saved its eyesight. Two days later Sabetta's child was born. Don Cipriano came from Lama for the christenings. A delegation of Pietrasecca fathers, led by Pasquale Gerametta, approached the parish priest of Lama.

"The wrath of God is unleashed against us," Gerametta said. "The innocent have been made to suffer for the guilty. Now we have no doubt left. There is mortal sin in our valley."

"Our afflictions in this life will redound to our advantage in the next," the old priest replied.

"There is mortal sin in our valley," Gerametta went on. "In the *refugium peccatorum*, near the stream. A young man of good family and a witch who came from the plain are living together in the house of the damned. Now we have no doubt left. If the authorities don't put a stop to it, we shall be compelled to put a stop to it ourselves, by force!"

Don Paolo was also sent for.

"Now we have no doubt left," said Gerametta. "God wished to punish the mortal sin."

"We ought to burn the house down," Campobasso said.

"We ought to demolish it," said Mastrangelo. "We ought to blow it up while the two are in bed."

Don Cipriano volunteered to attempt a pacific solution of the difficulty, provided Don Paolo, who knew the woman, came with him. Don Paolo had no wish for the authorities to intervene, so he consented to accompany the parish priest.

Giacinto Campobasso carried the two priests on his back across the still flooded stream, and they went on towards the house alone, sinking into the mud up to their knees at every step. One half of the double front door was missing. Don Paolo called Bianchina, but there was no reply. The inside of the house was like a cavern. The floor was a huge puddle. The roof was half blown away. Bianchina was curled up at the foot of the chimney, barefooted and unkempt. She was weeping silently. Near her Alberto was lying on a heap of damp straw, with a beard of several weeks, disheveled hair, the government party emblem in his buttonhole.

"Have you brought anything to eat?" Bianchina asked.

Don Cipriano had prepared a little exhortation. Bianchina interrupted him.

"Haven't you got anything to eat?" she asked.

Don Cipriano turned to Alberto.

"I christened you, and prepared you for confirmation and for your first communion," he said. "It is I who am responsible before God for your soul. It was I who consecrated you a tertiary of St. Francis."

Alberto looked at him blankly. Bianchina wanted to say something, but Don Cipriano silenced her.

"When St. Francis inaugurated the Third Order for the salvation of us all, in the castle called Cannario," he said, "the air was full of singing swallows. He gently asked them to be silent, and the swallows obeyed. Try, signorina, to imitate them."

"But you are not St. Francis," Bianchina retorted.

Don Cipriano ignored the interruption and started talking of the Franciscan virtues, particularly that of purity, addressing himself to Alberto.

"In one of the *Fioretti* we are told how the saint was once preaching in one of the countries of the Saracens, by order of the Sultan of Babylon. One night he went into an inn to rest, and there he met a Saracen woman, beautiful in body but impure in mind."

"I'm not a Saracen!" said Bianchina.

"The woman invited St. Francis to sin. 'I accept,' said St. Francis. 'Let us go to bed!' "

"There's a saint for you," said Bianchina.

"St. Francis led the woman to an enormous fire. He undressed and entered the flames and invited the woman to follow him and lie with him in that marvelous bed. But the woman was afraid."

"The woman was afraid?" exclaimed Bianchina.

"The woman was afraid," Don Cipriano repeated.

"If she had really loved St. Francis, she wouldn't have been afraid," said Bianchina. "I shouldn't have been afraid!"

"You would not have been afraid?" the priest of Lama exclaimed.

"Why wasn't St. Francis burned by the flames?" Bianchina said. "Because the fire within him was stronger than the fire of burning wood. Why was the Saracen woman afraid? Because she was cold and loveless. St. Francis invited her, and she was afraid. That Saracen woman was a disgrace to the female sex!"

Alberto got up, went outside, and came back with some wood for the fire.

"It's cold," he said, and lay down on the straw again.

Bianchina lit the fire. The wood was damp, and it was difficult to make it catch. For lack of tongs Bianchina was compelled to use her fingers. She ended by burning them, and burst into tears.

Don Cipriano had the bad taste to take his revenge.

"Oh," he remarked, "so you are afraid of fire?"

This remark exasperated her.

"I certainly wouldn't throw myself into the fire for you," she replied. "Or for my uncle, the parish priest of Fossa, either!"

"There is another fire," the priest went on. "An everlasting fire, for the damned. The air is full of blinding smoke, the stench of burning flesh, and groans and gnashing of teeth."

"We know," Alberto said. "We shall confess."

"And if you don't have time?" said Don Cipriano. "Suppose you had perished in the storm the other day?"

"We should have talked to God and tried to make him understand," Bianchina replied. "If He wouldn't understand, so much the worse for Him."

So far Don Paolo had not spoken.

"Why don't you get married?" he asked.

"My family wouldn't allow it," said Alberto.

"Have you asked them?"

"My family wouldn't allow it," Alberto repeated. "I know them."

The two priests took their departure.

"Marriage is the only solution," Don Cipriano said to Don Paolo. "You had better talk to the family."

Giacinto Campobasso was waiting for them to help them over the stream again.

"What are they going to do?" he asked.

"The whole thing will be arranged," Don Cipriano said. "You can tell that to the others. The whole thing will be arranged."

Don Paolo regretted his assumption of the task of talking to the Colamartini family. He felt himself quite unsuited for the rôle of matchmaker. He therefore put off the matter from day to day.

One afternoon a priest from Chieti arrived at Pietrasecca for a short visit. He had been Cristina's spiritual director and confessor at school. He arrived in a carriage, and he wished to see Don Paolo Spada before leaving again, two hours later.

"Signorina Colamartini spoke of you with great admiration," the priest said to Don Paolo. "As I was passing through the Marsica, I made a point of making a détour to Pietrasecca, yielding to the prayers and wishes of the Mother Superior and the sisters, who are very fond of Signorina Colamartini, and are sad that she is not yet among them."

Don Paolo was anxious not to raise the slightest suspicion about his identity in the priest's mind.

"I have remained a complete stranger to any discussions that may have taken place within the Colamartini family," was all he said.

"And so have I," replied the spiritual director, "nor has it been my intention during my visit here to exercise any pressure on the young lady. Nevertheless, I thought it my duty to find out what is making her postpone obeying a vocation to which she is called beyond any possibility of doubt."

"Signorina Cristina might also be very useful here at Pietrasecca," Don Paolo permitted himself to observe.

"Undoubtedly," the spiritual director replied. "Undoubtedly, provided Signorina Cristina's purely human qualities only are taken into account. But I do not see how her truly exceptional intelligence and sensibilities can develop and be put to account in a place as primitive as this. And in Signorina Cristina there is something else. She is one of those predestined beings who on this earth already form part of the generation pure as light, and carry on their brows the name of the Lamb. Their clothing is tinted with the blood of their daily immolation. They do not look where they go, but blindly follow where the Lamb leads them."

The fluency and unction of the spiritual director's ornate eloquence reminded Don Paolo of the Jesuit preachers who had visited his school.

"Signorina Cristina has made a profound impression on me, too," he said. "Nevertheless, I would not say it was an evil for her to remain a little while longer among such needy people."

The spiritual director, disappointed, took his leave, and departed in his carriage.

One night Don Paolo was invited to the Colamartini house. He was received by Don Pasquale in a big kitchen with smoke-stained walls. Three old women, white, cold, and silent, were seated round a big nutwood table. Cristina introduced him.

"This is my grandmother, this is my aunt, this is my mother."

An odor of wax and honey hung in the air. Don Paolo had a

feeling of simplicity and freshness, as though he had become a child again. But the three old women sitting round the table recalled memories of other landowning families. Matalena had, of course, gossiped about the Colamartini. Cristina's mother, she had told him, was half-witted. She was always laughing, but her intelligence was that of a child of five. Moreover, she was ten years older than her husband, and Don Pasquale had married her solely for the sake of her dowry. The whole family had been living on that dowry for many years. The peasants hated the Colamartini for their meanness. Cristina's grandmother was a real tyrant. Don Pasquale could do nothing against her will.

She told Don Paolo she was eighty-six years old and had had six sons, of whom two were dead, one was in the Argentine, and two were in North America. All had maintained the family honor, and the old woman could really not complain of her sons. But her grandchildren? Of her grandchildren it was better not to speak. The new generation was destroying what its fore-fathers had spent centuries putting together.

"I am not talking of Cristina," the old woman said. "Women are not the same as men. But when there is no man, woman must take his place. I was left a widow at the age of thirty-five, and I was father and mother to my children."

"You did not marry again?" Don Paolo asked.

The old woman looked at him in surprise.

"I loved my husband," she said. "How could I marry anybody else? My husband, may the Lord rest his soul, was a fine young man. He has been dead for more than fifty years, but I still love him."

Cristina was washing the floor. Don Paolo scarcely dared look at her. He discovered what purity meant; what it meant to make chastity the guardian over one's body.

The three old women got up and took their departure to go and tell their beads in their own rooms. Cristina remained to entertain the guest. She would tell her beads later, by herself.

The Colamartini kitchen reminded Don Paolo of his own home, which had been destroyed by the earthquake. Utensils of beaten copper, pots and pans and lids of all shapes, covered the whole of one wall. Two big grated windows looked out onto the garden, which contained few flowers but many box hedges, high as walls. Some beehives were at the bottom of the garden. To Don Paolo it was like reëntering familiar surroundings.

"My seedsman recently offered me some 'Queen Helena' dahlias, some 'Empire' carnations, and some 'Mother Italy' violets," Don Pasquale said. "I hastened to inquire whether this meant that the dahlias had been cultivated by Queen Helena, that the carnations came from the imperial gardens, and that the violets came from the gardens of the King's late mother. But I was told that the names had no relation whatever to the seeds, and that they might just as well have been called something else. So I did not buy them. I could not admit bastard flowers with titles of false nobility to my garden."

At one end of the table Cristina was ironing and folding table-cloths, towels, and napkins, and replacing them in wicker baskets.

"Do you know Don Benedetto of Rocca dei Marsi?" Don Pasquale asked the priest.

"Don Benedetto?" Don Paolo asked in surprise. "Why do you ask?"

"He advised Cristina not to take the veil," Don Pasquale answered. "Don Benedetto is an old family friend of ours; he is a saintly man and is hated by the ecclesiastical authorities. There is no doubt that there have been very few saints who have not been suspected and persecuted by the Church."

Cristina had finished her ironing, and now she lit the fire. She went down on her knees in front of the fireplace, and blew on the flames, which were slow to catch. The fagots were of fresh wood and were very smoky.

"I should like to know your opinion about what Cristina should do," said Don Pasquale. "That you did not hasten to express one gives me pleasure. But will you tell me if I ask you as a favor?"

For a moment Don Paolo made no reply.

"Here at Pietrasecca I have been reminded of three profound

words from the Bible," Don Paolo said. "*Jesus autem tacebat.* I cannot give you a better answer than that."

Cristina laughed whole-heartedly. She was sitting at the other side of the fire, with her head in the shadow of the chimney, and Don Paolo could not see her, because he was blinded by the flames. Her voice came from the darkness.

"God is everywhere, even at Pietrasecca," she said.

Don Pasquale offered Don Paolo some wine. A bottle of red wine and a bottle of white wine were on the table.

"The red wine comes from a country of sand, beaten by the sirocco," said Don Pasquale. "The white wine comes from a Malmsey vineyard, from a country beaten by the north wind."

The red wine was strong and left a sweet flavor at the bottom of the glass. The white wine was transparent, had a bitter-sweet taste, and gave one a sensation of shuddering in the bones.

"The wine for Don Benedetto's Masses comes from my cellar," said Don Pasquale. "I send him two barrels every year, as soon as they have fermented."

The fire went out. Cristina's head, neck, and shoulders emerged from the darkness. She was drinking her wine in little sips, like a sparrow.

"If there has been selfishness on the part of the family regarding Cristina, I ask you to believe that it has not been the dominant motive. Cristina is free."

"Even the wolves don't want me," said Cristina, in a joking tone.

"The wolves?" asked Don Paolo.

Her father told a story of Cristina's childhood.

"She was still in the cradle," he said, "and as she was very fond of sheep and it was warm in winter in the sheepfold, one evening we left her in her cradle among the sheep for a few hours. A wolf entered the fold and had time to kill two sheep. I heard the loud bleating of the flock and hurried to the fold with my dogs, but the wolf escaped."

"Was Cristina asleep?" asked Don Paolo.

"She was not only awake, but sitting up in her cradle. She had seen the wolf, but wasn't a bit frightened. No doubt she took it for a bad dog that was eating the sheep."

"As soon as I saw it biting the sheep I started calling father, but my voice was drowned by the bleating," Cristina said.

"Perhaps the wolf saw that she was too small, and intended to come back for her when she was bigger," said Don Paolo with a laugh.

"I'll be able to take care of myself," said Cristina.

Don Paolo reflected a moment, and then said:

"There are many kinds of wolves. There are wolves who look like lambs."

Cristina's father agreed.

"We are old and soon we shall die," he said. "A young woman cannot live alone. If a serious match presented itself, would it be prudent not to consider it?"

"I am already betrothed," Cristina replied.

Her father and Don Paolo looked at her in surprise.

"I am already betrothed," she went on, "to the Only Husband Who does not betray, the only One Who does not weary, the only One Who does not divorce, Who wants no dowry, does not die, and wants everything, body and soul, day and night, for the twelve hours of the day and the twelve hours of the night."

"And then the Colamartini family will come to an end," said Don Pasquale. "A scapegrace son, and a nun for a daughter."

"I spent many vigils and reflected much before understanding what is essential and what is illusory in life," said Cristina.

The three remained silent for a long time in the semi-darkness of the kitchen. Cristina went up to the first floor to put the ironed linen back in the cupboard.

"I have four pieces of land left," said Don Pasquale, "two planted with vines and two for sowing. Up to a few years ago I drew about seven thousand lire a year from the wine. Now, because of the plant lice, the yield of the new vineyards, reconstructed at great sacrifice, is not even so much as a few hundred lire. If I bought wine at market instead of getting it from my own vineyards, it would cost me only one-third as much."

The old man got up and fetched his account-book from a drawer.

"The lands for sowing," he went on, "barely yield enough to pay the laborers, although their wages have dropped to four or five lire a day, which isn't much. On top of it I have to pay taxes. For some years I have been wondering why I go on cultivating them. They do not even yield enough to feed me. Every year I have to find the money to buy eight hundredweight of wheat, two hundred lire's worth of greens and vegetables, and about three hundred lire's worth for cheese, meat, cod, and flour. On top of that there is the material for one's clothes and boots, because one cannot go barefooted. In all I have to draw five thousand lire every year from the family's last reserves, which represent the savings of fifty years."

"Depression," Don Paolo suggested.

"Bankruptcy," Don Pasquale answered. "We have a government which says it has saved law and order, but has brought us to a state of bankruptcy. We sink lower every year. If it were not for family pride, which prevents me from selling these lands, which have belonged to the Colamartini for centuries, I should have got rid of them long ago, in my own interest. The soil no longer yields anything. The city devours everything. I have an old house near Lama. It is now used as a stable, and I have let it. In order to comply with the laws I had to spend exactly six times the amount of the rent on it. Fourteen different dues and taxes are payable on the rent: stamp duty, transcription charge, tax on numbering agreement, emolument to notary, registration tax, tax for copying agreement, charge for formal transfer of lease, copies for registrar and parties to the agreement, various costs and postages, and receipt stamps."

"It's bankruptcy," said Don Paolo.

"It's the end," said Don Pasquale. "A hectoliter of Apulian wine costs forty lire, though the cost of production is more than a hundred. If you sell your wine you have to pay eighty-five lire consumption tax, or double the price of the wine itself. Fifteen years ago vineyards were worth about fifty thousand lire per hectare. Today there are no buyers at one-tenth of that amount."

"How do the small proprietors fare?" asked Don Paolo.

"In theory small proprietorship is a fine thing," said Don Pasquale. "Every peasant aspires to be a small landowner. Those who attain their ambition are worse off than the rest. You can't cultivate without capital. About seventy years ago Monsignor's land, the ecclesiastical demesne, was sold cheaply and divided up among the peasants. After a few years the peasants were forced to sell, and the whole area is now in the hands of two or three big landlords. You can't cultivate without money."

"How about the peasants?" asked Don Paolo.

"They are better off than I," answered Don Pasquale. "Flesh used to suffering doesn't feel the pain."

"They too are Christians of flesh and blood," the priest remarked.

"No peasant has ever died of sorrow," replied Don Pasquale, "though I have known one to die on hearing good news. Mastrangelo's father, may the Lord rest his soul, was a servant boy in my father's house. We were of the same age, so we did our military service together, at Ancona. On our last day we each bought a lottery ticket. Mastrangelo's ticket won. It was two thousand lire. I made the mistake of telling him the good news without preparing him for it properly. He collapsed and died on the spot. His heart could not contain so much happiness."

Cristina had finished putting the washing away, and she came down to keep the two men company again. Don Pasquale kept two cows, a mare, and a heifer in a stable behind the house, and he went to attend to them. Don Paolo was left alone with Cristina.

"Don Cipriano and I visited Bianchina and Alberto a few days ago," he said.

"I know," said Cristina.

"They are in a very bad way," said the priest.

"I can imagine it," the girl answered.

"They would like to get married," said the priest. "Perhaps that's the only solution."

"That's impossible," said Cristina.

The priest could not see why.

"The Colamartini cannot become connected to the Girasole," Cristina explained.

Don Paolo did not understand.

"My father would regard it as a disgrace not only to himself, but to all his forbears," the girl said.

"This has nothing to do with any forbears but with Alberto," said Don Paolo.

"It's impossible," said Cristina, with finality. "There can be no discussion about family honor."

"Is that what you think too?" said the priest, in surprise.

"Of course," said the girl.

They went on to talk about the storm.

"It did a lot of damage," said Don Paolo. "I do not understand why after every flood and every storm the houses are always rebuilt next to the stream and not behind your house, for instance, where they would be higher and perfectly safe."

"The land beside the stream is cheaper," Cristina said. "The land up there behind the stable belongs to my father, but the peasants won't pay the fair price."

"But next to the stream they are in constant danger," Don Paolo replied.

"Life is like that," said Cristina.

Don Paolo nearly retorted rudely. He checked himself in time. He felt profoundly disgusted with Cristina. He managed to control himself sufficiently to ask a question.

"Have you never thought of justice as an ideal capable of being realized in this world, among men?" he asked.

"Our Kingdom is not of this world," Cristina replied.

"But the land behind the stable is of this world. Why is it refused to people who would be safer on it than beside the stream?"

"God made rich and poor," answered Cristina. "Every man is answerable to God for what he has received. One must be content with one's lot."

"I do not understand," said Don Paolo. "You wish to enter a

convent and renounce the world, but you are unwilling to renounce the land behind the stable."

"I personally renounce everything," said Cristina. "But my family has a rank which it must maintain."

Don Pasquale returned from the stable, and the priest rose and went back to his hotel. He was furious with Cristina. The fascination she had exercised over him had vanished. The thing that had snapped inside him fifteen years before, when he had revolted against the cold and pitiless hypocrisy of the church people, snapped again inside him now. The cloth he wore had prevented him from speaking to Cristina as she deserved. He found it galling not to be able to speak out and tell this priggish little would-be saint exactly what he thought of her and her false religion. In the end, to relieve his feelings a little, he sat down at the table and started writing in his diary what he would have liked to say to Cristina if prudence had not forbidden it.

"Barnyard selfishness," he began, "is the most degraded and beastly kind of selfishness of all." And on he went in the same vein.

Chapter VI

SPRING passed and summer came, cherries were over and the corn was ripening. Don Paolo's health was much better, so he made efforts to escape the boredom of the female atmosphere that surrounded him. He avoided meeting Cristina and tried to establish relations with the peasants.

The peasants were away all day long. They returned to Pietrasecca in the evening, after sunset, in small groups, walking behind their donkeys, which were laden with their tools. Don Paolo would see them from his window, slowly coming up the valley, walking with their typical crouching walk, which they acquired from their perpetual bending over the soil, hoeing and weeding, and also from the force of suggestion, the habit of servitude. Now that Don Paolo was better, he left the house to escape from the continuous lamentations of Matalena, who was already living in terror of the next storm, to escape from the complaints of the other women, who were knitting and removing lice from themselves outside the inn, to escape from the breviary and the *Eternal Maxims*, and from the youthful phantoms which he had believed dispersed, but which, taking advantage of his solitude and physical weakness, had returned to haunt him. But above all he wished to avoid meeting Cristina.

He crossed the bridge, which still consisted of loose boards, took the road down the valley, and sat down on a stone to await the peasants returning from the fields. Don Paolo felt like a machine that has broken down and been to the repair shop, but is almost mended and works again and has resumed its usual rhythm.

The first to appear were old Sciatàp and his son, with Garibaldi a few paces ahead of them, laden with tools.

Sciatàp stopped and said:

"I've been wanting to speak to you for some time, sir, but I was told you had a cough, and I didn't want to disturb you."

"The cough is better now," said Don Paolo.

"It's about my son," the old man said. "He has been trying to join the carabinieri, the government militia, but so far they haven't taken him. Perhaps you could give him a recommendation, sir."

"Do you really want to join the carabinieri?" the priest asked the young man.

"Of course," he said. "People talk ill of them, out of envy. They work little and earn well."

"It's not a question of working little or much," the priest replied. "The point it this. You are a workingman, a peasant. If you become a carabiniere, your superiors may order you to shoot at dissatisfied peasants, as happened not far from here, at Sulmona, at Pratola, and at Prezza."

Sciatàp agreed.

"Don Paolo is quite right," he said. "To live at all well you've got to sell your soul. There's no other way. Once upon a time a big devil lived in a cave, clothed all in black, with a top-hat and his fingers full of rings, like a banker. Three peasants went to him and asked: 'What must we do to live well, without working?' The devil said: 'Bring me a soul, a living soul.' The peasants went away, took a cat, wrapped it up just like a new-born baby, and took it to the devil. 'Here is a soul, a really innocent soul,' they said. In return the devil handed them a book which gave all the directions for living well without working. But while they were going away with it the cat started miaowing. The devil discovered he had been tricked. The magic book disappeared in flames in the men's hands. A cat's no good. You need a soul, a real soul."

"Very well," said his son. "I shall do the same as the others. Meanwhile my application has not been accepted. There are too many applicants."

"There are too many souls," Sciatàp concluded. "The earth-quake and the epidemics and the war weren't enough. There really are too many souls."

"What remains to a man who has sold his soul?" the priest asked.

"There's always a way of arranging things as long as you're alive," Sciatàp replied. "What's the Church for? Does the Church forbid the carabinieri to shoot? When the Corpus Christi procession takes place at Fossa, four carabinieri always walk behind the Blessed Sacrament in full uniform. You said that at Pratola the carabinieri shot at the peasants. That means that afterwards they confessed. But what about the dead peasants? Who confessed them? In this life they suffered from cold, and in the next they'll suffer from fire."

"I am very sorry," said Don Paolo, "but I don't know anyone to recommend you to. I don't know any officers in the cara-binieri."

In the meantime the donkey had walked on.

"Garibaldi!" Sciatàp called out.

But the donkey took no notice and went on its way.

"He doesn't listen to me because he's hungry and knows that his stable and his straw are not far away," he said. "When he's hungry he even forgets his own name."

The old man and his son said good-night and walked on to overtake the donkey.

A little later a drunken peasant passed, riding a donkey. He was swaying from side to side. He kicked and struck the donkey each time he recovered himself.

"Will you go straight, yes or no?" he kept saying.

A group of peasants appeared, walking with Magascià's cart. Bersagliera, who was drawing the cart, was thinner than ever. Magascià introduced the other men to Don Paolo, who walked homeward with them.

"We've been to market," said Magascià.

"Did you sell well?" the priest asked.

"All the prices have gone down," said Magascià. "They had fixed maximum prices at which we were allowed to sell. We didn't want to sell, but we had to, otherwise they would have confiscated our produce."

"They fix maximum prices for country produce, but there's no price-fixing for town produce, which has gone up," one of the men walking beside the cart said.

"Giacinto Campobasso was arrested by the carabinieri for rebellion," said Magascià. "As soon as he heard about the price-fixing he wanted to go back to Pietrasecca without selling."

A big man, named Daniele Maglietta, wearing a large hat pulled askew over his bearded face, was walking beside the carter.

"Daniele had a sick donkey. It certainly won't live another month," Magascià confided to the priest. "He took it to market and sold it to a Fossa woman as sound in wind and limb."

"I shall confess next Easter," Daniele said.

The whole group laughed.

A youth named Luigi Banduccia, who looked as if he were drunk, was walking on one side of the cart.

"Banduccia went to a tavern at Fossa, ate and drank and stood drinks all round, and then went into the garden as though he were going to relieve himself, but he jumped over the wall and got away without paying," Magascià confided to the priest.

"I shall confess next Easter, too," Banduccia said.

Everybody laughed again. Don Paolo looked at these poor people, accustomed to being cheated and robbed, who had been legally cheated and robbed by the authorities that day, and tried to get their own back by cheating and robbing other poor people, and naïvely boasted of it. The manner of several of these poor peasants, their way of laughing and talking, betrayed craftiness, an animal-like selfishness; they looked like habitual thieves and pilferers; and this was reinforced by the respect in which they were held by the other poor people, who had no other defense.

"When the landlady, Signora Rosa Girasole, discovered I had gone, she tried to make Biagio Vaccaro pay my bill," Luigi Banduccia went on. "She said he ought to pay because he came from Pietrasecca, too. The poor lady made a bad choice. If people hadn't interfered he would have smashed the whole place. He picked up a log of wood and threw it at her. If it had hit her it would have killed her."

Biagio was the strongest peasant in the valley, and Don Paolo had heard him spoken of with great admiration before.

"Biagio has been to prison for violence three times," somebody else said. "He's a man who makes himself respected."

"It's no disgrace to hit; it's a disgrace to be hit," Banduccia said.

"The first time Biagio went to prison it was for breaking his father's arm with a hatchet," Magascià said. "Before he died the old man said to me, 'My son broke my arm, but I'm glad he's so strong.' "

The others went on telling stories of Biagio's prowess, but Don Paolo stopped listening.

Although the peasants talked quite freely in his presence, these casual encounters left him dissatisfied. He felt more like a tourist talking to people casually encountered by the wayside than a revolutionary working among the masses he represented. He felt he was in a ridiculous position, and this made him decide to try a risky experiment. He decided to try to surmount the obstacle of his priestly clothing, penetrate farther into the peasants' real feelings, and find out whether it was possible to make himself understood by them. It would, of course, be impossible to talk to them publicly or in a group, not only because it would be imprudent, but also because it would be ineffective. An agitator inciting to action must talk at the top of his voice and to a crowd. He must excite and be excited, exalt and be exalted. But to establish relations between man and man, to inspire confidence and have confidence, to exchange ideas and not words, two men must be alone together, talk softly and with many pauses, the better to be able to reflect. One by one Don Paolo reviewed in his mind those peasants whom he already knew, wishing to select one to make friends with. But for one reason or another he instinctively rejected them all. But there was a youth in the group now returning from market with Magascià who did not speak, but kept looking intently at the priest. He was barefooted, badly dressed, tall and thin. The hair ruffled over his brow gave him a wild look, which contrasted with his kind eyes, which were like those of a tame domestic dog. Don Paolo looked at him and smiled. The youth smiled too and came near him. After the group crossed the bridge at Pietrasecca and dissolved, Don Paolo took the youth by the arm and stopped him.

"I should like to talk to you," he said. "I should like to know what you think about some things."

The young man smiled and walked towards his cottage. Don Paolo followed him. Every now and then the young man turned and looked at the priest without speaking, but his eyes betrayed his emotion.

"I want to talk to you as man to man," Don Paolo said. "Forget for a moment that I am wearing a priest's clothing and that you are a poor peasant."

The young man's home was rather like a pig-sty. You had to bend to enter the door, which also served as chimney. In the darkness it was possible to discern with difficulty that there was barely room for a straw mattress, which was spread on the stone floor, and for a nanny-goat that was chewing the cud on some filthy straw. The stench was too much for Don Paolo, who sat down at the threshold, while the youth prepared his evening meal.

"There is a country," Don Paolo began, "a great country in the east of Europe. It is a great plain cultivated with wheat, a great plain inhabited by millions of peasants."

The young man cut some corn bread, sliced two tomatoes and an onion, and offered them to the priest with a piece of bread. There were still traces of earth on his swollen, scarred hands. The knife he cut the bread with looked as if it were used for everything. Don Paolo shut his eyes and tried to swallow the bread.

"There is a land," he said, "a great land, in which the peasants of the country have joined with the workers of the city."

Meanwhile Matalena had been going from house to house, searching for her lodger. At last she found him.

"Dinner has been ready for an hour," she said.

"I'm not hungry," Don Paolo said. "Go back to the inn, because my friend here and I have a lot to talk about yet."

"But haven't you noticed he's deaf and dumb and only understands signs?" Matalena asked.

The young man was sitting at the threshold of his hovel, beside the priest. Don Paolo looked him in the face, and saw that his eyes were slowly filling with tears.

"It doesn't matter. Go back to the inn, I'm not hungry," the priest said to Matalena.

The two men remained seated at the threshold of the hovel, alone; the one with the gift of speech was silent now, too. Every now and then the two looked at each other and smiled. Day had faded into evening, and now night came. Don Paolo coughed once or twice. The deaf-mute got up, fetched the blanket that covered his straw mattress, and carefully put it round his guest's shoulders. Then Don Paolo remembered that this man would have to get up early in the morning and go to work, so he arose, shook hands with him, and bade him good-night.

On the ground floor of the inn there was a bar to which peasants came every night to play and drink. It contained two greasy tables, some shaky chairs, and a colored print of the Moor of Venice. The corners of the room were used for storing provisions. There were sacks of potatoes, beans, and lentils. There was always a plate of salted roast chick-peas on one table, to make the customers thirsty. The customers chewed chick-peas, drank, chewed tobacco, drank again, and spat. This cycle went on uninterruptedly, so that when Don Paolo came in he always had to be careful not to slip. The older men were nearly always talking of famines and epidemics of days gone by, and the young men were nearly always talking about the town.

A boorish, grumpy old man named Fava was always seated in one corner. He was perpetually staring at the floor and moving his jaws, like an animal chewing the cud. He was the first to arrive and the last to leave, and when he went he was so drunk that he could hardly stand. His sons, his daughters, and his wife would come and try to fetch him home, but nothing would make him budge.

"There's wine at home. Why don't you drink the wine from our vineyard?" his wife asked him.

"I don't like it," he said.

Matalena exchanged some wine with Fava's wife.

"Now you must stay at home," his wife said. "We've got the kind of wine you like."

But the old man persisted in coming to the inn as usual. In the end his wife started berating Matalena.

"You mustn't give him anything to drink," she said. "If he wants to drink he must come home."

It made no difference. Every evening Fava came to the inn and sat in his usual place.

When Don Paolo entered, Mastrangelo was playing cards with Nicola Ciccavo.

"When I saw you talking to the deaf-mute, sir, I thought it was a miracle, but it was only a mistake," said Mastrangelo.

Don Paolo sat down at the table with the two men.

"It wasn't a miracle and it wasn't a mistake," he said.

"The lad is very intelligent," said Nicola. "Perhaps the Lord made him deaf and dumb as a punishment."

The two men went on playing.

"How will you get through the year now the crops are ruined?" Don Paolo asked.

"If it was possible to die of hunger we should have been dead long ago," said Nicola.

"Don't you think that one day things might alter?" asked Don Paolo.

"Yes," said Nicola. "When the patient's dead the doctor arrives."

Don Paolo grew reckless.

"Haven't you ever heard that there are countries where things are different?" he asked.

This time Mastrangelo replied.

"Yes," he said. "There are countries different from ours. God put grass where there are no sheep and sheep where there is no grass."

Don Paolo felt he was groping in the dark. He dropped all caution and asked:

"In the city, at least so I've heard, there are people who suffer from lack of liberty. Have you ever suffered from lack of liberty?"

The reply was slow in coming. Mastrangelo refilled his wine-glass, emptied it, went over to the door, then came back and sat down again, as though he had not heard the question.

"Liberty?" he said. "There's only too much of it. Once upon a time a girl was not allowed to be alone with her fiancé before marriage."

"I am not talking of that," said Don Paolo. "I am not talking of the behavior of engaged couples."

"I see," said Mastrangelo.

He lit his pipe and smoked. His pipe went out and he emptied the remains into his hand and put them in his pocket. After a long silence he produced his reply.

"I see, sir," he said. "You are talking of married people. With us things have remained as they were, but down in the plain there's only too much liberty."

"I see," said Don Paolo, and gave up trying to go on with the conversation.

On Sunday nights the bar was always full, and continual rows and quarrels broke out among the peasants. After drinking, they nearly always came to blows. Don Paolo, upstairs in his room, would hear men going and coming until late at night, and listen to the noise of the chairs and the clattering of the glasses, and the sudden flaring up of arguments, followed by shouts, cries, bangs, curses, tables and chairs being upset, and glasses and bottles being used as projectiles.

"Be quiet!" Matalena implored. "Don Paolo is upstairs, asleep!"

"I want to talk to him!" Francesco Grascia started shouting. "Make him come down! I want to talk to him!"

"It's impossible," said Matalena. "He's asleep."

"I must talk to him! I must talk to him!" Grascia went on shouting.

Don Paolo dressed and came downstairs.

"Who wants me?" he asked.

The quarreling stopped, and everybody started offering the priest drinks. He thanked them, tried to excuse himself, but in the end he was forced to make the circuit of the bar, touching every glass with his lips.

"Who wants me?" he asked again.

Francesco Grascia came forward.

"My patron saint is San Francesco of Paolo, the Calabrian saint," he said. "I've got a picture of him at home. When I need help I make my wife pray to him. To be perfectly frank, he doesn't grant many petitions, but I used to think it was my wife's fault for not being able to convince him."

"I am not interested in these things," said the priest.

"I used to think it was my wife's fault," Grascia went on, "but it's not her fault at all, but the picture's, which is a false one. In my picture San Francesco has a beard, but I went to a church at Sulmona, where I saw a picture of San Francesco of Paolo without a beard. My picture was sold me by Don Cipriano, the priest of Lama. How can a priest sell false saints?"

"What did Don Cipriano say about it?" Don Paolo asked.

"When I got back from Sulmona I went to see him about it straight away," Grascia said. " 'Through your fault I've intrusted my life to a false saint,' I told him. 'Whenever I had toothache I used to light an oil-lamp before that picture, and the oil got used up, but the toothache remained.' Don Cipriano told me that the resemblance was of no importance, and that what mattered was the devotion. But if the resemblance isn't important, why have the picture? If my son, who is a soldier, sends me his photograph, and I see that it isn't his photograph, but somebody else's, is there any reason why I should hang it on the wall? Why should I have any respect for it at all?"

A profound silence had fallen on the bar, and everybody waited for the priest's reply.

"Magascià has a beard," the priest said. "If he had his photograph taken now, he'd have a beard in the picture. But if next year he shaved his beard off and had his photograph taken again, there would be no beard in the picture. Which of the photographs would be true and which would be false?"

"They would both be true," Grascia replied.

"How many Magascià's are there?" asked the priest.

"Only one," said Grascia.

"So, although there's only one Magascià there would be two different pictures of him. That is what happened with San Francesco of Paola."

Don Paolo's reply had an enormous success. Everybody present shouted and offered him drinks. He had to make the circuit of the bar and touch everybody's glass with his lips again. Then he said good-night and went up to his room. But before he was in bed they were shouting for him again.

Four youths playing settemezzo had started a quarrel about the king of diamonds. In settemezzo the king of diamonds is the most important card. Matalena only had two packs of cards, and in both the king of diamonds was so worn and easily recognizable that it was impossible for the game to be fair. Daniele Maglietta made a proposal to avoid disputes.

"Since the king of diamonds is recognizable, let us substitute, say, the three of spades, for it. The king of diamonds which is recognizable, will count as the three of spades, and the three of spades, which is indistinguishable from the rest, will count as the king of diamonds."

"That's impossible," Michele Mascolo objected. "It would be impossible, even if we all agreed to it."

"Why?"

"It's obvious," said Mascolo. "The king of diamonds is always the king of diamonds. He may be filthy, or marked, or have holes in him, but he's still the king of diamonds. This, for example, is a pipe. You ask me why. It's obvious. It is a pipe because it is a pipe. In the same way the Pope is the Pope. Why? Because he is the Pope. The king of diamonds is the king of diamonds in the same way. That's what he is and that's what he remains."

"It doesn't matter if we all agree," said Daniele. "If we all agree, it will be perfectly all right. And it will be a better game, because no one will know in advance who has the king of diamonds."

Mascolo remained unconvinced.

"You say it won't matter if we all agree?" he said. "I say it will matter. You say that the game would be the same? Perhaps it would, but it would be a false game. It would be like a wife committing adultery with her husband's consent. Isn't that a sin? It's a double sin, even if everybody agreed."

Sciatàp, who was sitting at the other table, the old man's table, had overheard the argument.

"You must ask Don Paolo," he said.

Don Paolo came down from his room once more and the arguments were repeated for his benefit.

"Tell us who is right," Sciatàp asked him.

The priest held up the king of diamonds.

"Do you think this card has any value in itself or that its value was given to it?" he asked Michele Mascolo.

"It's worth more than the others, because it's the king of diamonds," said Mascolo.

"Where do cards come from?" the priest asked.

"From the printer's," several voices answered.

"What was this card before it was printed?" the priest asked Mascolo.

"A piece of paper, like all the rest of the pack," various voices answered again.

"So its value was given it by the printer," the priest went on. "It had no value in itself, but its value was given to it. And that's not all. Is its value constant or does it vary? Does the king of diamonds have the same value at all games, at tresette, briscola, and scopa, for instance?"

"It has different values in different games," said Mascolo.

"And who invented the games?" the priest went on.

Nobody answered.

"Don't you think the games were invented by the players?" the priest suggested.

Everybody agreed, including Mascolo. The games had been

invented by the players, and the value of the cards was different in different games and was therefore fixed by the players.

"So if this card has a value," the priest concluded, "not in itself, but because a value was attributed to it, if it has a value which differs according to the players' whim and fancy, it means that you can do what you like with it."

Enthusiasm for the priest broke out again. "Hurrah!" they shouted. "Bravo! Bravissimo! Never has there been such a wise man of God in our part of the world!"

Don Paolo turned to Sciatàp and said:

"Once upon a time there was a man here, at Pietrasecca, named Carlo Campanella, and now there's a man in New York named Mr. Charles Little-Bell, Ice and Coal. But are Carlo Campanella and Mr. Charles Little-Bell, Ice and Coal, one man or two?"

"They're the same man!" a number of voices replied.

"Sha-tap!" Sciatàp shouted. "It's I who ought to answer that question!"

He answered it.

"They are the same man under a changed name," he said.

"If a man can change his name, why can't a card?" the priest asked.

"A king is always a king," Mascolo replied.

"A king is only a king as long as he reigns," said Don Paolo. "A king who no longer reigns is no longer a king, but an ex-king. There is a country, a big country, in the direction the sun comes from, which used to have a king. Let us call him a big king of hearts. He used to rule over millions of peasants, but from the moment the millions of peasants stopped obeying him, he no longer reigned, and so he wasn't a king any longer. Not far away, in the direction in which the sun sets, there is another country where there used to be a king. Let us call him the king of diamonds. But from the moment his subjects ceased obeying him he ceased to reign. He ceased to be a king and became an ex-king, and now he is a political exile, which is a thing that even a peasant can be. So go on playing at settemezzo how you like, and good-night!"

Don Paolo handed the cards back to Daniele, once more said good-night to everybody, and went up to his room, followed by acclamations.

"As you're worn and filthy, from this moment you cease to reign and are not king any longer. You're barely even an ex-king," said Daniele to the king of diamonds.

Then he addressed the three of spades.

"From now on you take the place of the king of diamonds at settemezzo," he said. "Don't get filthy or marked, or you'll lose your crown to another card!"

The other players laughed and agreed, and the game was resumed. But in the days that followed, the deposition of the king of diamonds was the subject of much comment and argument among the peasants of Pietrasecca.

Next day Signorina Patrignani, the village schoolmistress, came to Don Paolo and complained.

"In the big children's class it was impossible to give my lesson today," she said. "The boys kept on talking about that affair of the king of diamonds and the king of clubs, and repeating what you said last night."

The schoolmistress wore the emblem of the government party over her heart. When she breathed, it bobbed up and down like a boat on troubled waters.

"The people here are very ignorant," she went on, "and when they listen to educated people like us they nearly always understand the very opposite of what we mean."

The schoolmistress had with her the latest number of *The News of Rome*, the wall newspaper. It was to be posted on the church door. Before putting it there, it was her duty to read and explain the most important news to the peasants, who gathered in Matalena's bar for the purpose. Rumor had spread that the priest was going to speak, too, so the bar was more crowded than usual. Some of the peasants the priest had never seen before, dull-witted, weather-beaten faces on twisted and contorted human stumps, deformed by illness and labor. They looked like people who had been betrayed and were mistrustful. Young men among them looked wild and quarrelsome. An audience of about thirty men gathered in a short time, seated on the floor, one against the other.

A vague odor of manure and dirty clothing exuded from them, a stench as of goats, a mustiness that gave one a catch in the throat. Don Paolo sat near the schoolmistress, at the foot of the staircase.

In the presence of the strange priest the schoolmistress was more garrulous and excited than usual. She told her audience to pay close attention and not be afraid to ask for explanations of the difficult words. Then she started reading *The News from Rome*.

"We have a Leader," she read, "for whom all the nations of the earth envy us. Who knows what they would be willing to pay for him . . ."

Magascià interrupted. He did not like such generalities. He asked how much other nations would be willing to pay for him.

"It's only a manner of speaking," the schoolmistress explained.

"What a thing to say!" Magascià protested. "Are they or are they not willing to pay for him? If they are, how much do they offer? And who offers most?"

The schoolmistress repeated that the phrase was only a manner of speaking.

"You mean, in other words, it isn't true that they are willing to pay for him?" Magascià said. "And if it isn't true, why say so?"

The schoolmistress glanced at the priest and sighed, as if to say, Now you see what kind of people we have to deal with!

The next item she read concerned the rural population.

"Who are the rural population?" asked Mastrangelo.

"You are," said the schoolmistress. "I've told you so before."

She went on reading.

" . . . the rural revolution has attained its objectives all along the line . . ."

Sciatàp interrupted.

"Are we the rural population?" he said. "The rural revolution was made by us?"

"Exactly," said the schoolmistress.

"What revolution did we make?" Sciatàp asked.

"It is to be understood in a spiritual sense," the schoolmistress explained.

This did not satisfy Magascià.

"This is a newspaper the government sends us," he said. "It says the rural population, which you say means us, has made a revolution, and that this revolution has attained its objectives. What objectives have we attained?"

"Spiritual objectives," said the schoolmistress.

"What spiritual objectives?" Mastrangelo asked.

The schoolmistress grew flustered, and everybody was completely bewildered. At last she had an inspiration.

"The rural revolution saved the country from the Communist peril," she said. "Nevertheless, that peril still exists, and the government is perpetually on the watch."

"Who are the Communists?" Francesco Grascia asked.

The schoolmistress heaved a sigh of relief. She was saved. She had no more need to think, because she knew the rest by heart.

"The Communists are wicked people," she reeled off. "They meet at night, in the lowest criminal haunts of the towns. To become a Communist you have to trample on the crucifix, spit at it, and promise to eat meat on Good Friday."

The schoolmistress added other details of the Communist program. They made Matalena's hair stand on end and did the same to the older peasants. The others remained rather more incredulous.

"The Communists go round the country at reaping-time, setting fire to the sheaves of corn," the schoolmistress said.

Pasquandrea confirmed this detail. He had recently met a larger number of carabinieri than usual in the Fucino and asked what they were all doing in the open country. They had told him there were Communists about who wanted to burn the corn.

The schoolmistress added other details. She expressed herself like the books censored for the use of schools. Francesco Grascia rose to his feet and said:

"For my part I don't agree!"

The schoolmistress asked him what he didn't agree with, and he didn't know. Nevertheless he repeated:

"I don't agree!"

He put his hat on and went out into the street. Don Paolo slipped out for a moment and asked him, with a smile:

"You can tell me what you don't agree with," he said.

"I said it to annoy the schoolmistress," Grascia whispered in the priest's ear.

Grascia found it intolerable for grown men to be instructed by a woman. Once upon a time the alphabet had been taught at monasteries and by the parish priests. Then came schools and schoolmasters, and that was all right. But now one saw nothing but schoolmistresses everywhere. It was all right if they taught babies, but to set them to instruct grown men . . .

"When women teach men how to make children, the children are born hunchbacks," Grascia said.

The last announcement the schoolmistress read out was about the coalition of the Protestant countries against Italy.

"Which are the Protestant countries?" Luigi Banduccia asked.

Sciatàp answered before the schoolmistress had time.

"The Protestant countries are the rich countries, the countries that have managed to sell their souls," he said. "But if they flourish in this world, in the next they will go to hell."

Sciatàp's explanation was not found adequate. This made him angry.

"Mr. Charles Little-Bell, Ice and Coal, turned Protestant and made a fortune!" he shouted.

"If they are rich, why do they protest?" several men wanted to know.

The schoolmistress told the story of Luther.

"Luther was a monk," she said, "and he had taken the vows of obedience, chastity, and poverty. One day he made the acquaintance of a nun, and fell madly in love with her. He asked the Pope's permission to marry her, but the Pope refused. So Luther started protesting. All the monks who found the vow of chastity vexatious joined him, and that was the origin of Protestantism."

This story was no invention of the schoolmistress's. Don Paolo remembered that when he was a boy an aunt of his had explained the origin of Protestantism in the same way. In many villages of the Abruzzi the word "Protestant" is used as an insult. As such it comes halfway between "blackguard" and "Turk." If you are disrespectful to your father you are a blackguard. If you are rude to your sister you are Protestant. But if you insult your mother you are a Turk.

The schoolmistress concluded her reading.

"The coalition of the Protestant countries against us is headed by England," she said.

This piece of news worried Sciatàp greatly.

"Queen Victoria is rich, very rich," he said. "If she opposes us, things will go badly with us."

The schoolmistress left, because it was late, and Don Paolo remained in the bar with a small group of peasants, who went on talking about queens.

They knew of very few queens, but these they knew thoroughly. They were Queen Giovanna, who had a bull for a lover; Queen Semiramis, whose love was fatal to her lovers; Queen Christina, who distributed all her possessions among the poor; Queen Taitù, the consort of Menelik; Queen Victoria, who was the richest in the world; and a few others. These queens survived in a world in which a difference of centuries vanished; the peasants even had stories of squabbles and tiffs between them.

"What has always been the ruin of us is sentiment," Magascià declared. "If a king marries a rich queen, it means the country has less to pay in taxes. Why did our king marry the daughter of a Montenegrin goatherd? For sentiment! The world is big, and there are plenty of rich women. He might have married an American or a Frenchwoman. Of course, Frenchwomen are frivolous, but the king can shut his wife in a castle, and have it surrounded by a cordon of carabinieri, with orders to shoot any young man who comes anywhere near it. But no! you can't command the heart! He must go and marry a woman with no money."

"Marriage is a private affair," said Matalena.

"And we suffer for it," said Magascià. "Because we have to

pay the taxes. When I heard our prince had got engaged to a Belgian, I went to the post-office at Fossa and asked the clerk whether this Belgium we were going to be connected with was big. 'It's rather small,' the clerk told me. 'Is it rich at least?' I asked him. 'It used to be rich,' he told me, 'but it suffered badly in the war.' Sentiment again! The same old story. Why should we connect ourselves with a country that suffered badly in the war? There are so many rich countries."

Brother Antifona, all covered with dust and mud, arrived at the inn for alms. The bag he carried over his shoulder was nearly empty.

"Few alms?" Don Paolo asked him.

"Not even enough to pay for the wear of my sandals," the Capuchin friar replied.

Matalena offered him a glass of wine and a piece of bread. The monk raised the glass to the light, then lifted it to his lips and sipped a little. Satisfied, he dipped his bread in it.

"They now have insurance in the plain," he said. "If I ask for alms for St. Francis to protect the crop against hail, they tell me the crop is already insured. 'Then St. Francis will protect you against fire,' I tell them. But they tell me they are insured against fire, too. What I wonder is, why, in spite of all these insurances, everybody always lives in fear."

"A poor peasant always lives in fear," said Matalena. "If he has a house, an earthquake comes. If he is healthy, illness comes. If he has a bit of land, he has to sell it."

"My father was a peasant, too," Brother Antifona said, "and he was burned to death in a fire. One of my brothers is in prison for murder, and another lives in poverty in Brazil."

"Life is better in a monastery," Mastrangelo said.

"In a monastery you live badly, too, but you are safe," said the Capuchin. "You have no family life, but you have no fear, either. Moreover, there is hope."

"What hope?" asked Don Paolo.

The monk pointed towards heaven.

"It's not a way for everybody," said Mastrangelo. "We can't all become monks."

"The demon of property lures people," said Brother Antifona. "My father wanted to buy a vineyard behind the cemetery in our village, but he died before he managed it. My brother wanted to buy the same vineyard, but ended up in prison because of it. My other brother went to Brazil, intending to make enough money to come back and buy that vineyard, but in Brazil he only earns just enough to live on. Meanwhile the vineyard passes from hand to hand. Every three or four years it passes to somebody else. How many people is it sending to damnation!"

"So in your opinion one ought not to work?" Mastrangelo said.

"When I'm not going round collecting alms I work, too," said the monk. "Behind the monastery there is a large expanse of fields, which are cultivated by the monks. We don't live well, but in security."

Matalena asked the monk whether there would be another storm like the last one.

"My husband is dead," she said, "and if my house is carried away by a flood, who will rebuild it for me?"

"There is even worse to come," said the monk. "One night when I was praying in my cell, I saw, in the direction of Rome, on the horizon, which was as black as pitch, a red phantom, a kind of red devil, who was peeping out between the clouds."

Brother Antifona took his departure, to continue his quest for alms from house to house. He hoped at least to get something at the Colamartini house.

"Good-by," he said to Don Paolo. "If we do not meet again down here, we shall at any rate meet above."

"Above? Where? In the mountains?" the priest asked.

"I mean in heaven," said the monk.

Don Paolo admired this way of making appointments.

Nicola Ciccavo was summoned to a meeting of the government syndicate of agriculturists at Fossa as the representative of the Pietrasecca tenants. Don Paolo went to see him as soon as he came back. He felt sufficiently protected by his priestly habit to start talking to some of the peasants about the common oppression and the necessity of shaking it off. Ciccavo's cottage was one of the highest on the slope of the little hollow in which Pietrasecca lay. The priest went through the entrance gate and up the insecure and broken stone steps. The room into which he went, which served as both kitchen and bedroom for Ciccavo's four sons, was cut out of the living rock. Ciccavo looked like a good, hard-working, home-loving man. When the priest entered he was amusing his sons by imitating a goat and a cow.

"Whether he's like a cow or like a goat you can't milk him," his wife said to the priest.

The two men were left alone. Ciccavo said that by government decree the eleven thousand tenants of the Fucino basin had been incorporated into the landed proprietors' association. The provincial president of this organization was Prince Torlonia; thus he, the landlord of the eleven thousand tenants, was also their official representative; so that when a conflict of interests arose between Torlonia and them, their legal representative would be Torlonia himself.

"The speaker who explained this excellent idea to us," Ciccavo said, "was very anxious to make us realize that the government has conferred a great honor on us tenants by putting us in the category of landlords, so that no more conflicts between landlords and tenants will be possible, and perfect peace will reign."

"Weren't you asked whether you agreed to this arrangement?" asked Don Paolo.

"What need was there to ask us? We are obviously always in agreement," said Ciccavo. "As a matter of fact, after today's meeting I asked the speaker whether, since I am always persuaded of the justice of everything he says, I might have permission to stay away from future meetings and remain at home, where there is always plenty to do. But he refused to give me permission. 'How do you know what will be said at future meetings?' he asked me. 'Know? I'm a poor tenant,' I told him. 'How should I know?' 'Then how can you be in agreement already?' he asked me, with a glance at the others. 'Of course I'm in agreement already,' I said. 'What do you take me for, sir? How could I be anything else?' I said. He understood what I was getting at, and he praised me for it. 'Bravo!' he said to me in front of all the other delegates. 'Bravo! You are an enlightened Italian. But you must never stay away from meetings.' At the end he proposed sending a long series of telegrams of greeting, one to the government, one to Prince Torlonia, one to the prefect, and others to other people whom I do not remember. 'Do you agree to sending these telegrams?' he asked me. 'Do we agree?' we answered. 'Of course we agree! The idea of such a thing! How could we possibly not agree?' Then he made some calculations on a piece of paper and said 'That will be one lira twenty each for sending the telegrams.' Several men pretended they wanted to relieve nature and tried to slip away, but the speaker had the door shut. As a matter of fact, I had a few lire in my pocket, but I bent down and slipped them inside my boots. 'I'm very sorry,' I told him, 'but I haven't got any money.' He made me carefully go through all my pockets, but he didn't think of making me take my boots off, so he didn't find anything. So I got the better of him in spite of all his chattering and his education."

"Now that nobody can overhear us," Don Paolo said to Ciccavo, "do you really agree with all that is said at the meeting?"

At that Ciccavo lost patience.

"What do you mean by always talking about 'agreeing,' sir?" he said, angrily. "What has that got to do with it? When it's fine or when it rains, do you ask if we agree? Rain is a fact, not a word. Facts are one thing and words are another, like men and women. A thousand women don't make one man!"

Don Paolo did not lose his patience, but asked again:

"Don't you believe that something ought to be done to escape from the wretched conditions in which we live today?"

Ciccavo understood at last. He thought for a moment.

"The roads abroad are closed. How can one escape?"

Don Paolo understood, too. He went away.

The schoolmistress had posted *The News of Rome,* on the church door. Somebody, probably a youth, had written "The Lies of Rome" underneath.

Don Paolo met Magasci.

"Evidently there's somebody who doesn't believe what the wall newspaper says. Why?"

"Well, first of all it doesn't cost anything," Magascià replied. "When it first came we didn't want it, because we thought there would be something to pay. But the schoolmistress told us it didn't cost anything. We thought it a pity to waste such a lot of paper. But really the present government doesn't shirk expense, and wherever you go you see an enormous waste of paper. You heard the schoolmistress reading the newspaper last night. Every time she reads it to us she tells us we are not to take it literally, and that it's all to be understood in a spiritual sense."

"Has no newspaper that says the opposite of what *The News of Rome* says ever come this way?" the priest asked. "I mean, a newspaper that was against the government?"

"May be," said Magascià. "May be. But you can't pay attention to every bit of paper that's given you. Once upon a time paper was a rare and precious thing. Every piece of paper was carefully put away in the chest of drawers. Instead of saying 'Going to America' you said 'to have your papers.' Without papers you ended up in prison. For 'getting married' you said 'the papers were ready.' There were papers that came only once in a lifetime. Before leaving for military service, you said your 'paper had come.' If you didn't obey the paper, the carabinieri would come for you. A piece of paper was always an important thing. In those times, in our part of the world, nobody, speaking with respect, would have dared use a piece of paper to wipe himself. You would never see dirty paper behind the bushes, sir. Everybody managed as best he could, with stones, or leaves from the trees. But now we've gone to the other extreme, and so much free and lying paper is handed out that it actually makes you shudder to touch your own body with it."

Don Paolo went back to his room to reflect on the peasants and their lives, and the perpetual fear in which they lived. The idea occurred to him of using his remaining time at Pietrasecca to finish his essay on the agrarian question. He took his notebook from his bag and started reading the notes he had started in exile. He read them through, and was astonished and dismayed at their abstract character. All these quotations from masters and disciples on the agrarian question, all those plans and schemes were the paper scenery in which he had hitherto lived. The country which was the subject of those notes of his was a paper country, with paper mountains, paper hills, fields, gardens, and meadows. The great events recorded in them were mostly paper events, paper battles, and paper victories. The peasants were paper peasants. The heresies and deviations against which he fought had been paper heresies and paper deviations, too. Don Paolo, just like Magascià, felt himself filled with disgust at the vast accumulation of paper. He was seized with a great fear of abstractions. Memory of his recent days of struggle with the shadows returned to plague him. Am I, too, dominated by fear? he wondered. Cristina was afraid of her own body, and wanted to shut herself in a convent; Brother Antifona was afraid of the vineyard behind the cemetery in his native village, and took refuge in a monastery; the peasants were afraid of hunger and aspired to be petty landowners. Was it possible that Don Paolo was seeking refuge in action because he was afraid of thinking?

Remaining inactive here and philosophizing about social reality won't get me anywhere, he said to himself. It won't even lead to a greater understanding of social reality. To understand social reality one must be inside it, participate in its movement and its struggles.

This was no new discovery, but the repetition of an old idea in different words. But it seemed a discovery to him. It suddenly illumined his whole being, kindled something in him. It touched a chord in him, roused something deeply rooted in him, something that was, perhaps, the essence of his being. Hence its prompt, instantaneous effect. Revolutionary action had always seemed to be demanded of him by the collective good. The ideal of the collective good had been inculcated into him from his earliest years by his Christian education. His subsequent intellectual development had modified the premises on which his original adherence to Socialism had been based, but he had not been able to modify the internal structure of his mind.

His chief dissatisfaction came from the fact that, though he had been at Pietrasecca for three months he had not succeeded in finding a single point of support among the peasants. His attempts to approach them had amounted to nothing but a series of detached, disjointed episodes. It had been impossible to follow up next day a conversation begun the day before. The relations among the peasants themselves appeared to be unstable, frail, and fugitive. It was impossible to build anything on them. The peasants' submission to the dictatorship seemed to him to be entirely independent of government propaganda. He realized now that the peasants were not susceptible to words. They submitted only to facts. The idea of conducting counter-propaganda, of which Don Paolo had thought on returning from abroad, was therefore entirely futile. Facts could be met only with other facts. The facts of dictatorship must be confronted, not with the words of liberty, but with the facts of liberty. The dictator's henchmen must be opposed not with other henchmen, who merely spoke differently, but with men who lived and acted differently. The peasants must be offered two sets of conflicting facts, and then, perhaps, they will make their choice and move, Don Paolo said to himself. He crumpled his notes on the agrarian question between his hands and looked out of the window. The sun, not a paper sun, but the real sun, was about to dip behind the horizon. The moon, the real moon, was just rising on the opposite horizon. A long cloud of dust was advancing along the valley road. This was the hour when the shepherds left the plain with their flocks and started back to the mountains. The sheep could just be distinguished in the cloud of dust, and Don Paolo could hear the distant voices of the shepherds.

Don Paolo tore his notes into little pieces and went downstairs and threw them on the fire—Matalena had started to cook the evening meal.

"I'm leaving tomorrow," he said to Matalena.

"For good?" the woman asked, in surprise.

"That depends on what the doctor says," the priest replied.

Chapter VII

D ON PASQUALE COLAMARTINI had to go down to
Fossa, too. He willingly offered to take the priest in his
trap.

The morning was bright, the air was pure, and a fresh scent
of dewy grass ascended from the valley. Don Paolo felt well. He
had not looked so well for a long time. While the old gentleman
was putting the mare between the shafts and slowly adjusting
the harness, the blinkers, and the bit, Cristina came to say
good-by to Don Paolo.

"Are you going?" she said. "Aren't you ever coming back?"

"I do not know," the priest replied.

Don Paolo's exasperation with Cristina had passed, but a certain sense of annoyance and disappointment remained. She would
do better to occupy herself a little less with God and a little
more with the poor people, he said to himself. But at heart he
was indifferent to her now. His mind was on other things. The
prospect of returning to the life of the political underworld attracted and excited him.

Cristina was about to say something else, but the trap started
and she was left there, slightly embarrassed.

"The mare is named Diana," Don Pasquale said. "I bought her
fifteen years ago for hunting. Good times that will not return!"

The shape of the trap, its high seats, its small front wheels and
big back ones, the trappings of the horse, the embroidered
cushions on which the two men sat, even their way of dressing,
also belonged to other times. Times that were passing away.

When the trap passed the *refugium peccatorum* Don Paolo
said:

"The two young people seem to have gone away. They certainly couldn't live there."

"I am not interested," the old man said.

Don Paolo said no more. Even a father's heartlessness towards his own son could not irritate him now. He thought of his own home surroundings, his own grandparents, his own uncles—all of them excellent people, but hard and pitiless whenever the good name of the family was at stake. Men that were passing away.

Though the old man had said he was not interested, at heart he was very interested indeed, for he added:

"Do you think those two scoundrels might marry without my knowing it?"

"Alberto is of age," the priest replied. "It would therefore be perfectly legal for him to marry."

"The law was made for the city. Here the father rules the roost," Don Pasquale replied.

Don Paolo did not continue the conversation. These things did not interest him. Were landowning families disintegrating? All the better. They were passing away, too. Don Paolo was preoccupied with thoughts of the underground work he proposed beginning among the peasants. On what elements was he to rely? Where was he to find them? How was he to assure his contacts? In the meantime Don Pasquale was explaining why marriage between Alberto and Bianchina was out of the question.

"Between the Colamartini and the Girasole there is an abyss," he said. "Nobody even knows where the Girasole come from."

Don Paolo was thinking that the first step to take would be to find some peasant who had belonged to the old Leagues of Resistance that had once existed round the Fucino. These leagues had been dissolved by the government, but there must still be some trustworthy elements at Luco, at Ortucchio, or at Pescina. But how was he to get in touch with them? What should he do to avoid rousing suspicion?

"Old Girasole," Don Pasquale was saying, "appeared in our part of the world at the time of the last cholera epidemic, selling lemons. He went from village to village, barefooted, with his box of lemons on his head. He did well, and when the epidemic was over he settled at Fossa. Of course, everyone has the right to live. But if the Girasole imagine the time has come when they can be connected with the Colamartini, the matter ought to be reported to the head of the lunatic asylum."

A man riding a donkey appeared, driving several other donkeys ahead of him. The donkey he was riding was small, and the man's feet almost touched the ground. The man took no notice of the trap, but looked steadfastly at the stream.

"He's a tenant of a small piece of land of mine, and he hasn't paid the rent for three years," Don Pasquale said. "Whenever he meets me he looks the other way."

Don Paolo was thinking that the first thing to do would be to think of some new plan which would enable him to get rid of this odious priest's clothing and get in touch with one or two members of the old leagues. Undoubtedly he would find them intimidated by the long years of dictatorship. It would be necessary to live among them for some time, gain their goodwill, and wait for a silent moment when it would be possible to start asking questions. "Don't you believe," he would say, "that we ought to unite and struggle against this dictatorship which is stifling the whole country and reducing it to ruin? Don't you know that the struggle has already been begun by the workers in the cities?" The rest would come by itself.

The trap overtook a cart going down to the valley, laden with a few sacks of grain. The carter was walking behind it. He had applied the brake and was leaning on it to increase the weight.

"Have you had a good crop?" Don Pasquale asked.

"That is the whole of it," said the carter. "It's all there, and I've got to take it to my landlord before it is seized."

The trap left the valley of Pietrasecca, crossed the bridge, and went in the direction of Lama. As they draw nearer and nearer to the Fucino the pink tints of the valley gradually yielded to ashen-gray. The country sloping down towards the former lake was checkered with yellow, bare patches formed by the recently reaped fields of stubble. High ricks could be seen in the distance, with men moving about them like ants. Women passed,

carrying baskets on their heads and leading pigs to market. Other
women passed with babies in their arms, like the Madonnas in
the churches, black and bad-tempered Madonnas, taking food to
their men-folk threshing in the fields. The midday heat began
to make itself felt, and the mare was surrounded by a swarm of
flies. The flies seemed to be short-sighted, because they all buzzed
around the mare's tail. The hillside above Lama was slanted
with vines. The vines were small and thin, and grew meagerly
in rare and irregular lines. Near the houses there were a few
pergolas, where the vines were higher and supported by stakes;
at a certain height they were tied together and hung in curves,
from which dangled clusters of sour, unripe grapes.

Collarmele, Cerchio, and Aielli came into sight in the distance, with Paterno and San Pelino beyond, and still farther
away a gray pall of smoke betrayed where Avezzano was. Don
Paolo felt himself getting younger every minute. He was filled
with a new sense of freedom and independence. He felt ready
for anything, and afraid of nothing.

The trap passed through Lama and slowly went down towards
Fossa. The road was hard and was freshly graveled. A group of
soldiers were sitting around a tent in a field, with rifles between
their knees. A small donkey was standing in the middle of the
road, and all the heat of the day seemed to be concentrated on
it. Don Paolo thought the poor beast was going to drop dead.

Donkeys laden with sacks of flour were coming from the Fossa
mill. Peasants with bundles under their arms were walking towards the station. Even in the heat, people who were going
away put on everything they owned, as if they never expected to
return. When peasants go on a journey they always look a little
like refugees in flight.

An acquaintance of Don Pasquale's, a clerk in the tax office
at Fossa, named Don Genesio, mounted the trap and started complaining of the hostility of the people in the valleys.

"In the eyes of a peasant, every man who wears a collar is a
clerk, and every clerk is a parasite," he said. "For some time past,
whenever I've had to go to any of the valleys I've taken off my
collar and put it in my pocket. And I get my shoes nice and dusty

and take off my party emblem, in order not to look like a clerk," he said.

"You can't blame it all on the peasants," Don Pasquale said. "The city's remedies for the country's ills are offices and rubber stamps. Every generation has its own plague. Sixty years ago there was the mildew disease, twenty years ago there were the plant lice, and now we have bureaucrats. As soon as a new government office is opened, strangers come and set themselves up as masters. The descendants of the old families are now confined to the mountains, like the bears in the caves of Monte Marsicano."

"How big is the population round the Fucino basin now?" the priest asked Don Genesio.

"There are about thirty thousand mortgages," was the reply. He made a sweeping gesture, embracing the whole landscape. "There's a mortgage on everything you see," he said, "on every house, on every clod of earth, on every tree. We are a nation of debtors."

Don Genesio told a story to illustrate his theme.

"A peasant from Fossa had a strange liver disease," he said. "He was sent to the city hospital in Rome. The hospital's pathological laboratory offered him money for the right to dissect his liver after his death. He took the money, and he isn't dead yet. He's still living at Fossa with his mortgaged liver. When this became known every peasant who believed he had any anatomical peculiarity, any organ that was too big or too small, started going to the official doctor in the hope of raising a small loan."

The sound of liturgical chanting became audible in the distance. Pilgrims were descending from the mountain trails and trooping on to the main road. In a meadow, on fires improvised with earth and stones, old women were preparing a turbid brew, the soup for the pilgrims. The pilgrims were already hoarse from excessive shouting and singing, and their chant consisted of four or five words, which they repeated over and over again in a monotonous and dirge-like cadence.

"Where are you going?" Don Genesio called out to them. "Which saint are you going to?"

"San Domenico," the pilgrims replied. "San Domenico of Cocullo."

"San Domenico," Don Pasquale observed to the priest, "is the saint who protects one against snake bites."

Among the pilgrims, though she was unkempt and covered with dust, Don Pasquale recognized Cassarola, the wise-woman. He stopped the trap.

"What is going to happen?" he called out.

Cassarola had the gift of prophecy, and Don Pasquale was superstitious.

"There will be war," the old witch replied, "and after the war there will be pestilence."

"That's no affair of mine," Don Pasquale remarked.

Some huge oxen, with enormous useless horns were munching the grass at the edge of the road. Two ancient motor-cars passed by with shrieking brakes and gears and rattling doors. On the roofs of the houses were tables spread with tomato pulp, put out to dry in the sun. Every now and then a girl went up to the roof to stir the red mixture with a large wooden spoon.

The trap reached Fossa. Don Pasquale put the priest down outside the Girasole Hotel and drove away immediately, in order not to have to greet Berenice, who was standing at the door.

Berenice hurried towards the priest, and received him with open arms.

"The Girasole family owes you a debt of eternal gratitude," she said, with emotion. "First of all you saved Bianchina at the point of death, and then you made her happy."

"I made Bianchina happy?" the priest asked. "On my word of honor, Signora Berenice, I swear to you that I refrained from doing anything of the sort."

"Wasn't it you who arranged the match?" Berenice replied. "Don't you know what an honor it is for the Girasole to become connected with the Colamartini? I shall invite all Bianchina's other relations to lunch today, to show you how grateful all the Girasole are."

Don Paolo did not know what to say. He hesitated to disappoint Berenice. But the woman would not stop.

"And of course," she said, "you must be the witness at the girl's wedding. Even if you go back to your diocese in the meantime, you must allow us to pay your fare. Do you know what we shall call the baby?"

"What baby?" Don Paolo asked in alarm.

"The future baby," said Berenice. "If it's a boy it will be christened Paolino, and if it's a girl it will be christened Paolina."

"The idea is a moving one, and it is easy to imagine its coming true," the priest said, "although, on my word of honor, I have not contributed to the situation in any way. The difficult part will be to get the Colamartini family to consent to the match."

"The Colamartini family will not consent?" Berenice asked, in amazement.

"Don Pasquale is opposed to it," he said. "He says it is impossible for the Colamartini family to lower itself by becoming connected with the Girasole."

Berenice went livid, and for a moment said nothing. Then she began abusing the Colamartini violently.

"Who do those people think they are?" she exclaimed. "Do they think that nobody knows their affairs? You come from another diocese, and there are some things you don't know, but just you ask anybody in our part of the world, and you'll hear fine things about the Colamartini."

"They do not concern me," said Don Paolo.

Don Paolo asked to be shown to his room, but Berenice refused to leave him.

"Don Pasquale married a woman ten years older than himself, and half-witted into the bargain, solely for the sake of her dowry," she said. "The whole Colamartini family now lives on the money the old idiot brought with her as her dowry. Don Pasquale prevented a sister of his from marrying in order not to have to share his inheritance with her. How can people as shameless as all that be proud and look down on others? Everybody here knows the story of the Colamartini!"

"The Colamartini at least have a history, an ugly history, but a history," Don Paolo said. "But Don Pasquale says that nobody knows where the Girasole come from. . . ."

To Berenice this was the last straw. Like a raging fury she proceeded to tell the family history of the Girasole. If she did not actually go back to the Crusades, it was probably for the sake of brevity. But there was no doubt that the Girasole had a history, too.

"Who hasn't got a history?" said Berenice. "All of us have histories."

"A philosopher of the Marsica, a certain Benedetto Croce, of Pescasseroli, has demonstrated that everything is history and that there is nothing apart from history," Don Paolo observed.

"Are we perhaps born out of the air?" Berenice went on. "Are we not all children of men?"

"Even the Girasole are descended from Adam," Don Paolo concurred, "though the exact ramifications of the family tree are not known. The documents have been lost in the course of ages. But the head of the Girasole family was undoubtedly Adam. Thus, since Adam was born and lived in a garden, it is quite conceivable that his name may have been Adam Girasole."

"How can you say such a thing?" the woman asked.

"It's a pure hypothesis, a pure hypothesis," Don Paolo replied. "But a philosopher has said that hypotheses are the lighthouses of science. In the writings which speak of Adam his surname is never mentioned. He is invariably described solely by his first name, Adam. Hence nothing prevents us from supposing that his surname may have been Girasole."

"But Don Pasquale might also say his name was Adam Colamartini," Berenice objected.

"To do so would be entirely fallacious," the priest replied. "Colamartini is a combination of two family names, the family of Cola and the family of Martini; and, since neither of these two families existed before the time of Adam, his name cannot possibly have been Adam Colamartini, while it is permissible to assume that it may have been Adam Girasole. All this, of course, is pure conjecture, pure conjecture."

Berenice, however, found it disturbing.

"I'll ask my brother, the parish priest of Fossa," she said.

Don Paolo tried to dissuade her.

"Why worry him?" he said.

"I do not understand these things, myself," Berenice replied. "We made great sacrifices to enable one member of our family to study, and thus have an educated person in the family. If we didn't consult him in cases like this, what would be the use of it?"

As soon as Berenice left him, Don Paolo wrote an express letter to Dr. Nunzio Sacca of Acquafredda, asking him to come to Fossa dei Marsi at once, saying he had need of him, as a doctor and a friend.

Meanwhile the usual crowd of idlers had gathered outside the Girasole Hotel and were lounging on the seats, because it was *apéritif* time. There were men with beards a week old, in shirt sleeves and slippers, their trousers and collars unbuttoned, and hulking youths of the most various occupations, but all looking like barber's assistants, with copious, well-oiled hair and impeccable creases in their trousers. An older man in a broad-brimmed hat, who looked like a retired provincial actor, with mustaches sticking up and a little pointed beard sticking down, was holding forth at the center of a group of younger men. He had made himself thoroughly comfortable, using four seats for the purpose. He was sitting on one, had his feet stretched out on another in front of him, and his arms on two more at either side. A pretty girl passed, and the man jumped to his feet and made an enormous bow. His eyes flashed, his mustaches bristled, he bared his teeth, and panted like a seal. The girl blushed and passed on.

"She's too provincial," one of the young men remarked.

The girl certainly looked healthy. She had pink cheeks, was ample-bosomed, and well built. Her passing was the first important event of the morning.

The imminence of the morning's second important event was signaled by the baker's boy from the corner of the square. This was the appearance of the station master's daughters. The youths outside the Girasole Hotel fell into formation like soldiers presenting arms. Two girls with plucked eyebrows, flaxen hair, mascaraed and enlarged eyes, and an affected gait passed by.

This exhausted the morning's big events. The usual argument then opened. The admirer of the provincial beauty defended her with great eloquence, basing his argument on a contrast between raw steak and boiled meat.

"Who is that man?" Don Paolo asked Berenice.

"That's our greatest lawyer," Berenice said, "Marco Tuglio Zabaglia, known as Zabaglione."

The priest had heard the name before.

"Wasn't he once the head of the Maximalist Socialists in this part of the world?" he asked.

"That's right, but he's a nice man," said Berenice.

Zabaglione noticed the presence of the strange priest at the entrance to the hotel and came forward and introduced himself.

"I am the lawyer Zabaglia," he said. "I am most honored to meet you. Excuse me, but are you perhaps from the curia?"

"What curia?" Don Paolo asked.

"The episcopal curia. The reason I ask is that I should like to know if the sacred orators for the ceremony of the departure of the conscripts have been appointed yet, and which orator will be coming to us."

"They will be appointed during the next few days," Don Paolo replied. "But I come from another diocese, the diocese of Frascati."

As a boy Don Paolo had always heard Zabaglione spoken of with hatred by the landowners and with love by the poor, and he was naturally impressed to find himself face to face with him now. Zabaglione was famous for his forensic eloquence. On days when the court was sitting, if it was known that Zabaglione was going to plead, the cobblers' shops, the tailors' shops, the carpenters' shops all emptied, and everyone who could went to hear and applaud him. His most famous perorations remained proverbial. In the eyes of the accused the question of their own conviction or acquittal was less important than the oratorical success of their advocate. In the course of time Zabaglione became a kind of popular Orpheus. When the change of government came about, a squad of militia was sent to arrest him. But he harangued them from his balcony.

"My fellow-countrymen, blood of my blood, my brothers . . ." he began, and the soldiers stopped to listen to him and went away without carrying out their orders. Then a squad of carabinieri was sent. These took him by surprise, bound him, gagged him, and took him off to prison. On the way Zabaglione begged for his release with heart-rending gestures, rolling his great bovine eyes, invoking now heaven, now the depths of the earth, and foaming at his tightly gagged mouth; the carabinieri were compelled to look away. He was kept gagged even during his interrogation. The police commissioner, who was specially sent from Rome, explained that he need answer only yes or no, that therefore there was no call for him to make speeches, and that it would be enough for him to answer the questions with movements of his head. After a few days, however, he was set free by order of the superior authorities. Ever afterwards Zabaglione had taken great pains to wipe out all memory of his political past. He altered his little pointed beard from the style of Mazzini to that of General Balbo, and to give himself a swashbuckling air he made his old mustaches, which had always drooped in a pacific and democratic manner, stand up. These, of course, had been the most visible and therefore the most painful sacrifices which the former tribune of the people had had to make. But who could count all his minor, daily sacrifices, such as having to renounce his own ideas, speak cautiously about the government, and break off relations with everyone who was politically suspect? Although Zabaglione did his level best, he had never succeeded in completely rehabilitating himself. He was always kept a little outside of things under the new régime.

Don Paolo, having made his acquaintance, decided to take advantage of it to sound him out cautiously and, if possible learn what remnants of the Socialist movement still survived in the Fucino basin.

"If I can be of any service to you with the curia," he said, "I shall be most happy."

Zabaglione nearly embraced him.

"Do me the infinite honor of coming to lunch with me," he said.

Don Paolo parried a little and then accepted. To reach Zabaglione's house you had first to cross the old part of the town, with its dark and ancient alleyways, bearing the names of saints and local benefactors, and its silent little squares, inclosed by old stone houses, blackened by time. Geraniums and creepers protected the windows, as with gratings, and behind them girls of good family looked out and sighed. Zabaglione greeted them all by name, with large gestures, rolling his eyes and showing his teeth. After the old town came the new. This had been rebuilt after the earthquake, with roads and avenues too big for local needs, houses constructed in imitation of villas, with bright green shutters, garden gates of imitation wrought iron, cement pillars painted to look like marble, and brass shields polished to look like gold. The street names extolled episodes and dates in the history of the government party as though they were momentous events. The heroic slogans of the dominant party were to be seen in large letters on the housefronts, the fountains, the trees, the garden gates. They were scrawled with charcoal, chalk, or tar, or painted in various colors. They were also to be seen in relief, carved in wood or stone, and even fused in bronze.

A group of bricklayers were sitting on the ground outside Zabaglione's house, with knives in their hands, eating their lunch of bread with red and green peppers. Around Zabaglione's house was a wall surmounted by jagged bits of glass. The flower-beds in the garden were surrounded with barbed wire. In the garden a little man was kneeling on the gravel path, attending to a flower-bed laid out like the Italian national tricolor.

"I love flowers," Zabaglione said. "There are some things that only flowers can express."

An elegant, good-looking, and well-groomed woman, with permanently waved hair, appeared at the door. She was Zabaglione's wife.

"Kiss the priest's hand and leave us," her husband said. The lady kissed the priest's hand and retired.

Three young women, dressed in black, all very thin, very pale, looking like larvæ, or three plants that had grown up in the dark, came forward in the hall. They were Zabaglione's daughters.

"Kiss the priest's hand and leave us," their father ordered.

The girls kissed the priest's hand, curtsied, and retired.

In the dining-room there was a large nutwood sideboard, with fruit, bottles of wine, and jam-pots displayed on it. The heroic words: *Dulce et decorum est pro patria mori* were carved on the sideboard.

"That sideboard was a bargain," said Zabaglione, "but I had the inscription carved on it myself. A man does not live by bread alone, you understand."

Sure enough, no sooner had the two men sat down than *pasta asciutta* was served.

Zabaglione had a splendid appetite. He called out to his wife and daughters in the kitchen and said so. A purple hue suffused his cheeks, his eyes sparkled happily, and every now and then he stroked his big mustaches with the voluptuousness of a cat. He tucked his napkin round his neck like a big, rubicund, greedy baby, and talked to the priest with effusive, good-natured, country cordiality.

"The young people of today," he announced with a gesture of disparagement, "do not know how to enjoy their food. That's why they are not worth anything."

"The old culture is passing away," the priest said.

Zabaglione, however, was no despiser of spiritual values.

"I send my daughters to mass every Sunday," he said. "If you don't believe me, ask Don Girasole, the parish priest of Fossa. What would women come to without the restraining influence of religion?"

Meanwhile the women were eating in the kitchen. The spectacle of Zabaglione wielding his fork, twirling it violently on his plate and vigorously shoveling the macaroni into his mouth, nearly took Don Paolo's breath away. He'll choke, Don Paolo said to himself. But Zabaglione had the mouth of a great lawyer.

The priest did not forget the purpose of his visit. He brought the conversation round to the subject of the peasant leagues that had been dissolved by the government.

"Before the present government was established," he said, "I was engaged in the organization of the Catholic peasants. Then our organizations were dissolved and absorbed. Hence there is, to a certain extent, a resemblance between your situation and mine. What is the state of mind of the old Socialist leaguers in this part of the world? Have they all passed over to the government party? Have many of them remained hostile to the government?"

Suddenly Zabaglione became reticent. He stopped eating. He filled his glass and emptied it. He used a toothpick, several toothpicks. He filled his glass and emptied it again.

In order to encourage Zabaglione to talk, Don Paolo invented a few details about the situation in the diocese of Frascati.

In the end Zabaglione made up his mind to speak.

"The truth is officially as follows," he said. "Bolshevism reigned here, and religion, morality, and private property were being trampled under foot. Then came Etcetera Etcetera, and religion, morality, and private property were restored."

"We are now neither in the market place nor in the pulpit," Don Paolo said, familiarly. "The official truth we know. But what is the semi-official truth?"

"The semi-official truth," said Zabaglione, "is that what reigned here was ignorance and hunger. The poor people started organizing themselves into leagues. Then came Etcetera Etcetera, and destroyed the leagues, but not the hunger, which has increased since."

"What are the old members of the leagues doing?" the priest asked. This was the question that kept him on tenterhooks.

"Officially they have all been reborn and spiritually regenerated in the spirit of Etcetera Etcetera, who has renewed the face of the country," said Zabaglione.

"But semi-officially, have they remained Socialists?" Don Paolo asked.

"It would be too much to say that," Zabaglione replied. "The peasants joined the leagues in order to get a little protection. In their minds, Socialism meant a little security. What Socialism meant to most of them was the chance to work and eat till their stomachs were full, to work and sleep in peace, without having to be afraid of the morrow. In the league premises at Fossa, next to the bearded portrait of Karl Marx, there was a picture of Christ in a red shirt. On Saturday nights the peasants came to the league to sing 'Up, brothers! Brothers, arise!' and on Sunday morning they went to Mass to say 'Amen.' The permanent occupation of a Socialist leader was writing recommendations. Now the recommendations are written by the local head of the government party or by the parish priest. My recommendations are now worthless, so the peasants take no more interest in me."

"But weren't there any real Socialists?" the priest asked.

"The only real Socialist, so to speak, was myself," said Zabaglione. "There were some other intelligent members among the peasant leagues, and Etcetera Etcetera's regenerative efforts were directed towards them. On January 19, 1923 (I do not know why I remember that date, but I can't get it out of my head) a squad of regenerators invaded the house of the man who was then the head of the league at Rivisondoli. They bound him, and all twenty-two of them raped his wife. It took from eleven o'clock at night until two o'clock in the morning. An incident. A few peasant leaders fled to France or to America. But the great mass started seeking in the government corporations that bit of protection which they had previously found in the leagues. Officially they are no longer called peasants, but agriculturists."

"Nevertheless, discontented elements must still exist," said Don Paolo. "If conditions have gone from bad to worse, there certainly must be some who remember the time of the leagues, when the workers could at least defend themselves . . ."

"Between ourselves," Zabaglione said, "I confess that I liked Socialism. I liked it just as I like women. The best speeches I ever made were about Socialism. I say so semi-officially, between ourselves. Apart from that, what Etcetera Etcetera has done has been providential."

"Don't you believe," said Don Paolo, "that sometimes it is necessary to make sacrifices?"

"Sacrifices—ah! a beautiful word," said Zabaglione. "Sacrifice is what I admire most in the Christian religion. What exposed Marxism was its materialism."

Don Paolo did not know whether Zabaglione was talking earnestly or in jest.

"I know very well," Zabaglione went on, "that there have been Socialists who have sacrificed their comforts, their careers, their lives. But what is all that compared with what I have sacrificed? I have sacrificed something far more elevated and precious—my ideas. A spiritual sacrifice costs far more than a material sacrifice, whatever the Marxists may say. But who can understand the meaning of spiritual sacrifice better than a priest?"

"You are a hero," Don Paolo murmured.

"An unrecognized hero," Zabaglione continued. "After twelve years of sincere and complete loyalty to Etcetera Etcetera I am still regarded with suspicion. It was only as a result of superhuman effort that I succeeded in becoming a member of the present municipal council, in which I am charged with the honorable and gratuitous duty of being consulted on questions of punctuation. The mayor, officially a genius, semi-officially a noodle, intrusts me with the task of giving a grammatical form to his decrees and to his most important correspondence."

Lunch was over, and the two men went into the drawing-room for coffee. There were blue divided curtains over the windows; bookshelves full of dusty books against the walls; three pictures— Mazzini looking lugubrious, Garibaldi in a red shirt, and Etcetera Etcetera; some faded photographs on the table; wicker chairs, which had been painted green, in which one could dawdle and nap.

Zabaglione's usual guests arrived punctually for coffee. These were the captain of the municipal guard, Don Genesio, the clerk at the tax office, and Don Senofonte, the chemist.

The captain of the municipal guard was in a uniform as resplendent as that of a pre-war general.

"How many guards do you command?" Don Paolo asked.

"For the time being, one," the man replied. "The commune is a poor one and only grows slowly."

Don Senofonte was a handsome man, with mustaches in the King Humbert style, hair like Mascagni, and a goatee. He said:

"I assure Your Reverence that I send my wife to Mass every Sunday. If you don't believe me, ask the parish priest, Don Girasole. In my opinion religion is to women what salt is to pork. It preserves the freshness and the flavor."

Don Genesio was also impeccably combed and oiled, and he, too, regularly sent his wife to Mass.

Don Paolo was surprised to observe the rôle that mustaches, beards, and hair still played in differentiating the professional class from the peasants and the landlords. He realized also why the various classes were indicated in dialect by the word "race"— the "race" of husbandmen, the "race" of "artists" (artisans), the "race" of landowners. The son of a petty landowner who studies, and therefore inevitably becomes a state or municipal employee, promptly tries to obliterate the fact that he comes of the "race" of husbandmen by brushing his hair in the style of his new station. If one observes the style of hair-dressing these people adopt, together with their way of speaking, rolling their eyes, frowning, setting their jaws, and smoking, no great effort of the imagination is needed to think one is at the theater.

"Any news? Any news?" Zabaglione asked.

"The news that the bank has shut its doors has now reached the people in the valleys," said Don Senofonte. "I met Don Pasquale Colamartini of Pietrasecca. He looked as if he were completely out of his mind. He hadn't known the bank was in difficulties. All that was left of his half-witted wife's dowry was on deposit."

"In the old days a bank failure would have led to a fine lawsuit," said Zabaglione. "Nowadays all that sort of thing is liquidated within the bosom of the Etcetera Etcetera family."

"Have you ever heard of a man called Pietro Spina?" the captain of the municipal guard asked.

No one in the room had ever heard of him.

"He belongs to the Spina family of Rocca dei Marsi," the captain of the municipal guard explained. "He's a crazy revolutionary. He was an *émigré*, and it appears that he returned to Italy for the purpose of assassinating Etcetera Etcetera. The police were on his trail for three months. He was reported in this neighborhood, too, because it appears that he wanted to set fire to the sheaves of corn on the threshing-floors. But news came today that he has been arrested in Rome."

"That's one maniac the less," said Zabaglione. "Some one who doesn't know the meaning of self-discipline and sacrifice."

"Did you say Spina? Of Rocca dei Marsi?" Don Senofonte asked. "I know the family. I was at school with the boy's father. His father was a good fellow. He perished in the earthquake. Another old family coming to a bad end."

"How did they know he wanted to burn the corn?" asked Don Paolo. "Was he seen in this part of the world at reaping-time?"

"He has never been seen in this part of the world," said the captain of the municipal guard, "either now or in previous years. He has always carried on his propaganda in the cities. But at reaping-time this year there were inscriptions on the walls, scrawled in red, saying 'Long Live Pietro Spina.' This is the first time it has ever happened. It proves that Spina must have been in the neighborhood."

"Do you think he came here to write on the walls?" the priest asked.

"Not he, but his followers," said the captain of the municipal guard.

"Oh, his followers," Don Paolo blurted out. "Are there, then, any rebellious peasants?"

In his zeal he forgot his caution.

"There's a lot of ferment among the young people," said the captain of the municipal guard. "The things they say under the pretext of talking about the corporate state are enough to make one's hair stand on end."

"The young generation is the dangerous generation," Don Senofonte said, "the generation that presents the bill. The youngsters take literally the idea that the corporate state spells the end of capitalism. The young generation wants capitalism to be destroyed."

"That is the root of the trouble," Zabaglione said. "Taking

things literally. No regime ought ever to be taken literally, otherwise what would the world come to? Suppose a French citizen took it into his head to live according to the Declaration of the Rights of Man! He would end up in prison. Have you read the papers today? In Russia the death penalty has been reëstablished for adolescents. Why? Probably because they took the Soviet constitution literally. There ought to be a rule that a country's constitution only concerns lawyers and older persons who understand the meaning of discipline and sacrifice, and must be rigorously ignored by the young."

The captain of the municipal guard agreed.

"I was put in charge of the public library," he said. "What real need there was for a library I do not understand. People who want books ought to buy them. Nevertheless, the library was opened. The books came from Rome. Boys came and started asking for the collected works of the head of the government. 'Look!' they started saying, 'here it says that the Church, the royal family, and capitalism ought to be overthrown.' I tried to explain that those books were written for grown-up people and not for boys, and that at their age they ought to be reading novels. But they would not be put off. In the end, with the permission of the higher authorities, I was forced to withdraw those books from the library and put them in a drawer under lock and key."

"Too late," said Don Senofonte. "Too late. My son tells me a typed copy of extracts from those books is circulating among the younger people. Some young men meet in the Villa delle Stagioni, on the other side of the stream, to read and discuss it. My son says there must be a second revolution to bring about all the things in those books . . ."

"Are they young peasants?" Don Paolo asked.

"Three or four young students," the captain of the municipal guard said. "The authorities know all about it, and at the right moment they will break up the game."

Zabaglione shook his head.

"When boys start taking seriously the things they read in books, it is the worst of evils," he said.

I, too, when I was a boy, took the Bible and the writings of the Church Fathers seriously, Don Paolo said to himself, and look what has become of me. A stranger in my own country, not ten miles from the village in which I was born; an invalid, and hunted like a wild beast.

The priest and the chemist left the house together.

"Did you know Pietro Spina's father when he was still a student?" the priest asked him. "Was he mad, too, like his son?"

"I knew him at Naples," Don Senofonte said. "We were republicans, like most students at that time. Giuseppe Mazzini was our god, and Alberto Mario his prophet. Then we returned to the Marsica, and married at about the same time. He came to see me a few years later, and he had changed almost beyond recognition. I shall never forget what he said. 'The poetry is over and the prose has begun,' were the words he used. The dreams of youth are poetry, and real life is prose. Every generation goes through the same experience. The authorities now complain to me that my son is inciting his comrades to talk of a second revolution. 'It's his age, the age of illusions,' I tell them. 'Now he's at the poetry stage, but later he'll settle down and marry, become a state employee, and the prose will come.' Alas! What if there were no poetry in life, and if the prose did not come after it!"

"What would happen if men remained faithful to their youthful ideals?" Don Paolo asked.

Don Senofonte raised his hands to heaven, as though to say it would be the end of the world.

"There comes a time," he said, "when young people find the bread and wine of their own homes insipid. They look elsewhere for their nourishment. The bread and wine of the inns, which they find at the crossroads, on the highways, can alone appease their hunger and their thirst. But man cannot spend all his life in inns."

Don Senofonte showed the priest some of the sights of the town.

"That is the new orphan asylum," he said. "That is the new

home of the Dopolavoro. This is the new post-office. That is the new theater. We have all the luxuries but lack the necessities."

The two men entered the headquarters of the Corporation of Commerce for a moment.

"This used to be the private warehouse of two wholesalers who bought the fruit and vegetables of the Marsica and resold them in the capital," Don Senofonte said. "They have not changed their business address. They still carry on their business from here. The only difference is that the rent and the employees' wages are now paid by the state."

On the walls were two marble tablets, with inscriptions. One said "Corporations Represent the Downfall of Capitalism," and the other, "Who Is against the Corporations Is against the State."

"What a beautiful thing marble is!" Don Senofonte remarked.

In the distance the priest saw an old man walking with difficulty. He recognized him as Don Pasquale. He said good-by to the chemist and went to join him. At first old Colamartini did not recognize him. Then he almost fell into the priest's arms, trembling all over. He seemed on the point of collapse. He breathed with difficulty and could hardly speak.

"Courage," said the priest. "I know everything."

Don Paolo accompanied Don Pasquale to the trap. He helped him to adjust the harness. Then, with great difficulty, he managed to get him into the driver's seat and put the reins into his shaking hands.

The old man's eyes were filled with tears. He said:

"This is the end," he said. "This really is the end."

"Isn't there anyone who could accompany you back to Pietrasecca?" Don Paolo asked him. "Isn't there some friend who could go back in the trap with you?"

The old man shook his head.

"No one," he said. "No one. This is the end."

Don Paolo went back to the hotel to see if there were a reply from Dr. Sacca, but there was none. Perhaps Sacca will come tonight or tomorrow, without warning, the priest said to himself.

Berenice had learned that the Colamartini had been ruined by the failure of the bank, and she was laughing maliciously.

"This is retribution," she said. "Don Pasquale married an old half-wit to have much money and few children. This is his retribution. He loses his money, his children leave home, and he's left with the old half-wit."

The priest asked Berenice whether she knew the son of Don Senofonte, the chemist.

"He's a nice young fellow, but he'll be the ruin of his family," she said.

The train from Rome had arrived and the passengers leaving the station passed in front of the hotel. Two carabinieri stopped a young man with a leather case under his arm.

"What do you want here?" they asked him.

"I'm a fruit dealer," the young man said.

"Have you got your license?"

The young man searched in his wallet and produced it.

"Have you got your corporation card?"

The young man produced it.

"Have you paid your taxes?"

The young man had even paid his taxes.

"Very well," one of the carabinieri said to him. "All your papers are in order, so there's no need to arrest you. You will remain in Fossa until the next train comes in and then go straight back to Rome."

"But I came here to buy fruit," the young man said.

The two carabinieri expressed themselves with the precision and exactitude of the slogans on the marble tablets.

"The times of capitalist speculation are over," one of them said.

"The corporation attends to the buying of fruit," said the other.

The young man was in a cold sweat. He declared himself convinced.

"You've had a narrow escape, young man," Berenice said to him. "You're very lucky not to have been locked up. What on earth were you up to? Why didn't you stay at home?"

"Thank you," said the young man. "Thank you for your kind words." And he went back to the station to take the train to Rome.

Bianchina had heard of Don Paolo's arrival and came to see him.

"Where are you living?" the priest asked her.

"In a country house called the Villa delle Stagioni," she said.

Don Paolo had one object in his mind.

"Do you know Don Senofonte's son?" he asked.

"Pompeo?" Bianchina said. "He's a great friend of Alberto's. He often comes to the Villa delle Stagioni."

"Take me to the Villa delle Stagioni," Don Paolo said.

Bianchina looked better and not so thin. She was neater and tidier, and had lost the somewhat bedraggled look she had at Pietrasecca. She looked a little older, too. But perhaps that was appearance only.

"Have you become a good girl now?"

"The wolf loses his hair but not his vice," Bianchina answered, with a laugh. "But that is only a manner of speaking, because as far as hair is concerned I have more than enough to spare."

The Villa delle Stagioni had formerly been a manor house that had been abandoned and was now put to agricultural uses. It had once been the summer residence of a baron who had died ridden with debts. The park wall that surrounded it had tumbled down in many places. The park gates had been taken from their hinges and were propped up against the wall. Nettles and poppies grew freely along the carriage drive. What had once been a peacock inclosure was used for a chicken-run. A Renaissance-style pavilion, entirely covered with ivy, which had once been a small temple of Venus, was used as a storehouse for straw. The villa consisted of two wings, set at right angles to one another. The upper floors were abandoned because rain came in through the roof. Horses and cows were kept in some of the ground-floor rooms, and some peasants lived in the others. Between the balconies were four empty niches where once there had been four statues representing the seasons of the year. On the walls, which were weather-worn and stained with saltpeter and damp, were a number of inscriptions scrawled in big red letters: "Long live the corporations without Prince Torlonia!" "Down with the bureaucracy!" "Long live the second revolution."

Alberto and another young man were sitting at the edge of a big pool built in the granite pavement.

"It was once a trout pool," Bianchina said. "Now it's used for watering cattle and horses."

Alberto introduced Pompeo, the chemist's son. Don Paolo sat down next to the young men, at the edge of the pool, and remained silent.

One of the corner rooms of the villa served to store the sporting equipment of the government youth organization. It was also used by Bianchina and Alberto, who lived in it. Two more young men came from the room and joined the others beside the granite pool.

Don Paolo spoke:

"How I should like to stay here with you in silence, all night, sitting round this pool, as we are now," he said.

"Bianchina has spoken to us about you," Pompeo said.

"There is a kind of silence," Don Paolo continued, "in which the hard, thick shell which normally covers and protects us, the thick shell of fiction and prejudice and ready-made phrases which separate man from man, begins to crack and open. There is no need to fear such silence. There is no need to be afraid of throwing off all formulas, commonplaces, and sententious phrases."

"We are not afraid," said Pompeo.

"We must not be afraid," Don Paolo went on. "We have reached a stage at which a member of the government youth organization must not be afraid of talking to a Communist, an intellectual of talking to a peasant."

"Do you mean that all distinctions between men are artificial?" Pompeo asked.

"Certainly not," Don Paolo replied. "But there are many artificial distinctions which are created with the specific object of concealing the essential ones. There are divided forces that ought to be united, and there are artificially united forces which ought to be divided. There are many distinctions that are distinctions of words only. There are many alliances that are alliances of words only. In no century have words been so perverted from their natural purpose of putting man in touch with man as they are today. To speak and to deceive (often to deceive oneself) have become almost synonymous. So far has this process gone that I, wishing to speak to you sincerely and fraternally, with no other object in mind than that of understanding you and making myself understood by you, if I begin to search for the right words, remain in perplexity, so false, equivocal, hackneyed, and compromised are they. Therefore it is perhaps better to keep silent and to trust the silence."

Four young men, a girl, and a priest were sitting by the pool, and they kept silent.

A peasant came, and opened the stable doors. The cows came out slowly, two by two, and drank at the pool. They were thin, black-and-white working cows, with big, arching horns. They drank slowly, looking aslant at the group sitting silently round the pool, and then went back to their stalls. The cowherd shut the door and came and sat down at the edge of the pool.

Pompeo spoke.

"There was a man who saved his country from ruin and showed it the way to regeneration," he said. "His words were clear and not ambiguous. He came into power, and we were astonished at the contrast between his words and all his actions. We asked ourselves: Is it possible that he has betrayed us? A few weeks ago some one came to us and revealed the truth. He whom we suspected of treachery had in reality been made a prisoner and he is confined in a cellar under the Banca Commerciale in Rome; and a double has been put in his place, to be shown at parades and ceremonies."

"That explains everything," said Alberto.

"That makes the whole thing perfectly clear," the cowherd said.

"What we wonder is how it would be possible to set him free," said Bianchina.

"It would not be easy," Pompeo confessed. "His worst enemies have established themselves in the seat of government. They still exploit his name in order to deceive the young, but all their actions are the very reverse of what he taught."

"All the same, an attempt ought to be made to set him free," Bianchina said. "Something ought to be done."

"Only a second revolution could set him free," said Pompeo.

"What do you think?" the cowherd asked the priest.

"I cannot tell you for certain whether the man of whom you speak is really a prisoner of the bank," Don Paolo replied. "Some people, of course, believe it. But in any case it is not just a matter of one man alone. What is certain, and what anyone who has his eyes open can see for himself, is that the whole country has been made a prisoner of the bank."

Pompeo agreed.

"The bank exercises a dictatorship over the whole country, under the mask of the corporations," he said.

"What is to be done, then?" Bianchina asked.

"I, too, believe in the necessity of working for the second revolution," said Don Paolo. "I too believe in the necessity of setting our country free from servitude to the bank. It will be a long and painful task, full of snares and pitfalls. It will not be a less worthy enterprise for that."

Don Paolo spoke calmly, in a matter-of-fact voice, as though he were saying the most natural thing in the world. Nevertheless, there was a note of firmness in his voice that left no doubt. Bianchina threw her arms around his neck and embraced him.

"Who would ever have imagined that we would have a priest with us for the second revolution?" said Alberto.

"Don Paolo is not a priest, but a saint," said Bianchina.

"In every revolution," Pompeo said, "there have been priests who have blessed the cause of the people."

Pompeo's remark must be understood in its true, southern Italian, Catholic sense. A priest's function in a revolutionary movement rather resembles that of a military chaplain. Would a peasant, even an atheist peasant, advance to the attack if he did not know there was a chaplain in the rear? The presence of a consecrated person in the revolutionary ranks is welcomed in the same way. It gives a sense of greater security; not because you are afraid of the other world (a southerner is not afraid of anything!), but because (after all, you never know) his presence is always a protection. Besides, if after death you really had to appear before the Almighty on the Judgment Throne (a pure hypothesis, of course, but it's as well to take account of everything) you could always say, "Excuse me, but did You not notice that even priests were on our side."

"I must confess to you," said Don Paolo, "that I do not attach much importance to my priestly clothing."

"It's more prudent for you to remain a priest," Pompeo remarked.

"Let us respect prudence," the priest said, with a laugh.

"But what are we to do now—at once?" said one of the young men who had not yet opened his mouth.

"With your permission," Don Paolo replied, "I would rather discuss that with Pompeo alone."

The priest and the chemist's son departed together. They left the park of the Villa delle Stagioni, jumped a brook, and took a path between some vegetable gardens surrounded by hedges of hawthorn. They walked for some distance without talking. Then Don Paolo spoke.

"We belong to two different generations," he said. "My generation grew up in the war, and your generation grew up within these last five years. The difference is enormous. Nevertheless, in our different generations, we are the same kind of young men; in the southern dialect I might say we belong to the same 'race' of young men. The 'race' to which we belong is distinguished by the fact that it begins by taking seriously the principles taught us by our own educators and teachers. These principles are proclaimed to be the foundations of present-day society, but if one takes them seriously and uses them as a standard to test society as it is organized and as it functions today, it becomes evident that there is a radical contradiction between the two. Our society in practice ignores those principles altogether. It is this discovery that leads one to become a revolutionary. Society preserves those principles as a fiction. But for us, who have nourished them with our life blood, they are a serious and sacred thing. They are the foundation of our inner life. The way society butchers them, using them as a mask and a tool to cheat and fool the people, fills us with anger and indignation. That is how one becomes a revolutionary."

At this point the two men had to jump another brook. The path continued along a row of almond trees, between fields of burnt stubble. There were a few bushes of ripe mulberries, and the two stopped to pick some. Pompeo pricked his finger. Don Paolo went on:

"We belong to two different generations. Our points of departure were different. But both took seriously the things they told us, and so we reached the same point. Our most important task now is to unite our two generations, or at any rate those of the same 'race' belonging to our two generations."

The path led out onto the provincial road. It was full of donkeys, carts, and peasants returning from the Fucino.

"There are Torlonia's niggers," said Pompeo. "Torlogne's niggers, I should say, belonging to the so-called Roman prince, who really comes from the Auvergne, like many of the adventurers in Balzac's novels."

"And Monsieur Laval," Don Paolo added.

The two started laughing. Then they noticed that they had walked a long way from Fossa. Don Paolo was tired, and leaned on Pompeo's arm. They went back by the provincial road, which was quicker, and Pompeo slackened his pace in order not to tire his companion. He would have liked to be silent, because he liked walking with this man, listening to him breathing in silence.

"But, to be practical, how are we to start? What are the first steps we must take?"

Don Paolo started talking of practical things. Speaking softly, he gave Pompeo some of his own ideas, encouraged him to make objections, and discussed the most minute details with him. Don Paolo drew on the technical experience of his past work as a conspirator, but he did this sparingly, because he knew that conspiracy is an art and not a science, and that there is only true art where there is originality and imagination, not just wooden plans and repetitions. Besides, coöperation with the younger generation was an entirely new experience for him, and he intended to push it to the uttermost without encumbering it with formulas. Nothing was more repugnant to him than to present himself as a master and as an initiate, particularly to youths whose experience had been entirely different from his own. Undoubtedly he would be able to tell them many things, but only after they themselves had spoken and said what they had to say.

The two friends separated before reaching Fossa, to avoid being seen together.

The raucous voice of a talkie filled the main street of Fossa, which was crowded with children. The noise followed the priest as far as his room. Don Paolo went to bed, tired but joyful.

The first stone is laid, he said to himself.

Chapter VIII

A NOTE from Dr. Sacca arrived next day. He excused himself from paying Don Paolo a visit, on grounds of prudence. But Dr. Sacca could not be very useful to Don Paolo in his new venture. The first stone has been laid, Don Paolo repeated to himself, and now I must find the second. Outwardly, nothing unusual had happened. But two men had talked together, and that was something extraordinary. Don Paolo could hardly sleep for thinking of it. Thus it was that great events were born. But people passed by without noticing anything—the carabinieri, the centurions, the Scribes and the Pharisees, Zabaglione, Don Senofonte, and Berenice—and not one of them noticed anything. But two men had talked together. That was how every conspiracy began.

Don Girasole, the old parish priest of Fossa, whose thin features bore a strange resemblance to Bianchina, came to invite Don Paolo to inspect his church. But Don Paolo briefly excused himself, saying that he had no time. He burned Dr. Sacca's note, went to the station, and took the train to Rome. The first stone has been laid, and now I must find the second, he said to himself. I must get assistance from the workers, and then the struggle will begin. His clerical garb enabled him to pass safely through the close police watch kept on the Termini station at Rome; but it left him perplexed when he thought of making contact with any of his old acquaintances. To present himself in priest's clothing would be ridiculous, and dangerous besides.

Don Paolo had in his bag a coat, a cap, and a tie, the minimum equipment necessary to transform himself into a layman. But the transformation could not possibly take place in the street or in a hotel or in any other place that might be under observation, because he would be detected at once. After wandering about for a long time in the neighborhood of the station, he reached the Lateran quarter. In the great sunny square between the basilica of San Giovanni and the Church of the Scala Santa an amusement park was being dismantled. Its gaudy and spurious decorations had been removed and workmen were taking down the scaffolding. Tents, colored posters, lamps, wooden horses, and tin swords were being packed into lorries. Plaster statues, a painting of a phantom boat on a stormy sea, and a skin of a sanguinary Bengal tiger lay on the ground in the dust. Don Paolo made his way across the littered square and sought refuge in the cool shade of the Church of the Scala Santa. A few women dressed in black were mounting the big staircase to the church on their knees. According to a medieval legend, the staircase after which the church was named came from the house of Pontius Pilate in Jerusalem, and various objects, retrieved from Golgotha by St. Helen, are imbedded in the steps, namely the remains of the Cross, one of the nails used to crucify Jesus, and some thorns from the crown that was put on His head when He was mockingly called the King of the Jews. Don Paolo waited for the women to finish their weary ascent and go away, but he had to wait a long time, because they stopped at every step, sighing painfully, and recited interminable prayers. The stairs were many, and the poor women's knees must have hurt dreadfully. Paying tribute to the Roman proconsul at Jerusalem must have been a tedious business. Don Paolo waited patiently at the foot of a marble group representing Pilate showing Christ to the people. On the pedestal were the words *Hæc est hora vestra et potestas tenebrarum*. A little darkness would have been very convenient for Don Paolo. When at last the women got to the top of the steps and came down one of the side staircases Don Paolo rapidly mounted the Holy Stairs. He remained at the top for a short time and when he came down he was entirely transformed. Don Paolo Spada had entered the church, but Pietro Spina came out of it.

He could not help laughing a little, but once in the street, in broad daylight, he felt embarrassed walking without his soutane. He felt as a woman must feel the first time she goes out in a ski-suit. He felt that everybody must be looking at his legs, and this made him walk quickly, almost run. He looked down several times to see whether his trousers were properly buttoned. Thus he passed the Porta San Giovanni and went down the Via Appia Nuova. Then he took a side street to the right and walked through a suburb grouped about several cinemas and a new church. Beyond this quarter there was a vast and dreary expanse of fields. It was a domain of cats, lost dogs, and boys playing truant from school. The fields were furrowed by trenches and ditches, and were also used to dump wood, bricks, piping, and corrugated iron. A few months previously, when Spina had had to fly from the police, he had taken refuge here in a hut of an old man named Mannaggia Lamorra, who came from the same village as he. As a boy Mannaggia had been a servant in his father's house at Orta, and he had spent many years abroad. He had sold mineral water in the Barrio La Boca at Buenos Ayres, had worked in a brick-factory at St.-André, near Marseilles, and after that he had spent some years working in a sandpit near Rome.

"How do you earn a living now?" Spina had asked on meeting him again.

"I get along," Lamorra had answered without offering any details.

Spina had no difficulty in finding Lamorra's wooden hut with its corrugated iron roof. Lamorra came forward happily and deferentially to receive him.

"Are you in this part of the world again, sir?" he said.

Spina handed him an address and said:

"Go and find out if a foreman builder named Romeo still lives there; find out if he's working and where he's working, but don't attract attention to yourself."

Lamorra went off and Spina entered the hut to wait for him. While he was waiting he fell asleep.

Lamorra came back late, drunk and hatless, but with precise information. Spina had prepared two beds inside the hut, but

Lamorra wouldn't come in. He lay down outside, overcome with a sudden respect.

"The hut is small," he said, "and how could I sleep beside my master?"

"You're the master here," said Spina, "and I'm your guest."

But Lamorra shook his head.

"Your father was a good man," he said. "When he was angry he used to beat me, but he was a good man all the same. He gave me a shoulder of kid once at Easter. The taste of that kid is in my mouth tonight."

Spina tried to go to sleep on a camp bed inside the hut, and Lamorra lay outside on the ground near the door. The bed was teeming with bugs and fleas. They pounced greedily on Spina's flesh, which was fresher than his host's. Spina turned and tossed, but dared not complain to Lamorra, for fear of offending him. But Lamorra noticed his discomfort.

"There must be 'Abyssinians' in the bed," he said. "If you pretend not to notice them they leave you alone."

"Good-night," Spina replied.

Lamorra, under the influence of the wine, started recalling the most beautiful episodes in his long life.

"Once," he began, "your father gave me a Tuscan cigar. What a cigar! It was on a Saturday night, and I smoked it on Sunday morning, in the square outside the church, while the women were coming home from Mass. What a cigar!"

Spina went to sleep, but Lamorra continued with his reminiscences.

"At Buenos Ayres there is a little river called Riachuelo, and the Italians live along it. They are called *gringos* and also *tanos*. Once there was a beautiful, fat negress . . ."

Early next morning Spina went to wait for Romeo near the Porta San Giovanni. It was not long before the foreman builder appeared, but since other workmen were with him, Spina did not approach him, but followed some way behind him. Workmen came trooping along from every side, and there was a beauty in the air that moved Spina deeply, the marvelous beauty of Rome at dawn, when there is no one in the streets but honest

people going to work, walking quickly and talking little. At the
Porta San Giovanni, Romeo went down the Via delle Mura
Aureliane, and at the Porta Metrovia he left his companions and
went alone down the Via della Ferratella. Spina walked behind
him and hummed a tune that Romeo had often sung when the
two of them had been deported to the isle of Ustica. The song
started:

> *Never a rose without a thorn,*[1]
> *Never a woman without a kiss. . . .*

Romeo looked round, but pretended not to recognize him. He
went on to the place where he worked as foreman, where a number of bricklayers were waiting for him. Perhaps there was some
one from the Abruzzi among them who might serve for Spina's
plan. The first stone has been laid, he said to himself, and I
must find the second. May it be a worker.

The building on which Romeo was at work was still at the
initial stages. The walls only reached to the bricklayers' chests,
and scaffolding was necessary in order to continue. Romeo gave
directions to his men.

"The first pole has been erected, and now we must erect the
second," he said.

Spina walked past.

"Are you the owner of that terrace that needs repairing?"
Romeo called out.

"Yes, I am," answered Spina. "I want to know what it will
cost."

The two walked away to discuss the repairs to the terrace,
and went and sat down between the lime-kiln and the tool-shed.

Spina drew a plan of the terrace on the ground.

"I've got to find a very reliable man," he said. "If possible he
must be a worker. He must come from the Abruzzi and still be
in touch with his native village. I want him to go back to his
village and work in conjunction with me. Without a worker to
help me I shall not be able to build anything lasting."

"You're asking too much," Romeo replied.

---

[1] Thorn in Italian is Spina.

"The man has got to be found," said Spina.

The foreman builder reflected for a moment. Then he described the situation.

"The reaction against the people from Apulia, the Abruzzi, and Sardinia who were among us has been terrific. The police nearly all come from the country themselves, and you cannot imagine their fury whenever a revolutionary who is not a townsman but a countryman falls into their hands. If a townsman believes in liberty it is a grave crime, but if an ex-peasant is for liberty it is sacrilege and all the hatred of the authorities is unleashed against him. He is nearly always killed, but if he does escape with his life he's such a wreck when he comes out of prison that his fellow-villagers are terrified of him and run away."

"What has happened to Chelucci?" Spina asked.

"He was arrested again a month ago for distributing an anti-war pamphlet, and now he's in Regina Coeli. He's nearly blind."

"What is Pozzi doing?"

"He's a bit suspect at present," said Romeo. "Nobody can understand why Chelucci was arrested and not Pozzi, for the police found them together. But the police may have done it on purpose, to discredit and isolate him. How can one know the truth? There have been several cases like his, and they have been the saddest."

"Aren't there any others from the Abruzzi in the groups?"

"We used to have Diproia, until he got married. But as soon as he married he wouldn't have anything more to do with us. Now every Sunday he goes to Mass with his wife in the morning, and in the afternoon he goes to the races with his blonde mistress. When he mentions his revolutionary past he says he feels as if he had thrown off a nightmare. There used to be a student named Luigi Murica, but he has completely disappeared. I've had inquiries made several times, but I have never managed to find him. He was a nice young fellow."

"What is Pecetti doing?"

"He now writes poetry about birds and flowers," Romeo said. "I've been shown a paper with a poem of his, all about birds and flowers, but even so the police won't leave him alone, because he refuses to denounce his former friends."

"Some active and trustworthy member of the groups has got to be found," said Spina. "It is absolutely necessary."

"Come back here tomorrow night when we stop work," Romeo said.

Spina had no desire to go straight back to Lamorra's hut, so he went down the Via della Navicella and the Via Claudia towards the center of the city, in order to see it once more. But the beauty of Rome had faded. The workers had disappeared from the streets, and no one was to be seen now but men in uniform, government clerks, priests, and nuns going shopping. Rome was now a different place. And between ten and eleven, when the big parasites began to appear, the hierarchs, the higher officials of the ministries, and the monsignori with their violet stockings, Rome suddenly became odious in his sight. Spina went down the Via Labicana and returned to the outskirts of the city, after buying some insect powder to dispose of Mannaggia Lamorra's "Abyssinians." He gave himself a lot of trouble for nothing, for the "Abyssinians" scattered and hid during the day, their tactics being guerilla warfare at night.

Mannaggia Lamorra was out all day. He came back towards evening, looking more dead than alive. He had a huge black eye, one of his hands had been bitten, and his clothing had been torn. Spina tried to find out how he had managed to get himself into such a state, but Mannaggia, instead of replying, took a small bottle of iodine from a box and applied it to his injured hand.

"You lack the greatest necessities, but you've got a bottle of iodine," Spina said. "Do you often get beaten up like this?"

"Once or twice a week, according to the time of year," Mannaggia replied. "But now I'm fed up with it. This is the last time."

Spina tried hard to find out who it was who beat him so regularly, and why, but Mannaggia sought to change the subject. At last he confessed.

"He'll probably be coming here later, and you'll see him,"

he said. "You know him already. Do you remember an engineer from our part of the world named Achilles Scarpa?"

Spina remembered him well. Scarpa had been dubbed Fleet-footed Achilles when Spina was still a student, having earned that Homeric title as the hero of one of the most inexplicable episodes of the Great War. For it seemed established beyond all possible doubt that at nine o'clock in the morning on the day when the retreat from Caporetto began he was at Palmanova, near the front, and at ten o'clock on the same day he was at Rome, which is about six hundred kilometers away. Not even an airplane could have covered the distance in the time; and what made the story even more remarkable was that Scarpa was an infantryman, and maintained that he had traveled from Palmanova to Rome on foot. Apart from this incident, he had always been a normal, even a timid and retiring man.

"Signor Achilles, being out of a job, has assumed the task of protecting foreign women and girl tourists who come to Rome," Lamorra said. "He hangs around certain hotels and pensions to spot the new arrivals. He follows them, and when he finds one of the type he likes, the blonde, fragile, nordic type, he sends for me. When the girl goes unescorted to some lonely place, such as the Colosseum at certain hours of the day, I have to accost her, say coarse things to her, follow her, and frighten her. An elegant young man who just happens to be going by intervenes on the young lady's behalf. He, of course, is Signor Achilles. A dramatic struggle takes place between us. It lasts until he finally has the advantage over me and beats me to the ground, in accordance with the agreement. Signor Achilles then makes a beautiful bow, offers the young lady his arm, and escorts her back to her hotel."

"So that's your occupation now?" said Spina.

"And a very hard one it is," said Mannaggia. "Signor Achilles calls me the Monster Outside the Gates. He says the most dreadful things about me to the young ladies he rescues, and that, of course, only increases their gratitude to him."

"It must certainly be a lucrative occupation," Spina remarked.

"It might be," the Monster replied, "if Signor Achilles did

not have scruples. The first few times, after accompanying the young ladies back to their hotels, he would suddenly notice he had lost his wallet in the fray, and the young lady would nearly always compensate him adequately. But now, or at any rate so he says, he finds this stratagem repugnant and only has recourse to it when he is completely broke. Otherwise he contents himself with glory alone."

"What glory?"

"The glory of risking his life to save the honor of inexperienced young ladies who come to our country from abroad and are beset by the Monster Outside the Gates. Signor Achilles always says we must show foreigners that the traditions of ancient chivalry in our country are not dead."

"But the whole thing is a sham," said Spina. "Both the assault and the rescue."

"Do you think my wounds are a sham?" Mannaggia replied. "Do you think I let myself be knocked about without hitting back? If only it all went according to the agreement! But unfortunately Signor Achilles, as he himself admits, has a romantic and passionate temperament. He nearly always loses his head. He becomes inflamed in the ardor of the battle, forgets the agreement, and starts hitting out in earnest, though he expects me to take it lying down. But that is impossible. I have to defend myself, and I hit back."

"But are the young ladies taken in so easily as all that?" Spina asked.

"They fall into our hands like ripe plums," the Monster replied. "Perhaps it is the effect of the Italian sun. There have been three, so far, who did not even allow time for Signor Achilles to intervene, but yielded to me at once, almost as soon as I approached them. Thus I have known some elegant women, with fine embroidered and initialed underwear, and expensive scents, who have never done a day's work in their lives. However, the effect of these unexpected successes was to make Signor Achilles furiously jealous. He was wild with me, and insisted on my dirtying my face and making myself look as repugnant as possible before he would let me approach any other girl he pointed out."

A man with a limp and a bandaged head was to be seen coming across the ditches, putting the stray dogs and cats to flight.

"There he is!" exclaimed the Monster, arming himself with a knotted stick.

The anger of Fleet-footed Achilles sounded terrible in the distance.

"Come on out, you loathsome pig!" he cried. "Come out of your sty!"

"If you come any nearer I'll crack your skull!" replied the Monster, brandishing his stick.

"Now show your courage, treacherous coward! Now show your strength, obscene gorilla!" cried Fleet-footed Achilles.

"If you come near me, I'll crack your skull!" the Monster repeated.

The two remained some distance apart, hurling defiance at each other and uttering the most blood-curdling threats. This went on for a long time. In the end Spina came forward as peacemaker. Fleet-foot had some difficulty in recognizing him at first, and when he did he expressed himself as being astonished to find an educated person living in a pig-sty with this disgusting chimpanzee.

"I have no money to go to a hotel," said Spina.

Fleet-foot offered him the hospitality of his own flat, and the Monster had no objection, hoping Spina's society might have a mollifying effect upon his partner and cause him to observe the agreement more faithfully.

The flat to which Spina now removed consisted of a single third-floor room in the Via dei Marsi, near the Porta San Lorenzo. The room was adorned with war trophies, photographs of various film stars, and a portrait of Etcetera Etcetera. Fleet-footed Achilles cast himself wearily on the bed.

"What a life!" he exclaimed.

"Have you been devoting yourself to the protection of young ladies from abroad for a long time?" Spina asked him.

"For two years," the man replied. "At first I used to take

what came—Poles, Hungarians, Swiss, Brazilians, anything. But nowadays I confine myself to women who come from countries whose currency stands higher than the lira. I find them more cultivated and sensible, with the exception of the Irish pilgrims."

Fleet-foot had a box in which he kept a large number of photographs and letters from women he had saved from the Monster's wiles. He had another box of inlaid wood which was full of curls and strands of hair of the same origin—tender mementoes in all gradations of blonde, red, and chestnut, all tied with blue ribbons.

"When I am old," said Fleet-foot, "I shall make a little cushion of them, to rest my head on in the hour of the siesta."

"You might also use them for rheumatism," said Spina. "I hear that nothing is more effective."

"That fellow-villager of yours, Mannaggia Lamorra, has remained a vulgar peasant," said Fleet-foot. "All he cares about is money. He cannot understand the divine beauty of two blue eyes saying thank you for having been preserved from profanation."

The bell rang and a smart, perfumed young woman came in, with her arms full of marmalade-jars, boxes of biscuits, several bottles, and a large bouquet of red roses. She was a fair and voluptuous Dutch girl whom Fleet-foot had saved from the Monster's clutches that very day. To express her gratitude she consulted a small pocket dictionary for every word.

"Marvelous," she said, "tenderness, gratitude, for which, beautiful, dear, with which, oh!"

With the help of the bottles the conversation became even plainer. Spina discreetly retired into the tiny bathroom. He removed a heap of dirty washing and a lot of engineering books from the bath, and settled down to spend the night in it. Suspicious noises soon began coming from the neighboring room, where the bed seemed to be moving backwards and forwards on its rollers as though an earthquake were in progress. Spina did all he could to shut his ears to what was happening, particularly to the whimpering cries of the Dutch girl and Fleet-foot's ferocious roars, which continued, with only brief interruptions, all night long. When it grew light next morning Spina was so tired that he fell asleep.

He was late for his appointment with Romeo. All the workmen had gone home. The foreman was waiting for him behind the tool-shed. A boy was with him.

"This lad is the 'contact,'" Romeo said.

"Money and a Czechoslovakian passport for you arrived from abroad a month ago," the boy said to Spina.

"How do you know it is a Czechoslovakian passport?"

"I opened the envelope."

"You shouldn't have done that," said Spina.

"We distributed the anti-war leaflet at San Lorenzo yesterday," the boy said.

"What did the leaflet say?"

"I haven't had time to read it yet," the boy said.

"Did you help distribute it?"

"Yes. There are very few of us left, and we have to do a little of everything."

Romeo lost his temper.

"What?" he said. "You're doing both propaganda and contact? Don't you know that every time the two have been combined the whole thing has failed from the start?"

The lad was embarrassed and confused.

"What is your trade?" Romeo asked.

"I've done a bit of everything, but I haven't really got a trade."

"That's the trouble," the foreman said. "If you don't know a trade, you'll never be able to do illegal work properly. A builder putting up a scaffolding first plants the uprights, then joins them with crosspieces, then puts up the scaffold-boards. A builder knows that a pole can't be used as a crosspiece, otherwise the scaffolding won't stand. It's the same in every job, the cooper's, the electrician's, the mechanic's. Every job has its own rules. Illegal work has its own rules, too; and if you don't know and observe them, you pay for it with long years of imprisonment and sometimes with your life. From today on you will no longer serve as contact man. Now go away and don't let yourself be seen in this neighborhood again. If we see each other you will pretend you don't know me."

The youth, crestfallen, went away.

Romeo gave Spina the addresses of some men from the Abruzzi who had been out of the groups for some years.

"You're the man best fitted to try to get them back into the movement," he said. "The war scare has created a situation in which some members who are now passive may be galvanized into action again."

"What do the masses think of the prospect of war?" Spina asked.

"The masses don't think about it at all. They behave as if the war were no affair of theirs. From that point of view the leaflet from abroad that we have started distributing is entirely mistaken. It might have been written expressly to rouse the sympathies of the masses in favor of the war, which it describes as a robber's enterprise. If we succeed in convincing the unemployed that there really is anything to steal in Abyssinia, many of them will promptly enlist. The only thing that holds them back now is the suspicion that Abyssinia has nothing worth looting. Besides, there are many revolutionary workers who rejoice at the prospect of war, which they think will lead to the downfall of the present government and give us liberty."

"My stay among the peasants during the last few months has convinced me of the futility of pure propaganda," said Spina. "The peasants accept the dictatorship, not because they are convinced by its propaganda, but because the dictatorship is a fact. As long as the peasants have to choose between facts and words, they will always abide by the facts, even if they are evil facts. Facts are one thing and words are another. A peasant told me that a thousand females don't make a male. Therefore propaganda for liberty must be accompanied by courageous and resounding acts that demonstrate liberty in action. In short, what we want is a new kind of program that illiterates can understand."

"For instance?"

"Blow up the offices of the Fucino administration at Avezzano;

set fire to two or three tax offices; prevent the seizure of poor families' property by sudden raids."

"We shall talk of these things again," Romeo said. "Individual acts of violence have never appealed to me." Then he added, with a laugh: "Scratch an intellectual, and you always find an anarchist!"

Spina used the list of addresses that Romeo gave him. Next day he succeeded in finding the home of an old friend of his, Uliva, a violinist, whom he had not heard of since they had used to meet in a Socialist students' group. All he knew about Uliva was that he had spent many months in prison and had lived completely apart ever since. Spina found him on the fourth floor of a house in the Via Panisperna in the Viminal quarter. A young, pregnant woman took him to Uliva's room, and Uliva received him with indifference, without pleasure or surprise. He was a bent, bespectacled little man, wearing a dirty black suit that gave him a sad and neglected look. Even after Spina had entered the room, he remained stretched on the divan, smoking and spitting. He spat in a wide arc, right across the room, in the direction of the washstand, but more often than not he missed it; traces of yellow tobacco juice were everywhere, on the fringes of the bed-cover, on the writing-desk, and on the walls.

"We haven't seen each other for a long time," said Spina. "I didn't think you would come to this."

"Did you think I'd become a state employee?"

"Is that the only alternative?"

"For us, yes," said Uliva. "There has never been any other alternative for us. Either you serve or perish. He who desires to live disinterestedly, with no other discipline than that which he imposes on himself, is outlawed by society, and the state hunts him like an enemy. Do you remember our student group? Those who didn't end up in prison or die of hunger have met a far worse fate, as state employees. After ten months' imprisonment for shouting 'Long live liberty!' in the Piazza Venezia, I spent some time sleeping in the public dormitories in winter, or under the bridges of the Tiber or in some doorway or on church steps in summer, with my coat under my head for a pillow.

Every now and then there was the nuisance of the police coming on their rounds, asking: 'Who are you? What is your job? What do you live on?' You should have seen how they laughed when, for lack of other identification papers, I showed my scholastic certificate and my musician's diploma! I even tried to settle in my native village in the province of Salerno. It was impossible. Our villages have not been in such a state since the Spaniards left the country."

"The time has come to emerge from isolation," Spina said. "The time has come to combine with the working-class. The time has come to convert the masses through a series of audacious acts."

"The working-masses are cowed, corrupted, intimidated, apathetic, classified, regimented, rubber-stamped, and famished," Uliva replied. "Hunger itself has been bureaucratized. There's the official kind that gives you the right to state soup, and the unofficial kind that gives you the right to throw yourself into the Tiber."

"Nevertheless, among the pulverized mass there are some living cells," said Spina. "We are in a grave situation. A man like you must not remain isolated. Isolated sacrifices are futile. Action is necessary to reawaken the masses."

"The situation is certainly grave," Uliva replied. "There is something corpse-like even about the dictatorship that stifles us. For a long time it has not been a movement, even a reactionary movement; all it is is a bureaucracy. But what is the opposition? Another bureaucracy that aspires to totalitarian domination in its turn, in the name of different ideas and on behalf of different interests. If it does conquer, as it probably will, we shall thus pass from one tyranny to another. We shall have a so-called economic revolution, thanks to which we shall have state bread, state boots and shoes, state shirts and pants, state potatoes and state green peas, just as we now have state railways, state quinine, state salt, state matches, and state tobacco. Will that be a technical advance? Certainly it will. But it will be the basis of an official, compulsory doctrine, a totalitarian orthodoxy which will use every means, from the cinema to terrorism, to extirpate heresy and tyrannize over individual thought. A Red inquisition will succeed the present inquisition, a Red censorship the present censorship. Instead of the present deportations there will be Red deportations, of which dissident revolutionaries will be the favorite victims. Our future bureaucracy will identify itself with Labor and Socialism and persecute everyone who goes on thinking with his own head, denouncing him as a paid agent of the industrialists and the landlords, just as the present bureaucracy identifies itself with patriotism and suppresses all its opponents, denouncing them as traitors bought by foreign gold."

"Uliva, you're raving," said Spina. "You have been one of us, you know us, and you know that that is not our ideal."

"It's not your ideal, but it is your destiny," Uliva answered. "There's no way out."

"Destiny is an invention of the cowardly and the resigned," said Spina.

Uliva made a gesture to indicate that it was not worth while continuing the discussion. But he added:

"You are very intelligent, but you are a coward. You don't understand because you don't want to understand. You're afraid of the truth."

Spina got up to go away. Uliva remained motionless on his divan. At the door Spina turned and said:

"There is nothing in my life which gives you the right to insult me."

"Go away and don't come back," said Uliva. "I have nothing to say to any emissary of the party."

Spina opened the door to go. But he closed it again and came and sat down at the foot of the divan on which Uliva lay.

"I shall not go away," he said, "until I have discovered why you have become like this. What was it that altered you to this extent? Imprisonment, unemployment, hunger?"

"I read and studied in my privations, and sought for at least a promise of liberation," said Uliva. "I found none. Every revolution, every single one, without any exception whatever, started as a movement for liberation and finished as a tyranny. For a long time I was tortured by that fact. Why has no revolution escaped that destiny?"

"Even if that were true, the conclusion to be drawn from it would be a different one from yours," said Spina. "If it were true that all previous revolutions had miscarried, we should have to say to ourselves, our revolution must not miscarry."

"Illusions, illusions," Uliva replied. "You have not yet won, you are still an underground movement, you have already become simply a group of professional revolutionaries. The regenerating passion by which we were animated in the student group has become an ideology, a network of fixed ideas, a cobweb. That is the proof that there is no escape for you, either. And you are only at the beginning of the parabola. That is the destiny of every new idea. It is crystallized in formulas so that it may be propagated. It is intrusted to a body of interpreters so that it may be preserved. That body is prudently recruited, sometimes specifically paid for its task, and is subject to a superior authority whose duty it is to resolve doubts and suppress deviations from the line indicated by the masters. Thus every new idea invariably ends by becoming fixed, inflexible, parasitical, and reactionary. And if it becomes the official doctrine of the state, no more escape is possible. A carpenter or a laborer can perhaps adapt himself even to a regime of totalitarian orthodoxy, and eat, digest, procreate in peace; but for an intellectual there is no escape. He must either bend the knee and enter the ranks of the dominant clerks, or resign himself to hunger and defamation and be killed off at the first favorable opportunity."

Spina was overcome with anger. He seized Uliva by the lapels of his coat and cried in his face:

"But why should that be our destiny? Why should there be no way out? Are we hens shut up in a hen-coop? Why should we remain the victims of an inexorable fate, powerless to fight against it? Why condemn a regime which does not yet exist and which we wish to create in man's image?"

"Don't shout," said Uliva. "Don't act the propagandist with me. You have understood very well what I have said. You pre-

tend not to understand, because you are afraid of the consequences."

"I am not afraid of anything," said Spina.

"But I know you," said Uliva. "I watched you when we were
both in the Socialist group. Since then I have discovered that
fear is what makes you a revolutionary. You force yourself to
believe in progress, to be optimistic, you make valiant efforts to
believe in free will, all because you are terrified of the opposite."

Spina felt a little perplexed. He made Uliva a small concession.

"It is true," he said, "that I believe in the liberty of man. I
force myself to believe at least in the possibility of the liberty of
man, and hence in the possibility of progress. If I did not believe
in them, you are right, I should be afraid of life."

"I do not believe in progress, and I am not afraid of life," said
Uliva.

"How did you reconcile yourself to it?"

"I am not reconciled to it," said Uliva. "I am not afraid of
life, but I am still less afraid of death. Against a life which is
dominated by pitiless laws the only weapon left to man's free
will is non-life, the destruction of life, death, beautiful death."

"I see," said Spina.

He saw, and it filled him with a great sadness. Further argument would be useless. They belonged to different worlds.

Uliva quietly whispered in Spina's ear:

"Life can control man, but man can control death—his own
death, and, with a little wariness, the death of tyrants."

The young woman who had opened the door to Spina came
in to fetch something. Uliva waited till she had gone and then
continued:

"My father died of drink at the age of forty-nine," he said.
"A few weeks before he died he sent for me one evening and told
me the story of his life, his failure. First he described his father's
death—that is, my grandfather's. 'I die a poor and disappointed
man,' my father's father said, 'but I rely on you to realize all
my hopes. May you have from life what I have not had.' When
my father felt his own death approaching, he repeated my grand-

father's words. 'I, too, my son, die a poor and disappointed man, but my hopes live in you. May you have from life what I have not had.' Thus illusions, like debts, are passed on from generation to generation. I am now thirty-five years old, and I am where my father and grandfather were. I, too, a failure, and my wife is expecting a child. But I am not stupid enough to believe that my son may get from life what I did not get. I know that he will not be able to escape the same destiny. He will either die of hunger or become a state employee, which is worse."

Spina rose to go.

"I do not know whether I shall return," he said.

"It's not worth the trouble," Uliva replied.

About fifty young men wearing students' caps were creating an uproar in the Via Panisperna. They were carrying a big tricolor flag and banner on which were the words, "Long live the war!" The students were escorted by a number of policemen, and were shouting, yelling, and calling out to the passers-by, and singing a new song that said: "We shall make a brush of the Negus's beard, to polish our Leader's boots." People looked at them curiously from the doors of their shops and windows, but made no comment. In the Via dei Serpenti, Spina met another group of students with a similar flag and a similar banner, singing the same boot-polishing song with a similar police escort. Spina recognized in the busy throng the footsteps of those hurrying home or to some destination, the uncertain footsteps of the unemployed, the footsteps of those who had no destination, and he himself was drawn into following the students' procession. Near the Colosseum, Spina stopped to watch some boys drilling. They belonged to the Avanguardista machine-gunners and artillery. Boys of fifteen and seventeen were learning the mechanism of their lethal weapons, how to load and unload them, and how to pass from marching order to action. The boys were serious and attentive, like little men, and carried out the exercises with great speed and precision.

Spina had an appointment with Romeo in a tavern in the Tiburtine quarter, in the Via degli Ernici, near the Acqua Marcia viaduct and the railway. The railway gave its gloom to the whole street, and the smoke from the engines entered the houses. The tavern was almost deserted. In one corner a carabiniere was eating *spaghetti al sugo* with a mournful and ferocious air, as though he were dining off the entrails of a Communist. The floor was strewn with sawdust to absorb the spittle. The only picture in the room was of an enormous transatlantic liner speeding across the ocean at night, under a full moon, with every porthole brilliantly lighted. Later porters and bricklayers began to drift in. They ordered their half-liters of wine, drank, looked at the liner on the wall, furtively, so that the carabiniere should not see them, and silently embarked for America. Then they paid for their wine, disembarked, spat, and took their bad tempers home. Romeo arrived very late, drank a quarter of a liter of wine, coughed, and left, without approaching Spina. Spina followed him into the street and kept some distance behind him. This was no easy task, because Romeo changed direction at every corner, evidently to find out whether he was being followed by the police. In the Vicolo della Ranocchia, Romeo slowed down and let Spina overtake him.

"The contact lad has been arrested," he said. "They are certain to torture him dreadfully to make him tell what he knows. One must always count on the worst on these occasions. We must be very careful, or we shall be caught. Here's the money that came for you from abroad a month ago, and here's the Czechoslovakian passport. We must avoid seeing each other for the next few weeks."

"I've got no time to lose," said Spina. "I've been back in Italy six months and I haven't done anything yet, and I'm tired of waiting."

"An illegal organization is a fabric that has constantly to be woven and rewoven," Romeo said. "It's a fabric that costs blood and patience. How many times has the organization of the Rome groups been destroyed by the police, and then reconstructed again? What trouble it costs to establish contacts, and then for what a short time do they last! How many friends have I seen go to prison? How many have disappeared without trace?

How many we have to shun because we suspect them? All the same, we've got to stick to it."

"All right," said Spina, "I shall be patient."

The two shook hands and walked away in opposite directions. With the foreign passport Spina might easily have gone to a hotel, but the youth who had been arrested knew about the passport, and it would be impossible to use it until one knew for certain how far the youth had been able to resist the police torture. He looked a good lad, Spina said to himself, but in these cases one must always count on the worst.

Back in the flat in the Via dei Marsi, Spina found Signor Achilles, very downcast at the Dutch girl's departure. She had left him a big signed photograph of herself, several curls, and a strand of hair, and had also promised to write to him at least twice a week. But all that was too little to console the love-sick Fleet-foot.

"War demonstrations have been taking place in the center of the city," Spina said. "Most of the people just looked out of their windows, indifferent or apathetic, and here you are sighing for a girl you didn't know the day before yesterday."

This offended Fleet-foot.

"I offered you the hospitality of my flat because we are from the same village, and because I know that you come of a good family," he said, angrily, "but I beg you not to interfere with me in questions of honor and sentiment, of which you know nothing. And as for the war, only students and provincials believe there will be one."

"Don't you believe there will be a war?"

"There will be a war, but not the kind you think. With our government there's no need to be afraid."

Spina did not understand, so Fleet-foot explained.

"Everything the government does is for the benefit of the tourist industry," he said. "The town parks, the new monuments, the motor-roads, the trains that run on time, the whole thing is done to please the tourists. You are no longer allowed to spit or piss against the walls, or put your feet on the seats, or wipe your nose with your hands. And why have these sacrifices been imposed? To attract foreigners. Nevertheless, in spite of it all, the number of foreign tourists has been diminishing for some time. The hotel business has slumped. There is only one way left of bringing foreigners to our country—the heroic way of declaring war."

"What on earth makes you think that?" asked Spina.

"All along the Tyrrhenian, from the Riviera to Calabria, the government has been taking a census of all the available accommodations. I asked a friend of mine, an officer in the artillery, the reason for this. He told me it was a precautionary measure in case of a war with England. That makes the whole dodge clear. There is a slump in the tourist industry. There are few visitors to our seaside places. The government will declare war on a rich, honest, and unsuspecting people like the English. The English will be compelled to land on our shores. They will occupy all our best resorts. The hotel industry, the ice-cream industry, and the picture-postcard industry will boom. The government, with the help of the League of Nations, will try to protract the war as long as possible, so that our guests will remain with us indefinitely. When they have become thoroughly bored and want to go home, we shall show our hand and present the bill."

"Do you think the English will pay?"

"Of course. An English gentleman cannot leave a hotel without paying his bill. That is the reason why we shall have the war with England, who is our traditional friend, and not with Russia, for instance. Of course the Russians would come, too, and they would eat twice as much as the English, but not only would they not pay, but they would say they ought to be paid themselves. But with the English the trick is infallible."

Spina was uncertain whether Fleet-foot was not pulling his leg.

"After all," he said, "Italy is not a nation of defeatist lickspittles, but a people of serious workers. A war would be a horrible calamity, and the apathy with which the people are allowing themselves to be dragged into it is terrible to contemplate."

"Are you by any chance an opponent of the present government?" Fleet-foot asked.

Spina did not reply.

"No, you're only a provincial," Fleet-foot went on. "You're thinking of war, with dead and wounded. You do not realize that nowadays no one wants a bullet hole in his stomach. The dispute with England will probably end with a football match. Conceive, if you can, a football match here, in Rome, between the Arsenal of London and the Juventus of Turin, played in the presence of the two governments! Imagine how tourists would flock to see it. Conceive, if you can, what glory would redound to our country if the English were inclined to give a guarantee that they would allow themselves to be beaten!"

"Impossible!" Spina exclaimed. "The English would rather evacuate Malta and Egypt than allow themselves to be beaten at football."

"In that case it will be a hard match," Fleet-foot concluded.

Spina cut the discussion short on the pretext of being tired and wanting to go to sleep. In reality he wanted to think what to do next, now that his contact with Romeo was interrupted. He could not go back to Fossa without having done anything, without having found some one to help him ferret out the best elements of the dissolved peasants' leagues in the Marsica, to coöperate with him in his future work, and to act as a substitute for him in case of his arrest. Spina no longer insisted that his accomplice be a worker, so long as he was reliable. Romeo had spoken to him of a student, a certain Luigi Murica, who came from Rocca dei Marsi, as being intelligent and brave, and as having disappeared without trace some time ago. But how and where was he to find him? And even if he did find him, how was he to present himself to him and prove his authenticity? Spina once more felt the ground slipping away beneath his feet. The unnerving struggle with the shadows was beginning again.

Next day Spina sent the Monster to inquire discreetly after Murica. The Monster was out all day, but his search was fruitless. Murica was entered in the address register as having left Rome nearly a year before. It was therefore useless to go on looking for him.

Spina went to the Via Morosini, at Trastevere, to visit the

wife of Chelucci, the worker who had been rearrested a month previously, and, according to Romeo, had become nearly blind in prison. The woman knew Spina well, and was nervous at having him in her house. Her mother-in-law, an old peasant woman who had come from the Abruzzi as soon as she heard her son was in prison, was with her. She and her daughter-in-law were alone in the house. The daughter-in-law was a Milanese, a worker and the daughter of workers, and her mother-in-law was an illiterate peasant woman, but it was obvious at once that they got on well.

"Have you come on account of the relief?" the younger woman asked Spina.

"What relief?"

"The groups have suspended the small relief they pay to the wives of political prisoners. They told me my case was going to be discussed."

"Why? What have you done?"

The woman blushed and said:

"I go to Mass now."

"That's no reason for stopping your relief, and it certainly won't be stopped. . . . But why do you go to Mass now?"

The woman fumbled for words to begin her story, and then said:

"My husband is in prison, and I am not allowed to visit him. He is ill and I cannot send him a doctor. He is alone and almost blind. The first few days I dashed here, there, and everywhere, but with no result. There was nothing that could be done. His mother, whom I hardly knew, came here. We were together all day long. I was in despair and she was calm. She was with me from morning to night, and I saw her lips moving, praying for her son. I had never seen prayer in my family; it always seemed very stupid to me. But the old lady came and started praying for her son, and trying to help him that way. The first few days I stayed with her all day in silence, and she prayed and moved her lips, and sometimes she smiled at me, and sometimes tears came into her eyes. I just stayed with her and did nothing. Then I saw that at bottom she was doing, or trying to do, something for her son. I saw that she was sustaining him, or trying to sustain him, while I, his wife, was doing nothing and had abandoned him. One evening I couldn't stand it any longer, and I asked her to show me how to pray. She showed me, and now we pray together. Together we try to help him. I'm sure you'll laugh at us."

"Have you ever heard of a student from the Abruzzi, named Luigi Murica?" Spina asked.

"He disappeared nearly a year ago," the woman replied. "Annina Pecci knows where he is. She used to be very friendly with him. She's a friend of mine, a dressmaker."

Spina asked the woman for the dressmaker's address.

"Since Murica disappeared Annina lives in seclusion and has even retired from her group," Chelucci's wife said. "But I shall tell her about you. Her room is on the fourth floor right under the roof, and if you see a pot of geraniums in the window it will mean she expects you."

The dressmaker lived in the Via della Lungaretta, also at Trastevere. Spina went three or four times and looked up at the window, expecting to see the geranium pot, but it did not appear. In the end he lost patience and went up. He found Annina Pecci bent over her sewing-machine in a small, untidy room, which was both bedroom and workshop.

"Chelucci's wife will have mentioned me to you," Spina said "I have come for news of Murica."

The girl looked at the intruder in indignation and surprise. She was very young, and had sharp, delicate, fresh features, and her eyes were beautiful in spite of her anger. Spina remained at the door, in some confusion, until the girl offered him a seat. Now that he was near her, she looked at him with a sad smile, which betrayed a sudden emotion that she could not altogether conceal.

"Do you know there is a strange resemblance between you and the man you are looking for?" she said. "You even resemble him in your rude way of paying visits. Besides, he was born at Rocca dei Marsi, which I think is not very far from where you were born."

"Less than ten kilometers," said Spina. "Where is he now?"

"He used to speak of you," the girl went on. "He often said he was sorry he did not know you. But the life of the groups was so split up that it was difficult to get to know people."

"How long since you have seen him?"

"It's nearly a year now. Several people have come and asked for him since then."

"Might he be in prison?"

"No," the girl answered, positively. "He was arrested last year and was in prison for a few months, and when he came out he swore he would kill himself rather than ever go to prison again."

Footsteps were heard on the staircase. A little girl came in with a dress to be mended and went away again.

"Have you known Murica long?" Spina asked.

This question worked a wave of memories that broke down all the girl's self-control.

"We met in the group about three years ago, and liked each other at once," the girl said, blushing to the roots of her hair. "It wasn't just love, it was madness. I was still living with my family then, and my mother always grumbled at me, and rightly because I forgot everything, and had no concern for anything in the world but him. It is difficult to describe what it was like. He was my son, my brother, my father, my husband, and my lover, all at the same time. I could not imagine that I would ever be able to live without him. He was very fond of me, too."

The girl turned her back to her guest and moved away to hide her tears. When she came back and sat down again in front of her sewing-machine her eyes were red.

"I do not want to remind you of things you have forgotten," said Spina.

"It's not a case of anything forgotten," the girl said. "I have the painful memory always before my eyes, and it will not go. It has become the master of my life."

"Listen," said Spina. "We revolutionaries are few and weak. Against us there is a whole world of self-interest and fear. To hold out and not allow ourselves to be annihilated we must concentrate our energies, support each other in every way we can. Instead, we waste our best strength on sentimental stupidities."

"Our friendship did not in any way diminish our participation in the work of the group," the girl said. "On the contrary, we were among the most active. We organized excursions and reading evenings, and chose novels dealing with social questions for the discussions. We even gave up marrying, setting up house, and having children, in order to have more time for the group."

"I can imagine the rest," said Spina. "Love faded, and with it all interest in the group."

The girl's mind was elsewhere and she did not hear Spina's interruption.

"This is the first time I have told this story," she said. "But you come from the same region, you resemble him, you probably think as he does, and have the same faults. I can tell the story of our calamity to you. When he was in prison last year he was beaten a great deal, but what affected him more than the blows was the moral outrage—having his face slapped and being spat upon. When he came out of prison he was unnerved and depressed. I attributed it to physical weakness, but the weeks passed, and the thought of the police and the possibility of being arrested again still preyed on his mind. 'Rather than go back to prison I'll kill myself,' he used to say. The police had warned him to break off all his old contacts, including his friendship with me, because I was politically suspect too. So when he was with me he was always nervous. The noise of a motor-car in the street would make him blanch. We were at a loss where to meet each other. He still loved me, wanted to be often with me, was furiously jealous if he did not see me for two days, but since he was in danger whenever he was with me, it made him almost hate me, too. Our meetings were no longer care-free as they had been before. 'The police might surprise us at any moment,' he would say. Even his physique was affected, and he suffered from all sorts of complaints, with his heart, and his digestion, and he got any number of gray hairs. A policeman often came here to look for him. He was from Apulia, had red hair, and he would come at the most unlikely hours, preferably at night when I was in bed. He wanted me more than he wanted Murica. Several times I had to defend myself by force, and in the end I invited a cousin of mine to sleep with me for safety's sake. On Christmas Day last year I had lunch with Murica at a restaurant outside the Porta San Paolo. He was in an unusually calm and good mood, almost care-free, as he had been in the old days. It had been a long time since we had been alone together, and I asked him to come back to my room for the afternoon. We bought flowers, fruit, sweets, and a bottle of Marsala on the way. He was helping me to arrange the flowers in a vase when there was a sudden knock at the door, which I had locked. 'Who is it?' I called out. 'Police!' was the answer. Murica sat down on a chair to prevent himself from falling, and signed to me not to open the door. But the knocks became more and more violent. 'I shan't go back to prison,' Murica muttered. 'I'll throw myself out of the window, but I shan't go back to prison!' Meanwhile the police had nearly broken the door in. That balcony leads on to a little terrace, and it's easy to climb from the terrace on to the roof; so I told Murica to hide on the roof. As soon as he had disappeared I opened the door. Two policemen came in, the one from Apulia and another whom I did not know. They knew my friend was with me, because they had seen us coming home together. They looked under the bed and in the wardrobe. The one from Apulia said, 'If he isn't in the room he must be on the roof.' I barred the way to the balcony. 'You won't arrest him! You won't arrest him!' I started screaming. The policemen tried to get me out of the way by force, but I fought them with my hands, my teeth, and my feet. 'You won't arrest him!' I screamed. 'On one condition we won't arrest him,' the police-man from Apulia said. 'I'll give you any condition you like,' I said. I would willingly have given my life to save Murica from prison, but the policemen wanted something else. They took me, put me on the bed, and stripped me. I do not know how long they remained. Much later I remember hearing Murica's voice from behind the half-closed balcony shutters. 'Have they gone?' he asked. He came into the room. 'What are you doing?' he asked. 'Are you asleep?' He went over to the window and looked out into the street to see if the house was being watched. 'There's no one in the street,' he said. He took a biscuit from the table and ate it. He went over to the door and listened to find out if anyone was on the staircase. Then he came over to me. 'What are you doing?' he asked again. 'Are you asleep?' I was covered with a sheet, and he uncovered me. He saw I was naked, and on the sheet he saw the traces of the two men who had gone. He made a grimace of disgust. 'Whore!' he said, and spat on the bed. He swept all the things we had bought for Christmas off the table and on to the floor. He upset the sewing-machine, threw the bottle of Marsala at the big mirror, and smashed it to fragments. Then he went away. I did not move and did not speak. What had happened had happened."

The girl stopped. A man's footsteps were heard coming up the staircase. Spina got up and said:

"If it's the policeman from Apulia, this time it will be you who will go out on the terrace, and I shall throw him out of the window."

It was not the policeman, however, but a messenger from a fashion house which sent its work out. The messenger handed in a parcel and went away.

"The policeman from Apulia has had the prudence not to show his face here again. His colleague has not appeared, either. Once or twice I thought I saw them in the distance in the street, but they moved off immediately."

"What do you think has become of Murica?" Spina asked.

"He is sure to have gone to his home at Rocca dei Marsi."

"Haven't you ever thought of finding him and trying to talk to him?"

"What has happened has happened," the girl replied.

"I shall go and talk to him," said Spina.

Spina went back to his refuge in the Via dei Marsi and was received by Fleet-foot with open arms.

"You have been sent by Providence," he exclaimed. "Listen. Today I saved not one but two foreign women from the wiles of the Monster Outside the Gates, while they were walking on the Palatine. They are mother and daughter."

"Where do they come from?"

"I don't know, but they are blonde, very blonde indeed," Fleet-foot replied. "They must be Germans or Norwegians. They told me they came from Copenhagen, which must be in one or other of those countries. They are very grateful to me, very grateful indeed. They will be here directly, and you'll see them. I shall need your help."

Spina did not comprehend.

"I'll look after the daughter, and you will do me the favor of looking after the mother."

"How old is the mother?"

"Age is of no importance," Fleet-foot replied. "Experience is far more important. Besides, she is very young-looking, as you will see for yourself. People from that part of the world live entirely on cod-liver oil, so you can imagine what she's like. Old hens make good soup."

Fleet-foot proceeded to give a whole series of recipes for making soup of old hens while Spina considered his own problems: whether to go back to the Abruzzi at once, look for Murica, and put him in touch with Pompeo, or to wait and see Romeo again and go on searching for some suitable worker in Rome.

The two women from Copenhagen arrived with their arms full of presents. The older woman was a living and walking advertisement for cod-liver oil. The younger one still had plaits down her back and did not look more than fifteen. The older woman said she had come to Rome because she was interested in archæology.

"My friend here is a well-known professor of archæology," said Fleet-foot.

The older woman also said that she was very fond of country walks.

"My friend here is a celebrated excursionist," Fleet-foot announced.

The girl said she was fond of flowers, was learning Latin, and knew some lines of Virgil by heart.

"Flowers and Virgil are my passions," Fleet-foot said. "What would life be without flowers and Virgil?"

The conversation continued on the same level. At one point the older woman apologized for not yet having mentioned that she had been to the police station to report the Monster Outside the Gates, and had given her rescuer's address, so that he might be suitably rewarded by the authorities.

"A policeman will be here directly for more details about the Monster," she said.

Spina picked up his bag and his hat and made for the door.

"I'm going to buy some cigarettes," he said. "I shall be back directly."

From the Via dei Marsi he went down the Via degli Ernici and walked straight on. At the Porta San Lorenzo he had a feeling that some one had recognized him and was following him, but he kept on walking straight ahead, hoping to be able to jump on a tram in motion as soon as he got a chance. At the Piazzale Tiburtino he summoned a taxi and heard some one behind him whistling a song he knew.

> Never a rose without a thorn,
> Never a woman without a kiss . . .

The taxi was free and Spina jumped into it with Romeo.

"To Portonaccio," Romeo said.

Before reaching Portonaccio station he stopped the taxi and dismissed it.

"Do you know about the explosion in the Via Panisperna?" Romeo asked Spina.

Spina did not.

"Uliva's flat blew up, burying him and his wife and the lodgers on the floor below. The papers have been given orders to say nothing about it, because it wouldn't harmonize with the press campaign now going on in preparation for the war, and would be liable to cast doubts on our much-vaunted national unity. But the explosion took place in the center of the city, and the news of it spread like lightning. Uliva seems to have been preparing an enormous attempt to blow up the church of Santa Maria degli Angeli at a ceremony which the whole government is going to attend in the next few days. A fireman friend of ours who helped clear away the débris reports that a big plan of the church was found among Uliva's papers, with a lot of technical notes."

"I went to see him two days ago," Spina said. "I thought he was preparing a big funeral."

"If the porter saw you go in, he's bound to remember you," said Romeo. "You've got a face that isn't easily forgotten. That's another reason why you should go away."

The two men jumped over a fence into a sandpit. When they re-emerged in the Via Tiburtina, Pietro Spina had become Don Paolo Spada again. He went straight to the station to take the train to the Abruzzi. There was a big crowd outside the station, and groups of soldiers, militia, and carabinieri.

"What is happening?" Don Paolo asked.

"Mobilization takes place tomorrow. The war begins tomorrow," some one told him.

Tomorrow? There had been talk of war for some time. But just because it had been spoken of so much, it had come to appear improbable and strange. Now the improbable was about to happen; or, rather, it was already behind the curtain, and tomorrow it would make its appearance on the stage.

Chapter IX

DON PAOLO spent the night at Avezzano and continued his journey to Fossa by the first train next morning. His compartment was crowded with young men who had been called up. Two gentlemen wearing government party emblems in their buttonholes were talking of the war. The other travelers listened in silence.

"With the new invention at our army's disposal, it will be over in a few weeks," one of them said. "The death ray will pulverize the enemy."

"The bishop is going to bless the Avezzano conscripts today," said the other. "The death ray will open the way for the Pope's missionaries."

Sitting among the youthful conscripts was an old peasant with a concertina. His son was asleep, with his head on his father's shoulder. "Play us a tune," his neighbors said, but the old man shook his head, for he did not want to miss the conversation of the two gentlemen who were talking about the war and the mysterious death ray. Both gentlemen had shotguns with them, and full cartridge-belts, and they were going to the Fucino to shoot quail.

"The quail were late this year," one of them said. "But they are fatter than last year."

"There's always a compensation!" the other replied, and laughed. His laughter indicated that he had uttered what was intended to be a witty remark, so his neighbors, a trifle late, started laughing, too, in order not to seem stupid.

The train stopped at every little station and more conscripts got in. Nearly all of them smelled of drink and of the stable.

Those for whom there was no room on the seats lay down on the carriage floor. Among them, besides peasants, there must have been builders, mechanics, artisans, but it was impossible to distinguish between them. Poverty had made them all look alike. They all looked ragged young paupers, with bodies molded by generations of famine, scarred by inhuman toil, deformed, tattooed, marked and marked again, by unemployment, alcohol, and epidemics. A few took pieces of corn bread from their bags and ate. The old man with the concertina passed around a bottle of wine. The wine gurgled noisily down their parched throats. "Play us something," his neighbors asked the old man, but again he shook his head.

Don Paolo was curled up in a corner of the compartment. His ancient, battered hat, his old, worn, and torn cassock made him look like a poor old priest from a mountain parish, but his burning, feverish eyes were inwardly fixed on something new. He was eager for danger, determined to break the unanimity which stupidity and fear had created. By many small signs he was able to distinguish the inhabitants of the villages, those of the plain, those who had descended from their shepherds' huts; people whose capacity for suffering was without limit, people inured to isolation, ignorance, and suspicion, to sterile hatred between family and family, to being cheated in isolation, exploited in isolation, insulted in isolation, made miserable in isolation. And now the government bureaucracy, on the brink of bankruptcy, was about to resort to the bloody diversion of war. But to do this it had to conscript them, bring them out of their isolation and make them combine. It had to mobilize them and put arms into their hands. One knew how mobilizations of the hungry and poverty-stricken began; how they ended no man could foretell.

Every time Don Paolo thought he recognized some one from Orta, his native place, in the crowd of travelers, he hid his face behind his breviary and lowered his hat over his eyes. His eyes fell upon the words *Venit hora mea*. He looked at his neighbors and smiled. Perhaps, slaves, our hour is approaching, he repeated to himself.

The country the train passed through was no longer his old
Marsica, but a new and strange country. It was the Land of
Propaganda. Government party war slogans were everywhere,
on the train, on the stations, on the telegraph poles, on walls,
pavements, trees, public lavatories, church towers, garden gates,
bridge parapets, schools, and barracks. Everything belonging to
ordinary, humble, everyday life that was able to peep through
the rhetorical, artificial landscape that had been superimposed
on it looked tamer, more intimidated, more resigned than ever.
Fossa was completely unrecognizable beneath its multicolored
decorations, its announcements of meetings, its festoons, flags,
slogans lauding war and massacre, scrawled in white lead, var-
nish, lime, tar, or charcoal on every wall. The Girasole Hotel
had become the mobilization center of local good society.

Berenice was in a great state of excitement, but she had
time to kiss Don Paolo's hands effusively and wish him welcome.

"What good fortune to have you here on this glorious day!"
she said.

There was a continual coming and going of youths and men
in the dining-room and on the stairs. A group of men wearing
the government party emblem were sitting round a table, discussing the arrangements for the spontaneous and enthusiastic
demonstration due to take place in the afternoon. They were
already hoarse from an excess of talking, and it was their business to take rigid precautions to secure the spontaneous and
enthusiastic participation of the whole population of Fossa and
the surrounding country.

"Shall we send lorries to Pietrasecca as well?" one of them
asked.

"Of course," another replied. "And we must send carabinieri
with the lorries, so that the population will understand that
they have got to come spontaneously."

At another table a number of sleek, plump, and well-fed gentlemen were heatedly discussing the menu for the evening's banquet, under the artistic direction of Zabaglione. Zabaglione was
so excited that he did not notice Don Paolo's arrival. A grave

difference of opinion had arisen, a difference on a matter of high principle, and the excitable Zabaglione ended by making it a question of personal prestige.

"I swear," he cried, "I swear to you on my honor, on my wife's honor, and my daughters' innocence, that if white wine is served before red I shall leave the banquet!"

"That is blackmail!" other members of the committee shouted indignantly.

But Zabaglione folded his arms and stuck to his point.

"Principles are principles," he declared.

The voluntary enlistment committee was in session in Berenice's bedroom on the first floor. Those of its members who did not have chairs were sitting or lying full length on the landlady's bed. Her pillows were elegantly embroidered, with the words "Happy Dreams" in the center of the pattern. Over the head of the bed was a colored print of a guardian angel caressing a dove. The mobilization of the paupers and the hungry at Fossa also involved the mobilization of the insolvent. The directors of the Fossa Bank had asked to be sent to Africa to forestall their trial for fraudulent bankruptcy, and their patriotic example had been widely followed. The haberdasher in the public square opposite the Girasole Hotel had failed and been compelled to put up his shutters, but that morning he had reopened, put his wife behind the counter and a large notice outside the shop, saying "Creditors are informed that the proprietor of this shop has voluntarily enlisted." Henceforward no authority would dare decree the sequestration of the goods of a war hero. . . .

"This is a mortgage war!" the tax-office clerk remarked, running his eye down the list of volunteers.

Don Senofonte, the chemist, was looking for his son everywhere. He could not find him. He would have good reason to despair if everybody else's son volunteered and his did not, for he, too, had bills that would soon be falling due. Should he have to pay them through his son's fault?

"Have you seen Pompeo?" he anxiously asked everyone he met. "Where on earth can he be? If I find him and he hasn't volunteered, I'll shoot him, as God is my witness!"

Don Paolo also wanted to see Pompeo. He wanted to discuss with him what ought to be done to transform the war against the peasantry of Abyssinia into a civil war for liberty. He said nothing to Don Pompeo's father, but went to look for him at the Villa delle Stagioni. It was silent and deserted. Near the pool he found Bianchina, alone. She was singing to herself, and playing with some paper boats. When the girl saw him she leapt to her feet and embraced him.

"Where is Pompeo?" he asked.

"He's gone to Rome," Bianchina said. "He was sent for."

"Who sent for him?"

Bianchina did not know for certain.

"It must be for the second revolution, I suppose," she said.

"Where is Alberto?"

"At Pietrasecca, with his family. He left me because he was jealous of Pompeo."

"Where is the cowherd?"

"At the moment he's taking the baroness out in the carriage."

"What baroness?"

Bianchina told what sounded like a story out of a popular illustrated magazine about the baroness of the Villa delle Stagioni. At the age of sixteen, on leaving her convent school, the baroness had been married to a baron burdened with years, the most varied debts, and assorted diseases. The baron had received a fatal pistol-shot in a duel, and the baroness, being still young and pretty, had gone on living gaily in the city. But now she was reduced to poverty, and had taken refuge here, in company with her lover, an old man who had been a colonel in the Piedmontese cavalry and was said to have taken part in the Crimean War, and who treated her as though she were an army mare. The cowherd had fixed up a room for them on the first floor. It contained a large bed that had a canopy adorned with a baronial crown. But since the roof had not been repaired for many years, the rain came in. Thus the canopy was not purely for decorative purposes, since in bad weather it served to protect the baroness and her colonel from the rain.

"If they would only sleep," Bianchina added.

"Do they suffer from insomnia?" Don Paolo asked.

"Every night the colonel kicks up such a row that it reminds me of the Turco-Russian War as it was described to us at school"; said Bianchina. "It doesn't worry me, but the cowherd suffers from it terribly."

"Let us leave these stupidities," Don Paolo said. "I have a great favor to ask of you."

Bianchina made a graceful bow.

"*Ecce ancilla Domini*," she said. "Behold, thy handmaiden is waiting."

Don Paolo asked Bianchina to go to Rocca dei Marsi and find a certain Luigi Murica.

"Tell him an acquaintance of his from Rome would like to see him," he said. "Ask if he will come. You mustn't tell him anything else, even if he tries to make you."

Bianchina went off to Rocca and Don Paolo returned to the Girasole Hotel.

As the hour approached for the radio broadcast proclaiming the outbreak of war, the crowds swarming in the streets became denser and denser. The authorities arrived from the right, and the peasants from the left. From the right came motorcycles, motor cars, lorries loaded with police, carabinieri, militia, officials of the government party and the corporations. From the left came donkeys, carts, bicycles, and lorries full of peasants. Two bands marched and countermarched over and over again, *ad nauseam*. Most of the bandsmen were workers, dressed up in the uniforms of animal-tamers at the circus or porters in big hotels, with double rows of metal buttons across their chests. Outside a barber's shop was a huge placard portraying Abyssinian women, with long breasts hanging down to their knees; a crowd of boys were laughing and staring at it with greedy eyes.

Peasants, small landowners, charcoal-burners, shepherds, kept pouring in from the left; representatives of the government party continued to arrive from the right. A loud-speaker, adorned with flags, had been set up at the end of the public square, between the government party offices and the town hall. From it would issue the voice that would proclaim the outbreak of war. As the people arrived they packed themselves round that small magical instrument, on which the country's destiny depended. The women squatted as at church or at market, the men sat on the packs or saddles of their donkeys. Everyone knew the reason for this gathering, and cast furtive glances at the small mechanical object from which the announcement of war would come; but, finding themselves all together like this, they felt sad, bewildered, and doubtful. By now the square and the adjacent streets were packed with people, but the influx from the surrounding countryside still went on, silently and steadily. The general mobilization of poverty and hunger went on. The lame came from the quarries, the blind from the smelting-furnaces, the bent and halting from the fields. The men of the hills came, with their hands red from the sulphur and the lime, and the men of the mountains, with their legs bowed from the labor of mowing. Each man was ready to come because his neighbor was. Should the war bring misfortune, it would be misfortune for all, and therefore only half misfortune. But should it bring fortune, one would have to secure one's share in it. And so they all came, leaving the pressing of the grapes, the cleaning of the vats, the preparation of the seeds, and crowded into the town. The inhabitants of Pietrasecca came, too, and were unloaded and dumped at the side of the Girasole Hotel. The schoolmistress told them all what to do, what to shout, and what to sing, but her voice was drowned out in the general confusion. Sciatàp lost patience.

"Leave us alone," he shouted. "We're not children. I've been to America!"

Don Paolo talked to Magascià and old Gerametta about what had happened at Pietrasecca since his departure. Magascià started by describing the death of Don Pasquale Colamartini.

"You remember the day he went down to Fossa with you, sir," he said. "That night he came home dead. The mare, Diana, brought his dead body in the trap right up to the house. Several people passed him in the valley and greeted him on his way home, but nobody noticed he was dead. As a matter of fact, he was sitting a little crookedly, and his head was on his chest, as if he were asleep, and he was still clutching the reins."

"Another old family come to a bad end, ruined by the bank," Gerametta observed.

"Mastrangelo broke his leg," Magascià went on. "He slipped and fell one night coming out of the house of his brother-in-law, Nicola Ciccavo. He thought it was only a sprain, but as the pain didn't go he was brought down here to Fossa to see a doctor, who said he really had broken it. It was too late to mend it, so now he's lame."

The peasants of Pietrasecca waited in silence for the ceremony to begin. The women were more impatient and inquisitive than the men. Gesira suggested that the women should go to church "before the machine started talking," but Filomena Sapone and Annina Stradone were against it, for fear of losing their places, but as the other women went, they went, too. Meanwhile the men passed round a bottle of wine and drank out of it noisily.

"What time will it start talking?" Giacinto Campobasso asked Don Paolo, pointing to the magic instrument.

"I don't know," the priest replied. "I think it may start any minute now."

This piece of news was passed from mouth to mouth, and the silence and tension increased.

Cassarola, the wise-woman, had been unwilling to climb down from Magascià's cart, which was drawn by Bersagliera. The women came back from the church and tried to make her.

"Come down here!" they called out. "Come and sit with us!"

The sorceress did not even answer, but continued staring fixedly at the sky. Every now and then she softly repeated her grim prophecy.

"There's a yellow comet in the sky," she said. "There will be war and then there will be pestilence."

The other women were unable to see the yellow comet, but they all made the sign of the Cross.

"Which saint ought we to pray to?" Gesira asked.

"Prayer is no use," the wise-woman said. "God reigns over

the earth, the waters, and the sky, but the yellow comet comes from beyond the sky."

Sciatàp offered her the bottle of wine. She put it to her lips and drank. Then she spat and resumed her sky-gazing. Magascià got into the cart and whispered in her ear.

"Tell me the truth," he said. "What can you really see?"

"A yellow comet," she said. "There will be war and then there will be pestilence."

Girls circulated among the nervous and anxious crowd, carrying baskets of tricolor cockades. Don Paolo recognized Zabaglione's three daughters among them. They came towards him and pinned a cockade on his breast. They were perspiring, breathless, and excited.

"Oh, padre!" they said. "What a wonderful day! What an unforgettable day!"

A sudden movement of the crowd, caused by an influx of new arrivals who wanted a view of the loud-speaker, carried the girls out of sight.

Peasants flocked in from the most distant villages. Shepherds with goatskin trousers, sandals on their feet, and gold ear-rings appeared, offset by Don Concettino Ragù, in the uniform of an officer of militia.

To avoid the risk of being recognized by his former schoolfellow, Don Paolo retired to his room on the second floor of the hotel. He hid behind the shutters, from which point he could watch the crowd and the rest of the ceremony. A memory of his childhood came to his mind. He had been looking out of the window of his own home, just as he was now, when the street had been suddenly invaded by a long procession of ragged pilgrims, chanting the praises of the Blessed Virgin. The pilgrims had come from afar and still had far to go, and the greater part of them were barefooted and covered with sweat and dust; and he remembered the fear and revulsion with which his childish mind had been filled at that sad spectacle. Looked at from the second floor, the assembly around the magic instrument below resembled a gathering of poor, tired, and anxious pilgrims at the shrine of a miracle-working idol. From his hiding-place Don

Paolo could see two or three church towers over the house tops. The bell towers were packed with boys, like dovecotes with pigeons. All at once the bells began to ring. Members of the government party made their way through the crowd and placed patriotic fetishes around the magic instrument—tricolors, pendants, flags, and an image of the Great Chief, with jaw protruding in an exaggerated manner. Members of the government party emitted barbaric cries of "Eià! Eià!," cries devoid of all intelligible significance, while the mass remained silent.

A space near the magic instrument was cleared for the "mothers of the fallen," a number of poor old women who had been wearing mourning for fifteen years, and were decorated with medals, and condemned, in return for a small pension, to hold themselves at the disposal of the marshal of the carabinieri on all occasions when the dictatorship might need them for propaganda purposes. The parish priests of the neighboring villages, affable old priests, gloomy-looking priests, athletic and impressive-looking priests, and one pink-and-white canon who looked like a well-nourished wet-nurse, and was chatting with Don Girasole, were placed next to the "mothers of the fallen." A number of country landlords, with unkempt beards and shaggy eyebrows, clothed in hunter's velvet, had collected outside the town hall. The clerks—that is, the members of the government party—were gathered in the middle of the square. With them was a solitary woman, Donna Evangelina, with her carpenter husband, whom she had forced to enlist voluntarily.

"Not only did she find a father for her natural son," said Berenice, "but what a father! A hero!"

"Donna Evangelina was born to be a war widow," Don Senofonte observed. "She won't be happy till she's in mourning and wearing a medal."

The bells went on chiming, the boys taking turns at pulling the ropes. People in the crowd signaled to them to stop, so as not to interfere with the imminent broadcast, but the boys either did not understand or pretended not to. At least a dozen bells were being rung simultaneously, with might and main, and the streets were filled with their clangor. Militiamen appeared in

the nearest bell towers and tried to make the boys leave the
ropes, but as the bells in other towers did not stop, the boys resumed their ringing as soon as the militiamen had gone down
again, so as not to be left out of it. The first hoarse mutterings
of the magic apparatus passed unnoticed; but a loud shout arose
from the groups of carabinieri, militia, and members of the government party, a rhythmical cry, an impassioned invocation of
the Great Chief. ". . . CHAY DOO! CHAY DOO! CHAY! DOO!
CHAY DOO! . . ." This chant was slowly taken up, first by
the women and boys, but gradually it spread until the whole
mass of people, even those farthest away and those looking out
of the windows, had taken up the melancholy hieratic refrain:
". . . CHAY DOO! CHAY DOO! CHAY DOO! CHAY DOO!
CHAY DOO! CHAY DOO! CHAY DOO! CHAY DOO! . . ."
That name which nobody dared pronounce privately, either in
praise or blame, because to name it brought misfortune, they
now shouted with all the force of their lungs in this general
gathering, in the presence of his feared image, in the presence of
the patriotic fetishes, as a piece of propitiatory magic, in a kind
of religious frenzy. ". . . CHAY DOO! CHAY DOO! CHAY
DOO! CHAY DOO! CHAY DOO! . . ." Those nearest the loud-
speaker motioned to the crowd to be silent, so that the speech
from Rome might be heard, but the people massed in the adjacent streets went on intoning the magic invocation, calling
on the Great Chief, the Witch-doctor, the Thaumaturge, who
disposed of their blood and their future. The shouting of the
crowd, with the added confusion of the ringing of the church
bells, made the speech that came over the wireless completely
inaudible to Don Paolo. Below, at one corner of the hotel, he
saw the women of Pietrasecca prostrate on the ground, and the
men gathered round Magascià's cart shouting the propitiatory
syllables just like the rest of the crowd: ". . . . CHAY DOO!
CHAY DOO! CHAY DOO! CHAY DOO! CHAY DOO! . . ."
Cassarola, sitting in the cart above the level of the crowd, was
still gazing fixedly at the sky. From time to time she moved her
lips, and there was an expression of mysterious anguish on her
darkened countenance. Meanwhile the cries of those about her

rose to a deafening, frenzied, hysterical, delirious clamor:
". . . CHAY DOO! CHAY DOO! CHAY DOO! CHAY DOO!
CHAY DOO! . . ." The whole crowd was now shouting, including those near the loud-speaker, the militia and the carabinieri
and the other officials; they were all convinced now of the utter
impossibility of attempting to understand a word of the speech
being broadcast from Rome. The rhythmical cry of "CHAY
DOO! CHAY DOO!" hammered the air with the dirge-like
monotony of penitents imploring mercy of a wrathful god. The
two syllables ended by losing all ordinary, intelligible significance,
and sounded like the incantation of a magical formula, chanted
to the accompaniment of the sacred music of the bells.

From behind his shutters Don Paolo watched the scene in
trepidation. There came to his mind the fear he had once felt
when he had attended a séance, an experiment in collective hyp-
notism, when he was a boy; the fear he had always experienced,
even in later years, whenever he was faced with any manifesta-
tion of the primitive and irrational forces that lie dormant in
individuals and in the mass. How was one to reason with poor
people who had fallen under the spell of a hypnotic wizard?

Those nearest the loud-speaker made signs to show that the
broadcast was over.

"War is declared!" Zabaglione shouted, and indicated that he
was about to make a speech.

But his raucous voice was drowned by the rhythmical clamor
of the crowd, which went on intoning: ". . . CHAY DOO!
CHAY DOO! CHAY DOO! CHAY DOO! . . ." The radio was
silent. No one had heard three words of the whole transmission.
No one had really tried to listen. No one really minded not having heard; for in reality there was no need for anyone to understand what had been said, nor had there been anything to understand. He who had spoken into the microphone had not thought
of explaining, of persuading, or trying to convince. In the Land
of Propaganda everything is presented as being indisputably self-
evident. The poor people in the street were caught in the Land
of Propaganda like fishes in a net. There was little to understand.
The net was there. For the fish the net was a reality, the only

reality that counted. Whether the Propaganda was right or wrong was a problem for idle brains. But for the poor peasant, things were like that, *a priori,* and not otherwise. The man looking through the shutters, with a foreign passport in his pocket, might think the Propaganda was fictitious, artificial, and abstract, relying for its prestige in the poor people's eyes on an irresistible hypnotic force. But the poor people were not up there behind the shutters, but down in the street. Down in the street things looked different. If one man shouted, all the others shouted. If one man raised his arm in the Roman salute, his neighbor raised both arms, to go him one better. Everyone within the net of Propaganda sought a little security for himself. Everyone sought recommendations, influence, and that was all that mattered. What the Propaganda said was only of secondary importance. It was therefore useless to attempt to refute it; it was useless trying to discuss it. Don Paolo's arms sank to his sides. What could he do? If it was impossible to talk to these poor people, because talking was a secondary thing, the primary thing being living (no matter whether living well or ill, but living), it would be necessary to act. But how? Where was he to begin? With whom? Don Paolo calculated how long it ought to take Bianchina to go to Rocca, find Murica, talk to him, and return to Fossa with a reply. If Murica's reply was satisfactory, he would go to Rocca at once, abandon his priest's clothing on the way, and discuss with him what ought to be done. In the meantime Pompeo might have returned from Rome. He would talk to the cowherd, and it might be possible to get Alberto to come down from Pietrasecca. Thus all his hopes depended on the young. The masses will be awakened by deeds, he said to himself.

"There will be war, and then there will be pestilence," the wise-woman was repeating from the top of Magascià's cart.

"The war will do it for us," Don Paolo said. "And if the war isn't sufficient, the pestilence will do it!"

The crowd's chanting was suddenly interrupted by the noise of motors being started up. The automobiles and motorcycles of the authorities made a way through the throng and departed for the local capital. When Don Paolo saw that Concettino Ragù had taken his departure, he left his refuge and went down into the street.

Zabaglione received him with open arms.

"Did you see my daughters?" he asked, with pride. "Did you see them distributing cockades? They were completely transfigured by patriotic emotion."

"They were as lovely as angels!" Don Paolo said.

Zabaglione blushed and was visibly moved by this compliment.

"I have talked of you to the bishop, and I hope I may have helped you," Don Paolo added. At that Zabaglione wanted to kiss him.

"My dear friend," he said, "my dear friend. I have heard you spoken of as a saint, but I did not know there were any saints as kind as you in the Church."

The lawyer took the priest by the arm and led him home through the beflagged streets.

Zabaglione's wife opened the door. She was pale and trembling.

"Kiss the father's hand and leave us alone," said Zabaglione. His wife curtsied and kissed Don Paolo's hand.

"The girls have not come home yet," she said, before withdrawing.

Zabaglione frowned.

"Send the maid out to look for them at once," he said.

In the dining-room Zabaglione offered the priest wine.

"Why did the Lord chastise me?" he asked the priest. "Why did he give me daughters and not sons? At this hour they would already be in Africa. For want of sons I have made my clients volunteer before their cases come on. Most of them won't be accepted for service, but the gesture remains."

The priest looked at him good-naturedly, as though to say that, between friends, semi-official language was more appropriate than official language.

"The war will be a hard one," he suggested.

"Even if it comes to the worst, we shall gain something," the lawyer replied. "Our country has expanded as the result of every war, particularly as the result of every defeat. The defeats of

Custozza, Novara, Lissa, Adowa, Caporetto, have made Italy great. If we lose this time, too, we shall certainly get something out of it to console ourselves with. But if we win . . . the Lord protect us from England! I say so, of course, semi-officially, between ourselves."

"I noticed that you wished to make a speech after the broadcast," the priest said.

"That was in the program, but the popular enthusiasm made it impossible," the lawyer replied. "Besides, I was only going to introduce the official speaker, a certain Concettino Ragù, who was to have spoken on 'the resurrection of the Roman tradition among the rural masses.' He gave me his speech to read beforehand, and a proper schoolboy's farrago it was."

"The crowd didn't miss much," Don Paolo remarked. "If the peasants allow themselves to be mobilized for war, it is not in homage to Roman tradition."

Annoyance at not having been chosen as the official orator still rankled in the lawyer's breast. He was pleased at having some one to whom he could unburden himself.

"Between ourselves, as between friends," Zabaglione said, "all this about the Roman tradition is sheer nonsense. In our part of the world, and throughout southern Italy, where the Roman tradition ought to be strongest, there is no trace of it whatever. Our only traditions are Bourbon, and Spanish, on a basis of Christian legend. All you hear, if you listen to our old people, is talk of calamities, famines, the cholera, hangings, and saintly miracles. There was no Roman influence here even in Roman times. The religion, language, alphabet, customs, race of the people who lived in this part of the world were entirely different from those of Latium. The only event of antiquity that left any trace in popular tradition was the Social War against Rome, which the Italic peoples fought under the direction of the Marsi. Its memory is still associated with terrible catastrophes; women gave birth to mice, statues sweated blood, fruit trees became sterile as a result of the Roman victory. These cannot be said to be happy memories."

In the warmth of his feelings Zabaglione had let himself go, and feared he had overstepped the mark. But Don Paolo reassured him.

"I permitted myself to speak of you to Monsignore and to recommend you highly to him," he said, "just because I appreciate your sincere and unprejudiced way of expressing yourself. By the way, do you imagine that there may be any subversive elements among the peasants who are opposed to the war?"

"Poor people!" Zabaglione said. "The peasants haven't got enough to eat. How can you expect them to take any interest in politics? Politics are a luxury reserved for the well fed. Nevertheless, among the young some disloyal elements do exist. . . ."

Don Paolo thought of Murica, Pompeo, and the cowherd. It also occurred to him that Bianchina might have returned from Rocca dei Marsi by now. So he quickly bade the lawyer good-by and hurried to the Villa delle Stagioni. On entering the park he thought he saw a girl lying in the straw beside the peacocks' cage. Slowly he drew near, and discovered a little too late that it was not Bianchina, but one of Zabaglione's daughters, with a soldier. Warned by this experience, when he saw two girls talking to two soldiers on the other side of the Temple of Venus, he did not assume that Bianchina had doubled herself, but recognized the girls as Zabaglione's other daughters. There was no trace of Bianchina or the cowherd. The Villa delle Stagioni was empty. Swallows were flitting to and fro in the broad, empty courtyards, swallows that were also about to spend the winter in Africa. Disappointed, Don Paolo went back to his hotel. Zabaglione had said that the young people were disloyal, and this gave him hope. Nevertheless, there was no time to lose.

There were still a lot of people in the streets of Fossa, particularly around the taverns. Berenice had put a roast suckling pig on sale outside the hotel. It was laid on a table, with a skewer right through it. It had been cooked whole in the oven, full of rosemary, fennel, thyme, and sage, and abundantly seasoned with salt and pepper. People crowded round it, but there were few who bought, apart from soldiers who had just joined up and drawn their first pay. The peasants not in uniform gazed at it, showing their teeth like hungry wolves. A corporal of militia was eating a lovely slice of the pork on a piece of white bread. He cut it with a new knife, one of those instruments with blades, punch, corkscrew, and scissors. This knife attracted the attention and admiration of the whole crowd.

A booth had been erected next to the town hall, with a big placard announcing that enlarged colored views of Abyssinia were to be seen within. It cost ten centesimi to enter. Don Paolo payed his ten centesimi, lined up with the other spectators, and passed before a series of peep holes provided with magnifying lenses. Putting his eyes to the lenses, he gazed upon a series of Abyssinian women, with bare, hairy legs and protuberant breasts. The last picture was that of the Empress. This artistic and patriotic spectacle lasted longer than Don Paolo would have liked, because he was shut in by the queue and those in front remained absorbed for a long time before each picture. A timid request that they should make haste drew down on him the jibes and protests of the whole line. When at last he was able to get away his patience had reached its limit. He walked hither and thither, tired and unnerved to the point of committing an act of recklessness, tempted to shout, "Down with the war!" in the middle of the square. Twice he went back to the Villa delle Stagioni, and on both occasions he could distinguish the underwear of Zabaglione's daughters among the straw and the grass. But of Bianchina and the cowherd there was no trace.

Thus evening fell. Local good society gathered at Berenice's hotel for the banquet, while the peasants of Fossa, the artisans and little shopkeepers excluded from the banquet, and those from neighboring villages who had lingered in the town, gathered at the Buonumore tavern. The Buonumore tavern was at the edge of the stream. Many benches had been put out into the open for the occasion, and local wine was being offered at reduced prices. A big barrel had been placed under an old nut tree, near the path that ran along the stream, and mine host was filling half-liter bottles from it, which a number of serving-girls bore to the thirsty. Among the latter Don Paolo found a group from Pietrasecca, and he sat down and talked to Mastrangelo, Pasquandrea, Magascià, Sciatàp, and others. They were already three parts drunk. Bersagliera was asleep behind a bush, near Magascià's cart. Don Paolo tried as hard as he could to find out what these peasants really thought about the war, but he only obtained disjointed replies. Pasquandrea was of opinion that it would soon be possible to emigrate again, "and that was the great thing." Campobasso said there were bound to be immediate requisitions of horses and mules, "but he who had only one donkey had nothing to fear." Sciatàp wanted to know whether the death ray could destroy the seeds in the earth. The others listened and drank, stupefied, stunned, and silent. A people so poor and primitive that for several centuries it had read only one book, *Il Guerrin Meschino*, a people whose wisdom was summed up in a few proverbs passed down from generation to generation, had been literally submerged and overwhelmed by propaganda.

"Sir, you would do better to drink and not waste time asking us things we do not understand," Magascià said to the priest. "At Pietrasecca a joke or a funny story lasts for many years, and passes from father to son and is repeated an endless number of times, always in the same way. But here you hear so many novelties in a single day that it ends by giving you a headache."

Zabaglione came down the path beside the stream. He took the priest to one side. He was ashen pale, and he asked Don Paolo anxiously whether by any chance he had seen his daughters.

Many of the drinkers recognized Zabaglione. They surrounded him and started shouting.

"Speech! Speech! Speech! We want a speech!" they cried.

They demanded a speech as they might have demanded music, a ballad, or a fox-trot, whichever the pianist preferred. Zabaglione parried and resisted, but gave in when he noticed that there were some municipal employees among those who were beseeching him. He forgot his daughters and remembered that the post of mayor was vacant. A few youths lifted him ponderously on to a table next to the barrel.

He preened himself, stroked his mustaches, ran his hand

through his hair, raised his arms towards the starry sky, and then his deep baritone boomed forth.

"Descendants of Eternal Rome," he began, "O thou, my people. . . ."

Thus the music started, and what lovely music! The orator addressed the drunken peasants as though they were an assemblage of exiled kings and emperors. Memories of ancient glories emerged from the wine fumes.

"Tell me," he said, "who was it who brought culture and civilization to the whole Mediterranean and to all known Africa?"

"We did!" voices replied.

"But the fruits were gathered by others. Tell me again, I pray you, who brought culture and civilization to the whole of Europe, even to the misty shores of England, and built towns and cities where savages had grubbed for food with wild hogs and deer?"

"We did!" voices replied.

"But the fruits were enjoyed by others. Tell me again, I beg you, who discovered America?"

This time everybody rose to his feet and shouted:

"We did! We did! We did!"

"But others enjoy it. Tell me again, I beg you, who invented electricity, wireless telegraphy, and all the other things on which modern life is based?"

"We did!" voices replied.

"But others enjoy them. And tell me again, if you please, who are the people who have emigrated to all the countries of the world to dig mines, build bridges, make roads, dry swamps?"

This time everybody rose to his feet again.

"We did! We did!" they shouted.

"And thus you have explained the origin of all your ills. But now, after centuries of humiliation and injustice, Providence has sent us the man who will give our country all its rights that others have usurped."

There were a few shouts of "To London! To London!"

"To New York! To America! To California!" others cried.

"To São Paulo! To the Avenida Paulista! To the Avenida Angelica!" one old man shouted. Others called out:

"To Buenos Ayres!"

Sciatàp, who was next to Don Paolo, was seized with a sudden paroxysm of excitement. Although he was so drunk that he could hardly stand, he insisted on standing on a bench. He imposed silence and shouted:

"To Forty-second Street! To Forty-second Street!"

Silence was reëstablished, and Zabaglione spoke of the marvelous death ray, the latest invention of Italian genius, the decisive arm by which the Empire would be resurrected.

"The death ray can stop engines, bring trains running over the earth and ships furrowing the sea to a standstill, deflate bicycle tires, dry up women's breasts, stop clocks and watches, make the birds of the air lose their plumage, the clappers of bells fall to earth, and turn the enemy soldiers into salt! No one will be able to oppose our victorious advance. The Man of Providence has announced it himself to all the world today. The hour of reckoning has come!"

"To New York!" the whole crowd started shouting now. "To Forty-second Street!"

The crowd pressed around Zabaglione's table to urge him to go on, but he had seen three girls in the distance walking arm in arm with three soldiers along the path beside the stream. So he jumped down from the table, forced his way through the throng, and ran after them.

"In New York," Sciatàp began telling his neighbors, "at Mulberry Street, there's a scoundrel who calls himself Mr. Charles Little-Bell, Ice and Coal. He's the one who ought to be punished first. My idea (of course anyone with a better one is at liberty to propose it) is to take him prisoner and make him pass in front of a regiment of soldiers. Each soldier must give him a kick in the pants with nailed boots. If he complains, every soldier must yell 'Sha-tap!' at him. He'll know what it means!"

Campobasso drew Sciatàp to one side.

"What is there at Forty-second Street?" he asked.

"That's the entertainment quarter," said Sciatàp. "The entertainment quarter for the rich. Beautiful women you see there, perfumed women . . ."

He stopped because he saw his son approaching, comically arrayed in an ill-fitting uniform. His sleeves were too long and were folded over his wrists, and his trousers were too short and only came down to his knees.

"Have a drink!" his father said.

He drank.

"Have another drink," his father said. "You're lucky to be young!"

He drank again.

"Now you listen to me," his father said. "Don't forget what I tell you. If the government decides to send the soldiers with the death ray to New York, just you step forward and volunteer. Tell the government that your father has been there and has a lot of old scores to settle. Well, when you disembark at Battery Place, turn to the right and ask for Mulberry Street. When you get there ask for Mr. Samuel's old-clothes shop. He's a Polish Jew who talks Neapolitan. He's a little old man who knows everything. Whatever you ask him he can tell you. He knows where there's good food and where there's good drink and where the rich people live. It's a big city, and if you don't want to lose your way about, go and see him!"

The son laughed open-mouthed and looked gratefully at his father.

"Have another drink and listen to me," Sciatàp went on. "I'm an old man and don't need much. But if you want to please me you can bring me home three or four pairs of boots. The kind I want are called 'Regal,' and I want them broad at the toes. Samuel will tell you where to get them. Don't bring me narrow ones, because I suffer from corns. . . ."

At a near-by table there was a stonecutter from Bergamo, still dressed in the manner of his native place, with a skin hat and a velvet coat. He had come to the Marsica at the time of the earthquake, on the work of reconstruction, but had married a Fossa woman and settled down. He was talking of the work done by Italians in Switzerland.

"I spent the whole of my youth from the age of fourteen in Switzerland with my father, who was a miner," he said. "There's not a tunnel in Switzerland that wasn't dug mainly by Italian miners. My father was killed digging the Lötschberg tunnel. He was buried by a landslide with twenty-four others. I was sixteen years old at the time. Afterwards I worked in the Trimbach tunnel, the Grenchen tunnel, and the Vallorbe tunnel. The Italian huts at Trimbach were all built together, and the new village was called Tripoli. A special post-office was kept open as long as the work lasted, and 'Tripoli' was written up over it."

"Why 'Tripoli'?" Campobasso asked. "You weren't Arabs!"

"That's just it," said the man from Bergamo. "The Swiss are good people and pay well, but we did all that work for them and not for ourselves. As soon as it was finished we had to go. Some left an arm or a leg behind. Poor people attract misfortunes just as old donkeys attract flies. While we were excavating for an electric station at Grimsel, near Berne, a small piece of rock, no bigger than a man's hand, was hurled into the air by a charge of dynamite, and hit a fellow countryman of ours, who was peacefully having his breakfast about two hundred yards away. It struck him from behind, at the back of the neck, and killed him on the spot. He might have been picked off by a sniper."

A group of drunks had gathered round the wine barrel and started singing an old emigrants' song:

> *After thirty days in the steamship*
> *We got to America. . . .*

At a more distant table an old chair-mender was talking of his days at São Paulo in Brazil.

"At São Paulo there was a district the Brazilians called Abbasce 'o Piques, where we Italians lived, and it was the Negro quarter, too. You used to have to spend all day mending chairs, and in the evening you had to use your knife to protect your life. Going out without a knife would have been like going to war without a rifle. My father used to say it was always best to mind your own business, but when it came to stabbing, it was always better to give a knife thrust than to take one. Brazilian lads who wanted to show off used to come down at night to the

Abbasce 'o Piques, but they generally went home with their entrails hanging out. All the work done around São Paulo was done by Italians. Some made their fortunes and bought themselves places in the Avenida Paulista, but most of them remained in Abbasce 'o Piques or the Praz quarter, with the Turks, the Portuguese, and the Negroes. If the day of reckoning really has come, we are entitled to a good part of Brazil. That's what I say, and I know the country."

It was a painful sight for Don Paolo to see the peasants shaking off their usual apathy, their almost geological resignation, and getting drunk on propaganda.

A noisy diversion was created by some soldiers who left the bar without paying for their drinks. The serving-girls shrieked, and the landlord brandished a kitchen knife at them.

"Collect from the government!" the soldiers shouted from afar.

Around the barrel, which by now was nearly empty, about a dozen peasants were still singing the emigrants' song. Some of them were clinging to the cask, like men clinging to a boat tossed on an angry sea.

> *After thirty days in the steamship*
> *We got to America;*
> *We slept on the bare earth;*
> *We ate bread and sausages. . . .*

Magascià woke up and put poor Bersagliera, who had been lying down behind the bushes, between the shafts. The men from Pietrasecca went home, because it was late. Don Paolo got up to leave too, and although he was so tired that he could scarcely stand, he went once more to the Villa delle Stagioni, to look for Bianchina and the cowherd. He crossed the bridge and went down a path with gardens on both sides. The emigrants' song followed him in the darkness.

> *We ate bread and sausages,*
> *But the industry of us Italians*
> *Founded towns and cities——*

The priest met the cowherd near the park walls.

"I want to talk to you," said Don Paolo.

"I want to talk to you too, sir," said the cowherd.

The two men went along the dark drive and sat down at the edge of the granite pool outside the villa.

"War has begun," said Don Paolo, "the war of the bank. The war will be fought by the Italian peasants against the peasants of Abyssinia. I have been looking for you all day long, because I want to talk to you about what can be done against this madness."

"I have been out with the baroness all day," the cowherd replied. "Perhaps you can help me, sir, before I go mad."

"What is the matter with you?" the priest asked. But the cowherd did not answer. "The war began today," the priest went on, "the war of the bank . . ."

The cowherd interrupted.

"The baroness and I are almost the same age. When we were small we played together here, round this pond, along the drive round the peacocks' cage and the Temple of Venus, until she got old enough for her parents to shut her up in a convent. But we went on liking each other . . ."

"I know your story," Don Paolo interrupted.

"Then you know that the baron, that is, her husband, was killed in a duel. It was a real visitation of God. Instead of coming back here, the baroness started living gayly. She isn't bad, but she's weak."

"How do you know?" asked the priest.

"The baroness has always written to me," said the cowherd.

"Did she tell you her adventures in writing?"

"Indirectly, yes," said the cowherd. "She has always been very religious, and she is very frightened of death. Every Saturday she goes to confession. Her confessor must be a severe man, and as a penance for every mortal sin he makes her recite one Ave Maria and lick a little cross on the ground with her tongue. That kind of penance is also used in our part of the world, but for a priest to impose it on a baroness is really shameful. She always recited the Ave Maria herself, I don't deny that, but she always left the licking of the crosses on the ground to me. I am not telling you this in any complaining spirit. Since it was for her, I always did it with pleasure. Well, every Saturday night she used to write me a postcard, from wherever she might happen to be, Rome, or Monte Carlo, or St. Moritz, and she put down the number of crosses that had to be licked. At first, when the baron was alive, there were only a few crosses every week, but after his death the number quickly went up to twenty or thirty. Just imagine it, sir! Such a fine lady, and thirty mortal sins a week! Recently the number has nearly always been twenty-one, and that's not a little. It's an average of three a day."

"Three a day is certainly not a little," Don Paolo agreed. "Do you still lick the crosses on the ground?"

The cowherd stammered in confusion.

"It's the only contact I had left with her," he said. "If I had refused, she would have had it done by somebody else, and I shouldn't have heard from her at all."

The cowherd led the priest into the stable, took a lantern, lit it, and showed him innumerable tiny little crosses drawn on the wall in charcoal, covering an area of several square meters.

"So as not to forget or make mistakes, I always draw the required number of crosses on the wall," he said.

The little black crosses, drawn on the damp stable wall, reminded Don Paolo of a war cemetery he had seen near Gorizia. But this was the cemetery of the baroness's mortal sins.

The two men went back and sat at the edge of the pool.

"The baroness came back here a few days ago," said the cowherd. "You can imagine how glad I was! She told me she had come back because she had no money to go on living in town. I told her that as long as I was here she wouldn't want for anything. Next day her lover arrived too, a Piedmontese cavalry colonel. Bianchina says he looks as if he might have fought in the Crimean War, but I wasn't frightened of him. So on the evening of the day he came I took him aside and told him if he wanted to leave the Villa delle Stagioni alive, he had better take the next train back to the Crimea. But the baroness intervened on his behalf. Since then my life has been like hell itself. I can't sleep a wink, and the nights seem endless. Things certainly can't go on like this. The night before last the baroness came to me and asked me to lick the usual twenty-one crosses on the ground. 'No!' I said, 'I certainly won't do penance for the mortal sins you commit with that man.' The baroness looked at me in amazement, and tears came into her eyes. 'Then shall I have to do them myself?' she said. In the end I promised to do the penance once more, but for the last time. Now, every day when evening comes and the two of them go to their room, I feel my head beginning to whirl. I get the craziest ideas. I don't get a moment's peace and I can't think of anything else. It's useless to talk to me about anything else!"

"Do you know when Pompeo is coming back from Rome?" Don Paolo asked.

"No."

"I sent Bianchina to Rocca. Do you know if she is back yet?"

"She's not back yet," the cowherd replied. Then he added: "You, as a priest, ought to talk to the baroness."

"I am very sorry," said Don Paolo. "War has started, and I am unable to think about anything else."

The streets of Fossa were deserted and badly illuminated. The flags, the trophies, the streamers, the words of which were indecipherable in the darkness and the colors of which were indistinguishable, gave a carnival-like air to the sleeping town. Don Paolo hesitated and stopped outside the Girasole Hotel, because the sound of voices and singing was coming from the dining-room. Evidently the guests at the banquet to celebrate the opening of hostilities against Abyssinia had not all gone home. To avoid having to pass through the dining-room and be compelled to talk to these people whom he detested, Don Paolo walked round the hotel building and tried the kitchen door, which was at the bottom of a yard full of boxes, stacks of vine branches, and heaps of charcoal. Don Paolo suddenly remembered an incident of his school days, when he was in the second elementary class. The whole school had mutinied against a master, Don Vincenzo Limone, who had broken a boy's arm while beating him. Don Paolo, who had been seven or eight years old at the time, had written vindictive slogans such as "Down with Don Vincenzo!" and "Death to the tyrant!" on all the white walls he passed on his way to school. Sounds of washing-up were coming from the kitchen, and Don Paolo was unwilling to go in. He filled one of his pockets with charcoal, and in the semi-darkness made a short reconnaissance of the streets of Fossa. The road to the station was empty, the station was silent, and a beggar with a dog was asleep in the waiting-room. The last train must have gone. Don Paolo took a piece of charcoal and wrote, "Down with the war! Long live liberty!" in large letters over the ticket window. Then he crossed the station yard and entered the old part of the town. He went down a dark, winding alley to the church of San Giuseppe. The church walls were rough and would not take the charcoal, but the three broad steps that led up to the church door were smooth and clean and seemed to be waiting for someone with a piece of charcoal in his hand. On the first step Don Paolo wrote "Down with government soup!" On the next step he wrote "Long live home-made soup!" On the third step he wrote "Down with the Pope who's in favor of the war!" When he had finished and was walking away, he turned two or three times to admire his handiwork. The inscriptions, in big, black, bold, block letters really looked splendid beneath the church. At a turning in a narrow street he met a drunkard lurching from side to side and singing the emigrants' song at the top of his voice. The man seemed startled at the priest's appearance. Then he burst into idiotic laughter and started following him, whispering:

"Darling! Darling! Stop a minute!"

The priest lengthened his stride to escape the revulsion with which this pursuit filled him, but the drunkard refused to abandon the chase. So Don Paolo waited for him under a lamp-post and made ready to punch his head. Only then did the drunkard perceive his error; he made a comic gesture of surprise and started muttering:

"What a mistake! What sacrilege was about to take place!"

Don Paolo came to the tax office, which had the government sign on the door and solidly barred windows. Next to the door he carefully wrote: "Down with the war and the mortgages! Long live liberty!" He heard other drunken voices in neighbor-

ing streets, so in order to avoid further encounters he went back
to the hotel and entered by the kitchen door. The kitchen was
now deserted. He found Pompeo sitting and waiting for him in
his room.

"I came back from Rome tonight, by the last train," the chemist's son said. "As soon as I knew you were here I came to see
you, and I've been waiting for you, because I want to talk to
you."

"I have been looking for you and waiting for you all day,"
said Don Paolo. "The new war has begun, the war of the bank
against the poor people, and what are we doing?"

Pompeo went pale.

"No, you are making a mistake," he replied. "This is a war
for the people and for civilization."

"What makes you think that?"

Pompeo described his visit to Rome. He and a friend, who was
also in favor of the second revolution, had gone together, and
they had spent many hours walking in the vicinity of the bank
where they suspected the Chief of the Revolution was held
prisoner. They had put their ears to the walls, had watched to
see whether anything resembling a prisoner's food had been
taken into the building during the day, and had even tried to
get into conversation with two carabinieri who were on guard
outside. But they had not been able to find out anything for
certain. They had spent all their evenings in friends' houses, the
houses of rich people, and to his surprise Pompeo had heard
great merchants and a banker expressing doubts about the economic utility of the new war, which they seemed actually to regard as a risky and expensive undertaking. "Then why was the
war being waged?" the two lads had started asking. But all the
answers given them had been vague, and no one had dared pronounce *his* name. Was it possible for people to be so very
frightened of a prisoner? Was not the double who had been put
in his place said to be a docile slave of the bank? What, then,
was the reason for the war? It was revealed to them in the Piazza
Venezia.

"A speech by the Head of the Government had been an-

nounced for four o'clock in the afternoon," Pompeo said. "My
friend and I went there, and we stood right in front of the balcony of the Palazzo Venezia. We had to wait a long time, but
when he appeared on the balcony and his voice started booming
over the crowd, all doubt disappeared. It wasn't a double, it was
He!"

Don Paolo was about to say something, but he hesitated to
oppose rational arguments to this act of ingenuous faith. He put
his right hand, which was black from the charcoal, into his
pocket.

"The war that started today," the lad went on, "will serve to
provide our unemployed with land which is now uncultivated
and uninhabited. Not till our national economy is freed from
the dead weight of surplus labor will an effective struggle against
the bank and private monopoly be possible. The second revolution is only postponed. The war must be won first."

Pompeo produced a piece of paper from his pocket and showed
it to the priest.

"I enlisted voluntarily today," he said.

"In that case we have nothing further to say to each other,"
the priest said, and showed the youth the door.

But Pompeo, after some hesitation, still had something important on his mind.

"Promise me," he said, "that you will do none of the things
we spoke of together."

Don Paolo hesitated. He did not want to lie, but he was afraid
of being denounced to the authorities as a priest hostile to the
government. If he were arrested his identity would be easily established. The idea of arrest frightened him less than the thought
of the scandal that would be caused at Fossa and Pietrasecca
among those who had known him in his priest's clothing.

"Promise!" said Pompeo.

"I promise," Don Paolo said. "Bon voyage!" he added. "I hope
you return safely from the war. Then we shall talk again."

Pompeo embraced the priest affectionately, promised he would
write to him from Africa, and left. The laughing and singing of
the banqueters who still remained in the dining-room came

floating up the staircase. Don Paolo washed the charcoal from his hand. The wash basin smelled disgustingly. He looked at his face in the mirror which had been fouled by hundreds of flies. His face was livid and looked older than ever. His black clothing made him look like a mournful clown. Uliva's words returned to his mind: "You are a fool. You are a revolutionary because you are afraid of reality." He was seized with an attack of obstinate, dry coughing, and suddenly he felt a warm, sweet, saliva taste in his mouth. Light-red foam appeared between his lips. He lay down on the bed and remembered the words of the breviary. *Venit hora mea.* Perhaps my hour has come.

He was still lying on the bed, fully dressed and wide awake, when he heard some one tiptoeing towards his room and listening at the door. "Come in," he said. Bianchina came in.

"I saw a light at the window," she said, "and so I came up."

The girl was all painted up and smelled of alcohol.

"There were some small celebrations at Rocca on account of the outbreak of war," she said, "and the boys, of course, were only too pleased to entertain me. But that Murica is an idiot. I had to go all over the place, but in the end I found him in a garden, looking after the cabbages. I told him that a friend of his from Rome had sent me especially to say that he would very much like to see him and would come and see him if he wanted him to. He didn't even thank me or offer me a glass of water, but said he didn't want to see anybody."

Don Paolo was breathing with difficulty and he was afraid of another fit of coughing.

"Why don't you say anything?" Bianchina asked him. "Why aren't you in bed yet? Are you feeling sad?"

Don Paolo nodded his head.

"Why are you sad? Are you in debt? Are you in love?"

Don Paolo almost smiled.

"I've got it," said the girl. "You're in love with a nun. I read a story in a book once, about a priest who was always sad because he was in love with a nun. But there are so many other women in the world!"

The coughing came back and shook the sick man. He rested

his head on his shoulder, and a thin trickle of warm blood oozed from one side of his mouth. Bianchina went pale, and Don Paolo saw she was on the point of calling for help, but he took her hand, smiled, and murmured:

"Don't be afraid. It's nothing."

Bianchina dipped some handkerchiefs in cold water and put them on his forehead and on his chest. She took a light-blue shawl from her shoulders and wrapped it around the electric light to dim it. She hurried down to the kitchen and fetched a glass of salt water, which she made Don Paolo sip, and fetched two pillows from the next room, which was empty, and propped up the priest's head with them. Then she slowly and carefully undressed him, so that he did not have to make a single movement, pulled a sheet and a blanket from under him and covered him properly, opened the window to let in fresh air, and carefully washed the traces of blood from his mouth and chin. Every now and then she changed the cold compresses on his forehead and chest, and each time she stroked his hair and whispered:

"There! There! It's nothing serious, you'll see!"

Bianchina forbade the priest to speak. She gave him a pencil and a piece of paper to use in case there was anything he wanted to say. Don Paolo wrote down: "Telephone tomorrow morning to Dr. Nunzio Sacca of Acquafredda."

"And now it's time to go to sleep," the girl said. "Good-night!"

Bianchina lay down on the stone floor beside the bed. But neither she nor Don Paolo managed to go to sleep.

"Did you celebrate the beginning of the war, too?" the sick man asked her during the night.

"Yes."

"Why?"

"I did what the others did."

Next morning Bianchina told her aunt all about the priest's illness and went to the post-office to telephone to the doctor at Acquafredda.

Dr. Sacca arrived towards midday. Don Paolo was very glad to see a friendly face, but the doctor was embarrassed and reserved. He examined him hurriedly and distractedly. As soon as he was alone with the patient he said:

"Now you will be convinced that your return to Italy was an act of folly. In any case, if one insists on being a hero, it shouldn't be at the cost of others."

"You weren't obliged to come," Don Paolo answered. "One can die quite well without a doctor."

"As long as you are disguised in this way I am compromised, too," the doctor said. "The police would easily discover that Don Paolo Spada arrived at Fossa in a carriage from Acquafredda, and that the carriage was hired at Acquafredda by me."

"No one compelled you to do it," Don Paolo said.

"I obeyed a stupid, sentimental impulse," the doctor confessed. "It's your duty now to relieve me as quickly as possible of the permanent risk that hangs over my head. Besides, even from your point of view, you ought to be convinced that for the time being there is nothing you can do in Italy. Go and have your health looked after in a sanatorium abroad, and wait for better times."

"I must tell you," Don Paolo replied, "that I accepted your help because at one point I believed you were of a different breed from the common run of my former school-fellows. Now I see you are as worthless as the rest. You may even be more worthless. A state of war creates many opportunities for a doctor to advance himself in his career. A doctor like you, with the bishop's influence to help him, has excellent prospects in wartime. Is that what makes you afraid?"

Bianchina entered the room and prevented Dr. Sacca from replying.

"You may go," Don Paolo said to the doctor. "As soon as I can stand I shall leave."

The doctor departed, and Bianchina told the priest that certain inscriptions written in charcoal on some of the public buildings during the night had caused an uproar in the town. While Bianchina was tidying up the room she discovered large black stains in the wash basin, which looked as if a charcoal-burner had been washing his hands in it.

"What's this?" she asked.

But instead of waiting for a reply, she hurriedly cleaned away the stains. Then she went over to Don Paolo and said to him in a tone of reproach:

"Do you know you are a big baby? A bold and reckless baby?"

But she regretted reproaching the sick man, and added, "You are a nice baby all the same."

"Bianchina," Don Paolo replied, "what good fortune it is that there are women in the world besides the calculating swines of men!"

Bianchina reflected a moment, and then said:

"Perhaps you say that out of pure selfishness. If there were no women in the world, who would there be to bring babies into the world?"

The sick man protested.

"Even if science discovered another way of producing babies, it would be a blessing if, in addition to men obsessed with their careers, there were women . . ."

"But having babies is not the important thing," Bianchina said. "In fact, quite often people have them by mistake and against their will. The important thing is suckling them."

This idea had never occurred to Don Paolo, and it gave him great pleasure. He looked at the girl as she washed the floor. Her breasts resembled ripe oranges. A few months ago they had been like bitter lemons.

Chapter X

SUCH was Don Paolo's apathy that he lost all desire to think of the disappointments he had suffered. With a flick of his hand, as though a swarm of flies was buzzing round his head and annoying him, he dismissed the troublesome thoughts that sometimes came to pester him. He had no idea what to do or where to turn in order to remain among the peasants and begin the task he had mapped out for himself. The ground had sunk beneath his feet. Nothing was left for him but to go. But he felt no hurry or anxiety even to do that. He would go when he was in a fit state, and not before. The only thing that annoyed him was the mirror. He avoided approaching the washstand in order not to see himself in the mirror. He knew he looked absurd and ridiculous. He knew now that ruining his face with iodine and disguising himself as a priest had been nothing but a stupid and idle prank. But he did all he could not to think about it.

"As soon as I am able to leave, I shall go abroad," he said to Bianchina. "I cannot go on living in this country. I am tired and disillusioned."

"Find me a job and I'll come, too," the girl said. "I don't know what to do here, either, and it won't be long before my aunt turns me out again. Besides, I should adore to travel!"

The idea of meeting Bianchina abroad made Don Paolo smile.

"If you come abroad," he said, "I shall tell you a lot of things that will make you laugh."

"Can't you tell me now?"

Bianchina believed in not putting off till tomorrow what could be done today. But Don Paolo was not to be cajoled.

Berenice looked after the priest according to Dr. Sacca's instructions. Dr. Sacca, on leaving the patient's room, had met Berenice on the stairs, answered her greeting curtly, brushed rudely past her, left the hotel, and hurried away towards the station. But later he had returned, apologized for his previous haste, left some prescriptions, ordered a special diet, and particularly recommended Berenice to distract the patient from his black humor and, if possible, make him laugh and think of other things.

The latter task was conscientiously undertaken by Bianchina. Don Paolo being an invalid, she was somewhat restricted in her choice of entertainment. She knew plenty of pastimes and diversions that would have amused Don Paolo, but would not have been good for him, and these she had to renounce; but being a resourceful young woman, she called on the memory of her school days for a whole series of more innocent but not less entertaining pastimes, such, for example, as tickling the soles of the feet and fly-catching. Fly-catching had been actively practiced at her school, particularly during school hours, the object of this form of sport being to catch the flies in flight without injuring them and without the sister noticing it. Pins or feathers were then delicately laid on the captured flies' backs, and they were put down and lined up on the bench and encouraged to run races, which were called "towing races." Bianchina had made quite a name for herself at this sport, but when she tried catching flies now she sometimes injured them.

"I'm out of practice," she said by way of apology. "You learn such a lot of things at school, and then, later, when you want them, you've generally forgotten them."

The towing races took place on Don Paolo's bed, the black leather binding of his breviary serving as the course. Some flies would make straight for the finish, others would go crooked and leave the course, while others would only move a little way and then stop dead.

"Those that won't go are the wives," Bianchina said. "They slow down to let their husbands win. Feminine sentimentality as usual!"

Don Paolo discovered that fly-racing, when carefully studied, was as full of surprises and entertainment as horse-racing or motor-racing, apart, of course, from the difference in dimensions.

In spite of Bianchina's precautions, an echo of the excitement caused in the town by the writing on the walls reached the sick man.

"So many policemen have never been seen in Fossa before," Berenice announced. "Anyone would think we were a town of criminals."

Bianchina made no comment. Gelsomina, acting as substitute for her husband, the haberdasher, who had enlisted, stood at her shop door and stopped all passers-by.

"Have you heard any news?" the good woman asked each of them. "I'm sure it must have been a stranger!"

"It was such a beautiful celebration, with everybody happy and everybody in such complete harmony," Berenice lamented. "Whoever could have thought of writing such stupid things on the walls?"

"Envy is never absent," said Don Senofonte. "Some one who couldn't enlist and had no sons to enlist relieved his feelings that way."

"It was such a beautiful celebration! Such a unanimous celebration! And just on the eve of the appointment of the new mayor!" said Zabaglione.

"Never a funeral without a smile, never a wedding without a tear," the chemist observed.

"Night birds are birds of ill omen," said the haberdasher's wife. "It's lucky there's the law!"

"There's fire smoldering among the peasants," said Berenice. "You don't notice it in the daytime, but you can see the sparks at night!"

"The peasants? Out of the question!" said the chemist. "They can't write! The inscriptions were in block capitals. No peasant wrote them!"

"There are one or two youngsters who have lost their heads," Zabaglione observed. "Of course I am not alluding to anyone."

The insinuation was not lost on Don Senofonte.

"Just to let you know," he answered, with asperity, "let me tell you that my son has enlisted voluntarily. The honor of a volunteer is beyond suspicion. Besides, while we are on that subject, my son has never been a Socialist!"

- This was a home thrust. Zabaglione went livid with rage.

"Your repartee has misfired," he replied. "Everyone knows I sacrificed my ideas a long time ago. Who is there who has never been a Socialist? Even Etcetera Etcetera was once a Socialist!"

"Everybody gives what he can," the haberdasher's wife said, to restore peace. "Some give their money, some give their lives, some give their ideas, some give their sons, some give their daughters."

But Zabaglione took every word amiss.

"My daughters? What's that about my daughters?" he exclaimed, turning angrily on Gelsomina. His cheeks had now turned purple.

The poor woman did not understand the question, and attempted to extricate herself by uttering innocuous lamentations.

"My husband is going to Africa, the shop is head over heels in debt, my sister is consumptive, we've had to take a second mortgage on the house, and with all that, how can other people's affairs interest me?"

But Zabaglione did not relent.

"Answer me," he said. "What have you got to say about my daughters?"

The poor woman was terrified and started babbling confusedly.

"Yes, yes, of course, let us be perfectly open with one another. Hasn't my husband volunteered? Has he or has he not?"

"If the person who wrote on the walls isn't found, the whole town will be punished," the tax-office clerk said. "We shall be given a special commissioner instead of the new mayor."

"What's that? What's that?" said Zabaglione, going pale. "If I find the scoundrel, I'll tear him to pieces with my own hands!"

The words "Down with government soup" on the steps of the church had upset Donna Adalgisa Colantuoni so seriously that they nearly made her ill. She took them as a personal insult. Her father said she ought to have nothing more to do with the government soup.

"It is not worth while to sacrifice yourself for the ungrateful rabble," he said. "You ought to threaten to resign."

"But if I resign, what shall we have to eat?" his daughter objected.

"I didn't say resign, I said threaten to resign," her father explained.

Bianchina told Don Paolo she couldn't understand why there was such a lot of fuss about a few inscriptions on the walls.

Don Paolo was surprised, too. He tried to explain it.

"The Land of Propaganda is built on unanimity," he said. "If one man says, "No," the spell is broken and public order is endangered. The rebel voice must be stifled."

"Even if the voice is that of a poor, solitary sick man?"

"Even then."

"Even if it belongs to a peaceful man who thinks in his own way, but does nothing evil apart from that?"

"Even then."

These thoughts served to sadden the girl, but gave the man new heart. He felt ashamed of his previous discouragement.

"In the Land of Propaganda," he said, "a man, any man, any little man who goes on thinking with his own head, imperils public order. Tons of printed paper repeat the government slogans; thousands of loud-speakers, hundreds of thousands of manifestoes and leaflets, legions of orators in the squares and at the crossroads, thousands of priests from the pulpit repeat these slogans *ad nauseam*, to the point of collective stupefaction. But it is enough for one little man to say 'No!' murmur 'No!' in his neighbor's ear, or write 'No!' on the wall at night, and public order is endangered."

The girl was terrified, but the man was happy again.

"And if they catch him and kill him?" the girl asked.

"Killing a man who says 'No!' is a risky business," the priest replied, "because even a corpse can go on whispering 'No! No! No!' with a persistence and obstinacy that only certain corpses are capable of. And how can you silence a corpse?"

Berenice came in.

"Pompeo knows who wrote on the walls, and he has just gone to Avezzano to tell the higher authorities," she said.

"How do you know?" the priest asked.

"He told Gelsomina himself."

Bianchina took a shawl and hurried to the station.

"Don't poke your nose into things that are no concern of yours!" her aunt called after her. "Don't go on being the ruin of the family!"

But by this time Bianchina had gone.

Don Paolo jumped out of bed to pack his bag and escape. His temperature had been normal for several days and his cough was much better, but he was still so weak that he could scarcely stand. Where was he to go? There's only one railway line, he said to himself, and if I take the train it will be easy to catch me. Should he go over the mountains and spend a few nights in the open? Impossible in the weak state he was in.

He unpacked his bag and renounced the idea of flight. Everything considered, his arrest at Fossa, a town already in a state of ferment, would be more "useful" than an arrest at Rome station, where it would pass unnoticed. Orta, his native village, was only a few kilometers away. Don Benedetto was only a few kilometers away. One or another of his former friends was in every village in the neighborhood. Concettino Ragù himself might be among those who would arrest him. News of his arrest would spread quickly throughout the Marsica and would come to the ears of the peasants, and in the long winter nights, the poor, hungry people, sitting over their empty hearths, would think of him. "What has happened to that lad from our part of the world, Pietro Spina?" they would say to themselves. "What will he be thinking? Will he come out of prison alive?" And there would certainly be some who would say: "If only he were among us. . . ."

From Fossa to Avezzano was only an hour's journey by train, but Bianchino and Pompeo did not return till late in the evening.

"We've eaten and drunk," Bianchina told her aunt and the priest, "and on our way back we passed a cinema, so in we went."

"You are the ruin and disgrace of the Girasole family," her aunt said. "You mean to tell me you allowed yourself to be taken to the cinema?"

"Didn't you say you had quarreled with Pompeo?" the priest asked. "And didn't Pompeo go to Avezzano to denounce somebody?"

Bianchina, with her aunt in the room, had some difficulty in explaining what had happened.

"Pompeo behaves as though he were a little Robespierre, but with women he's more like Danton," she said.

Berenice was obviously very proud to have her niece express herself in such an educated fashion, but she still wanted to know what had happened.

"Whom did he denounce?" she asked. "Will he be arrested at once?"

"At Fossa station, when we got into the train, Pompeo was perfectly certain he knew who it was. We had a long argument about it, and we nearly tore each other's hair out. The police were waiting for us when we got out of the train at Avezzano, but Pompeo had changed his mind."

"But whom did he denounce, for Heaven's sake?"

"A cyclist he saw coming along the road from Orta," Bianchina said. "Pompeo is sure he saw him, but he wasn't able to recognize him in the distance. I told the police I could corroborate this myself, because I saw a man on a bicycle coming along the road from Orta with my own eyes that night."

"From Orta?" said Berenice. "So Gelsomina was right. It was a stranger!"

She dashed to the haberdasher's shop with the news.

"We were right!" she exclaimed. "It was just as we said. It was a stranger, a man from Orta, who wanted to compromise the people of Fossa!"

The news spread rapidly, and of course many other people said they had seen the man on the bicycle coming from Orta that night; but since he was not one of those who generally came to the Tuesday markets, no one had recognized him. The outrage had been committed by an unknown man, perhaps the Mystery Man himself!

Now that the tension was over, Don Paolo felt better. He became high-spirited. His zest for battle and adventure revived. He decided to make Rome his headquarters and undertake a series of nocturnal raids throughout the Marsica. At Orta, his native village, an uncle of his had formerly owned a timber-yard immediately behind the tax office. It must be there still. It would make a lovely bonfire to begin with. Near the station at Avezzano there was a chemical factory which was now turning out poison gas for civilizing the Abyssinians. That would also be highly inflammable. Perhaps even the illiterates would end by understanding and follow his example.

While he was reflecting on these designs, Don Girasole, the parish priest of Fossa, came to invite him to visit the parish church, and he accepted. Don Girasole was about sixty, but looked older. His hair was entirely white, his face was thin and yellow, and he walked slowly, with bent shoulders. He told Don Paolo he was the oldest of ten brothers and sisters, of whom only he and Berenice survived. His religious duties kept him busy from early morning till late at night. Besides Masses, confessions, rosary, funerals, novenas and tridua, and religious devotions of all kinds which he had to either direct or attend, there were christenings and weddings, there were the illiterate women who made him read them the letters they received from America, there were the Daughters of Mary, there was the San Luigi Boys' Club; also he had to teach the catechism in the elementary schools, and prepare boys for confirmation and for their First Communion; there was the Congregation of Charity, there was the Confraternity, there were the Tertiaries of St. Francis. . . .

"I have to use the odd moments left over to me," he said, "to say my breviary and retire into myself a little and prepare myself for the death which I feel to be at hand, but which, nevertheless, creeps on me so slowly."

In the evening he was so tired that he could scarcely stand. And sometimes he was called to the bedside of a dying man in the middle of the night, and occasionally this would happen in the worst season of the year. But he did not complain; quite the contrary. "The man of God must always be tired," he said. "For idle thoughts occur in idle moments, and behind them lurks the Evil One, who is always on the watch."

A crowd of boys were playing football in the little square opposite the church. They stopped their game to let the two priests pass.

"Don't forget that catechism begins in a quarter of an hour," the parish priest reminded them.

Don Girasole stopped for a moment on the steps of the church to recover his breath.

"You will probably have heard of the sacrilege that was committed here," he said to Don Paolo. "A masked stranger came here one night, to the very threshold of the church, and scrawled the most outrageous things on the steps."

"By the way," said Don Paolo, "what do you think of the war?"

A woman was waiting for the parish priest at the church door to arrange the date of a christening.

"A country priest has many things to do and little time to think," Don Girasole replied. "For the rest," he added—

> "There are the Old Testament and the New,
> And the Pastor of the Church to guide us."

"Forgive me. I expressed myself badly," said Don Paolo.

The usual variety of many-colored votive tablets, erected by those of the faithful who had had their petitions granted, adorned the side walls at the entrance to the church. They varied according to the favors received: hands, feet, noses, nipples, and other parts of the body were represented in their natural size. The interior of the church seemed dark when one first went in, but one's eyes soon got used to it. A large part of the uneven, disjointed stone pavement was occupied by women all dressed in black, praying and whispering to one another, squatting in the Oriental manner as a sign of humility and familiarity with the house of God. An old woman was crawling on hands and knees towards the Chapel of the Blessed Sacrament, with bent head, licking the floor and leaving in her wake irregular traces of saliva, like the silvery trail of a slug on the old stones. Her son, in soldier's uniform, was walking slowly by her side, looking clumsy and embarrassed. Don Girasole genuflected before the tabernacle, and Don Paolo followed suit. On the altar there was a picture of the body of Christ on His Mother's knees. She was wearing mourning. Christ looked like a peasant who had been killed in a quarrel and whose corpse had started decomposing. The wounds in the hands and feet and the deep rent in the breast looked as though they were in an advanced state of gangrene, and the reddish hair looked as if it were full of dirt and vermin. The Mother looked like the widow of a rich merchant who had been overwhelmed by misfortune. Two paraffin tears shone on her handsome pale cheeks; her dark eyes were turned upwards, as though to avoid the sight of her son, of whom she had had high hopes but who had come to the worst possible end. A finely embroidered veil covered her waved hair and came down halfway over her brow; an elegant lace handkerchief was tied to the little finger of her right hand, and on the pedestal at her feet, in letters of gold, were the woeful words: *Videte si est dolor sicut dolor meus.*

The soldier's mother finished her procession.

"Please find out whether we cannot get the allowance at once," she said to Don Girasole. "Otherwise how are we to live?"

"What allowance?"

"Four lire a day," said the soldier. "The mother of every man called up gets an allowance of four lire a day. It says so in the paper today."

"To whom should we apply for the allowance?" another woman came and asked the priest. "The post-office? The town hall? Couldn't you apply for us?"

No sooner were they in the sacristy when another woman came up and said her son had scarlet fever; she asked permission to dip a piece of cloth in the oil of the lamp that burned beside the tabernacle, to lay it on her dying baby's heart. Don Girasole granted her request.

"A parish priest can reflect about the war but little," he said to Don Paolo, "because he has continually to run hither and thither. Now the prayers for dependents' allowances are beginning, soon there will be prayers for the safe home-coming of prisoners of war and those reported missing; then there will be prayers for leave to be granted to those who are needed to work on the land, prayers for pensions, prayers for orphaned children. The poor people could apply to the government offices for all these things, but they distrust the officials, and are generally treated rudely when they do go to them, so they come and weep in the sacristy."

"Many years ago, at Rome, on the occasion of a jubilee, I met a certain Don Benedetto of these parts," Don Paolo said. "If I am not mistaken, he was, I think, at that time Greek and Latin master at a diocesan school. Is he still alive? Do you ever see him?"

Don Girasole seemed not to have heard the question. He showed Don Paolo the parish treasure. He went to a big cupboard that occupied the whole of one wall and, with some difficulty, opened its two enormous, inlaid wooden doors. He showed Don Paolo the gold work and jewels on the top shelves, a silver bust of St. Antony in a special niche on the middle shelf, and a large number of chasubles, dalmatics, and richly embroidered stoles hanging as in a wardrobe at the bottom.

The sacristan came in and served two glasses of wine.

"Don Benedetto," the parish priest finally said, "is a very rash man of God. For seventy years he lived an exemplary life. In learning and virtue he was the master of us all. But now, on the brink of eternity, his habitual disdain for the opinion of men and his excessive confidence in God prompt him to utterances that border on heresy. If only you had known him during the first years of his ministry! . . . When he was ordained I was still a pupil at the divinity school, and I was full of admiration for him, for his dignified and noble calm, his candid love of the classics, the unstained purity of his private life. He insisted on celebrating his first Mass in a prison chapel, and his second in a hospital. You can imagine how shocked his relatives were, for a first Mass is generally considered a social event. His brusque way of flying in the face of public opinion worried his superiors even then. For that reason they were unwilling to intrust him with a parish, and he was sent to teach in a school. The study of the classics and the company of the young seem to have had a mollifying effect upon his character, but his relations with his superiors did not improve. That he was not ambitious and did not try to advance himself was regarded as shocking by the majority; and offense was taken at his preference for the company of his pupils to that of his colleagues and superiors. So he was relieved of his post as a teacher. I always tried to preserve my friendship for him in his solitude. But now it is really no longer possible."

"Has his character changed a great deal?" Don Paolo asked.

"A man from Fossa, one of my parishioners, who worked for a few days in his garden, heard him say that the real name of the present Pope was Pontius XI. This was repeated from mouth to mouth at Rocca dei Marsi, where Don Benedetto lives, and everybody believed him and took what he said literally, because of their naïve ignorance and the respect that they have for him. That parishioner of mine came to me here, in the sacristy, and asked me whether it were really true that the Church had fallen into the hands of a descendant of Pontius Pilate, who, when he had to deal with any grave matter, washed his hands of it."

"And what did you tell him?" asked Don Paolo.

The parish priest looked at his guest in surprise.

"I beg your pardon," said Don Paolo, "I expressed myself badly."

The sacristan came and told the priest that the women were waiting in the church for the rosary and that the boys had started arriving for catechism.

"The provincial committee for deportations has actually begun investigating Don Benedetto's case," said Don Girasole. "That is the pass he has come to! A former pupil of his, Concettino Ragù, who has a good deal of influence in the government party, and I did all we could to save him. We went to see him for the single purpose of helping him. We suggested that he should sign a quite general declaration of submission to the present government and the present policy of the Church. It would have sufficed. He received us politely. When I started explaining that the Church often had to make the best of a bad business in order to avoid worse evils, he interrupted me. 'The theory of the lesser evil may be valid in a political society, but not in a religious society,' he said to me. I tried not to argue with him on an abstract level, because the worst heresies are capable of seductively insinuating themselves into abstract discussions. So I replied: 'Imagine what would happen if the Church openly condemned the present war. What persecutions would descend on its head! What moral and material damage would result!' You will never imagine what Don Benedetto replied. 'My dear Don Girasole,' he said, 'can you imagine John the Baptist offering Herod a concordat to escape having his head cut off? Can you imagine Jesus offering Pontius Pilate a concordat to avoid crucifixion?'"

"Speaking in the abstract," Don Paolo observed, "Don Benedetto's reply would not appear fundamentally anti-Christian."

"But the Church is not an abstract society," Don Girasole said. "The Church is what it is. It has nearly two thousand years behind it. The Church is no longer a young lady who can commit acts of foolishness and indiscretion. The Church is an old, a very old lady, full of dignity, respect, traditions, bounden rights and duties. The Church was, of course, founded by Jesus, but after Him there were the apostles and generations upon generations of saints and popes. The Church is no longer a small, clandestine sect, but has a following of millions and millions of human beings who look to it for protection."

"Sending them to war is a fine way of protecting them," Don Paolo exclaimed. "Besides, in the time of Jesus, the old Synagogue was also an old, a very old lady, with a long tradition of prophets, kings, lawgivers, and priests, and a multitudinous following to protect. Nevertheless Jesus did not treat it with much respect."

Don Girasole was still sitting over his untouched wineglass. He closed his eyes as if seized with a sudden weariness, and remained like that for several moments. There was a blue transparency about the lids of his eyes, and a light, nervous tremor. "O God, O God, why do you torment me?" he murmured.

The sacristan returned and told Don Girasole that the women were still waiting for the rosary and the catechism boys had started to make a terrific row.

Don Girasole rose wearily to his feet and went towards the church, where the faithful were waiting. Don Paolo went back towards his hotel.

On the way he came upon a noisy crowd outside the town hall. Two peasants who had happened to come to the town because of a lawsuit had been recognized as natives of Orta and had been set upon by about a hundred citizens of Fossa, half beggars and half small tradespeople, who attacked them from every side with a most varied assortment of weapons. A squad of carabinieri had had considerable difficulty in rescuing the two unfortunates, who were completely ignorant of the cause of this sudden outburst of hatred, from the fury of the mob, which continued to hurl the most terrible threats at them from the public square, though they had now been safely locked up in the town hall. Zabaglione, at the request of the authorities, tried to calm the mob, but with scant effect. Their wrath was not appeased until it was announced that the two peasants from Orta had been put under arrest and would be taken to prison as presumed accomplices of the author of the unpatriotic writings on the walls.

At the entrance to the hotel Don Senofonte was loudly commenting on this healthy popular reaction to the cowardly deed committed by the Mystery Man from the next village. So the feelings aroused by the writings on the walls and by the measures taken by the authorities had crystallized into hatred of the stranger. Don Paolo learned that a letter of loyalty to the dictatorship had been signed by all the unemployed who received the government soup at midday, and by their wives. These facts perplexed him. He had not expected great positive results from the few words he had written on the walls, but he had certainly not looked for a sequel as discouraging as this. All his plans for

nocturnal pyrotechnic expeditions now seemed misguided. He
was driven this way and that, pushed one way by his determination to do something, pulled another by a baffling reality that
lured him on like a will-o'-the-wisp, and then snapped its fingers at him and eluded him. His mind reverted to his talk with
Don Girasole, and he promptly sent Bianchina to Rocca dei
Marsi, with a brief letter to Don Benedetto, signed with his
initials only, in which he asked if he might visit him. Bianchina
came back with a note on which there was written in a small,
clear, regular, perhaps slightly tremulous handwriting:

> . . . *tibi*
> *non ante verso lene merum cado*
> *jamdudum apud me est; eripe te morae.*[1]

This was the first time he had seen his old schoolmaster's handwriting since his student days, but he recognized it at once from
his memory of the corrections written on his exercise-books. The
message also reminded him somewhat of a school task, but the
task was easy and the invitation cordial. He left for Rocca towards evening, in a carriage hired for him by Bianchina.

The driver's name was Pratolano.

"Are you from Pratola?" the priest asked.

The man nodded his head.

"How long is it since you left there?"

"A year."

"Were you there at the time of the revolt?"

The man nodded again.

The carriage passed through a belt of vineyards. The grapes
had only just been gathered. The landscape was gentle, soft and
warm, relaxed.

"What are things like at Pratola now?" the priest asked.

"Just as they were before. Just as they've always been."

"Anyway, the Pratolani manage to make themselves respected,"
the priest plucked up courage to say. The driver turned slowly
round and looked at him.

"Those who opened their mouths now have them shut," he

---

[1] "There has for a long time been in my house for you a cask of old wine
not yet opened. Do not delay."—Horace, Book III, Ode XXIX, To Mæcenas.

said. "They are either in the cemetery or in prison. The others kept quiet before, and they keep quieter than ever now. I tend to my own business."

Grapes were being pressed in a big container between two houses on the outskirts of Rocca. Three women, holding their dresses above their knees, were treading the grapes with their bare feet, in a kind of slow dance.

"Are you going to see Don Benedetto, sir?" the man from Pratola asked.

"Do you know him?"

He shook his head, but said:

"They talk a lot about him."

"What do they say?"

"They say, if only everyone were like him."

Don Paolo stopped the carriage in the little village square, told the driver to wait for him at a tavern, took the bag he had brought with him, and climbed the slope to where he saw Don Benedetto's cottage and garden. He dared not present himself to Don Benedetto dressed as a priest, so he had brought a coat, a collar, a tie, and a hat with him. That was all he needed to transform himself into a layman. The road was empty and winding, and had a brier hedge on one side. He stepped through a gap in the hedge and when he emerged a few minutes later the transformation had taken place.

He found Don Benedetto waiting on the threshold of his cottage, as if he had been expecting him to arrive at just that moment. They shook hands and greeted each other, both slightly embarrassed by the emotion they felt. The old man led the younger into the big room on the ground floor, which was full of garden tools and books. He made him sit in a big armchair by the fireplace and sat down next to him on a low stool. He was bent with age, and seemed much smaller than his former pupil. The younger man tried to control his emotion and appear unconcerned.

"Behold the lost lamb that returns to its shepherd of its own accord," he said with a laugh.

Don Benedetto looked with surprise at his guest's prematurely aged face. He did not laugh, but shook his head.

"Here, among us, one cannot tell who is the lost lamb," he said, bitterly. "One cannot tell which of us it is who really has need of the other's pardon; which of us it is who really feels humiliated and afflicted in the other's presence. It is sad, my friend, to make certain discoveries at my age. It is not those who say Mass and call themselves the ministers of the Lord who are most faithful to Him in spirit."

Hearing the old man talk of God, as in olden times, the young man feared he might be laboring under a wrong impression that would falsify the whole encounter. Did the old man think he was still religious?

"I lost my faith in God many years ago," the young man said, and his voice changed. "It was a religious impulse that led me into the revolutionary movement, but, once within the movement, I gradually rid my head of all religious prejudices. If any traces of religion are left in me, they are not a help, but a hindrance, to me now. Perhaps it was the religious education I received as a boy that made me a bad revolutionary, a revolutionary full of fears, uncertainties, complexities. On the other hand, should I ever have become a revolutionary without it? Should I ever have taken life seriously?"

The old man smiled.

"It does not matter," he said. "In times of conspiratorial and secret struggle the Lord is obliged to hide Himself and assume pseudonyms. Besides, and you know it, He does not attach very much importance to His name; on the contrary, at the very beginning of His Commandments He ordained that His name should not be taken in vain. Might not the ideal of social justice that animates the masses today be one of the pseudonyms the Lord is using to free Himself from the control of the churches and the banks?"

The idea of God Almighty being forced to go about under a false passport amused the younger man greatly. He looked at his old schoolmaster in astonishment, and suddenly saw him in a very different light from the image of him that he had preserved during the long years since they had last met. Certainly he was much nearer to him now, but the thought of the pains and torments the old man must have gone through, abandoned and alone, to reach this point saddened him and made him silent.

"I live here with my sister, between my garden and my books," the old man said. "For some time, now, all my letters have been opened by the censor. My books and papers arrive late or get lost on the way. I pay no visits and receive few, and most of them are disagreeable. All the same I am aware of many things that go on, and they fill me with consternation. The Church has made religion a drug for the poor people. What belongs to God is given to Cæsar, and what ought to be left to Cæsar is given to God. The spirit of the Lord has abandoned the Church, which has become a formal, conventional, materialistic institution, obsessed with worldly and caste worries. It was to such a Church that the Baptist spoke the words: 'O generation of vipers, who hath warned you to flee from the wrath to come?' I was summoned to Rome, to be reproved and threatened. The few days I spent there were decisive in my mental life. The impression the papal court makes upon one is of Oriental sycophancy, of manifest and pompous sovereignty. Wherever I went I was received with rudeness and irony by young prelates promoted to high rank through the influence of banker or landlord uncles. Old acquaintances refused to receive me for fear of compromising themselves. In my absence my luggage was ransacked and notebooks and papers were stolen. If I asked those prelates what they thought of the war that was about to break out between two Christian peoples, they fled as if from the presence of an *agent provocateur*. If one of them, after looking carefully all about him, dared to reply at all, he would talk in sibylline words. 'From one point of view it is true that so-and-so is the case,' he would say. 'But from another point of view it is also true that such-and-such must be taken into account. . . . Nor must it be forgotten that so-and-so. . . . And it must be admitted that such-and-such. . . . From which our attitude is perfectly clear.' In the face of all this poltroonery, all this concern for miserable material advantages, I started asking myself: Where then is the Lord? Why has He abandoned us?"

"That is a very pertinent question," the young man said. "Where is the Lord? If He is not a human invention, but an objective spiritual reality, the beginning and the end of all the rest, where is He now?"

His voice was not that of an atheist, but that of a disappointed lover.

Marta, the old man's sister, came in to greet the young man. She put two glasses and a jug of red wine on the table, and went back to her room.

"There is an old story that must be called to mind every time the existence of the Lord is doubted," the old man went on. "It is written, perhaps you will remember, that at a moment of great distress Elijah asked the Lord to let him die, and the Lord summoned him to a mountain. And there arose a great and mighty wind that struck the mountain and split the rocks, but the Lord was not in the wind. And after the wind the earth was shaken by an earthquake, but the Lord was not in the earthquake. And after the earthquake there arose a great fire, but the Lord was not in the fire. But afterwards, in the silence, there was a still, small voice, like the whisper of branches moved by the evening breeze, and that still small voice, it is written, was the Lord."

Meanwhile a breeze had arisen in the garden, and the door of the room in which the two men were sitting creaked and swung open. The young man shuddered. The old man placed his hand on his shoulder and said, with a laugh, "Do not be afraid. You have nothing to fear."

He got up and closed the door.

"So I asked myself: where is the Lord and why has He abandoned us?" he went on. "The loud-speakers proclaiming the outbreak of the war in all the market-places were certainly not the Lord. The bells that rang to summon the ragged and hungry crowds round the loud-speakers were certainly not the Lord. The shelling of African villages and the bombing raids of which the papers tell us every day are certainly not the Lord. But if a poor man, alone in his village, gets up at night and takes a piece of chalk or charcoal and writes on the village walls: 'Down with the war! Long live the brotherhood of all peoples! Long live liberty!' behind that poor man there is the Lord. In his contempt for the dangers that threaten him, in the secret love he nourishes for our so-called African enemies, in his love of liberty, there is an echo of the Lord. Thus, when I read in the papers of bishops being tried in the courts for smuggling money, and behaving before the judges like fraudulent merchants caught red-handed, and when I read in the same paper of workmen being condemned to death for having claimed the liberty of their own consciences, even if those workmen consider themselves atheists, I have no need of much reflection before deciding on which side the Lord is. Now you can imagine what it means to make such a discovery at my age, at the age of seventy-five, almost on the brink of the tomb, when a man turns back to contemplate the road he has traveled and make an audit of his past life. A barren audit! And if I then avert my gaze from myself and consider my former pupils as a whole, I have still greater reason to consider myself a failure. A tree is judged by its fruit, and a teacher by his pupils."

The reverence and admiration that the young man had always preserved for his old schoolmaster now yielded to such a lively feeling of tenderness and affection that he got up and embraced him.

"I used to console myself a little by thinking of you, but I was mistaken," the old man went on. "You have yourself reminded me that the good you have done in your life was not because of your education, but against it and in spite of it."

The young man remained a little perplexed, and then he answered:

"We have not seen each other for fifteen years, and perhaps after this we shall never see each other again. You are an old man, and I am ill and the times are hard. Let us, then, try not to waste the precious minutes left to us in mutual compliments. I am sincerely convinced that I am no better than any of my school-fellows. I am also convinced that the society in which we

live has reached such a state of putrefaction that it is bound to
contaminate anyone who does not completely break with it.
I have had a better fate than my school-fellows because at the
right time, and helped by a series of circumstances, I broke with
it. If I had remained within it I should have run the risk of end-
ing up like them. Instead, I live outside the law. I live under a
false name. In my pocket, in case I have to flee, I have a foreign
passport. I certainly run risks on the material plane, the danger
of prison, the possibility of torture, and, if it came to the worst,
the possibility of being shot. But in exchange for that I live
secure from compromise. A few days ago I saw Dr. Nunzio Sacca.
He certainly used to be no worse than I, but what a wretched
state he is reduced to now! We have reached a point at which it
can be said that only he can save his soul who is prepared to
throw it away."

"There is no other salvation than that," the old man said.
"Poor Nunzio has now realized his family's fondest dreams. He
was appointed director of the government hospital a few days
ago. What intrigues he had to descend to, what humiliations he
had to submit to, what fairytales he had to tell, to establish his
political orthodoxy and eliminate the other candidates! . . .
He came to me after his first encounter with you, at Acquafredda
last spring. He described the internal crisis he went through,
almost in the words that you have just used. He said: 'In a dic-
tatorial regime, how can one practice a profession that depends
on government good-will and remain an honest man? Spina is
lucky to be out of it.' "

"I saw Concettino in the distance at Fossa on mobilization
day," the young man said. "He, too, has adapted himself and
made a career."

"Not only that," the old man said, "but he now makes
speeches on behalf of the war and adorns them with Latin quotations. Thus my instruction has at least served for something.
Now he has felt himself obliged to leave as a volunteer for
Africa. 'They are all going, so I've got to go, too,' he said to
me. He's a kind of obligatory volunteer."

"Have you news of the others?" the young man asked. "What has happened to Antonio Speranza?"

"He used to have a provision shop, but it failed, it seems not altogether honorably," the old man said. "Now he has volunteered, but he has not yet been accepted."

"What has happened to Verdone?"

"He is still a minor official in a tax office. But he hopes to become the head of an office during the war. There is certainly a great future for his profession. If Italy wins the war, what else will she be able to do but set up a magnificent tax-collecting organization?"

"The Abyssinians are poor, and very bad payers," the young man observed. "What about Battista Lo Patto?"

"Concettino Ragù says he is absolutely unbeatable at scientific scopone," the old man said. "Perhaps that is the reason why they have made him head of a syndicate."

"A syndicate of workers or employers?"

"I do not know, and in any case it amounts to the same thing, a government syndicate. So now he will be able to go on playing scopone and draw a salary at the end of the month as well."

"What has happened to Di Pretoro? Is he still with the railway?"

"He was dismissed a long time ago because of his Socialist views. He is now reduced to living in his village, where he has married a dressmaker. He is no longer interested in Socialism, but is sent to prison every now and then in memory of his former opinions. He was arrested on mobilization day, and does not seem to have been released yet."

"What about Don Piccirilli?"

"He used to be a parish priest near here, but at the beginning of the new scholastic year the bishop appointed him a teacher at the seminary. He has thus achieved his ambition. What he is capable of teaching I do not know. Gymnastics, perhaps. He too, of course, now makes speeches in favor of the war, and adorns them with Latin quotations. Thus he maintains that this is not a war, but a crusade for the pacification of Africa, a struggle for true peace, Roman peace. These, then, Piccirilli, Concettino,

Verdone, Antonio Speranza, Battista Lo Patto, are the fruit of my tree."

"A tree may have good fruit," the younger man said, "but before it ripens a robber may come and steal it, or hail may fall and destroy it, or worms may gnaw at it and taint it. When we left school no one could foresee that our destiny would be as hard as it has been. But to talk of destiny is no doubt an exaggeration."

The old man refilled his glass, and held it up against the light to test its clarity, because it was from a new barrel. Then he slowly drew it to his lips and sipped it.

"Each one of us has within himself his own thief, or his own worm, or his own hail," he said. "Circumstances can only help them. One must frankly admit that in the post-war years the circumstances were ideal for the thieves, worms, and hail that each one of us carries about within him. But that does not absolve any of us of responsibility."

"I watched a popular demonstration at Fossa on the occasion of the outbreak of war," the young man said. "It almost made me afraid to see a whole crowd fall a prey to the most primitive instincts. The poor peasants believe in the Leader as in an all-powerful wizard, the priests believe in him as the Man of Providence."

"If the priests allow themselves to be deceived, it is their own fault," the old man interrupted. "They have been warned for two thousand years. They were told that many would come in the name of Providence and seduce the people, that there would be talk of wars and rumors of wars. They were told that all this would come to pass, but that the end would be not yet. They were told that nation would rise up against nation and kingdom against kingdom; that there would be famines and pestilences and earthquakes in divers places; but that all these things would not be the end, but the beginning. The Christians were warned a long time ago. Many will be horrified and many will betray. And if some one (even if it is the Pope himself) says: 'Here is a Man of Providence! There is a Man of Providence!' we must not believe him. We have been warned. False prophets and false saviors shall rise and shall show great signs and wonders, and shall deceive many. We could not demand a plainer warning. If many have forgotten it, it will not change anything of that which will come to pass. The destiny of their Man of Providence has already been written. *Intrabit ut vulpis, regnabit ut leo, morietur ut canis.* He will come in like a fox, reign like a lion, and die like a dog."

"What a wonderful language Latin is!" the young man exclaimed.

"I often wonder what I ought to do," the old man went on. "At the age of seventy-five one can change one's ideas, but not one's habits. A retired life is the only one that suits my character. Even when I was young I lived very much apart. I always kept aloof from politics because of my repugnance to vulgarity. Taste and an æsthetic education always withheld me from action. Besides, my aversion to the present state of things is not political. It is not as a voter but as a man that I find this society intolerable. And then I ask myself what I am to do. I look around me and see very little that I can do. Among my parishioners? Nothing. Those among them whom I know personally avoid me now and are frightened of meeting me. In the last fifty years every priest who has left the Church has done so because of some scandalous infraction of the rule of celibacy. That is sufficient to give an idea of the spiritual condition of our clergy. If the news were spread in the diocese that another priest, one Don Benedetto, of Rocca dei Marsi, had abandoned the priesthood, the first explanation that would naturally occur to the faithful would be that yet another priest had eloped with his housemaid. I may also tell you that the only reason why I go on celebrating Mass is because I respect the simple souls about me and dislike to shock people uselessly. What am I to do?"

Comparing his own mind with that of the old man, the younger one found some deep harmonies between the two, the existence of which he had not suspected before. He plucked up courage and revealed his own bewilderment, described his own disappointments, his vain efforts to find some form of action that would rouse men's minds, his discovery at Pietrasecca of the peasants' indifference to all forms of propaganda, his recent conversation with the man from Pratola, revealing the sterility of many acts of violence. What was he to do?

Both now remained silent. Pupil and master were in the same quandary. Two lives, so different, had converged.

"One must be careful not to be led astray in the heat of the struggle by the artificial, the deceptive, the abstract," the old man said. "One must be careful not to chase apparent success. The evil I see around me is deeper than politics. It is a canker. You cannot heal a putrefying corpse with warm poultices. There is the class struggle, the town and the country, but underlying all these things there is man, a poor, weak, terrified animal. The canker has penetrated to his marrow. . . ."

The younger man was in an exceptional state of receptivity. He listened to the old man, hung on his words for a suggestion, waited for guidance and advice. The old man felt this, and suddenly his words became more cautious.

"What then is to be done?" the young man asked again.

"In different measure and in different ways I have passed through the same experiences as you," the old man said. "I tried arguing with some of my former pupils, I took the trouble of refuting point by point the ideology of the dictatorship, that obscene hash of inanities concocted out of the spurious erudition of a handful of drunken doctors and propounded in the name of the State. It took me a long time to find out that I was wasting my time, because those to whom I spoke did not take the nonsense seriously themselves. Nevertheless, they are faithful servants of the dictatorship; they compete desperately for the honors it has to bestow, and outdo each other in acts of devotion to it at every opportunity. Even in the Marsica there have been isolated acts of violence, dictated by despair. They have not, however, reanimated the weak. On the contrary, they have only made them more intimidated than ever."

The old man stopped, and the younger man waited for him to go on. He remembered his school days, when the master had given his pupils a too difficult problem and refused to help them solve it. "If you don't know, why should I know?" he had said, with pretended seriousness. But this time the master was also at a loss. The old man and the young were at the same point. What was to be done?

"What our country lacks is not the critical spirit," the old man went on. "And it is often not without anonymous acts of violence either. Perhaps what it lacks is men. There are malcontents and there are perpetrators of violence, but Men are lacking. I, too, ask myself: what is to be done? . . . I am convinced that it would be a waste of time to show a people of intimidated slaves a different manner of speaking, a different manner of gesticulating; but perhaps it would be worth while to show them a different way of living. No word and no gesture can be more persuasive than the life, and, if necessary, the death, of a man who strives to be free, loyal, just, sincere, disinterested; a man who shows what a man can be."

The old man talked of a visit he had paid to Orta, the young man's native place.

"The people there talk of you, though they do not know what you are saying or what you are doing. They think of you because you represent a different race of men, a different way of living; and, since you were born among them, you represent what every young man at Orta might become."

"Is that enough?" the young man asked. "I do not think it is enough."

"For the time being I do not see anything else," the old man said. "One must respect time. Every season has its own work. There is the season for pruning the vines, the season for spraying them, the season for preparing the barrels, the season for gathering and pressing the grapes. If in spring, when the vines are being tied to the stakes, some one passes by and says: 'It is not worth while doing that, because if the barrels are bad the wine will be spoiled; the first thing to do is to attend to the barrels,' you can answer him and say: 'Every season has its own work. This is not the season for cleaning out the barrels, but for pruning the vines and tying them to the stakes. Let me, therefore, remove the useless branches from the vines, let me prune and tie them to the stakes.' "

Marta came in to bid the young man good-night before she went to bed. The young man rose and said good-by to Don Benedetto, too, because it had grown late and the carriage was waiting for him at one of the village inns. Before he left he wrote an address on a piece of paper, put it in an envelope, and gave it to the old man.

"I expect to go back to Rome in a week's time," he said. "Here is my address for the next few days, in case you should have need of me."

The man from Pratola was waiting for Don Paolo with his carriage at the bottom of the hill. The priest had changed back into clerical garb and took his place without speaking.

"How is Don Benedetto?" the driver asked.

"Very well."

"If only everyone were like him!"

The great hollow of the Fucino was dotted all round with lights, as in a fairy tale. A north wind was blowing from Pescina and the plain seemed to be swelling like an inlet of the sea.

When Don Paolo reached his hotel he found Bianchina in his room, sewing and mending in the midst of a heap of washing, which was spread all over the chairs and the bed.

"That's my outfit for going abroad," she said. "I'm mending some old chemises my aunt gave me. I'm putting my initials on everything. It would be absurd to go to Paris without my initials on everything!"

"Are you thinking of going to Paris?" the priest asked.

"Didn't you promise to take me with you?" the girl replied.

"You're quite right, so I did," Don Paolo admitted. "I had completely forgotten it. But I must tell you that I no longer wish to go there now."

The girl had been thinking of the journey every day, and working at her outfit every night. Not only was she bitterly disappointed, but she was furious with Don Paolo for forgetting to tell her that he had changed his mind and letting her go on dreaming about Paris.

"Why don't you take me seriously?" she grumbled at him.

"I don't take you seriously because you are a little fool," the priest was thoughtless enough to reply.

This caused her to burst out crying. She sat down on the floor and covered her aunt's chemises with tears. Don Paolo was annoyed, but let her go on weeping, and waited for her to go away so that he could go to bed. When the tears were on the point of ceasing Bianchina, between one lament and the next, promised to be a good girl, but insisted on being told whether she really deserved to be insulted like that.

"Why am I a fool?" she said. "Please tell me why I am a fool. Is it because I go with men? Or because I'm not married yet?"

"Have you ever thought of working?" the priest asked her.

"What has work got to do with it?"

"Working is not a certain way of becoming a serious person, but it often helps," the priest replied.

Bianchina was disappointed. Was that the only reason why he thought her a fool?

Next day she raised the subject again. In the end she seemed convinced. She decided to go to Rome. Don Paolo gave her the money for the journey and two letters. One was to the wife of the political prisoner, Chelucci, asking her to help Bianchina find some kind of work. The other was to be delivered to Romeo by Chelucci's wife. It was written in lemon juice, announcing his early return to Rome and asking Romeo to find him a safe place to stay.

Chapter XI

DON PAOLO went to Pietrasecca for a few days, intending to remain just long enough for Romeo to find him a safe place to stay in Rome. One evening he kept Matalena company on the ground floor of the inn while she prepared the flour for baking. At Pietrasecca bread was baked once a fortnight in a communal oven; bread-making was a rite with rigid rules. Matalena had covered her hair with a cloth, rather like a nun's veil, and was passing the flour through a sieve over an open bin. She was separating the white flour from the chaff, and the fine flour from the ordinary flour. The chaff was used for the pigs and chickens, the ordinary flour for bread, and the fine flour for pastry. The woman's face and hands were powdered with flour dust raised by the rhythmical movement of the sieve. Americo, on his knees before the hearth, wept copiously while lighting the green wood underneath a caldron in which potatoes were to be cooked. They were to be added to the flour to make the bread heavier and more filling. Don Paolo looked on in silence, thinking of how the bread was made in his own home at Orta, of the care and assiduity with which his mother carried out every detail of the ceremony, first of all making the sign of the Cross. He remembered the voice of the baker's wife calling out in the night from the street—the first call for the yeast needed to make the dough ferment; the second call for the preparation of the loaves; and the third call for taking the trays to the communal oven.

Matalena stopped shaking her sieve when an unknown young man, who appeared to be something between a peasant and a workman, entered the inn and asked for Don Paolo. He handed

Don Paolo a note. It consisted of a few words written in Don Benedetto's fine, tremulous handwriting.

"*Ecce homo,* my friend," it said. "Behold a poor man who has need of you; perhaps you also have need of him. Hear him to the end."

The young man seemed surprised and embarrassed on seeing Don Paolo. He made as if to go away, but stopped and apologized.

"Don Benedetto told me he was sending me to a man in whom I could have full confidence. To tell the truth, I did not expect to find a priest," he said.

Don Paolo took the young man upstairs to his room and sat down by his side.

"If you had come to me as one goes to a priest," he said, "quite frankly I should have told you to apply elsewhere. But if you can forget my priest's clothing and regard me solely as a man, a man like yourself, who knows? Perhaps Don Benedetto may have been right in sending a poor man like you to me. . . . How long have you known him?"

"We belong to the same village," the young man said. "Every family at Rocca knows every other. Everybody knows everything, or almost everything, about everybody else. If you see somebody going out, you know where he is going. If you see him coming home, you know where he has been. My family has a vineyard next to Don Benedetto's garden, halfway up the hill, above the village. We draw water from his pond when we spray our vines, and he uses our stakes for his tomatoes, beans, and peas. My mother always consulted him about my education. His advice may not always have been right, but his intentions were. He has always liked me, ever since I was a child."

As the young man spoke, his features became better defined. True, at first sight, he looked half a workman and half a peasant, particularly because of his patched and shabby clothing, the many earthy scratches on his hands and face, and his unruly and untidy hair. But, looked at more closely, his eyes were exceptionally lively and intelligent, and his ways were modest and polite. And he did not talk in dialect, but in correct and fluent Italian. The confidence both men had in Don Benedetto drew them together. The young man started telling his life story.

"When I was a boy I was weak and delicate," he said, "and I was an only son, besides. For that reason my mother decided I should not grow up to till the soil. 'All our forefathers tilled the soil,' my mother said, 'and we always remained where we were. We have raked, dug, sown, fertilized the soil for countless generations, and always remained poor. Let us make this son study. He is not strong, and needs an easy life.' My father was against this. 'The earth is hard but safe,' he said. 'Education is for the sons of gentlemen. And we have no influence to help us.' Our influence was Don Benedetto. 'Since the lad is well-disposed to study, let him study,' he said. He helped my mother with his advice. As long as I was at the lower school my family could still consider themselves well off. Besides the vineyard, my father owned two fields, on which he grew corn and vegetables, and he had a cowshed with four cows. The money for my schooling never came regularly, but it came. During my three years at the upper school my family's position went from bad to worse. There were two bad harvests and my father was taken ill with pleurisy, and on top of that there was the heavy expense of my education. My father had to sell one of his fields to pay his debts. Two cows were taken ill and died, and the two others were sold at market and the cowshed was let. 'It doesn't matter,' my mother said. 'When our son has finished his examinations he will be able to help us.' Three years ago I passed the state examinations and in October I went to Rome, where I matriculated in the faculty of arts. My mother did not know where to turn to find the money to keep me in Rome until I took my degree."

"Why did you choose the faculty of arts?" Don Paolo asked. "It doesn't offer the best prospects for earning a living."

"Don Benedetto thought I had more talent for arts than for science," the young man answered. "In his mind that settled the question. At Rome I started a life of great hardship. I lived in a room with no light. At midday my only nourishment was coffee and bread, and in the evening I had soup. I lived in perpetual hunger. I was oddly clothed. I had no friends. My provincial appearance meant that when I tried approaching other students they laughed at me and made stupid jokes about me. Two or three incidents like that were sufficient to make me shyer than ever. I often used to weep with rage and mortification in my little room. I resigned myself to a life of solitude. I felt ill at ease in the noisy, vulgar, cynical student world after the atmosphere of warm affection in which I had grown up at Rocca. What most of the students were interested in was sport and politics, because both provide frequent opportunities for collective rowdiness. I cared nothing for football or for politics, and understood less. One day I witnessed a typical piece of student rowdiness. I was in a tram. About a dozen students of my faculty started beating a young workman in the middle of the street, till the blood flowed. I remember the scene very well. The workman lay on the ground, in the roadway, with his bleeding head on the tram line, while the students stood all around him and kicked him and beat him with sticks. 'He didn't salute the flag,' they shouted. Some policemen arrived and congratulated them on their patriotic action and arrested the injured man. A big crowd gathered, but kept completely silent. I remained alone inside the stationary tram. What cowardice, I muttered to myself. A dozen youths against a single, defenseless man! I heard some one whisper behind me, 'Yes, it's shameful.' It was the conductor. That was all we said to each other that day, but as he was often on duty on the line that went down my street, we saw each other every now and then and got into the habit of greeting each other as though we knew each other.

"One day we happened to meet in the street. It was his day off. We shook hands and went to a tavern and had a glass of wine. We told each other our life stories, and made friends. He invited me to his home, where I met other people, nearly all of the same age. These people, five of them in all, constituted a 'group,' and these gatherings were the 'group meetings.' These were strange and new things to me. The tramway man proposed me and I was admitted to the group. I started attending the weekly meetings regularly. Because of the lonely life I had been leading, these were the first personal contacts with townsmen that I had. As I was a student, the other members of the group, who were workers and artisans, were favorably disposed towards me. My purely human pleasure in these meetings kept me from realizing at first the importance and gravity of the step I had taken. At the meetings we read badly printed little papers and pamphlets, which spoke of tyranny with hatred and of the revolution as a certain, inevitable, and imminent event, which would reëstablish fraternity and justice among mankind. We indulged in a kind of weekly dream, a secret and forbidden dream, which made us forget the wretchedness of our everyday life. It was like taking part in the occult rites of a secret religion. There was no link between us apart from these weekly meetings, and if by chance we met in the street we pretended not to recognize each other.

"One morning, on leaving my house, I was arrested by two policemen. I was taken to the central police station, put in a room full of more policemen, and for a whole hour my ears were boxed and I was spat upon. Perhaps I might have borne more violent blows more easily than the treatment I actually received. When the door opened and the official who was to question me came in, my face and chest were literally covered with spittle. The official rebuked, or pretended to rebuke, his subordinates; he let me wash and dry my clothes, and took me to his office. He said he had studied my case with benevolence and understanding. He knew that I lived in a little room, he knew the dairy where I took my midday coffee and the inn where I went for my soup in the evening. He had detailed information about my family, and knew of the difficulties which made it doubtful whether I should be able to continue my studies. But he said he could only make surmises concerning the impulse that had led me into the revolutionary groups. He said the impulse was not in itself a reprehensible thing. On the contrary, he said, youth was by nature generous and aspiring. 'Alas if it were not so!' he added. But it was the rôle of the police, an unwelcome rôle, perhaps, but a socially necessary one, to keep a close watch on the dreams and generous impulses of youth. . . .''

"In short," Don Paolo interrupted, "he suggested you should enter the service of the police. And what did you reply?"

Matalena appeared at the door and said supper was ready. Should she lay for two?

"I am not hungry this evening," the priest said.

He rose from his seat and lay on the bed, because he was tired. The young man resumed his story. At first Don Paolo barely heard what he said; he was almost deafened by a sudden pounding of his heart and a loud humming in his ears. The young man continued in a weary voice:

"I was given a hundred lire to pay for my room, and in exchange I wrote a short report, in the form of an academic essay, on 'How a group works, what its members read, and what its aspirations are.' The official read it and praised it. 'It is really well written,' he said, and I was proud that he was pleased with me. I undertook to remain in contact with him in return for a salary of five hundred lire a month. This enabled me to have soup at midday as well as in the evening and to go to the cinema on Saturday nights. One day the official gave me a packet of cigarettes as well. I had never smoked in my life, but I learned how to, out of politeness."

"And what did you write in your next reports?" Don Paolo asked.

"My next reports were quite general in nature, too, and that made him start grumbling. I always sent him copies of the literature distributed in the groups, but that didn't satisfy him; no doubt he received the same things from other sources. Eventually he advised me to change my group and enter a more interesting one. I had no difficulty in doing so, because as soon as I said I would like to be transferred to a group in which there were other 'intellectuals,' my friends agreed. In the new group I joined I met a girl, a dressmaker, and made friends with her, and we became fond of each other at once. She was the first woman I had ever known, and what a woman! Very soon we were inseparable. It was with her that I began to feel the first remorse; it was with her that I first caught a glimpse of a clean, honest, and disinterested way of life. I had never believed in the possi-

bility of such a thing before. Thus my group life led to a deep-
ening of my moral sensibility, but at the same time I was digging
an insuperable abyss between my outward and my secret life.

"There were days when I managed to forget my secret, when
I worked for the group with devotion and enthusiasm, translated and typed whole chapters of revolutionary novels sent us
from abroad, and stuck propaganda leaflets on the walls at night.
But I was only deceiving myself. When my comrades in the new
group admired me for my activity and courage, they only reminded me that in reality I was betraying and deceiving them,
and then I tried to shun them and avoid their presence. Besides,
I said to myself, I too have the right to live. I received no more
money from home. When I was hungry, or had no money to pay
my rent at the end of the month, I forgot all my qualms; I could
not see any other way. I decided that politics was grotesque—
nothing but an artificial struggle between rival degenerates.
What did it all have to do with me, I told myself. I should certainly have preferred to live in peace, eat three or four meals
a day, go to the university, practice a profession, and let both
the 'necessity of imperial expansion' on the one hand and 'economic democracy' on the other go to the devil; but unfortunately it was impossible. I had no money for either food or rent.
But all my cynical arguments along these lines collapsed when
I was with my girl. We were desperately in love. In my eyes she
did not represent a different kind of politics, a different way
of arguing; as a matter of fact she argued very little, but generally kept silent and willingly listened to others; she represented much more a way of existing, a way of living, a way of
giving oneself in an unparalleled pure and human manner.
I became unable to think of life without her, for she was more
than a woman; she was a flame and a light, the concrete proof
of the possibility of living on this earth honestly, cleanly, disinterestedly, striving wholeheartedly for human truth and justice.
My spiritual life seemed to have begun only at the moment I
met her. But in her presence, in the face of her ingenuous faith
in me, how could I not remember that I was deceiving and betraying? Thus our love was poisoned at the roots. Being with

her, although I loved her so much, was a torment, an insupportable pretense. . . ."

Don Paolo recalled the numerous cases of political denunciation he had known in his party life. A clandestine organization in a country under the heel of a dictatorship is continually engaged in a blind and desperate struggle against police infiltration. But Don Paolo had always pictured the informer in a somewhat conventional and uniform manner. For the first time he saw before him the writhing soul of a poor man in whom everything human and decent had been soiled, tarnished, and trampled underfoot.

"Why didn't you break with the police?" Don Paolo asked.

"Several times I tried to disappear," the young man continued. "Once I changed my address, but I was easily traced. For some time I tried to quiet my conscience by sending the police harmless, false, or reticent reports. That was at a time when my mother had started sending me a little money again every month. I tried to deceive the police by saying I had been excluded from the group because my comrades no longer trusted me. But the police had other informers who were easily able to prove the opposite. In the end I became obsessed with the idea that my position was irremediable. I felt I was damned and that nothing could be done. It was my destiny, from which there was no escape. I do not wish now to make myself out as less ugly than I was. I do not wish to make my case more pitiful. I wish to present myself in all my hideous nakedness. The truth is this. The fear of being found out was stronger in me than remorse. I said to myself: What will my girl say if she discovers I am a traitor? What will my friends say? I was obsessed with the fear of being found out. I trembled at the danger to my reputation, not at the evil I was doing. And everywhere about me I saw the image of my own fear. It is well known that the police have their informers in every section of every big factory, in every bank, in every big office. In every block of flats the porter is, by law, a stool pigeon of the police. In every profession, in every club, in every syndicate, the police have their ramifications. Their informers are legion, whether they work for a miserable pittance or whether their only incentive is the hope of advancement in their careers. This state of affairs spreads suspicion and distrust throughout all classes of the population. On this degradation of man into a frightened animal, who quivers with fear and hates his neighbor in his fear, and watches him, betrays him, sells him, and then lives in fear of discovery, the dictatorship is based. He who has had the misfortune to succumb to this shame is condemned to wishing that the dictatorship may endure. At the bottom of his humiliated heart he hates it mortally, but he dreads its disappearance, for then everything will be known and he will be found out. He is bound to his own shame by a chain of fear. Perhaps some element of these conditions exists within the framework of every state, but never before has a regime been built on the corruption of its morally weakest citizens and their accomplice, fear. The real organization on which the present system in this country is based is the secret manipulation of fear. As long as I remained at Rome I was its prisoner. I knew that I was watched by the police; that they no longer trusted me. So I stayed away from my friends, in order to avoid being compelled to denounce them. The police threatened me with arrest should I be in contact with my suspects without at once informing them. I had a mad fear of arrest. I tried to live as far as possible in solitude. Every encounter with my girl was agony. In spite of it she was always patient, gentle, affectionate. We celebrated Christmas Day last year in a restaurant outside the gates. . . ."

Don Paolo went on listening to the painful story he already knew. He heard every detail over again—the unusually happy lunch, the invitation to go home with the girl, the buying of the flowers, fruit, sweets, and Marsala, the arrival of the police, the hiding on the roof, the long wait. . . . But the young man did not finish the story. He hid his face in his hands and started weeping like a child.

"I came home," he said, when he was able to continue, "and told my parents the doctor had advised me to return to my native climate. I spent the whole winter at home, without seeing anybody. Sometimes I went to see Don Benedetto, who gave me books to read. In the spring I started working with my father, weeding the cornfields, pruning the vines, digging and threshing.

I worked as long as I could stand erect, until my very bones seemed to bend inside of me. I worked to the point of physical collapse. In the evening, immediately after supper, I would go straight to bed, and every morning I woke my father at dawn. He looked at me admiringly and said one could see I came of country stock. 'Who comes from the soil cannot free himself from the soil,' he said. But he who comes from the country and has lived in a city is neither peasant nor townsman. Memory of the city, of my girl, of the group, of the police, was like a gaping wound, a wound that still bled and had become gangrenous and threatened to poison the whole of my life. My mother said that the air of the city had ruined me and put sadness in my blood. 'Let me work,' I told her, 'perhaps work will cure me.' But even in the fields the lovely image of my girl would haunt me. How could I forget all that I had learned from her? After glimpsing the possibility of another life that would be clean, honest, and courageous, after that frank communion with another and those lovely dreams of a better humanity, how could I reconcile myself to life in a village? But, on the other hand, how could I undo what I had done? In my solitary brooding, which left me not a moment's peace, I passed from dread of being punished to dread of not being punished. I began to be obsessed with the idea that I was haunted by the evil I had done only because there was a possibility of my being found out. I started wondering whether my situation wouldn't be more tolerable if I could find an improved technique that would enable me to betray my friends without running any risk of eventual exposure.

"At heart I had never believed in God. I was baptized, confirmed, received communion, like everybody else, but I had never really believed in the reality of God. Consequently, at Rome, I had no difficulty whatever in accepting the so-called scientific theories that were disseminated in the groups. But in my meditations at Rocca these theories began to seem too comfortable. They suited my situation only too well. The idea that everything was matter, that the idea of good was inseparable from the idea of utility (even if it were social utility) and was based on the idea of punishment, became insupportable to me. Punishment by whom? The state? The group? Public opinion? But what if the state, the group, public opinion were immoral? Besides, supposing there were a definite method, a definite technique, of doing evil with assured impunity: what would then be the basis of morality? Could a technique which eliminated all danger of retribution destroy the distinction between good and evil? That thought terrified me. I became filled with dread of chaos, of the void. I do not want to bore you with these digressions, which may seem abstract and remote to you. I do not wish you to think I am trying to put myself in a more favorable light by mere empty verbiage. But those were the ideas that became the substance of my life. I did not believe in God, but I started wishing with my whole soul that God existed. I had need of Him to escape from my fear of the void. One night I could stand it no longer, and I went to knock at the door of a Capuchin monastery not far from my home. On the way I met one of the monks whom I knew, one Brother Antifona. 'I want so much to believe in God,' I said to him, 'and I cannot. Will you not tell me how it is done?' 'One must not be proud,' he answered, 'one must not try to understand everything; one must not strive but resign oneself, close one's eyes and pray. Faith is a gift of God.' But I was born without that gift. I wanted to understand everything. It was impossible for me not to try to understand. My whole being was in a state of extreme and agonizing tension. I could not resign myself. I wanted God, by force! I had need of Him, but He did not answer me.

"So I went to Don Benedetto, not because he was a priest, but because in my eyes he has always been the pattern of the righteous man. He has known me since my childhood, as I have told you. I went to him and told him that in reality he did not yet know me at all, because he had no suspicion of what was hidden in me. I made an agonizing effort, and told him everything. My confession lasted five hours, and at the end I lay prostrate and exhausted on the floor. He sent his sister, Marta, to tell my mother that I was going to sleep at his house that night, and that for the next few days I would help him working in his garden. I worked with him in his garden, and from time to time he would stop and talk to me. He taught me that nothing is irreparable while life lasts, and that no condemnation is eternal. He told me also that though one should not be in love with evil, nevertheless good was often born of evil, and that perhaps I might never have become a real man without the calamities and errors through which I had passed. When at last he let me go home, I was no longer afraid. I felt I had been reborn, and I was struck by the breeze that was blowing from the mountains. I had never breathed such fresh, pure air before. Having ceased to fear, I stopped battling with myself and started rediscovering the world. Once more I saw the trees, and the children in the streets, and the poor people working in the fields, and the donkeys carrying their loads, and the oxen drawing the plow. I went on seeing Don Benedetto from time to time. Yesterday he sent for me and said: 'I should like to spare you the repetition of your suffering, but there is a man in the neighborhood of Rocca to whom I wish you to repeat your confession. He is a man you can trust completely.' He gave me the necessary directions, and I came."

It had grown dark. The young man's tired voice ceased in the darkness, and the voice of the other answered him.

"If I were the head of a party or a political group," he said, "I should judge you according to the party statutes. Every party is based on a definite ideology and is equipped with a corresponding morality, which is codified in objective rules. Often these rules are very like those with which every man is inspired by his own conscience, often they are the very reverse. But I am not, or am no longer, a political leader. I am just an ordinary mortal, and, if I am to judge another man, I can have nothing to guide me but my own conscience. Besides, it is only within the narrowest limits that one man has the right to judge another."

"I did not come here to seek pardon or absolution," the young man said. "There are wounds that should not be bandaged and hidden, but exposed to the sun. The usual ritual and sacramental confession, generally carried out behind a grating, is a ceremony towards which I have reservations, but a confession of one man to another can be like the cauterization of a wound."

"Luigi Murica," the other said, softly, "I want to tell you something that will prove to you how much I now trust you. I am not a priest, and Don Paolo Spada is not my real name. My real name is Pietro Spina."

Matalena had laid the table for two, and insisted that the two men come downstairs to supper.

"A convalescent mustn't miss his meals," she said. "And if he has a visitor, the least he can do is to invite him."

She had put a clean tablecloth and a bottle of wine on the table. The two men ate in silence. The wine was last year's and the bread last fortnight's. The two men dipped the old bread in the new wine. Murica wished to return to Rocca the same evening, and Don Paolo went upstairs to fetch his coat and accompany him part of the way. Matalena could not conceal a certain jealousy at this sudden friendship between "her" priest and this unknown young man.

"You've been talking all this time and you still have things to say to each other?" she said to Murica.

"I have been making my confession," the young man said.

When the two men parted down the valley road Murica said: "Now I am ready for anything."

"We shall talk again very soon," the priest promised him.

Voices could be heard, muffled by the distance, the voices of shepherds calling, dogs barking, the subdued baaing of sheep. A gentle scent of thyme and wild rosemary rose from the damp earth. It was the hour when the peasants put their donkeys back in their sheds and went to bed. Mothers, leaning out of windows, called to their tarrying children. It was an hour for humility. Man returned to animal, animal to plant, plant to earth. The stream at the bottom of the valley reflected innumerable stars. All that was visible of Pietrasecca, sunken in the shadow, was the cow's skull with the two big, curving horns at the top of Matalena Ricotta's inn.

In the daytime Pietrasecca had reassumed its usual torpidity. Now that the superficial excitement of mobilization day was over, the peasants had gone back to their normal, unchanging life. The village had been emptied of its youngest men, that was

all. The old peasants ate their soup in silence at the thresholds
of their hovels, looking neither to the right nor to the left, and
answered questions in bored and tired voices. A few mothers
of soldiers now received a small allowance and hoped in their
heart of hearts that it would last. As for anything else, it was not
worth troubling about, for what would be would be. War had
been coming, and war had come. If it really was going to be followed by a pestilence, very well, the pestilence would come, too,
and nothing whatever could be done about it. Everything destined to come would come; and in the end everything that came
would go away. The schoolboys now had battles with stones outside the church, Africans against Italians. Sometimes the Africans
beat the Italians, to the horror and indignation of the schoolmistress.

Magascià's wife heard from Matalena that Don Paolo had received permission to hear confessions, and came and implored
him to confess her husband, who had not been reconciled to
God for twenty-five years.

"He has no trust in the priests in this part of the world," she
said, "and the chance of a strange priest's coming to Pietrasecca
will not occur again. If you don't do him this favor, sir, he
will die in sin and go to hell."

The priest tried to explain that he had received no permission
whatever to hear confessions, but the woman went away and
old Magascià arrived. The tall, bearded, massive man, hat in
hand, nearly filled the doorway. His empty left sleeve was tucked
into his pocket. Don Paolo received him sitting in a chair beside
his bed and tried to say something, but the old man knelt at
his feet, made the sign of the Cross, kissed the floor, and recited
the *confiteor* with his face to the ground and struck his breast
three times.

"*Mea culpa, mea culpa, mea maxima culpa,*" he muttered.

Without raising his head, and lowering his voice still more, he
continued muttering in an incomprehensible fashion for several
minutes. All Don Paolo could make out was a low, sibilant sound
interrupted by brief sighs. When he stopped he remained prostrate on the ground, taking up half the room with his enormous

bulk. His gigantic stature reminded Don Paolo of a geological specimen, a fossilized, antediluvian monster. His beard and hair recalled wild vegetation, but the fear that his attitude expressed revealed him to be a man. He remained prostrate and silent for some time. Then he raised his head and asked in his ordinary voice:

"Well, is it finished? . . . Have you given me absolution? May I go?"

"You may go."

Magascià rose to his feet and kissed the priest's hand.

"I should like to ask you something I don't dare ask anyone else. Can one be prosecuted for murder after twenty-five years? Does one have to be tried in an assize court if one is found out after twenty-five years?"

"What murder?"

Magascià could not understand why the priest should now appear so ignorant, but since the question was a pressing one, he whispered in his ear:

"The murder of Don Giulio, the notary of Lama."

"Oh!" said the priest. "Yes, of course, I see. I had already forgotten it. . . . But I am not a lawyer, and I do not know the answer to your question."

The news that Don Paolo had received permission to hear confessions spread quickly.

Magascià had said:

"He is a confessor who understands and forgives everything."

"He is more than a confessor," Matalena maintained. "He is a saint who reads poor sinners' hearts."

People flocked to the inn to find out for themselves. Don Paolo's room became public property, with people continually going in and out. Everyone wanted to fix a time for his own confession. Children swarmed up the stairs and gathered round the doorway, not daring to approach the saint who could no longer hide or protect himself.

Old Gesira came in, turned everybody else out, closed the door behind her, went down on her knees, recited the *confiteor*, and started telling her life story. The old woman rasped like a pepper-mill, but a toothless pepper-mill, with yellow, shapeless lips. Beneath the filthy remnants of her hair she showed the priest her ear, of which only half was left, and explained that the rest of it had been bitten off by a donkey when she was a girl. She described in detail various injuries in various parts of her body which had been caused by her husband. Nobody had ever seen these injuries because, thanks be to God, she had never let anyone see her body, but the injuries were just as real as the spear wound in the side of the crucified Saviour. Her husband had been dead for twenty years, having perished in the earthquake.

"When the earthquake happened," Gesira said, "God willed it that I should be in the street. Three-quarters of Pietrasecca collapsed. My husband was in bed, and was buried beneath the wreckage of our house, which collapsed entirely, as if it had been razed to the ground. Now that I'm a widow, I'll choose my second husband a little more carefully, I said to myself at once. That, I must confess, was my first thought. Those of us who escaped the earthquake took refuge behind the cemetery, in the snow, in a few tents we rigged up as best we could. We had to keep huge fires roaring all night to drive the wolves away, and we gathered dry wood for the fires from among the débris of our houses. One evening, when I was collecting the remains of some of my household goods from the wreckage, I heard a faint voice coming from under the stones. 'Gesira,' it said, 'Oh, Gesira.' My husband was alive! I was so frightened that I ran away. If he's rescued, I thought to myself, he'll kill me for not getting him out at once. Besides, I thought, he's probably got a broken arm or a broken leg, so he'll be crippled for the rest of his life, and we'll be poorer than ever. Next day I went again to the place where he was buried, and again I heard his voice calling, but it had grown much weaker. 'Oh, Gesira!' it said. 'Oh, Gesira!' If God had wished him to live, He wouldn't have had him buried by the earthquake, I thought to myself. A few days later soldiers came to clear the débris and bury the dead. He was one of the first to be found and buried. My second marriage was no better than the first. After six months my second husband went to the Argentine. He took my money and never came back. Such is the lot of us poor women!"

Gesira waited for the priest to say something, make the usual little homily, ask her the usual questions, and give her the usual absolution. But Don Paolo looked at her doubtfully, without saying a word.

"May I go?" the old woman asked. "Is it finished?"

"It is not finished," the priest said. "But you may go."

Mastrangelo arrived, with Lidovina, his wife, and Marietta, his sister-in-law, holding him up, because his leg was still bandaged and he could walk only with difficulty. He could not kneel, so the two women helped him to a chair by the priest's side. Then they went away. Mastrangelo spoke into the priest's ear to prevent anyone from overhearing. His breath was foul; it stank of many years' drinking and nearly made Don Paolo's head reel.

"My wife has had eighteen children, but God has already taken back sixteen of them," he said. "Two remain. Some flesh is chastised as soon as it is born, and there is no help for it. Marietta, my wife's sister, has been chastised in a different manner. She was poor, but in good health. Before she married Nicola Ciccavo, when everything was ready and all the announcements had been made, he came to me and spoke to me privately and said he wanted to tell me a secret. He said he had been chastised by the war. He showed me his misfortune. That man, who looked so strong and robust, was no longer a man. He had been castrated in the military hospital, in order to save his life. The wretched man was alone in the world, without mother or sister, with no one to wash his shirts or make his bed or cook his soup; it was right that he should want to marry. He had a vineyard and a medal. If Magascià died, the salt and tobacco monopoly would go to him, because of the medal. Magascià was an old man even then, and it was reasonable to expect that he would die soon, and if he is still alive it isn't my brother-in-law's fault. So Nicola and Marietta were married. Marietta did not discover his misfortune till after the ceremony. Nicola said: 'Your brother-in-law, Mastrangelo, knew all about it,' so she sent for me and started crying. 'You're the ruin of me,' she said, 'and

I shall kill myself for shame!' Nicola left us alone, but before he went he said, 'Since God chastised me I have no right to be jealous; but only on condition that the family honor is saved.' Marietta has had six children, four of whom are still alive. Making children is like drinking. This glass will be the last, you say to yourself. But then you get thirsty again and have another glass. Just this last one, and then no more, you say. But who can control his thirst? Sometimes it is the woman who is thirsty and sometimes the man; sometimes both. At first relations between the two sisters were very difficult, but things accommodated themselves in time. We accepted it all with resignation, as God's will. Our honor has been saved; there has been no scandal; no one has ever known about it. But one day Nicola went and confessed to Don Cipriano; and Don Cipriano made him change his mind. Don Cipriano tells him that the punishments God has sent us are nothing in comparison with those we deserve and those we are still to receive; and those not visited upon us will be visited upon our children, who are the children of sin; and those that are not visited upon our children will be visited upon our children's children, even unto the seventh generation. But if God knows the truth, how can He go on punishing us? Have we not suffered enough?"

The penitent stopped and gazed at the priest with fixed and bloodshot eyes, waiting for a reply. The excited voices of some drinkers playing morra came floating up the stairs. "Five! . . . Five! . . . Five!" one of them shouted, and another called out, shrilly: "Three! . . . Nine! . . . Six!" On the window-pane the priest saw two flies on top of one another, surprised by death in the act of love. Outside it was raining. Don Paolo shuddered.

"Mastrangelo," he said, "I ask you to believe me, but I do not know what to say to you. I have never thought of a case like yours."

"What do the Scriptures say?" Mastrangelo asked.

"I shall see," said the priest. "I shall look."

Mastrangelo called Lidovina and Marietta, who came upstairs and helped their man out of the room, casting inquiring glances at him as if to divine the result of the confession.

Other penitents were sitting on the stairs, waiting their turn to confess. An acute and pungent smell came up the staircase, as if they never washed. Don Paolo put on his hat and coat and took refuge in the street, although it was raining. He remembered a visit he had paid to the sewers of Paris. He felt he had been visiting a sewer now. He had always instinctively avoided penetrating man's individual troubles and secrets—perhaps because he feared that the rather simple idea he had formed of human sufferings and their solution might be destroyed in the process; perhaps, also, because he was afraid of being confronted with sufferings that had no solution. Uliva's trenchant judgment of him suddenly returned to his mind. "You are afraid of the truth. You force yourself to believe in progress, to be an optimist and a revolutionary, because you are terrified of the opposite."

In order not to be drenched to the skin and to avoid returning to the inn, Don Paolo sought refuge in the Colamartini house. Cristina opened the door. He had caught only casual glimpses of her since returning to Pietrasecca. She looked thin and ill, and the black she wore in mourning for her father accentuated her appearance.

"We were talking about you," the girl said.

She led him to the big kitchen, where the whole family was assembled, Cristina's grandmother, aunt, mother, and brother.

Alberto was in the uniform of an officer in the government militia.

"I enlisted voluntarily," he explained. "I shall get a few hundred lire a month, instead of rotting away here doing nothing. If I hadn't volunteered I should have been called up anyway. It's better to make a virtue of necessity."

There was a slight mustiness in the kitchen, relieved by an odor of preserves and aromatic wine. The women remained silent. Through the window Don Paolo looked out at the garden wet with rain. It had taken on its autumn tints. The flowers had run to seed; the seeds had fallen to earth; and from them new flowers would grow. Cristina's aunt rose to retire and asked Cristina's mother to come with her. Cristina's mother had difficulty in understanding, and laughed stupidly, like an idiot.

Cristina and Alberto went out, too, to look after the mare in the stable.

"You were the last person to whom my son Pasquale spoke before he left Fossa. What did he say?" the old woman asked.

"He said: 'This is the end,'" the priest answered. "He did not wish to be accompanied. It was indeed the end, and that was all he said."

The old woman, dressed entirely in black, was sitting in an easy-chair covered with old red velvet, near one of the windows that looked out on the garden. She was small, wrinkled, and shriveled. She looked at the priest with glassy, inscrutable, absent eyes, and when she spoke she showed her empty gums. The other members of the family did not return.

"They left us alone because they want me to confess," the old woman said. "But I don't want to confess. I lack the repentance necessary to confess. Why should I repent?"

She held her hands crossed on her breast. They looked like two old utensils worn out by long and painful labor. Her thin, fragile arms were as two dry branches waiting to be plucked and put on the hearth.

"Why should I repent?" the old woman asked. "For eighty years I have wished for one thing only, a right thing, the only right thing, the honor of my family. I have never thought of anything else. I have never wished for anything else. I have never done anything else. For eighty years. . . . Am I to repent now?"

Her eyes suddenly dilated, revealing a hopeless anxiety, a long-repressed fear, a dismay so fixed and irreparable, an expression of despair so unguarded and so profound, that it took Don Paolo's breath away.

"Is it the end?" she asked. "Is it really the end? . . . Is it the end of everything or only of the Colamartini?"

The old woman saw that the priest was looking her in the eyes. She closed them. The shape of her skull, which was almost fleshless and practically hairless, reminded Don Paolo of a sparrow; a thing so fragile, and yet so resistant, so firm, so obstinate, so tenacious, so pitiless, so hard, with the hardness of eighty years. Cristina had told her grandmother that if she did not repent and confess she would go to hell. "Very well, I shall go to hell," she had replied. But now that she had an opportunity of consulting a priest, she hastened to ask him about a detail of procedure.

"Those who do not repent and therefore go to hell—how much time are they allowed before the Judgment Throne?" she asked. "Have they at least time to tell Him the truth face to face?"

Don Paolo was compelled to admit that he could not reply positively from his own knowledge; but that ordinary common sense inclined him to answer the second part of the question in the affirmative. That was enough for the old lady.

Cristina came back in time to see Don Paolo to the door, but before saying good-by she showed him a small room, next to the kitchen. It contained a spinning-wheel, at which she worked in all her free hours during the day, and sometimes till late at night.

"We don't know how to live now," the girl said. "You know that we lost all our savings in the bank failure? The land we have left yields nothing. The tenants don't pay."

Cristina had thought she might earn something by weaving, but had changed her mind.

"Wool is dear," she said, "and no one buys hand-woven stuff. It is a luxury. The few orders I have had were given me by friends, solely out of pity for me."

"You are no longer thinking of taking the veil?" Don Paolo asked.

"How could I now?" the girl replied. "These material difficulties are not the greatest evil. I only spoke of them because it breaks my heart to see old women like my mother, my grandmother, and my aunt uncertain of their daily bread right at the end of their lives. But the spiritual collapse is more painful than the material one. My father's death upset the family equilibrium. Things I never heard mentioned before are now the subject of continual argument and discussion."

Just when the priest was going, Cristina said she would like to make her confession to him in the next few days, at any time or place convenient to him.

"Oh no!" Don Paolo exclaimed, blushing suddenly.

The idea of having the secrets of her private life forced upon him was intolerable. He had to explain his refusal in some way, but could find no plausible excuse.

"I advise you to apply to your usual confessor," he said in embarrassment. "However, as I remember with much pleasure the conversations I had with you last spring, I should like to talk with you again before I leave for my diocese, now that so many things have happened."

Thus they parted, hoping soon to meet again.

Sciatàp was waiting for Don Paolo in Matalena's bar. He had just returned from the plain with a note from Marta, saying that Don Benedetto was in danger. "The person who warned us did so in terms that left no doubt of the seriousness of his warning. I don't know to whom to apply. Concettino Ragù is in Africa. Dr. Sacca is afraid of losing his position."

It was impossible for Don Paolo to go to Rocca himself to find out what it was all about and what precautions ought to be taken. If Don Benedetto was being watched and he went to see him, he would run the risk of being stopped, recognized, and arrested, and then Don Benedetto would be far more seriously implicated than he could possibly be now. Don Paolo decided to send Marta's note to Murica, who came from Rocca himself, and could therefore move about without attracting attention. Don Paolo added a few suggestions of his own. "As long as actual danger lasts, Don Benedetto must not leave his house alone," he wrote. "If he has to go out, his every step must be accompanied. You ought to go and stay in his house yourself and sleep there."

Don Paolo sent for Sciatàp again.

"How much do you earn a day?" he asked.

"From four to six lire."

"I shall give you two days' pay in advance if you take this letter to Rocca at once."

Sciatàp fetched Garibaldi from his stable, got on his back, and went off at a trot down the valley road.

Next day was Saturday. Cristina also received a letter from

Marta, speaking of the danger Don Benedetto was in. "The provincial commission for deportations," the letter said, "has not dared condemn him to compulsory domicile on an island because of the sensation it would cause. For the same reason he has not been arrested and denounced to the government tribunal. They are afraid of what he might say and write. The plan, so far as one can guess, is to make him quietly disappear." Cristina hurried to Don Paolo with the letter in her hand. Don Paolo's explanations disturbed her more than ever.

"But Don Benedetto never wished to have anything to do with politics whatever," the girl expostulated. "How can he possibly be persecuted as an enemy of the government?"

"We live in a society which has no place for free men," Don Paolo explained. "The only priests who are tolerated are those who put their religion at the service of the government and of the bank. The only artists who are tolerated are those who sell their art. The only philosophers who are tolerated are those who sell their wisdom. The others, though they are few, are imprisoned, deported, boycotted, or quietly made to disappear, as the convenience of the police may decide."

Cristina understood nothing of all this; she was not interested in politics, and did not wish to have anything to do with such things. But she was fond of Don Benedetto and his sister, and if they were now in danger and appealed to her for help she could not possibly abandon them. So, after asking her grandmother's permission, she left for Rocca, with the intention of staying there till Sunday night.

At Rocca everything seemed just as usual. Don Benedetto knew of the danger that threatened him, but he did not know that his sister had told anyone. He went about his everyday affairs with his usual cheerfulness. On the first night, when Murica asked his hospitality, he was not surprised, assuming he had quarreled with his parents. But when Cristina arrived and asked if she could stay with him, he was a little surprised. For Cristina to spend the night anywhere but at home was an event. But he left all these mysteries to be solved by his sister.

On Saturday night the sacristan of the parish of Lama came

and invited Don Benedetto to say Mass next day in the country church of San Martino.

"Why isn't Don Cipriano going?" Marta asked.

"He is busy," the sacristan replied.

As soon as he had gone Marta implored her brother to refuse the invitation.

"There is no reason why I should refuse," Don Benedetto said, and started talking of other things.

Cristina spent the night in Marta's room, Murica slept in the kitchen, and Don Benedetto stayed up late at his desk, tidying his papers and correspondence.

Next morning, when Don Benedetto left the house, Marta was waiting for him, and implored him not to go. There was no need for him to officiate in a church belonging to another parish, she said. Besides, she had dreamed an unlucky dream during the night.

Affectionately but firmly Don Benedetto said good-by to her. He laughed at her superstitious belief in dreams, but he allowed Cristina and Murica to go with him.

It took them nearly an hour to reach Lama on foot. The road was muddy, from the recent rains. Although the sun had risen, the air, suffused with the cold dampness of night, was slow in getting warm. Cristina walked on the old man's right and Murica on his left.

"Cristina," the old man said, "if the man now living at Pietrasecca, in Matalena's inn, ever has need of you, I beg you to help him."

"Do you mean Don Paolo?" the girl asked. "What need could he have of me?"

"Cristina," the old man said, "many things may happen that you will not understand with your head. Try to understand them with your heart."

Mist was rising over the hills from the hollow of the Fucino, like a silent flood, a silent sea. Small islands emerged from the sea; these were the church towers and the tops of the highest poplars.

Don Benedetto talked to the two young people of the time

when he had been their age and had had a temporary enthusiasm
for local archæology. He spoke of his frequent visits to the neighboring villages whenever he heard of any "interesting" stones discovered in the process of digging a vineyard, or of human bones
or skulls turned up in the course of building operations. He
enlivened his stories with jokes and amusing anecdotes, and made
his young companions laugh. When Lama came into sight and
the bells of San Martino were heard calling the faithful to
prayer, Don Benedetto became silent and absorbed. The church
of San Martino was old and neglected, and mass was said there
only a few times a year.

"You will be able to make the responses for me, won't you?"
the old man asked Cristina outside the church.

"Yes," she replied. "I often used to at the convent."

"I am glad you will make the responses for me today," the old
man said.

The façade of the church was of granite, blackened by time,
with a big, roughly carved door.

Don Benedetto went straight to the sacristy through a side
door, and Murica and Cristina went into the church through
the main door. The church floor was paved with gravestones,
dating from the times when cemeteries did not exist and the
dead were buried in the crypts. The interior of the church was
divided into three parts by a double row of columns supporting
arches. Ancient and of various sizes, the columns had no bases,
but rose straight from the floor, and were adorned with rough
capitals decorated in the most varied and haphazard manner.
At the other end of the church there was an altar that looked
like an unadorned stone block, with a wooden crucifix, painted
black, and four candlesticks on it. To the left of the altar was a
fresco representing hell, with black devils, of horrible and repugnant shape, tormenting the souls of damned peasants in the
most ingenious ways. Some were immersed in boiling caldrons
and others impaled on hooks. On the right there was a repre-
sentation of the legend of the three quick and the three dead, a
kind of satire of mediæval society in the form of a *danse macabre*.

The skeletons wore miters, tiaras, and crowns on their heads, and they struck one another in the fervor of the dance.

The sacristan lit the four candles on the altar and rang a bell to announce the beginning of the Mass. There was a congregation of about a dozen in the church, consisting of women and children. Don Benedetto, in his sacred vestments, stood before the first step of the altar, and Cristina knelt for the recitation of the *Introibo*. Cristina gave the responses slowly, speaking the Latin words syllable by syllable. Murica had remained near the door, by the font. A few men came in, late for Mass as usual, dipped their fingers in the holy water, and made the sign of the Cross. One man wore a piece of snake skin in his hatband against the evil eye; another had some badger's hair tied to his watch chain. Don Benedetto went up to the altar and arranged the objects destined to serve for the consummation of the mystery. He put the reading desk with the missal on the right of the altar, and read the Epistle. He moved the reading desk to the left of the altar, and read the Gospel. As the rite proceeded, the faithful participated in the mystery, knelt and rose to their feet as Don Benedetto genuflected, turned to the people, or prayed. Murica alone remained standing the whole time, a simple spectator, and followed in his heart the unrolling of another mystery and another sacrifice.

Don Benedetto genuflected before the altar each time he passed from one side of it to the other. Standing on the right of the altar were the cruet of wine and the cruet of water: Don Benedetto went towards them with the chalice, and poured wine and water into it. At the beginning of the consecration the faithful went down on their knees and bent towards the earth. Softly, Don Benedetto spoke the sacred words of consecration over the bread and wine. Three times he confessed his own unworthiness. Three times he repeated *"Domine non sum dignus."* Then he bent over the altar and consumed the Host; he raised the chalice to his lips and drank from it. The faithful rose to their feet. But Don Benedetto remained motionless at the center of the altar, leaning on it with his elbows as though he were about to faint. Slowly his knees gave way and he collapsed at the foot of the altar. Cristina hurried to him, asked him if he felt ill. A few frightened women started shrieking. Murica ran up the aisle, raised Don Benedetto by the shoulders, and, with Cristina's help, carried him into the sacristy. The faithful left the church and in the little square outside started excited conjectures about the priest's sudden illness.

"He fainted," one said.

"Poor old man!" said another. "The consecrated wine must have been bad for him."

Two militiamen arrived with strange promptness. All that was left for them to do was to confirm Don Benedetto's death. The body was relieved of its sacred vestments and a watch was kept over it until the authorities should arrive. All strangers were asked to leave the sacristy. Cristina and Murica refused and were forcibly ejected. The faithful who were waiting outside in the square surrounded and questioned them. Cristina was trembling with emotion. She was unable to articulate a single word. She gazed wildly around her and scarcely had strength to go back into the church, where she collapsed almost in a faint. Murica lost Cristina from sight, was at a loss to answer the people who questioned him, stammered confusedly, himself started asking those about him what had happened, how on earth a thing like that could have happened. He saw a trap passing. It was going in the direction of Rocca. He stopped it, asked to be given a lift, and was driven away.

Chapter XII

"AFTER all we have been through, we can no longer talk of politics like other people," Don Paolo said to Murica. "Politics have become something quite different for us."

Murica was walking in front of the priest, making a way for him through the brambles and down a steep path that led to the bottom of the valley and then for some distance skirted the stream that came from Pietrasecca. He told Don Paolo what happened after Don Benedetto's death.

"The intervention of the ecclesiastical authorities made it impossible to establish the truth about the cause of death," he said. "The bishop said to Marta: 'Madam, I promise you that full light will be thrown on your brother's death, but in the appropriate manner.' A post-mortem was not considered appropriate and was therefore not held. Marta sent for Dr. Sacca, of Acquafredda, and he went to the cemetery, but he was not allowed to examine the body."

"I am only just beginning to recover from the shock of Don Benedetto's death," Don Paolo said. "I did not know he was so important to me. Until very recently I had not seen him for fifteen years, and it was only rarely that I heard any news of him. It was his teaching that made me a Christian, but not a Christian in the 'appropriate' manner. When I entered real life after leaving school, I developed in a direction quite opposite to that of religion, and I slowly substituted Marxism for Christianity. Nevertheless, even when I was most engrossed in political agitation, it gave me pleasure in my heart of hearts to know that that old man was somewhere. I tried, of course, to shake off all remnants of his teaching, I mocked at the naïveté of all religious

symbolism, I wrote anti-Church articles in the party papers; but
I also wondered what Don Benedetto would say if some one told
him what I was doing. I did not then foresee that circumstances
would lead me towards him and him towards me."

The two walked in single file along the stream. They had to
stop, because the path was interrupted by a ditch. A cloud had
appeared in the sky. It seemed to hesitate which way to go, but
eventually made up its mind and went off in the direction of
the Fucino. In the ditch there lay the white jaw bone of an ass,
with teeth still on it.

"It seems to me now that for fifteen years I was only half
alive," Don Paolo confessed. "During that time I never ceased
trying to smother and repress my deepest impulses, solely because in my youth they had been bound up with religious symbols and practices. I tried, with an obstinacy and a determination
that sprang from my loathing of the Church, to substitute logic
and intellectual ideas taken from the world of economics and
politics for those deeper forces which I felt myself compelled to
distrust. When I returned to the Marsica I realized that my attempt at self-mutilation had not entirely succeeded. I had not
eradicated my religious ideas but only overlaid them with other
ideas. Nevertheless, what I saw of religion at Pietrasecca convinced me that all my distrust of it was justified. When I met
Don Benedetto I was prepared to understand that my vain en-
deavors to do effective work among the peasants, and my un-
satisfied ambition for real and immediate political success, were
the consequence of my internal conflict. I reflected for several
days on what he said. Your coming to Pietrasecca and your confession finally broke down my last resistance. Don Benedetto's
words penetrated to the depths of me. Within a few days all
that remained alive and indestructible of Christianity in me was
revived: a Christianity denuded of all mythology, of all theology, of all Church control; a Christianity that neither abdicates
in the face of Mammon, nor proposes concordats with Pontius
Pilate, nor offers easy careers to the ambitious, but rather leads
to prison, seeing that crucifixion is no longer practiced. This
resurrection of a part of myself for which I used to blush, which

I used to try to exterminate or conceal, now gives me a sense of well-being, even of physical well-being, and of strength and courage of which I did not believe myself capable.

"At Rome, in the group, I used to hear a lot about you, but I did not think you were like this," Murica said. "I used to feel rather frightened of you."

"A revolutionary is a man of flesh and blood, like everybody else," said Don Paolo. "There are some who appear to be made entirely of steel, but at heart they are flesh and blood like everybody else."

The two continued their way down the valley until they reached the place where the valley broadened out and their path rejoined the carriage road.

"Let us stop here," Murica suggested. "If we go on they may see us from the road and recognize us."

During the last few days Murica had been watched a great deal by the police. He did not want to be seen with Don Paolo.

"At Rocca," he said, "I have formed a small group of young writers."

"Writers?"

"Writers."

"I suppose you mean a group of correspondents of small local papers," said Don Paolo.

"They would never consent to contribute to the bourgeois press," Murica replied.

"How many of them are there? What do they write?"

"For the time being there are three of them," said Murica. "It might be possible to attract others, but it is better to be cautious. Besides, three are enough. They are good young fellows, and I know them well. They are poor, and went to elementary schools. They came to me after Don Benedetto's death and asked what ought to be done. We had a discussion, and agreed that the truth ought to be made known. Truth was what Don Benedetto loved best. Making the truth known was the only thing that would have pleased him. They were ready to do anything that would have pleased him. So they have formed themselves into a group of writers of the truth. At night they get on their bicycles, take pieces of chalk or charcoal, and go to neighboring villages and write the truth on the walls. The truth they write is 'Don Benedetto was poisoned.' We discussed whether anything ought to be added to that, but decided that nothing ought ever to be added to the truth, or it would cease to be the truth. We also agreed that it would be idle to add anything to reinforce the truth, because nothing is ever stronger than the pure and simple truth. So we decided that 'Don Benedetto was poisoned' should be written up everywhere, and that this should go on until everybody knew it. We decided to use just those few words by themselves, without even an exclamation mark, so that even those who do not want to understand will have to understand. When it looks as if some people are beginning to forget, we shall start writing 'Don Benedetto was poisoned,' again, and those who want to forget will be forced to remember. That, for the time being, is the function of those writers."

Murica referred to other scattered elements in the neighboring villages. There was a carpenter who had been twelve years in America, where he had been in touch with groups of anarchists; there was a peasant who had been at the head of a league of resistance before the war; there was a man from Pratola who was now a cab-driver at Fossa, and one or two more. But he was afraid he did not know the right way to approach them.

"What you said just now was quite right," he said. "After all that has happened, I cannot go back and talk of politics as before."

"One must talk as little as possible," Don Paolo said. "Try to make friends with the people you have just mentioned, and with any others you may get to know. When you have gained their confidence, you may then be able to make them understand that it is not a matter of putting new formulas, new gestures, or shirts of a different color into circulation, but rather a matter of a new way of living. To use an old expression, it is a matter of conversion. It is a matter of becoming a new man. Perhaps it is sufficient to say that it is a matter of becoming a man, in the real sense of the word. We are so far from manhood now that he who starts comparing his present plight with what he might be cannot fail to be disturbed. He discovers he is mutilated, disfigured, deformed, degraded. At heart every revolution puts this elementary question afresh: What, it asks, is man? What is this human life? There are neurotics for whom revolution is a form of intoxication, a kind of lyrical exaltation. 'Better a day as a lion than a hundred days as a sheep.' But for the poor people revolution stands for something else; it stands for liberation, a need of truth and simplicity, a repudiation alike of the destiny of the sheep and the destiny of the lion, and a vindication of the destiny of man."

"The revolution," said Murica, "is a need of being no longer alone, one man against another; it is an attempt to stand together and to be afraid no longer; a need of brotherliness."

"You cannot conceive what it would mean to a country like ours," said Don Paolo, "if there were a hundred youths ready to renounce all safety, defy all corruption, free themselves from obsession with private property, sex, and their careers, and unite on the basis of absolute sincerity and absolute brotherliness: a hundred youths, who would live among the people, in contact with the workers and the peasants, and refuse to be parted from them; a hundred converted youths, who would speak the truth on every question and on every occasion, nothing but the truth, and live according to the truth; youths who would be recognizable not because they wore emblems in their buttonholes or a uniform, but by their way of living. . . ."

A flock of sheep was grazing in a meadow where the path joined the carriage road. It was the time of year when the flocks are brought down from the mountains to pass the winter in the plain. An old shepherd was lighting a fire of brushwood in the meadow, while a youth blew on it and another youth searched for dry branches. The old man was Bonifazio Patacca, and he called Don Paolo to tell him he had dreamed about Don Benedetto.

"He was smiling," Bonifazio said, "and he wanted to give me a lira."

"Did he give you one?"

"No, he spent a long time fumbling in his pockets, but he couldn't find one."

Don Paolo laughed and gave him a lira.

"Do you know the story of the lake of Fucino, sir?" Bonifazio asked.

Don Paolo did not know it.

"Jesus was going about in search of work, dressed as a carpenter," said Bonifazio, "and He came to the Marsica. 'Have you any work for a poor carpenter?' He asked everywhere. 'Where do you come from? What is your name? Have you got a permit? Have you got a recommendation?' the masters answered Him. Evening came, and He had found no work. Then He said to all the unemployed He met on the road, 'Come with Me,' and they all followed Him. 'Don't turn round,' He said to them, and not one of them turned round. When they were on the mountain Jesus said, 'Now you can turn round.' Where Avezzano had been there was a lake. If things go on like this it won't be long before it is a lake again."

"There are said to be minerals in the mountain," Murica said.

"Heaven forbid!" Bonifazio replied.

Don Paolo asked why.

"As long as the mountain is poor, it is ours," the shepherd explained. "But if it is discovered to be rich, the government will take it. The government has one very long arm and one very short one. The long one is for taking, and reaches everywhere, and the short one is for giving, but it only reaches those who are nearest."

Brother Antifona, the monk, passed along the carriage road. Bonifazio called him to ask him the latest news from Africa.

"Has your son been called up?" asked the monk.

"At the end of the month."

Brother Antifona showed Bonifazio some medals of St. Francis "for the protection of the life of combatants."

"How much are they?"

"Fifty centesimi."

Bonifazio gave Brother Antifona the lira Don Paolo had given him and waited for his change. But the monk did not like to give change. He showed the shepherd other medals, bigger and therefore more efficacious, costing one lira. Bonifazio hesitated.

"One mustn't be niggardly when it's a matter of one's own son's life," the monk remarked.

Bonifazio sacrificed his lira.

Don Paolo protested.

"Did you give him the lira I gave you?" he said.

"No," the shepherd whispered in his ear. "I gave him a counterfeit one."

The priest and the monk walked together along the road up to Pietrasecca.

"Are the medals selling well?" the priest asked.

"Not badly," the other replied. "They would have gone better if we had started on mobilization day. But the Church is always late. The father provincial is too old and does nothing but pray. Our father superior, who really has the nose of a saint, wrote to him months ago and said: 'War is coming, and what are we doing?' 'War? What war?' the old father provincial replied. Thus time was wasted and we were taken by surprise. All the same, we mustn't grumble. The medals are well enough appreciated, in spite of the delay."

When they were halfway back to Pietrasecca they came upon a woman doing penance, going on her knees all the way from Pietrasecca to Lama. She looked like a bag of rags and mud, floundering this way and that. At first Don Paolo was afraid she was mad. She was not mad, but a mother whose son was at the war. She had made a vow to go on her knees from Pietrasecca to Lama, so that her son should return safely to her. The poor woman had been on the road since morning. Her voice was hoarse, her face unrecognizable, her eyes dilated, haunted, crazy. She looked as though she were going to collapse at any moment. Don Paolo wanted to make her get up and walk on her feet. He actually made as if to take her by the shoulders and lift her by force, but the woman defended herself with nails and teeth. She had made a vow and must fulfill it. If she failed and rose to her feet, her son in Africa would die. Brother Antifona was surprised at a priest who did not realize so obvious a thing as that.

Later they met two men, father and son, riding a small donkey. The monk offered his medals.

"How much do they cost?"

"Fifty centesimi."

The man had no money, but offered the priest a handkerchief full of apples, which the monk accepted. A handkerchief full of apples was not too much to pay for a son's life.

When the priest and the monk reached Pietrasecca the sun was setting. They parted before the bridge, near the little schoolhouse, because the monk wished to go round the village from door to door, starting with the schoolmistress. The air was cold, the sky gray. The top of the mountain behind Pietrasecca was white with snow. The hesitating voice of a little girl came through the open school window.

"A, e, i, o, u."

It was the beginning. The beginning of the school year. The beginning of spelling. For the little girl it was the beginning of life. A little boy's voice said:

"Ba, be, bi, bo, bu."

The priest stopped to listen. The little girl's voice came again:

"Fa, fe, fi, fo, fu."

Pietrasecca was invaded by shadows. Only the house of the Colamartini, standing higher than the rest, was still illuminated by the rays of the sun. Cristina was at a window on the top floor, and her face was like a mirror on which the setting sun was reflected. All Don Paolo could see of the village was that glowing face.

As soon as the sun disappeared the air grew frosty. Matalena was waiting for the return of "her" priest in the doorway of the inn, winding thread on a spindle.

"Snow is not far away now," she said, looking at the sky.

Snow came two days later. When Don Paolo woke up in the morning the landscape was transformed, as in a fairy tale. The snow was falling quietly and thickly, like something expected and inevitable.

Cristina came to see Don Paolo. Her eyes were dilated with suffering.

"Do you know that Don Benedetto left everything to his sister and to one Pietro Spina?" she said.

She showed Don Paolo a letter from Don Cipriano, telling her this news and taking advantage of the opportunity to insinuate that Don Benedetto must have lost control of his faculties.

"Is it true that this Pietro Spina is an enemy of religion?"

"Yes."

"So Don Cipriano was right?"

"No."

Cristina raised her pale, worried, suffering face to Don Paolo. Her expression was that of one who had grown weary of being put to the test and implored a little peace.

"There are dead with whom one must keep faith," Don Paolo said.

The girl looked at him with tears in her eyes, and nodded her head. All she said was:

"Help me."

That evening a number of people came to Matalena's inn to celebrate the first day of snow. Cristina came, too, a little later. Don Paolo was sitting next to the fireplace, with peasants, women and boys sitting all around in a big circle. On one side of the fire there was a dog, and on the other Teresa Scaraffa's baby, who was to have been born blind, but had been saved in time. The child had been put on the ground, in a wicker basket, like a cauliflower, and its face, reddened by the reflection of the fire, was like an apple. The people asked Don Paolo to tell stories, and Cristina specified sacred stories. In the end he could no longer refuse, and took his breviary, looked up the *index festorum,* and started telling in his own way the stories of the martyrdoms of which the breviary speaks. The story was always different, but always the same. There was a time of profound crisis; a dictatorship with a deified leader; a decaying old church, living on alms; an army of mercenaries who guaranteed the peaceful digestion of the rich; a population of slaves; incessant preparation of new wars of rapine to maintain the dictatorship's prestige. Meanwhile mysterious travelers arrived from abroad. They whispered of prodigious successes in the East. They announced the good tidings: liberation was at hand! The poor, the hungry, and the desperate met in cellars and secret places to hear them speak. The news spread. Catechumens abandoned the old synagogue and embraced the new faith. Nobles left their palaces, centurians deserted. Police raided clandestine meetings. Prisoners were tortured and handed over to a special tribunal. They faced execution with a smile on their lips. The young were thrown to the wild beasts, the old were poisoned. Those that survived kept faith with the dead, to whom they devoted a secret cult. . . .

Times changed, ways of dressing and eating changed, ways of working changed, languages changed, but at heart it was the same old story—the story of man.

The first to go to sleep was the dog lying by the fire; it was followed by the baby in its basket, and then by others. Those that did not go to sleep stared into the fire.

Cristina said:

"In all times, in all societies, the supreme act is to give oneself to find oneself, to lose oneself to find oneself. One has only what one gives."

The fire died out, the guests said good-night, and Don Paolo went up to his room. He picked up his note book containing the "Dialogues with Cristina" he had started at the beginning of his stay at Pietrasecca. He read the first few pages, full of tender affection for the girl, read, tore out, and destroyed the following pages dictated by depression and disillusion. Eight months had passed, and not in vain, either for him or for Cristina. He added a few lines to the "Dialogues" before going to bed.

"Cristina," he wrote, "it is true that one has what one gives; but how and to whom is one to give?

"Our love, our disposition for sacrifice and self-abnegation are barren if dedicated to abstract and inhuman symbols; they are only fruitful if carried into relations with our fellow-men. Morality can live and flourish only in practical life.

"If we apply our moral feelings to the disorder that reigns about us, we cannot remain inactive and console ourselves by looking forward to another, supernatural world. The evil that we have to combat is not that sad abstraction called the devil, but everything that sets man against man. . . ."

At this point Don Paolo hesitated. He knew what he wanted to say, but he did not know how to say it. He spoke aloud to Cristina. He had not forgotten that the social question is not a moral one and is not resolved by purely moral means. He knew that in the last resort the relations established among men are dictated by necessity and not by good will or bad. Moral preaching did not suffice to change them. But there came a moment when certain social relations revealed themselves as outworn and harmful. Morality then condemned what had already been condemned by history. A sense of justice caused the slaves to rise, put arms into the hands of the advance guard, kindled the souls of martyrs, inspired thinkers and artists.

"It is sufficient to look about us, dear Cristina, to see how far our present society has sunk in putrefaction," he wrote when he put pen to paper again. "Jumping up on tables and making speeches is not for everyone; entering a political group and struggling for the political transformation of society is not for everyone; nevertheless, a woman like you should have her eyes open to what is going on about her, and open the eyes of others who wish to keep them closed.

"What a great revolution there will be in the world when persons who possess such spiritual riches as you possess, almost as a natural gift, cease expending them upon religious symbolism and devote them to the collective life. Thus a new type of saint will be born, a new type of martyr, a new type of man.

"I do not believe there is any other way of saving one's soul today. He is saved who overcomes his individual egoism, family egoism, caste egoism, does not shut himself in a cloister or build himself an ivory tower, or make a cleavage between his way of acting and his way of thinking. He is saved who frees his own spirit from the idea of resignation to the existing disorder. Spiritual life has always meant a capacity for dedication and self-sacrifice. In a society like ours a spiritual life can only be a revolutionary life.

"Cristina, one must not be afraid, one must not be obsessed with the idea of security, even of the security of one's own virtue. Spiritual life and secure life do not go together. To save oneself one must struggle and take risks."

Don Paolo read through what he had written. He now saw clearly the path he had traveled since returning to Italy. He was content to have returned and found himself.

Snow fell uninterruptedly all night. The priest was still asleep next morning when Matalena called him. A group of peasants and boys had gathered round Garibaldi, Sciatàp's donkey, outside the inn. A wolf's carcass was lying across the donkey's crupper. It had been killed that morning on the mountain behind Pietrasecca. Its skin was gray, shaggy, filthy with blood and mud. Its teeth were white and very strong. There were two bloodstains where the bullets had entered its side and shoulder. According to custom, the wolf was being shown from door to door, for alms for those who had killed it. Luigi Banduccia still had his gun on his shoulder, and was telling the story of what had happened. This was the fourth wolf he had shot. He showed the sign of love on the nape of the beast's neck, the deep bite of a she-wolf. The love-making of wolves is a serious thing. Banduccia could tell a wolf's various kinds of howls from a distance: the howl of danger it lets forth when it is attacked with arms; the howl of prey, which means that it has found an animal to tear to pieces and calls its companions, because it does not like eating alone; the howl of love, which means it wants a female and is not shy about letting it be known.

Cristina's grandmother refused to give anything for the dead wolf, although Cristina, who had had a special respect for wolves ever since her childhood, urged her.

"Dead wolves don't bite," the old woman said.

Don Paolo received a letter from Rome, with a few banal words and an unknown signature. He warmed it in front of the fire and some yellowish writing in lemon-juice emerged between the lines.

"Romeo has been arrested," it said. "If you come, go cautiously to the Chelucci house."

Don Paolo left for Rome at once.

"I have to leave for family reasons," he told Matalena. "I shall return later to fetch the things I'm leaving now."

He could not tell whether he would need his refuge at Pietrasecca again.

Shortly before the train reached the station Don Paolo went to the lavatory, and when he came out and mingled with the crowd of other passengers who got off the train he was once more Pietro Spina.

He went straight from the station to the Via della Lungaretta, to see Annina Pecci, the dressmaker, Murica's friend.

"Murica sends you his best wishes," he told the girl. "He has suffered greatly, but now he is cured. When you see him you will not recognize him. He has become a new man. He still loves you."

"Will he not return to Rome?"

"No."

"Do you think that one day I might be able to visit him in his village?"

"He expects you, and has already spoken of you to his family."

The girl decided to leave next day.

Spina sent Annina to the Via dei Morosini to warn the wife of the political prisoner Chelucci of his arrival. He waited for the two women in a side street. It was a long time before they came. Spina walked up and down. The building he kept passing was a school. The sound of a little girl's voice came through the open window:

"A, e, i, o, u."

It was the beginning. The little girl's voice was hesitating. All beginnings were difficult. A little boy's voice went on:

"Ba, be, bi, bo, bu."

Spina stopped and listened. The little girl's voice came again:

"Da, de, di, do, du."

How bright and clear the sky was. High over Vatican City was an enormous captive balloon, with big letters on it advertis-

ing the effectiveness of a well-known purgative. It occurred to
Spina that most purgatives in Italy were called after the names
of saints; and he recalled that the rare advertisements to be seen
in the Italian Catholic press nearly always referred to purgatives.
Could it be chance? It could not be chance.

The Church is constipated, Spina said to himself.

This idea made him laugh. It would certainly have amused
Don Benedetto, too.

The two women arrived, looking cautiously all about them, as
though they were afraid they were being followed.

"Romeo has been arrested," Chelucci's wife said. "But they
found nothing incriminating on him, so perhaps he may be out
again soon."

"The government does what it likes with prisoners," Spina
replied. "The laws exist only for the benefit of law students and
foreigners. . . . Is your husband still in prison?"

"Yes, he's still awaiting his trial. Meanwhile he has gone blind.
He may have been blind for several months, but I only discovered it the last time I went to see him. To please him I put on a
shawl he gave me as a wedding present. We were separated by a
grating when we talked, but there was enough light for him to
have been able to recognize it. 'Don't you recognize what I'm
wearing?' I said to him. 'What is it?' he replied. 'Don't you
recognize it?' I asked him. 'Is it a fur?' he said. 'Who gave it to
you?' His mother was standing next to me. She is always so
upset that she can hardly speak. 'Where's mother?' he asked.
'Why didn't she come today? Is she ill?' Then we realized that
he was blind. If only they would bring him to trial!"

"The other trials are continually postponed, too," Annina
said. "The government doesn't want it to be known that there
are people opposed to the war."

"Romeo asked me to find you a safe address," Chelucci's wife
went on, "but I don't know what name you want to go under
here."

"I'll tell you."

"Besides, I want to talk to you about putting you in contact
with the new committee."

Spina asked about Bianchina.

"We tried to help her, but it was very difficult," Chelucci's wife said. "She's not a bad woman, but she's restless, lazy, and weak. She was bored to death with us. She found the little work there was to do so tiring that it nearly made her ill. One day she disappeared without saying anything. Two days later she came back entirely transformed. She asked after you and gave me a telephone number in case you came."

Chelucci's wife gave him the number. He gave Annina some directions for her journey to Rocca dei Marsi, made another appointment with Chelucci's wife, and went to a hotel near the Pantheon to take a room. He signed his name in the register, giving the particulars written in his Czechoslovakian passport. In the evening he telephoned to Bianchina and arranged to meet her at a café in the center of the city. Both arrived punctually.

"You must not be shocked if I have put off my priestly clothing," he said to her. "It is permitted to do so when necessary."

"You look a bit absurd in trousers, but it doesn't matter," the girl said.

She was painted up to her ears, was dressed with great elegance, and her hair was done in a striking fashion.

The café seemed rather a doubtful one to Spina. It was crowded. People were dancing to the accompaniment of a blaring orchestra. Shaded lamps were on every table. They reminded Spina of the night lights left at the bedside of the dying. The "dying" were smoking their usual *de luxe* cigarettes, had their hair smoothed down with the usual brilliantine, and were whispering the usual inanities to their neighbors. The atmosphere was one of palpable stupidity, sensuality, sweating armpits, and dirty feet. Bianchina sat opposite Spina with a tired and bored expression on her face. Perhaps she was waiting for him to speak.

"Have you become a serious person?"

This was a continuation of their talk at Fossa, after which Bianchina had decided to leave for Rome.

"Serious? . . . Only too serious," she replied.

"Where are you working now?"

"I'm taking a few days' rest."

"Is the pay good?"

"So-so."

"Do you like the work?"

"No one ever really likes his own work. Only characters in books for young ladies like their own work."

"Where do you work?"

The girl slowly lit a cigarette.

"Excuse me, but where do you work?" the man asked again.

"In a brothel," the girl answered, simply.

A newsboy came in, and Spina bought a copy of a special edition of the evening paper, which announced that the Italians had entered Makalé.

"Have we entered Makalé?" the girl asked.

"Yes, you have entered Makalé," the man replied.

That was all they said.

In the street, on the point of parting, the girl asked:

"Are you disgusted with me?"

"Really, I was not thinking about you but about something else," the man replied. But the girl would have her answer.

"Are you disgusted?" she said.

The man wanted to go about his business.

"I am under no obligation to answer."

"You must answer."

"Good-night," he said, and tried to go away.

The girl held him by the arm.

"Are you disgusted?" she asked.

The two sat down on a stone seat.

"When I was at school," the man said, "a novel about the lives of the 'pupils' of an 'establishment' of the kind to which you are now attached used to be passed around under the desks. I read the book myself. I was fifteen years old. I was so disgusted by it that ever since I have never been able to read books in which that sort of thing was even casually mentioned."

"Books like that used to be passed around at my school, too," the girl said. "I think they must be specially printed to be read secretly in religious schools. I read about a dozen of them, and they were all alike. Chapter one, Innocence. Chapter two, Temptation. Chapter three, the Fall. Chapter four, Guilt. Chapter five, On the Slippery Slope to Sin. Chapter six, the First Pangs of Remorse. Chapter seven, Repentance and Salvation. That is the invariable plot of those absurd books, written specially to make boys and kind-hearted young girls cry. But my story is neither to be laughed at nor cried over. It is a stupid, banal, boring story. It is not even a story; it is my life."

"Perhaps it is my fault," the man said. "I should not have urged you to leave Fossa."

"At Fossa I was bored to death," the girl said, "except, perhaps, on the rare occasions when you were there. At Fossa, I fed on yawns. Married friends are boring because they talk only about their husbands—'my Ciccillo, my Antonino, my Gigetto. . . .' They are only their husbands' shadows, and live in everlasting fear of losing them. Friends who are not married are even more boring; poor girls, they wait twenty years for a quarter-of-an-hour's pleasure, a quarter-of-an-hour that finally turns out to be banal, stupid, and absurd; and while they are waiting, interminably and everlastingly waiting, at the bottom of their hearts they are never really thinking about anything else. The men . . . let us not talk about them. They are not men, but clerks, tradesmen, landowners, peasants."

"At Rome you could have stayed with Signora Chelucci. She is an intelligent, unprejudiced woman, and she certainly would have helped to put you on your feet."

"I don't want to speak ill of her, as she is an acquaintance of yours," Bianchina answered. "She is certainly an excellent woman, but she moans from morning to night, worse than my aunt. She always has tears in her eyes. She does not speak, but sighs."

"Her husband is in prison, and he is blind."

"I know. I tried hard to understand her, sympathize with her, give her courage, distract her. I couldn't. Besides, the other women I met there were boring, too, although their husbands were not in prison. They were all obsessed with Socialism. Mind, I don't say it's a bad idea in itself. I say if you want Socialism,

very well, then, want it, but don't let us hear any more about
it. But those women talked about it and sighed about it from
morning to night, in their damp, filthy, unhealthy houses, while
outside the sun was shining. It was really pitiful to see young
people making themselves sad and ill and getting white hair,
all because of a fixed idea. Those poor women live for Socialism
like nuns living for the Sacred Heart. I don't want you to mis-
understand me. The people you sent me to are all unquestion-
ably good and worthy people, but boring, boring."

"The 'establishment' you took refuge in was certainly gay in
comparison."

"Have you ever been in that kind of 'establishment'?"

"No."

"Neither had I. At the house of an acquaintance of mine here
in Rome, one Giuseppina Sraffa, who was at college with me and
Cristina and is now kept by a soap manufacturer, I met a commendatore, a patriot, a member of the government party. After
a few days he asked me if I would like to go to Abyssinia. The
high command had asked for two thousand women, some for
the men, and others, of finer quality, for the officers. The commendatore said that in view of my youth and good education I
would do excellently for the officers. He said that if I didn't like
that kind of life, a job in an office or something could be found
for me in the colony. Only one thing made me hesitate. That
was you. I did not want to go a long way away from you. I had
illusions about you. In the end I yielded to the commendatore's
importunity and left. What attracted me most was the sea
journey to unknown countries, where people would talk a different language. Perhaps they would grumble there, too, but at
any rate I wouldn't be able to understand."

"Did you sail for East Africa?"

"I went to Naples. I was taken to a so-called 'salon of nude art'
to wait for embarkation. There were sixteen of us 'nude artists,'
at the clients' disposal. They were mostly soldiers passing through
the town on the point of leaving for the war. Among the nudes
there were some really fantastic and original ones, who had been
through the Great War. In the evening, soldiers and non-com-

missioned officers, in helmet and field uniform, came in. They
came from the training-grounds of Eboli, Cava, Avellino, Bene-
vento, Campobasso, Formia, Caserta. They had to stay a day
or two at Naples before they sailed, and naturally the poor
fellows tried to have a good time, but they did not succeed.
Those who came to our place were happy, noisy, and even vulgar
as long as they were together in a crowd, but as soon as you
were alone with them in a room they became gloomy and sad.
Most of them were peasants. When I looked at their faces while
they were enjoying themselves with me, their seriousness frightened me. If one of them ever did smile, he was most likely the
father of a family, and smiled to please me, more than anything
else. Grave men with big mustaches and enormous muscles
chirped like dicky-birds while enjoying themselves, and made
childish noises at me. 'Cli, cli, cli! Tiù, tiù, tiù!' But their voices
were sad at heart. Some of them showed me photographs of
their mothers, wives, and sons, with tears in their eyes. Just
imagine it, in a place like that! Unfortunately, they were not
allowed to stay in a room for more than a quarter of an hour.
Those who could pay double stayed half an hour, but you
mustn't think they enjoyed themselves more than the rest. After
they had finished, nearly all of them asked me to tell my life
story. At first I could not understand why. What interest could
my life have for them? Afterwards I realized it formed part of
their pleasure. So I told them; that is, I invented things to
increase their pleasure. 'I've got a little girl at school,' I told them
with a sigh, 'and I'm forced to live this life in order to give
her a Christian education. What wouldn't I do for my little
girl?' Sometimes tears would come into their eyes as they listened
to me. They were good people, country people, and bored people. One of them even sent me, by post, a pair of shoes for my
little girl. I've still got them in my bag. Now, in a sense, I feel
myself almost obliged to have a little girl. I've talked such a lot
about her, described her appearance so many times, her hair,
her eyes, her hands, the little dimple she has on her cheek when
she laughs! So many excellent people have been interested in
her, taken pity on her, almost wept for her! I've even got a pair

of shoes for her little feet! . . . Well, after a few days, life in
the establishment began to bore me. I was very tired, too. I had
a permanent ache in my legs, as after a long pilgrimage, pains
in my bones, aches in my muscles. But above all it was a monotonous sad banal life. A kind of restaurant with one obligatory
dish. Everyone who came wanted the same thing. My colleagues
were stupid enough to put cows to shame!"

"At your age you are already bored with everything," Spina
said, "normal life and abnormal life. What is there left for you?"

"A hope."

"What hope?"

"You."

"I am sorry," said Spina, "but . . ."

"What are you, anyway?" the girl said. "You're certainly not a
priest, nor a brigand, nor a devil, nor a commercial traveler.
What are you? You may be all these things, but I don't care,
I'm not interested, I don't want to know. What I do know is
enough. You are you. From the first time I saw you (do you
remember that first time?) from the first time I saw your eyes I
loved you. I am not interested in anything else. I love you from
head to foot. Everything else bores me. You are the only thing
that doesn't bore me."

"Bianchina, I must tell you . . ."

"Don't answer me at once. The longer you put off answering
me, the better for me, because my hope will last the longer. Let
me hope. It is the only thing that keeps me alive now, and it
doesn't cost you anything."

"We shall talk of this again," the man said.

They parted on that understanding.

Next day Spina met Chelucci's wife at a corner of the Via
Morosini, as arranged.

"I've just taken Annina to the station," the woman said. "You
should have seen her eyes sparkling with joy at the thought of
seeing Murica again."

"Who has taken Romeo's place in the organization of the
groups?"

"A man from Milan, named Bolla. I have told him you are here."

A vender of roasted chestnuts was sitting before her stove beside an inn door.

"That's a woman who helps us," Chelucci's wife whispered to Spina.

The woman gave Chelucci's wife a bag of chestnuts. A little way down the street she opened it. Among the chestnuts there was a piece of paper giving particulars of where Spina was to meet Bolla.

The two met on the steps of the Trinità dei Monti. They recognized each other because each was carrying a copy of an illustrated sporting paper in his left hand.

"We believed you had been arrested a long time ago," Bolla said. "We had no more news of you. I even think your arrest has been announced in our legal press abroad."

Bolla was a worker, but as "cover" he had assumed the occupation of commercial traveler, which he said he exercised with a certain amount of success. He called on about twenty hairdressers every day, with a bag of samples consisting of cheap perfumes, tooth pastes, brushes, and cosmetics. The most lucrative articles were now prohibited, because they were contrary to the government's population policy.

"How do the groups stand at Rome?" Spina asked.

"We are right at the beginning again. Romeo's arrest was a disaster. Most of our contacts are broken or unsafe. We've got to start all over again."

"Are any new members joining us?"

"There are some, but when they are discovered and threatened they generally don't put up much resistance. They tell everything they know. That is why we always have to start all over again. Sometimes we have to work for weeks to reëstablish a contact: we have to find people we have lost sight of, go from one address to another at random, make appointments at which no one turns up. And finally, when the contact is reëstablished, sometimes it only lasts a few days. And then you have to be patient and begin all over again from the beginning. Illegal work is a game of patience."

"What do you tell a new person who wants to join a group?" Spina asked. "What is he given to do?"

"We start by making him distribute a few leaflets, to test him."

Spina could not hide his disagreement.

"Don't you think it would be better to gain his friendship first of all?" he said. "Don't you think it would be better to see him in the evenings, in his free hours, go out with him sometimes on Sundays, and gradually start talking to him about everything, and not only about politics? That is, take advantage of his vague sympathy for us to win him entirely and make a man of him?"

Bolla had a certain respect for Spina, of whom he had heard a great deal before meeting him, but he also knew that he was a little peculiar, like many intellectuals, and he wished to avoid arguing with him.

"I have prepared a small illegal paper for students, to be sent by post to about a hundred addresses," he said.

"What does the paper say?"

"I wrote the leading article myself," Bolla said. "Also there's a splendid letter from a Catholic student."

"Who wrote it?"

"I did," said Bolla. "There's also a short but lively letter from a nationalist student, who says he has had his eyes opened."

"Who wrote it?"

"I did."

"Why do you go in for stunts like that?" Spina asked.

"One must give the impression that the students are beginning to wake up," Bolla replied.

Spina lost patience.

"We are not a party of hairdressers," he nearly shouted. "We are not working for appearances. The important thing for us is not to appear strong, but to be strong. The revolution is not a stunt or a conjuring trick. It's the truth, nothing but the truth!"

"And if the truth is demoralizing?"

"It is always less demoralizing than the most encouraging lie."

Bolla did not continue the argument. He knew Spina was a good comrade, but with strange susceptibilities.

"Since I'm going to stay in Rome," Spina said, "I should like to join a trade group as a simple member."

"You can enter the gas workers' group," Bolla suggested. "Chelucci's wife and Signora Rosa, the chestnut-seller, will put you in touch."

Chelucci's wife failed to keep her subsequent appointments with Spina. He dared not go to her house, fearing that the police might be watching it. Spina knew the rule of the political underworld by which, if some one fails to keep an appointment, it is tacitly renewed the three following days, at the same time and place. Between one wait and the next he spent the time at his hotel, writing a long report, to be sent abroad, on what he had seen and learned since returning to Italy. On the third day he went punctually to Trastevere in the hope of meeting Chelucci's wife, and took Bianchina with him, so that the time should not be entirely wasted if Chelucci's wife failed to appear. They chanced to pass the inn outside of which Signora Rosa sold her chestnuts. The old woman was sitting behind her oven, wrapped in a black shawl, holding a warming pan on her knees. Every now and then she got up to poke the fire in the oven and move the bursting chestnuts.

Signora Rosa recognized Spina, called him, and offered him a bag of chestnuts.

"These are for you," she said. "An acquaintance of yours paid for them for you."

Spina and Bianchina went on their way, eating chestnuts. Wrapped around one chestnut Spina found a note saying "Chelucci has been released. He wants to see you. Come late tonight."

Bianchina saw the note and waited for Spina to show it to her or tell her what it said, but Spina tore it into little pieces, threw them on a rubbish heap, and started talking of other things. Spina resigned himself to spending the evening with Bianchina, to fill in the time before going to the Via Morosini.

They dined together in a tavern and then went to an almost deserted café. For the first time Spina tried talking to Bianchina of serious things.

"Life," he said, "is in itself not necessarily either serious or stupid, boring or interesting. It depends on us."

Bianchina agreed.

"A silly life," Spina went on, "is based on appearances. It aims only at seeming. It wishes to seem interesting, intelligent, beautiful, well-informed; sometimes it even wishes to seem good, altruistic, courageous. To the stupid, *being* is not important, *seeming* is."

Bianchina promptly agreed again.

"Why do you always agree with what I say?" Spina suddenly asked.

"My dear," she said, "I shall always agree with whatever you say."

Spina stopped, discouraged. He was wasting his breath.

"Now I understand," he said. "You are a little goose."

"And you? Do you want me to say what you really are?"

"It does not interest me."

"You are a big donkey."

"Why?"

"A woman," Bianchina said, "a real woman, always agrees with the man she loves. She is Catholic if he is Catholic, Mohammedan if he believes in Allah, a collector of rare and precious stamps if he is a stamp-collector."

"So, in your opinion, a woman always pretends?"

"Excuse me, but now you really are a crocodile. A woman who really loves a man loves not only his mustaches but his ideas, and does so naturally and perfectly sincerely. Don't you think so?"

"What does a woman believe in if she is not tied to any man?"

"At the bottom of her heart she worships the unknown god who is still to appear."

"Supposing a woman has different ideas from her husband?"

"It means she is betraying him and that her ideas are her lover's."

"And if she is not betraying him?"

"She must be frigid."

Spina decided it was useless to go on with such a silly conversation. Bianchina was sorry he was so easily upset, and tried making a small concession to pacify him.

"Are you sorry I want to have the same ideas as you? Do you want me to think differently from you? If so, you've only got to say so. What more do you want of me? All I wish is to please you; I am ready to do and to think only what you want me to."

Spina tried hard not to lose patience.

"I want you to act according to your conscience and think according to your reason and common sense; and I want all that to remain independent of your private life."

"If that is what you want, I shall do it," said Bianchina. "But in return, will you love me?"

Spina got up, seized his hat, and made hurriedly for the door. Bianchina watched him in surprise, thinking he was joking. But when she saw he really was going out without even looking round, she only had time to call out:

"You're not a man but an ostrich!"

Spina, once outside the café, saw it was late enough for him to go and see Chelucci in the Via Morosini. He walked casually up and down the street outside the house two or three times, to make sure it was not being watched. Then he went in and quickly mounted the half-dark staircase. He found Signora Rosa acting as sentinel on the last landing. She was looking down the well of the stairs, resting her head on her hands because she was old and afraid of getting giddy. The Chelucci dwelling consisted of one poor room, which Spina already knew. The blind man was sitting at a table, between his mother and his wife. His wife whispered the visitor's name in the blind man's ear. The two men embraced at length. Then the blind man sat down again between the two women. He was thinner and seemed taller. He was not yet thirty, but had a lot of gray hair. He immediately started overwhelming Spina with questions.

"How do we stand now in Russia? How do we stand in China?"

His movements were hesitating, embarrassed, almost childish;

as he spoke he held his face forward, as though to see the man he was talking to, and then waited for the answer with his hands on his knees, like a well-behaved schoolboy. The lines on his face had altered and become gentler since Spina had last seen him, and this was still more apparent when he smiled and beamed with pleasure at being told that "his" affairs were going well in Russia and China. It almost seemed then that he could see. But he kept on asking for news.

"How do we stand in Vienna? . . . How do we stand at Barcelona? . . . How do we stand in France?"

The two women remained silent and looked at their blind man. They had combed, cleaned, and reclothed him; it really was a shame that he could not see himself in the mirror. They too, poor things, were cheered at heart that "their" affairs were going better, in several distant countries at any rate. Chelucci's mother, who had remained a peasant, said, to console herself:

"Sometimes God closes a window but opens a veranda."

His wife, who was a Milanese worker, said nothing. Her husband was there. What else was there to say? There would be an extra plate at table. There was a little oil-stove for cooking. When Spina had visited the women in the summer there had been two beds on the floor in opposite corners of the room. Now a third bed had been put between them, and it was the only one with blankets. Winter was just beginning, and the blind man would never know that his mother and wife were sleeping without blankets.

The blind man continued his questioning.

"How is the war going?"

"Yesterday they bombarded a hospital, as a reprisal," Spina said.

"Who did?"

"Those who intend to bring civilization to that part of the world."

"When do the rains start again?"

"In May."

"Only in May? Poor Abyssinians," the blind man said.

"If God wills, He may cause the rains to start two months

earlier," his mother said, seeing that this piece of information saddened him. "When there's no other hope, there is always the mercy of God to hope for."

Her son was unwilling to contradict her. He was sitting between the two women, his mother on the right, his wife on the left; on the right the country, on the left the town. He himself was both country and town.

"Is it true that Murica is with us again?" he asked. "Is it true he has made it up with Annina?"

"Yes," said Spina. "He has become a new man."

"And what do you intend to do? Stay here? Go abroad again?"

"I am staying here. I shall enroll in the gas workers' group."

"In our group?"

Signora Rosa came to warn Spina that it was time to go, because the sound of voices might make the neighbors suspicious. He gave Chelucci's wife the address of the hotel at which he was staying, and his Czechoslovakian name, warning her to learn it by heart and not put anything in writing.

Two days later Chelucci's wife telephoned and said an important letter had come from Annina, and she wished to show it to him. Spina met her at a dairy near the Pantheon, and she showed him Annina's letter. It consisted of several lines written in ordinary ink, and the following words written in lemon: "Murica was arrested yesterday. There is a lot of ferment here. Some young men who call themselves a group of wall-writers ask me what they ought to write, what the truth is. A man from Pratola came to see me too."

Spina decided to leave for the Marsica.

"They'll catch you," Chelucci's wife warned him. "There will be a lot of surveillance now."

"The place where you were born is like your own home," Spina said. "You're better known, but it's easier to hide in."

He hurried to find Bianchina. She was in her room. Her eyes were red and swollen from much weeping.

"I really need you," he said. "Murica has been arrested. You must leave for Fossa at once. You must take a trip to Avezzano. I want you to talk to everyone you know, but without attracting attention. I want you to try to find out everything that is happening and everything that is being prepared."

"Are you staying here?"

"I shall follow you tomorrow. Send the man from Pratola with his cab along the road between Fossa and Rocca dei Marsi shortly before midday. And I want you to find me somewhere to spend the night."

"Won't you go to my aunt's hotel?"

"No, because I shall not be dressed as a priest."

"Can we spend the night together?"

"Yes."

Bianchina jumped with joy. She packed her luggage and went out at once. Spina left Rome next morning. He took the tram to Tivoli, and from there the slow local train that went to the Abruzzi, stopping at every little station. He knew there was a regular police watch only on the fast trains. But he found the slowness of the train exasperating. He did not know what to expect in the Marsica. Annina had vaguely said there was much ferment, but that might mean anything. Was it possible for the network of friendships built up by Murica to have changed the old situation in such a short time? In any case he must act as substitute for Murica, and not drop any of the threads he had gathered. He recalled Don Benedetto's words: "Every season has its own work. There is the season for pruning, the season for spraying, the season for preparing the barrels, the season for gathering and pressing the grapes." Which season had they reached in the Marsica? He would try to find out by talking to the man from Pratola, to Annina, Bianchina, the wall-writers, and Murica's other friends. He would act and give the lead according to the season that he found.

The train from Tivoli went no farther than Avezzano, and he changed to another train waiting at the next platform. It was already full of peasant women and traders who had been to market and were going home to their villages.

"The market is always crowded before Christmas," a woman said to Spina. "And now, thank God, a lot of people are getting allowances for their sons who have been called up, so there's more money about."

The ring of mountains surrounding the basin of the Fucino was entirely white with snow. At some points the snow even covered the foothills that formed the first tier around the deep plain. Spina was wearing a black coat that came right down to his feet, with a black woolen scarf round his neck. Thus no one he might happen to meet who had known him as a priest would notice that he had put off his priest's cassock and collar.

At the same time it would be sufficient, in case of need, to unbutton his coat and remove his scarf to look like an ordinary citizen. His most ingenious idea was represented by his hat. It was of a material and shape that permitted it to pass as ecclesiastical or civil headgear at will. It all depended on how you put it on and dented it. This discovery had wasted a lot of Spina's time at a Rome hat shop, but in the end it had made him laugh like a happy child.

He got out at Fossa station without looking round, and walked down the street that led out of town in the direction of Rocca. The road wound slowly uphill, forming the boundary line between a rocky hill planted with vineyards and an expanse of grain fields. At a turning the man from Pratola overtook him in his cab. Spina got into it without saying a word, and the horse resumed its trot.

"Is there any news of Murica?" Spina asked.

"He died yesterday."

On the left the vines were losing their last withered leaves. On the right the fields were lined with the tender green of the new grain. Murica had died yesterday. The sky was gray and laden with snow.

"He told me that you knew each other and that you were friends," Spina said.

"We were friends," said the driver. "One spent time willingly with him. He was a good man, and made other people want to be good, too. He also used to speak to us about the revolution. 'To be together without being afraid of each other, that is the beginning,' he used to tell us."

"We must stay together," said Spina. "We must not let ourselves be divided."

"He had written on a piece of paper: 'Truth and brotherhood will reign among men in the place of hatred and deceit; living labor will reign in the place of money.' When they arrested him they found that piece of paper on him, and he didn't disown it. So they put a chamberpot on his head instead of a crown, in the yard of the militia barracks at Fossa. 'That is the truth,' they told him. They put a broom in his right hand instead of a scepter. 'That is brotherhood,' they told him. Then they wrapped his body in a red carpet they picked up from the floor. They bound him, and the soldiers kicked and punched him backwards and forwards among themselves. 'That is living labor,' they told him. When he fell they walked on him, trampling on him with their nailed boots. That was how the judicial investigation began. He survived it for two days."

"If we live like him, it will be as if he were not dead," said Spina. "We must stay together and have no fear."

The man from Pratola nodded his head.

"What can a man fear who is in search of justice?" Spina said.

"Murderers fear death," the man from Pratola said.

He pointed out the house of the Murica family at the outskirts of Rocca, in the midst of the fields, with a big farmyard on one side.

Spina walked down a grassy path towards the farm-house, after asking the man from Pratola to come back and fetch him later, if possible with Bianchina. It was a single-story house, but wide and roomy. The windows were all closed with the shutters drawn, and the big front door stood wide open, as is the custom during mourning. In the yard outside the door there was a big, square, solidly built two-wheeled cart, its sides painted red and blue and its shaft in the air. Next to the cart there was a plow, with earth still on it. People were going and coming from the house, paying the customary visit of condolence. Spina hesitatingly went in, but no one took any notice of him. On crossing the threshold he found himself in a big, stone-paved room, that ordinarily served as both kitchen and storeroom for agricultural implements. It was full of people. The women, dressed in black and yellow, were sitting on the floor near the fireplace, and the men were standing around the table, talking about the land and the crops. Spina saw Annina at the other end of the room, sitting on a stool, alone, pale, bewildered, trembling with cold and fear among all these strange people. She was not even weeping, because to weep one has to be alone or with people one knows. But as soon as she recognized Spina she could restrain herself no longer and started sobbing. The dead man's parents, dressed in black, came in from the next room. The woman went over to Annina, wiped away her tears, wrapped a big black rug about her, and made her sit beside her on another stool near the fireplace.

"Who is she?" the women asked each other.

"It's the *fiancée*," someone answered. "The *fiancée* from the city."

The father sat down with the other men at the head of the table. Relatives arrived from a near-by village, and a number of children. The mother, as is the custom, started praising her dead son. She had tried to save him; she had sent him away and let him study, in order to save him from the destiny that his weakness, his delicacy, his sensibility, had made her foresee. She had not saved him. The air of the city was not made for him. The earth had called him back. He had started tilling the soil, helping his father. He might have been expected soon to weary of it, because to till the soil every day is a real chastisement of God. But he had gradually begun to take pleasure in it. He had awakened his father in the morning; harnessed the horses; chosen the seeds; filled the barrels; looked after the garden. Every now and then the mother paused in her praise to poke the fire and add a dry branch to it. Marta, Don Benedetto's sister, came in, wearing mourning, too. Peasants of the neighborhood arrived. Others left. The cart and the plow could be seen through the big doorway. Old Murica, standing at the head of the table, offered bread and wine to the men around him. He poured out the wine and said, "Drink," and broke the bread and said, "Eat!"

"It was he who helped me to prune, spray, weed, gather the

grapes of which this wine was made. Take and drink this, his wine."

Beggars arrived.

"Let them come in," his mother said.

"They may have been sent to spy," some one murmured.

"Let them come in."

Many, giving food and drink to beggars, have fed Jesus without knowing it.

"Eat and drink," the father said. "This is his bread and this is his wine."

When he came to Spina, the father looked at him.

"Where do you come from?" he asked.

"From Orta."

"What is your name?"

Annina got up and whispered a name in the old man's ear.

"I knew your father as a young man," he said to Spina. "He bought a mare of mine at market. I have heard a lot about you from my son who has just been taken. Sit here, between his mother and his betrothed; and eat and drink, for this is his bread and this is his wine."

"The bread is made of many grains of corn," said Spina. "Therefore it stands for unity. Wine is made of many clusters of grapes, and therefore it stands for unity, too. Unity of similar, equal, and useful things. Hence also it stands for truth and brotherhood, things that go well together."

On Spina's right was his dead friend's mother, a country woman; on the left his betrothed, a worker. He himself, Spina, was town and country.

"It takes nine months to make bread," old Murica said.

"Nine months?" the mother asked.

"The grain is sown in November, reaped and threshed in July." He counted the months. "November, December, January, February, March, April, May, June, July—just nine months. Also it takes nine months for grapes to ripen, from March to November." He counted the months. "March, April, May, June, July, August, September, October, November—just nine months."

"Nine months?" the mother repeated. It had never occurred

to her before. It takes the same time to make a man. He had been born in April. She counted the months backwards. April, March, February, January, December, November, October, September, August.

"I remember when he was a baby and you were still young, and I used to take him for walks on the hills in my arms," said Marta. "Don Benedetto said you were like a vine and he like a cluster of grapes; that you were like the stalk and he like the ear of corn. . . ."

Bianchina appeared in the doorway and Spina went over to meet her.

"You must get away at once. You have been found out," the girl said to him.

"How do you know?"

"I saw Alberto Colamartini at Avezzano," she said. "He's still in love with me, and he isn't jealous any more, as Pompeo has left for Africa. I followed your advice and pretended to accept him. He is an officer in the militia now, and he told me a big photograph of one Pietro Spina has been on view in his office for some days past. When he looked at it he became positive that Spina and Don Paolo Spada were the same person. I tried to shake his conviction, but it was impossible. He reported it to his superiors this morning. It's extraordinary that you weren't recognized in the train or at Fossa station when you arrived today. You haven't got a minute to lose. All the carabinieri and militia stations in the neighborhood must have been warned already."

Spina spoke to Annina, and then asked old Murica to lend him a horse for a day. The old man led a fine colt, only tamed a few months, into the yard.

"It'll do it good to get a little fresh air," the old man said, and handed it over to Spina.

"What can I do?" Bianchina asked.

"Do what the man from Pratola tells you, and be serious," Spina said. "I am going straight to Pietrasecca, where I have left some papers I want to burn. After that I shall go in the direction of Pescasseroli, from there to Alfedana or Scanno, through

the plain of Cinque Miglia. I shall let you have news of me
as soon as I can."

He mounted the colt. In accordance with country custom, it
had neither saddle nor bit, but a simple halter of hemp round
its neck. As soon as it felt the strange man's weight on its back
it whinnied and dashed off in a wild gallop across the fields,
taking Spina, who had not ridden for many years, by surprise.
Pulling at the halter was of no avail. To avoid being thrown off,
Spina was forced to cling to the beast's mane and neck. However,
after the first fury had subsided, the colt became more reasonable and allowed Spina to guide it in the direction of Pietrasecca,
and trotted along the country lanes to the carriage road.

Just as Spina was leaving Lama behind, when he was only a
few paces from the bridge which marks the beginning of the
Pietrasecca valley, a militiaman appeared in front of him and
called out "Stop! Stop!" The colt, startled by the man's sudden
appearance, started galloping madly again, this time without
Spina making any effort to check it. Although the first stretch
of the valley of Pietrasecca was very steep, the colt covered it
without taking breath. It slowed down only when the road began
to be covered with snow. Every now and then Spina turned and
looked behind him, but there was no sign of pursuit. It was
unlikely that the militiaman would try to follow him on foot.
More probably he would report to the nearest barracks, giving
a description of the horseman. In that case a watch would be
kept at the end of the valley and a patrol of mounted carabinieri
or militiamen on motor-cycles would scour the valley all the
way to Pietrasecca. Spina felt caught in a trap from which he
saw no escape. He went on trotting towards Pietrasecca, but
the valley was a blind alley, with no way out. Where could he
go? To turn straight back and go down towards the plain would
be putting his head in the noose, because he would almost
certainly meet militiamen or carabinieri. But staying at Pietrasecca would be no better, for he would be caught there like a
rat in a trap. He could see no way out. The colt was panting,
steaming, and foaming, but still kept up a rapid pace. The
farther he went, the more the landscape altered. Much snow had

fallen and the gray sky promised more. The white walls of the valley had never looked so high and impassable. Apart from the difficulty of climbing them, it would be useless, because the villages beyond were also part of the Marsica, and no doubt the village militia and carabinieri had already been warned.

Pietrasecca came into sight. Spina adjusted his hat and buttoned his coat to give himself an ecclesiastical appearance. The mountain behind Pietrasecca was entirely white with snow. It had two summits, in the shape of two unequal humps, like a Bactrian camel. The bigger hump closed the perspective of the valley, and the smaller, more crushed one, joined the right wall of the valley. Between the two humps was a deep hollow called the Goat's Saddle; there was the source of the stream that flowed down through Pietrasecca. Spina knew that there was only one way over to the opposite slope, and this was a mule-trail over the Saddle; it would now, of course, be covered deep in snow. Spina remembered hearing Sciatàp say that in summer it took from four to five hours to cross the Saddle and reach the first houses beyond. But in winter? If he had been stronger than he was, it would have been the only way out of the trap into which he had fallen. But would it not be madness on his part to risk a long and dangerous mountain climb at this time of year? It would certainly be more advisable to stake everything on a clever stratagem; stay at Pietrasecca, pretend to fly in one direction or another, but really hide in some peasant's hovel, in the communal oven that was only lit once a fortnight, in a cellar, or an empty tub. But for this he would need an accomplice, and he had no one.

Still thinking of these things, he came to Pietrasecca. He tied the colt to the inn door and was about to enter when he heard some one coming behind him. He turned; it was Cristina, and there was such desolation in her face that it frightened him.

"My brother has written to me," she managed to say.

Spina feared some misfortune had happened to Alberto, but it was something else.

"Tell me the truth," the girl asked him. "Are you really Pietro Spina?"

"Yes," he replied.

Matalena came out of the inn and the two remained silent, each shaken by a different emotion. Spina went up to his room, sorted his things, and burned a lot of papers. Every now and then he stopped to look out of the window along the valley road. In tidying his papers he came upon the notebook on which he had written "Dialogues with Cristina." He hesitated, then wrote on the cover these words of dedication and farewell:

"My dear, my very dear Cristina, here you will find the truth, nothing but the truth; I mean the real and essential truth; in these evil times the hidden truth, the truth of the heart. Pietro Spina."

He put the notebook in an envelope, went down to the kitchen, gave it to Americo, and told him to take it to Cristina at once. At the same time he sent Matalena for Sciatàp, paid him a day's wages in advance, gave him the colt, and told him to take it back to its master at Rocca immediately. Then he once more retired to his room. Half an hour later Matalena went up to ask him what he would like for dinner, but found the room tidy and empty. Some money and a few words of thanks to Matalena for the hospitality he had received were on the table. What a strange way of going away, without saying good-by and only half an hour after returning! The woman went out into the garden and saw the man's footprints in the snow. Surprised, she followed them until she came to the brook. From there they went, not downstream, but upstream. The man must certainly be mad! Matalena met the deaf-mute and asked him by signs whether he had seen the priest. He answered that he had seen him running in the direction of the mountain. Magascià appeared and confirmed this strange report. The priest had been running like mad, and he must be a long way off by now.

"He must have gone mad!" Matalena exclaimed. "In summer he always stayed in his room, and now in winter, when there's three feet of snow, he goes up into the mountains!"

Not knowing what to do, she went and asked Cristina's advice. The girl had locked herself in her room, alone, and was in a state of utter prostration. She had just finished reading Spina's notebook.

"The priest has gone mad!" Matalena called out. "He slipped out of the back door without telling anyone, and now he has taken the path over the mountain!"

Cristina dashed to the window and looked in the direction Matalena indicated.

There was no sign of man on the white mountain slope that led straight up to the Goat's Saddle. He must therefore have taken the mule-trail, which was easier and longer and went up the mountain-side in a series of great zigzags after first skirting the stream.

"If only he had had something to eat!" Matalena exclaimed. "If only he had warmer clothes on!"

The course of the stream was so hidden by rocks and shrubs that it was impossible to see how far the fugitive had gone; besides, the air was not very clear.

"It will soon be dark," said Matalena. "He'll be caught in a snowstorm even if he does get to the Saddle."

Matalena went away, because she heard her son, Americo, crying. Cristina stayed at the window, her eyes fixed in the direction in which the man was flying. It was an adventure that might cost him his life. He was so weak in health, so ignorant of the neighborhood, and he had no food or special equipment with him. She was suddenly terrified by the peril he was in, and her anxiety made her forget all other considerations, and all prudence. She hid Spina's notebook under her pillow, searched in her wardrobe for all the woolen garments that might be of use —a coat, two vests, gloves, two scarves—and wrapped them in a bundle. Then she went to the kitchen and took a loaf of bread and a bottle of wine and put them in with the clothing. To avoid being seen or heard by her grandmother, she went out by the back door, with her bundle under her arm, as though she were going to the stable. But instead she made a short détour, passed behind the church and the cemetery, and slipped down a steep slope of about ten meters to a path beneath. Here she paused for a moment to get her breath, sitting on the snow as she had done when she was a girl.

The path skirted the stream. Cristina walked upstream, and as soon as she felt sure that no one in the village had seen her and was following her, she started running, because, if the fugitive had half an hour's start, there was no time to lose if she were to catch him. There were several different footprints in the snow along the path, and as she ran she tried to guess which were his. The footprints thinned out as she went along, but none of them led away from the stream. That was a sure sign that he had taken the longer way to the Goat's Saddle, the mule-trail. Cristina's only chance of catching up with him lay in taking a steep short cut three hundred feet up the steep incline that formed the right valley wall at this point. She knew that climbing it, even in summer, was an enterprise reserved for daring boys and goats. In winter it was still more dangerous. But there was no other way of overtaking the fugitive. She jumped the stream and started the ascent.

She climbed with hands and feet, clinging to stumps, shrubs, rocks that protruded through the snow. Several times she stumbled, fell with her face in the snow, and started slipping back. Luckily, where the slope was steepest the snow was thinnest, because the wind had carried it away. But between the rocks, where Cristina thought she could advance with the greatest safety, she plunged deep into the snow and had to struggle out with her hands. She was greatly hampered by her skirts and her bundle. Where a big overhanging rock formed a kind of dry cave she flung herself to the ground, exhausted and panting for breath. Mist was rising from the valley. A gray pall obscured the ravines, hid the houses, covered the fields, the hedges, and the walls. The earth looked shapeless and void, as though it were uninhabited, as though it were at the beginning again. But it was not entirely uninhabited, because it contained a man and a woman, a man who was alone and perhaps not very far away. So she got up, to meet him, to bring him succor in his loneliness.

The snow was harder now, which made it easier for Cristina to climb; but it also made it easier for her to slip. She was dripping with perspiration and her hands were bleeding, having been torn by the thorns to which she had several times been forced to cling to keep from being hurled into the abyss. Her heart was pounding so hard that she had to put her hand to her breast to hold it. When she got to the top of the chasm she had no idea how long her climb had taken. She had lost all sense of time, and was so exhausted that she could not go on. She had reached a big, open, almost rectangular space, called the Witches' Meadow. Beyond this the mountain continued to rise gently upwards. The snow lay trackless all around her. No one had passed that way. To go on towards the mountain top would be extremely exhausting, and useless as well. Cristina decided it would be better to skirt the mountain, and thus cut across Spina's path. So she set off in this new direction.

The landscape had completely altered. The valley of Pietrasecca had disappeared. There was nothing to be seen save the outlines and summits of the other mountains. Visibility was rapidly diminishing. There was a freezing wind that cut her face. Evening was coming on and so was snow. Cristina reached the edge of the hollow that divided the mountain into two humps and formed the Goat's Saddle. She could find no footprints in the snow. The ground was strewn with rocks and boulders that had been washed down from the mountain sides by storms and floods. With the snow nearly up to her waist, Cristina could not see far. She remembered the first time she had come up here, on a day in spring. She had been a little girl and her father had brought her. It was a less happy landscape now. Cristina resumed her climb towards the Saddle. She thought that if she got there it would be possible to overlook both slopes, see Spina more easily, or at any rate be seen herself. But a moment came when she could not go on, and she collapsed in the snow. To prevent Spina from passing without seeing her, she called him by name, with all the strength left in her lungs. She called him by his new name, his real name.

"Spina! Spina!"

He would certainly hear her if he passed. She tidied her hair, wiped the snow from her face, her eyelashes, her eyebrows, her ears, her neck. How surprised he would be to find her! She would say: "First of all take these woolen things and put them on." He would answer: "But how on earth did you get here before me?" She would say: "Now drink a little wine and eat a little bread; they are simple things that do one good." He would say: "Signorina Cristina, do you wish to continue the journey with me?" She would reply: "Things are not so simple as all that, my dear sir; you have forgotten that I have people and must go home." That is what she would say to him. So she went on calling "Spina! Spina!" with all the strength of her lungs.

She realized that if he did not come, her own situation would become perilous, too. "That is what we are like, we poor women; we want to help, and then we have to be helped ourselves." So she went on calling, with all her remaining strength.

A voice suddenly answered her in the distance, but not a human voice. It sounded more like the howling of a dog, but it was sharper and more prolonged. Cristina recognized it; it was the howl of a wolf; the howl of a beast of prey; a call to the other wolves scattered about the mountain; an invitation to the feast. And no coarse flesh awaited them now, but fine, tender, and clean flesh; baptized flesh. Through the driving snow and the darkness of approaching night Cristina saw a beast galloping towards her, appearing and disappearing in the hollows. In the distance she could make out still others. She knelt, closed her eyes, and made the sign of the Cross.

THE END

Bread and Wine
Set in Linotype Baskerville
Format by A. W. Rushmore
Manufactured by The Haddon Craftsmen
Published by Harper & Brothers, New York and London